Scattered & Breaking

Natalie Cammaratta

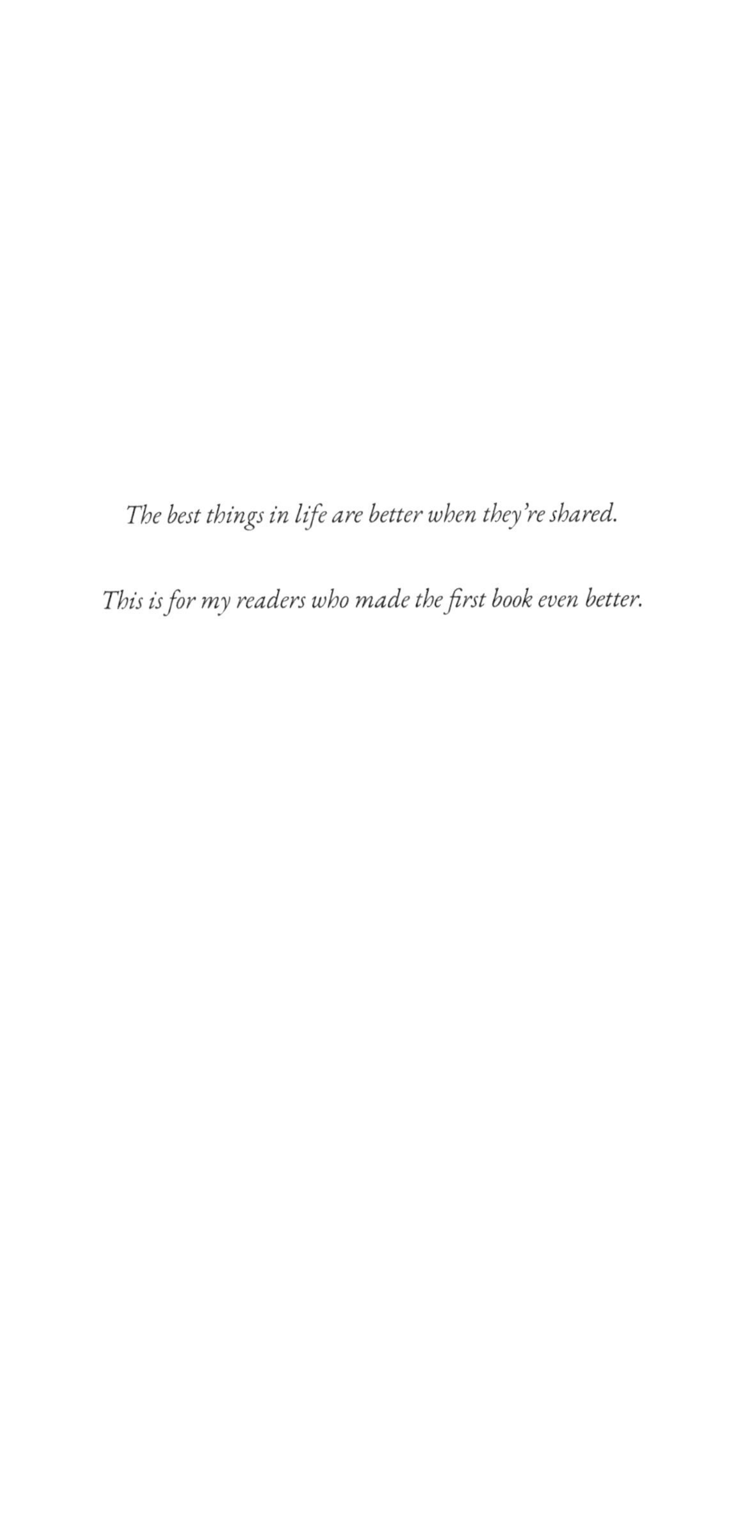

The best things in life are better when they're shared.

This is for my readers who made the first book even better.

Playlist

Nothing Is As It Seems – Hidden Citizens feat. Ruelle
Land of Confusion – Hidden Citizens
Natural – Imagine Dragons
Smoke and Mirrors – Imagine Dragons
Foreverglow – Lindsey Stirling
Wherever I Go – OneRepublic
Dream – Bishop Briggs
Wrecked – Imagine Dragons
How Can You Sleep at Night? – Tom Walker
Lions Inside – Valley Of Wolves
Big Guns – Ruelle
Dream – Imagine Dragons
We Are the Rulers – Hidden Citizens feat. Rayelle
Little Talks – Of Monsters and Men
IDK You Yet – Alexander 23
Boomerang – Imagine Dragons
Deep End – Ruelle
Believe – The Score
I Don't Mind – Imagine Dragons
Where Do You Run – The Score
Unleash the Power – Hidden Citizens feat. Sam Tinnesz & Rayelle

Everybody Wants To Rule the World – Lorde

Afterglow – Taylor Swift

Silence – Marshmello feat. Khalid

Here We Stand – Hidden Citizens feat. Svrcina

Stay Alive – Hidden Citizens feat. REMMI

Shots Fired – Hidden Citizens feat. Laney Jones

Phoenix – League of Legends, Cailin Russo, & Chrissy Costanza

Born Ready – Zayde Wølf

Silent Running – Hidden Citizens

Stronger – The Score

Oh My God – Alec Benjamin

Casualty – Hidden Citizens feat. Tash

Too Far Gone – Hidden Citizens feat. Svrcina

Lost Soul - RIOPY

Listen On

SCATTERED & BREAKING

Cast of Characters

Serenity Ward
Kaycian celebrity; Leadership student

Bram Eros
Marshal from Lawson

Jase Delgado
Health graduate

Vogue Taylor
Technology student

Frey Dempsey
Technology graduate

Krisalyn Laska
Health graduate

Dixon Blythe
Technology student

Tori Foster (deceased)
Security training captain

Sophos Verity
Director of Education and Placement

Adwin Lebeau

Visual Arts graduate

Grace Ward

Actress; Serenity Ward's mother

Anton Ward

Director of Cultural Affairs; Serenity Ward's father

Kolina Eros

Leader of uprising; Bram Eros' mother

Aren Eros

Bram Eros' younger brother

Emrys Eros

Marshal; Bram Eros' youngest brother

Casimir Agnar

Lieutenant Governor; Adwin Lebeau's grandfather

Espy Taylor

Fashion designer; Vogue Taylor's mother

Adelle Nemes

Former Director of Education and Placement;

Vogue Taylor's grandmother

Gernot Martel

Governor of Kaycie

Watt Kemp

Director of Security

Tevin Hickey

Director of the Health Department

Alima Karan

Director of Research and Technology

Flora Prosper

Director of City Planning

Cole Markey

Mayor of Eudora

Aster Rigby

Mayor of Gardner

Vaiana Mizuno

Mayor of Blue Springs

Hadia Desmond

Mayor of Lawson

Parisa Otto

Fashion student

Millie Gersemi

Public Relations Advisor

Rollin Karan

Leadership student; Alima Karan's son

Lanelle Kemp

Health graduate; Watt Kemp's daughter

Aldan Foster (deceased)

Health Department transfer from Gladstone; Tori Foster's father

Carista Campbell

Eros family friend

Reid Campbell

Marshal from Lawson; Carista Campbell's twin

Travick Campbell

Marshal from Lawson; Carista Campbell's older brother

Estrella Rinne

Former Director of Cultural Affairs

Aurora Bloom

Actress; Jase Delgado's mother

Snowflake

Serenity Ward's dog

Chapter One

BRAM

People say seeing is believing, but I had to touch it. I can't believe my eyes. I crouch down and press my hand into the silty mud. My mom and brother remain above me on the seawall; the sun rises behind them. A turtle scuttles by. Fish flop helplessly, gasping for breath.

I never thought I'd commiserate with a fish, but that's a fitting metaphor.

The sea fell as we initiated the uprising. It can't be coincidence, but what could cause this? Where did the water go? My chest squeezes into a tight ball. *What did we do?*

"Let's check in with the other islands," Mom says. "Time to see who needs help, and how far this stretches."

"Yeah," I mutter as I take another look around. Wiping mud on my pant leg is a fitting way to say goodbye to the uniform I've worn for five years. I climb onto the seawall like I'm floating through a dream. This can't be real.

My mom wraps her arm around my back. "I'm so glad you're home."

There's too much ricocheting in my head to appreciate it. Last night I killed four marshals, watched Tori die, lost Serenity, started an uprising, and apparently, drained the sea. Nothing about this is the homecoming I had envisioned.

As we walk back to the factory where Mom set up base, we pass by the Establishment Center. This squat concrete building being called the EC is a joke when compared to Kaycie's sleek glass tower. In the dim light of dawn, the crowd celebrates their apparent victory over the marshals and independence from the Establishment. People are hugging, kissing, clinking beers, jumping around.

A tall girl turns toward us. "Oh my gosh, Bram!" she says and wraps me in a hug. "I can't believe you're back."

Carista Campbell? She's Aren's age, so the last time I saw her she was thirteen. I barely recognize her all grown up. "Wow, hi."

She smooths loose brown strands of a messy ponytail. Her jeans and thin jacket are dirty and blood splattered. "We need to catch up. I have so many questions."

"I'm running on no sleep. You might want to wait a day for coherent answers."

"Yeah, I'm sure we all need a day." She wraps her arms around herself, trembling.

"I'm going to regroup with Sophos and the Kaycians," Mom tells her. "I'll be back to start organizing this mess as soon as I can."

"Take your time." Carista flashes a thin smile. "I'm not going anywhere. I'll see you later, Bram." She walks back into the crowd and the three of us continue to the factory.

"What's her role in this?" I ask Mom.

"Carista and Aren have been my extra eyes and hands. She's as good as family."

That's true enough. My brothers and I grew up with the Campbells, always popping back and forth between our neighboring houses.

A sense of nostalgia washes over me as we walk. Lawson is familiar, but being here is strange after all this time. This was my home, but it's like going back to a world in black and white after being over the rainbow. Dorothy knew home was better, but for me it's... *dingy* now. Were the storefronts always so clustered? Houses are even smaller than I remember. I can't think I'm above this place. *Damnit.* I've spent years feeling out of place in Kaycie, but now I'm not sure I belong here, either. Maybe I don't fit anywhere anymore.

Mom unlocks the door, and we file into the building. "Don't worry," she says. "The office has a window. We'll have some light once we're there."

In the dark, this place is creepy. The assembly lines and machinery loom in shadows like mangled trees on a moonless night. It would be a good setting for a horror movie. Cue the murderer popping out.

We make it without any blade-wielding psychos showing up and find a large office space with several desks lining the walls. Vogue sits on the floor in a corner, lazily pawing at a holoScreen with Krisalyn's head on her shoulder. Frey is at a desk, head down on his crossed arms. Dixon reclines back in a chair, tapping his fingers. Sophos jumps up to meet us.

"Kolina." He greets her warmly this time with a hug. "How did it go?"

"Better than I hoped for," Mom says. "The timing couldn't have been better."

Kaycie's Director of Security, Watt Kemp, said the timing was clever before our fight broke out last night. I didn't know what he meant by that, but apparently Mom and Sophos agree. I might have questioned Sophos on our way out, but I was preoccupied with Serenity. Later, I'll have to get clarification on that.

"Who have we heard from?" Mom asks.

"Gardner and Eudora are in the clear," Sophos says. "Vaiana radioed from Blue Springs that the marshals shut themselves into their Establishment Center without even being attacked. Nothing from Gladstone or Greenwood yet."

Gladstone's radio silence is no surprise based on the bombardment we saw from the top of the tunnel. Flashes from there lit the falling sea waters for us almost as well as the moon.

"All right. And the sea has receded everywhere?"

Sophos presses his lips together. "Yes."

Eudora and Gardner are at the opposite corner of the island chain from here. If the sea has run dry there, it's gone across the country.

"Good thing we blocked off the tunnels." Dixon marks his sarcasm with a shake of his head. Right—if we can walk from island to island (though in that case they aren't islands), the Establishment can too with their army from Leavenworth. Great.

"Okay," Mom says. "Let's get everyone settled and rested so we can figure this out."

The squad rises and offers thanks to my mom. She thanks them for their help, and we're one big, oddly mismatched family. As we walk the mile to my street, Mom explains she set them up with an empty house a couple doors down from us and collected some clothes for them. On that topic, I finally ask what they were doing last night to end up in the commotion dressed this way.

"We were at a nightclub." Frey's tone says this should be obvious.

"In case you needed further proof that the Kaycian lifestyle is charmed, I was getting my ass kicked and blowing up Kemp's office while you were out dancing."

Vogue shrugs. "You didn't invite us to that."

They look hilariously out of place as Mom shows them their temporary housing. Any one of their outfits would cost a months' rent in this two-bedroom house. Dixon and Krisalyn maintain appreciative looks, Vogue suppresses concern in sharp gazes, and Frey is too tired to care. Once they rest up, they'll need some training on how a kitchen works, but Mom gives them an open invitation to come to our house to eat anytime.

Sophos continues with us back home. This is so weird. Are my mom and Sophos a couple? He's been gone for years. What is their status? Is he going to live with us? That is seriously uncomfortable.

When we walk in, Carista's mom greets us. "Is everything all right?" she asks my mom.

"Everything is great. Is she up?"

Why is Mrs. Campbell here? And who is the *she* in question?

"Yes, she's getting dressed. I'll get out of your way and catch up later. Welcome home, Bram." She gives me a tight hug.

As I step farther into the house, I don't have a chance to ask who '*she*' is. A little girl with a head of wild dark curls runs out from the hall.

"Mommy!" she cheers as she leaps into my mom's arms.

My jaw drops as I watch *my* mom cuddle this little girl who calls her 'mommy.' "Libby, baby, this is your brother, Bram," Mom says to her.

My feet are cemented to the floor as *Libby* gasps, stretching her little mouth as far as her jaws will go. "I always wanted a bruhver!" she squeals.

"And what do you call Aren, silly girl?" Mom rubs their noses together.

"Well, I wanted another one."

"Bram,"—Mom smiles—"I'd like you to meet your sister, Libby."

Only now do I realize how tense my shoulders are. I take a deep breath to steady myself. The déjà vu from finding out about the islands is overwhelming. Just like the world, my family is bigger than I knew, people have been keeping information from me, and there's a pretty face breaking the news. Libby wriggles out of Mom's arms and skips over to me. I get down on one knee and lean forward to level with her. Her piercing hazel eyes are bright and full of joy, her round baby cheeks dimple as she smiles. She's beautiful.

"Hi Libby."

She wraps her little arms around my neck in a tight hug. I don't even know who I am anymore, because I just plunged into unrelenting devotion to this little girl, and the feeling is foreign to me.

"And Libby," Mom says, stroking her hair, "this is your dad."

Libby pops up out of my arms and stares up at Sophos. "Daddy?"

Chapter Two

SERENITY

My eyes creak open, pulling at my eyelashes, which are glued together by mascara. It takes me a moment to remember where I am. Room 326. Although I don't know where that is, anyway. The sound of the shower running reaches me. I roll over to see that Jase isn't here. My memory is fuzzy, but I think I'm on his side of the bed now.

Rays of sunlight peek through the curtains. I sit up and wrap my robe tighter around myself. Next to a dentalDrop are two pills and a glass of water. A dull headache lingers, so I take them gratefully.

The shower stops. "Curtains." My voice achieves nothing. I get up and open them manually to light the room. Outside the window are low, simple concrete buildings. A truck passes between them. I've never seen this part of the city. Staring out, I tap out a nervous, silent melody on my crossed arms.

Soon Jase comes out of the bathroom, hair wet, wearing a gray t-shirt and unflattering navy-blue pants. "Good morning. How are you feeling?"

If only I could define it. I shrug. "I'll be fine."

His lips twist to the side, giving me the impression he doesn't have much confidence in my answer. "You should get ready. We're supposed to be at a meeting in half an hour. There was a note on our door, along with some clothes."

"Oh." That answers the question of where his outfit came from.

"I hung yours up in the closet."

"Thank you. And for the painkillers."

"You should have taken something last night. I'm sorry I didn't think of it in the confusion."

I put on a thin smile as I go to the closet where a hideous navy-blue dress hangs. There are equally ugly plain black shoes underneath it. "I'm supposed to wear *this*?"

He smiles humorlessly as I take it into the bathroom with me to get ready. There are sub-par miniature toiletries, but I can get by. The dim lighting is a greater challenge. After I shower and put on the dress, a light knock sounds on the door.

My mother peeks in. "Good morning, sweetheart. Are you feeling better?"

"A little. Do you have any makeup?"

"Yes." She hands me a pouch. "It's all I could bring. They wouldn't let us take anything bigger than a purse, so we're stuck with security-issued clothing for now."

I nod as she goes back to the bedroom, closing the door behind her. There's nothing I can do with my hair, which feels so unnatural ending at my shoulders. At least there's makeup. It's enough to make me look human, even if I can't feel like myself. I go back out to my mother and Jase. Her hair is still holding its curl from last night, though not as neatly. Her makeup is simple, but the sack of a navy-blue dress she wears makes her look like a different person. I assume my matching one is doing the same for me.

"Do you know anything?" I ask.

She sighs. "There has been an uprising."

We can rise up. Words flash through my memory without context or source. I squeeze my eyes shut as I try to process it.

"I'm told everything is fine in the city," she continues. "They can handle the situations on the other islands."

They keep us away from the people on the islands. I shake my head as information ricochets around in it. "In the city… Where are *we*?"

"We're in Leavenworth," she says. "It's our military base."

Military base? This a lot all at once. "Why are we here if everything is fine in Kaycie?" Jase paces the small room as my mother and I talk.

"It's just a precaution," she says. "Your father and I have to be here with the council, and we wouldn't leave you behind. I'm sure we won't be here for long. Come now. There is a lot to catch you up on."

An uprising? My stomach knots as we leave.

Outside, people stop and gasp at a railing. I veer off our path to see what they're looking at, ignoring my mother's objections. Jase comes along with me as I hurry up the slight hill to the railing overlooking a drop-off. Beyond it, the ground is soaked with puddles extending as far as the eye can see. Jase gasps.

"It's like the land rose right up out of the sea," someone murmurs.

I look at Jase's stunned face and back to the expanse. Is this where the sea is supposed to be?

It's like the land rose right up out of the sea.

This isn't what I thought an uprising was.

A fishy, musty smell hangs like a fog. My gaze lingers on the seafloor as my mother pulls me away from the railing. Jase shakes his head as if to wake himself up and looks at me with concern painting every feature of his face. His eyebrows draw together, forming a crease between them, and his golden eyes drill into me. He takes my hand and comes along with us.

"What happened?" My chest tightens.

"I don't know." My mother leads us to the next building over. This one has electricity. "These are our offices here." On the ground floor, my father, Governor Martel, Lieutenant Governor Agnar, and Watt Kemp wait for us in a boardroom.

"Serenity," Agnar says. "I'm glad to see you're feeling better after last night's scare." He gazes down over his long nose—his countenance as stiff as his stance. If he were broad, Casimir Agnar would look formidable, but his height is like that of an Italian cypress, thin and stretching upward in a narrow column.

"Yes, I am. Thank you."

"It's a pleasure to meet you both. Let's talk over breakfast." Gernot Martel is probably in his early sixties, but he's looked the same for as long as I can remember. Not a single gray appears in his close-cropped black hair, his skin doesn't show any trace of wrinkles, and his smile is bright white.

An assortment of dishes are set out family-style. Pastries, eggs Benedict, shrimp, cheeses, and charcuterie. It all looks appealing, but my anxiety isn't doing anything for my appetite.

"Please sit and help yourselves," Martel says.

Jase pulls out a chair for me, and I slide into it. He takes the seat to my right. I serve myself a pastry and some cheeses as a server offers us coffee. Agnar requests tea, which sounds lovely, but I had the strangest night's sleep. Jumbled dreams that made no sense kept me from truly resting. This is a coffee kind of day. Jase eyes me as my coffee is poured and offers me sugar, which he adds for me. Heat permeates through me as I take a sip and eases me a little.

"Now then,"—Martel smiles once we are all situated with our breakfasts—"you know why you're here."

"I haven't the foggiest idea." All eyes turn toward my mother. "Serenity is not of age to be in Establishment meetings."

Agnar's jaw tightens. "Grace, it might be easier if we update you and Anton later on."

"I'm not going anywhere, Casimir."

"You won't have a choice in the matter if you don't let us speak to your daughter without interruption."

She looks at Martel indignantly, but he offers no assistance.

My father takes her hand. "Go ahead, Serenity. Do you know why you're here?"

"No, I don't." I glance at Jase from the corner of my eye. He doesn't add anything.

"Sophos, the ringleader of this little uprising, is your mentor," Agnar says. "All of your friends disappeared with him last night as they wreaked havoc on the city's systems, but you plan to tell us you were not involved?"

What is he talking about? "Who went with him?"

Agnar looks at Kemp, who pulls a note out of his pocket. "Frey Dempsey, Krisalyn Laska, Dixon Blythe, and Vogue Taylor," he reads.

"That's not possible," I say. "I live with Vogue Taylor. I'd know if she was involved with such a thing. There is no way she would do this." I have no idea if the rest of them would, but not Vogue. My stomach twists and I take a deep breath, trying to get a handle on myself. I look to Jase, expecting some support against the accusations, but he offers none. His silence is infuriating.

On the contrary, my mother couldn't remain silent if her life depended on it. "That's Adelle's granddaughter." Apparently that is as much defense as Vogue requires.

Kemp puts the note away. "Miss Taylor hacked into Leavenworth's systems and fired missiles at our power plants. It is a fact, not conjecture."

That is absurd! My head is spinning, my stomach tying itself into a tighter knot, and I swallow hard to try to keep myself from throwing up. It doesn't help. My stomach's roiling isn't only anxiety. I'm going to be sick. I push my chair out from the table to stand.

"Where is the ladies' room?" I ask, holding two fingers over my lips. Perspiration forms on my forehead.

"Are you all right?" Mamá asks, standing.

I nod with my eyes closed and gesture for her to stay.

"Out that door, turn right, it's on your left," Martel says.

I all but run out, making it to the bathroom just in time to vomit up the little breakfast I ate. My chest heaves as I sit back on the floor and lean against the wall, head pounding and eyes tearing up. This is a lovely addition to a great day.

My legs wobble under me, but I find my balance and go to rinse my mouth out. I take a few deep breaths, my hands pressed onto the countertop. Funny how it doesn't take much time feeling shaken up to forget what normal is like. My throat burns, my stomach is still in knots, and I don't understand anything going on.

I know Jase loves me, but I don't feel it. I know I'm innocent of any involvement with the uprising, but how could all my friends be involved without me noticing? My mind feels like a puzzle with an infinite number of pieces, and I can't sort through them.

One more deep breath. Roll my shoulders back. Slide into the role I've always known. It doesn't matter what I've got going on; I know how to be 'Serenity Ward', the symbol. One last look in the mirror before I go back.

I don't have anything to hide. I can do this.

When I renter the dining room, Jase stands and comes toward me. "Are you okay?" He looks as miserable as I feel.

"Yes, I'm fine." I smile weakly as he pulls me in for a hug. His embrace offers a sense of safety, if nothing else.

"Serenity," Agnar says, approaching, "if you're still unwell, you should get some rest. We can continue our conversation later on." I nod at him from the protective haven of Jase's arms. I *can* do this, but I don't particularly want to. If they are going to offer me a way out, I'll take it.

"I'll get her back to bed," Jase says.

My parents are huddled together in the corner, talking quietly. My father looks up at me and tells me they'll come to see me soon.

"Jase, we'll have Tevin meet us here to continue our conversation," Martel tells him.

"Of course." We walk out, Jase's arm around my shoulders.

Outside, the fresh air revitalizes me somewhat. "I'm all right, I just…"

"It's okay. Get some rest. I'll take care of it."

My chin drops to my chest and my fingers tap away on my arms. He wants to take care of me, but how can he fix this? We return to our scant room and sit on the side of the bed.

"It'll be all right," he says. "Don't worry."

"How can you say that?" Tears well up in my eyes. "Didn't you hear what they said about our friends? The whole world is upside down. I don't understand any of this!"

He wraps his arms around me, and I cry into his shoulder. "I know, it's scary." His hand strokes my back.

"Nothing makes sense." Including letting him see me break down like this, but I don't have the strength to stifle it.

"I'm sorry." He sighs into my hair. "I'm so sorry."

I pull myself away and wipe my eyes. "Don't be. It's not your fault."

His golden eyes glisten. "I have to go."

"What can you possibly have to speak to them about?"

"They want to ask me more about what our friends might have gotten into."

"But they couldn't have..." I don't know what's possible anymore. Kemp is positive that Vogue fired missiles. Seriously?

"I know. I'll tell them." He pulls back from me, and his mouth is twisted into a grimace. "Are you feeling all right now?" I nod in response. "Okay. We'll have to get more clothes at uniform issue. They gave me a couple of maps of the base." He pulls one from his back pocket and hands it to me. "I'll be back as soon as I can."

"All right."

He rises off the bed and pauses before leaving. He looks at me searchingly, but I don't know what he's looking for. I watch him leave and close the door behind himself. Alone, I twist over and lie face down, resting my forehead on my arms.

All I can manage at this point is to cry.

Chapter Three

BRAM

I don't immediately remember where I am when I wake up. It's an unsettling feeling, even if it only lasts a second. *Home.* I let Mom, Sophos, and Libby have their reunion. Exhaustion was settling in anyway. I had expected to feel relieved at this point, but I'm still anxious. There are so many unknowns right now: what happened to the sea, the Establishment coming to take back the islands, what's happened to Serenity. The last one is technically the least important, but it's the most haunting.

What time is it? My cuff is dead, but the clock on the wall shows one o'clock. Probably not enough rest, but I don't want to flip my whole sleep schedule. I stretch and muster up the motivation to sit up. I dig through Aren's clothes to find jeans and a T-shirt and go take a shower. Higher water pressure in Kaycie was something I forgot I had gotten used to.

When I come out, I find Mom sitting at the table, drinking a cup of coffee. She looks up at me over her cup and smiles. "I could get used to seeing you here. Can I get you something to eat? You must be starving."

"I'll get it," I say as I open the refrigerator.

"You must have a lot of questions for me." *You think?* I make a simple sandwich as she starts to explain herself. "It's not Sophos' fault that he didn't tell you about Libby."

"Honestly, that's not my biggest concern right now." Nothing should be more shocking than finding out I have a little sister, but there's a lot going on. Mom waits in silence for me to explain. Her eyebrows pull together as I sit down. "Last night, Kemp told us that our timing was clever, but dangerous. You said the timing was perfect. It was too easy to take control from the marshals. Why?"

"The Establishment has been distracted. They haven't only been hiding the islands from each other, they've also hidden other countries." She pauses to see if I'm okay, but my marshal mask is on.

Despite the prickling down my neck, I keep my face calm. "Countries. Multiple?"

"Eight, including us. They all keep to themselves."

Again? I close my eyes and take a slow breath. Finding out the world was so much bigger than Lawson was insane. I never thought I'd deal with the world growing again, but here we go. We're not the last ones. We're one of eight. Is our chain of eight islands a miniature model of the world? My stomach twists. If that's true, which island are we? Kaycie, or one of the lesser, cowering islands?

"There is a conflict with another country—Montica, the one on our continent. So the Establishment wasn't paying much attention to domestic concerns."

"On the same continent? There's another whole country so close?"

"Something like six hundred miles away."

Six hundred miles. Wow, I feel small.

"They pulled most of the marshals to Leavenworth," she continues. "It was a good opportunity."

"And what about the foreign threat?"

"The Establishment has its whole army. They can handle it."

How are we supposed to protect anyone if we are fighting amongst ourselves? Kemp's words resound in my mind. Not that I've ever trusted him, but he may be right about this. Sophos and Mom knew this the whole time but moved forward anyway. I want to trust their judgement, but it does seem risky. And lies are piling up on both sides.

"What is the conflict over?"

"A Montican craft flew into Kaycian airspace and was shot down. The Establishment is scrambling to keep them from engaging in war against Kaycie."

I press my fingers along my eyebrows. Perfect. Another threat. "I'm going to go check on the Kaycian kids." This is *not* how I wanted to reunite with my family. I need to get space from Mom before my temper gets away from me.

"Bram,"—her voice is patronizing—"you understand, don't you? The system has rolled over us for generations. This was our best shot to make a change."

"Yeah, I get it."

"Do you want to bring them a pot of coffee?"

"Not a bad idea. Thanks."

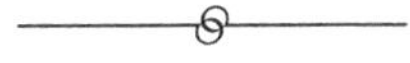

Krisalyn answers the door, and her eyes light up when she sees the coffeepot in my hands. "Oh, you're a lifesaver!" She rushes into the kitchen and starts throwing open cabinets until she finds mugs.

As I place the pot on the table, a bedroom door opens, and Frey appears looking disheveled. "I smell coffee."

Krisalyn brings mugs and starts filling them. "Do you think we have sugar?"

"I don't care," Frey mutters as he slides the first filled mug toward himself and drops into a seat at the table.

"Not yet," I tell her, "but we'll stock you up later."

"Thanks." She smiles as she carries two cups of coffee into the other bedroom.

I sit on the couch and watch as Frey sits huddled with his coffee like he needs it to live. He'd still be the best-looking guy in any room, but it's kind of nice to see him looking less than perfect. Coffee reminds me of the boiling water story, which reminds me of Serenity. She prefers tea. She said it to be a thorn in my side, but I think it's true.

Vogue trudges out with Krisalyn. She's another one who's lethargic look is a relief. Anyone can still see she's gorgeous, even with her hair mounded on top of her head, no makeup, and wearing sweats, but it's comforting to know she doesn't wake up looking perfect.

"Wow, Krisalyn can have you," Frey grumbles when he looks up at her. "You wake up looking rough."

She smiles contemptuously at him as she takes a seat across from him. "It must have been mind boggling that I was never attracted to you, but I'd have thought when you found out why, you'd start being nicer to me."

"That wouldn't be any fun." He sips his coffee. "You could have told me sooner."

"That wouldn't be any fun."

Krisalyn rolls her eyes. "Am I going to be an arbiter the whole time we live together?" "No," Frey snaps. "It has to be Dixon. You're biased."

She grins and shrugs as she sits next to Vogue.

"Vogue," I say, "if you were wondering what it would be like to have brothers and sisters, it's basically the relationship you have with Frey."

Her laugh is trill. "Well, thank goodness I was born in Kaycie and didn't have to suffer through this my entire life."

"Cheers to that," Frey says as he and Vogue tap their mugs together.

The front door opens, and Dixon enters, flushed and sweaty. "Finally! I thought you'd sleep all day. Hey, Bram."

"Hi. You're clearly not on the same schedule as everyone else."

"I can't sleep during the day. I went for a run—almost got lost. So, what's the status of everything?" It's refreshing to see someone who isn't fueled exclusively by caffeine.

"I don't know yet," I say. "I'll help you find food and then go see what I can find out."

"Yes, please, on the food," Vogue says. "But then I'm going with you. I'm not waiting around to find out what's happening."

"*I'm* not waiting around for you to get ready," I say.

"I only take a long time when I want to," she insists, standing up. "Five minutes!"

"Me too," Dixon says, disappearing into his bedroom.

I look at Frey and Krisalyn. "I don't suppose that you two are going to want to be left behind?"

"Nope!" Krisalyn smiles as she steps out of the room.

Frey seems to consider it for a moment before gulping down the rest of his coffee and standing up. "Fine. I'll come."

Fifteen minutes later—not five—we all walk out. In all fairness, none of them ever had to share a bathroom before. Mom isn't home, so we continue toward the factory. On the way, we stop to pick up burritos to eat as we walk. Vogue and Frey find some common ground over how very happy cheap, fast-food makes them. They're the last people I thought I'd ever want to be around, but they keep things interesting.

At the factory, Mom and Aren are tinkering with something when we walk in. "What's that?" I ask.

"A drone." Mom keeps her eyes on it. "We're trying to get visuals on Gladstone and Greenwood, so we don't go in blind."

"Except this won't get far enough on its battery," Aren says, putting it down.

"I can help with that," Dixon offers. "I work in product development."

"I used to, too," Vogue says.

"That would be great," Mom says. "Thank you."

"What happens next?" Krisalyn asks.

"We need to get a team on a train to Blue Springs to take their Establishment Center from the marshals,"—Mom taps the desk as she enumerates the to-do list—"check on Gladstone and Greenwood, and start sorting through the marshals."

"What are you going to do with them?" Frey asks.

"Try to get them home, but it won't be easy since they don't know their own names or where they're from."

"We'd like to help however we can," Krisalyn says. They all mutter in agreement.

Mom promises to make them useful, starting with the move into the Establishment Center. I recommend renaming it, since the Establishment has no place here. 'Townhall' is adopted as the new name.

Krisalyn and Frey help get things situated there with Sophos and Mom, while Vogue and Dixon work on the drone. Aren pulls me out of the factory to 'catch up' and we end up at the taproom's patio.

"It's been a long time since I had a beer." The one in my hand hisses open. Sneaking them as a kid was a different experience than this.

"What else doesn't exist in Kaycie?"

"Bar-b-que. I'm going to need burnt ends to happen real soon."

My description of the city doesn't do it any justice. Its appearance isn't so difficult, but how can I explain a lifestyle so unlike anything he's ever known? I guess he'll be able to see it someday. It's hard to imagine a reality in which we can all just pass between the islands—or whatever—freely, but now that we don't have to be isolated, it'll be possible.

On the other side of the windows, the lights in the taproom turn on. Aren's eyes widen for a second. "Looks like your crew made fast work of getting the power back on."

"It's the least they could do since they were the ones that knocked it out." *And probably drained the ocean.* This is a lot to deal with.

"Hey..." Aren's gaze drops. "Mom told me you didn't know about Libby. That sucks. I'm sorry you were kept in the dark."

"Not the first time," I grumble. "Did you know about the trouble with Montica?"

"Yeah, that worked out really well."

Am I the only one torn about taking advantage of the crisis? "Why did you get to know about everything as it was happening?"

"You were surrounded by the enemy. Wouldn't it be more dangerous for you to know everything?"

"I guess." I lean my chin on my fist. "I don't know that it was such a good idea to mix everything up when the country's forces might need to defend against an outside threat, though."

"Really, Bram? Would it be better when they could focus their forces on us?"

"No, I know, but—"

"There's no but. This doesn't hurt the Establishment's ability to defend the country, and if they battle it out maybe the military will be too weak to take back the islands afterward."

"A weaker military means marshals died in the conflict. You might remember Emrys is one of them." How far are we willing to go to abolish the Establishment? Mom and Sophos kept talking about the destination being worth the journey, but how many people do we have to lose along the way before it isn't worth it anymore?

Aren's lips press into a hard line. "Don't bring him into this."

"He's in it! I didn't put him in it, but he is a part of it."

"Bram, we already mourned Emrys. He's gone."

Seeing Emrys at Marshal Headquarters in Kaycie flashes through my mind. He didn't know me, but that didn't change the fact that he was my brother. "You can't tell me you don't care if he lives or dies now."

Mercifully, his radio goes off, interrupting our conversation. Mom's voice comes through the static. "Come to the Townhall. We've got a visual on Gladstone. It's not good."

We rush over, and I lead Aren to the office of Lawson's ousted manager. There we find everyone in various states of grief, horror, and outrage as they watch a projected screen.

The camera shows us smoldering ruins and scattered bodies.

Chapter Four

The horse skids to a stop, leaning back to counter his momentum. The rider—one hand on the reins, a rifle in the other—looks out at... what? A threat, or the untamed land he's set out to concur? The stoic expression on the statue's face gives away nothing. My sketch mirrors it. *Buffalo Soldier* is a relic of times long past. When the west was won by men like this. When power was the prize given to the strongest. Brute force and survival of the fittest winning the day. There's something to be said for the straight forwardness of it all.

Modern, manipulative politics created a whole new breed of soldiers. Soldiers who can overpower with silver tongues and plotting minds, in wars no less dangerous for the lack of bullets flying. We evolved, and so did warfare. But we still have our brutes, trying to shift power with violence. Perfect timing for me to come of age—able to step into my place in the Establishment.

I fill in the details and shadows of the statue on my sketch pad, wondering if I'll be of any use in this conflict we've found ourselves in. The mental game was the one I had been preparing myself for—so much as I could, given the limits of my placement. Art was perfectly acceptable until my grandfather told me I was meant for more. I floated through my first sixteen years of life, but for the last two, I've sharpened for a greater purpose. The art stuck though. It's an outlet I'm grateful for.

"Adwin." My grandfather's voice pulls my focus from the sketch in a near growl. He strides toward me in a quiet fury. "What *are* you doing?"

"Drawing." He thinks it a waste of time, but I consider visual arts to be an excellent education in dissecting hidden meanings, which is imperative to our station. "I was unaware of anything I might be needed for."

His eyes burn with rage. "Come with me."

I follow him to his office in silence. What have I done to earn this? The door is scarcely closed before I find out.

"You could have prevented the uprising. Was it really so difficult to date the girl?"

This again? My grandfather already delivered a reprimand when I broke up with Serenity five months ago. Somehow current events have made it a more egregious error on my part. *Lovely.*

"She knew about it?" Serenity is such a sweet, delicate little thing. I don't imagine she could have handled knowing about the uprising without falling apart. "I thought Anton and Grace weren't even telling her about the islands yet."

"That is correct. It's a fact Sophos Verity took advantage of." Grandfather smolders as he sits at his desk. "Serenity Ward didn't only *know* about the uprising, she was a principle participant! She got Sophos into the train control system, she brought Vogue Taylor in who hacked Leavenworth's systems, and she helped find the power plants which they *bombed.*"

"We can't be thinking of the same girl. Serenity Ward is a lovely little simpleton. She isn't capable of anything you're talking about."

"You are the incapable one, Adwin. Incapable of perception, selflessness, responsibility."

I wonder if my mother got these kinds of remonstrances from him as well. It seems like an easy way to secure her estrangement from him. Though his issues with us contradict each other thoroughly. My mother's crime against her father was in choosing to marry a man who he deemed to be featherheaded. How is it that he *wants* me to be with the fatuous Serenity Ward? This whole argument is ridiculous.

"Is there any point to this?"

His scowl is venomous. "Would it kill you to keep an eye on her *here*? You won't have nearly as many distractions, so I dare to hope you can handle it."

An impertinent smile creeps onto my face. "As much as I'd love to help, *you* brought her boyfriend here. I don't think she'll want me around." *Thank you for providing me with an excuse to avoid feigning that attraction again.*

"That will be falling apart now," Grandfather says. "By their own hands. She took an amnesia shot on her way out of Kaycie. She hardly knows him."

There's an argument I wasn't expecting. "Why would she give herself amnesia?"

"To protect Sophos and the uprising. As if I wouldn't be able to get the information I want, anyway."

"If she doesn't remember any of that, why do you want eyes on her?"

"The same reason I wanted eyes on her *before* she was recruited into the uprising. I don't trust the Wards. We are teetering on the brink of destruction, Adwin. I don't need them jolting us over the edge."

I don't have to ask if he means the country or our family. He only cares about the destruction of one. The country only matters by way of our place in it.

Chapter Five

SERENITY

Once my tears dry up, I sit up and comb my fingers through my hair. It ending at my shoulder is bizarre. My hair is on the ever-growing list of inconsistencies I can't sort out. My memory is both obscured and inexplicably straightforward. Veiled in a thick fog, but with sharp spotlights of clarity poking through it. Those spotlights are blunt though, and although I know the information they illuminate for me, there's something missing. I can't even find a way to describe it to myself. I couldn't possibly explain it to anyone else. Not that I have anyone I want to tell.

My relationships are the worst of this mysterious feeling. I know Krisalyn, Frey, and Dixon, but I can't think of anything particular about them. Of course I know Vogue, but I can't think of what it's like to live with her. Jase is the most confusing. I know he's wonderful; I know he loves me, but I don't feel any of that. How can I know I feel something, but not feel it? It's enough to make me want to pull out my awful, short hair.

The motivation to move is difficult to muster, but I push myself up onto my feet. I make my way to the bathroom to see if my appearance is reflecting the torment resounding inside me. My eyes are a little puffy, but overall, I look better than I feel. And isn't that what it's all about?

My hair isn't even as bad as I thought. Maybe I could grow to like it, or I could grow it back out. I wonder which will happen faster?

I glance down at the only jewelry I have here. Earrings that dangle in delicate twists of silver, and the necklace I don't remember obtaining. Are those forget-me-nots? Did I need to remember something? I hope it wasn't anything important, because my brain feels like it got pulled into a tornado.

There is a knock on my door, and I nearly call out 'open' before I remember I'm in this technologically deficient hotel instead of my home. I go to the door and find my parents on the other side.

My mother has her perfectly poised face on, but behind his glasses, Papá's eyes are misty. "Are you all right?" he asks.

"I'm okay."

My mother rubs my arm. "Do you think you can eat?"

I'm hungry enough to risk it. "I should try."

"Good," she says. "Your grandfather just arrived, and I told him to meet us in the dining room."

"Grandpa is here?"

The officers' dining room is two buildings over from the hotel. My grandfather waits outside for us and lights up when he sees me. "There's my girl." He wraps me in an embrace. "Why is it that I have to leave the city to see my granddaughter?"

"I'm sorry, Grandpa. I've missed you."

"And I you. Ah, my prodigal daughter."

"Hello, Father," my mother says as she kisses his cheek.

"Have you heard yet if everyone has arrived?" he asks.

"A few still unaccounted for who were on the islands."

"I'm going to leave the three of you to lunch," my father says. "It's a busy day." He looks at me regretfully. "There is a lot for you to learn, Serenity. I'm sorry I can't be present for all of it."

The three of us enter a decent looking restaurant with a wall of windows that overlook—well, nothing—but they used to have a sea view. It's about half full at the moment. My grandfather asks for a table in the corner, and we're seated.

"So much for retirement," Grandpa says. "I hadn't expected to see this island again."

"You've been here before?" I ask.

"Been here? I ran this place."

"As much as I'd prefer you over Watt Kemp," my mother says, "you aren't here in your former position, so behave."

After we order, I look back and forth between the two of them, waiting for someone to clue me in. "So...what on earth is going on?"

My mother sighs. "I'll start from the beginning. Before the oceans rose, humanity was greedy and combative, diseases swept the planet collapsing healthcare systems and economies, and the planet was abused. The flood gave the survivors an opportunity to start over—to mend their ways so they didn't recreate the same problems."

"You are so theatrical." My grandfather leans his chin on his hand as he looks at my mother incredulously.

"There has to be context, Father." She shakes her head to find her place again and continues. "Keeping communities isolated helped to quell the spread of diseases. Previously, one virus could impact the entire species. Unfortunately, if people know there are places to go, they don't want to remain still. Keeping the islands unknown to each other solved that problem."

My fingers tap my knee. "How could people be so afraid that they agreed to pass on a lie until the truth was lost?"

"Those were very different and very frightening times," she says. "The hope that our generations would be unable to comprehend such fear was the entire purpose."

Well, if the purpose was to give us easier and better lives, they certainly succeeded. But... *all come from the labors of people across the sea. They live as slaves to the Establishment.* Another spotlight shines through the fog.

"What about the people on the islands?" I ask. "They don't live as well as we do."

My grandfather frowns. "Life is different on each island. Not all people would choose to live the way we do."

Facts crash into each other in my mind, fighting for dominance. The spotlight ideas are tempting because they are so clear, but perhaps they're too clear. Now that I'm getting conflicting information, they seem false. Maybe they all are. But that doesn't make sense either. Other spotlight ideas include living with Vogue and being in a relationship with Jase. Those are real.

"Life on the islands varies greatly," my mother says. "Some are quite lovely—for the most part. Though I don't approve of Sophos' methods, the islands had reason enough to want to displace us."

"Always idealistic but can't provide an alternative." My grandfather and mother don't usually argue in front of me, but I know they tend to disagree.

"We *have* offered alternatives. They are consistently rejected."

"Because you can't replace people all together. There will always be a human element."

"What people?" Have they forgotten I'm here? "What are you talking about?"

"Marshals, and a few other positions in Kaycie, are filled with people from the islands," my mother says.

"But they're..."

"No," my grandfather says. "We haven't created effective cyborgs—"

"Demi-sapiens," my mother corrects.

"Whatever. That's the story, because most people can't handle the reality of the matter."

"Which is?" The glass through which I've viewed the world is already webbed with cracks. Can it stand any more? Marshals have always been nearly invisible to me. How can they be people?

"We *brainwash* the people selected to be marshals." My mother glowers at her father.

"I don't like it any more than you do, Grace."

My fingers play *Flight of the Bumblebee* on my lap as I try to steady my breath. Lunch might go the way of breakfast with my stomach flipping this way. "You can't be serious?"

My mother's chin dips down. "Many of us have been trying to end the whole thing."

"How many people know about this?" My voice sounds small.

"There are nine families—"

"Ten," my mother corrects my grandfather again.

He rolls his eyes. "Ten families hold the information and govern the island chain. The eight families which currently have council members, plus Nemes and Rinne. We rotate through council positions and management of the islands. All children in these families are to learn of this sometime between their sixteenth and eighteenth birthdays. *I* advised your mother to tell you already, but since I said it, she opted to wait."

"Father, there was a…" She sighs. "Never mind. Serenity, I'm sorry. I hadn't intended this onslaught. It shouldn't have been all at once like this."

I lean my forehead onto my hand. My mother presses the other one. "Are you all right?"

"This is a lot to take in," I say with my eyes sealed.

"I know, dear."

"The Nemes family too? So Vogue…"

"Found out on the first of the year," my mother says. "About the islands and marshals, anyway. They didn't tell her everything. She didn't know you'd be finding out, and she was sworn to secrecy."

"Why aren't you and Espy in Establishment positions?"

"We don't all have to be. There are more people than positions, so many of us choose to have other jobs. When major issues arise, we're all pulled in, though. We're like the board of directors. We don't all have to work there full time to run the company."

I nibble at my lunch without tasting it. If Vogue's family told her about the islands, then how did she get mixed up in the uprising? "So, we're here because the islands rose up against the Establishment?" And the Establishment is a collective of families including mine. I always thought it was bigger than that.

"If only." My mother grimaces. "We are here because there is a foreign country threatening war against us. Another country lies to the west of the Kaycian Islands."

My stomach drops and my eyelids press closed as I try to take a deep breath. Not only are there other islands, but another country too?

"I need to get some air." I push away from the table and stand.

"I'll go with you," she says.

"No, Mamá. I need to be alone."

"You don't know your way around," my grandfather says.

I wave the folded map from my pocket. "I'll be fine. It's not like I can get far."

They both frown, but neither argue with me. "Meet us here at seven-thirty for dinner?" she asks.

"Yes, I'll be here."

As I walk out, it occurs to me I should have said 'we'll be here.' Why didn't Jase leave that meeting at the same time as my parents?

The map leads me to a long walking trail. The open space helps center me. It isn't manicured like the green spaces in Kaycie—aside from the paved walkway it's rather wild. The tall grasses are starting to brown, and a few trees are showing some red and orange leaves. Autumn's changes have always enchanted me, but now the reminders of change are unsettling. There is too much change right now, and it's happening too fast. Still, it's a nice day, warm in the sun. I just wish I had music. That would clear my mind.

I glance at my cuff, which looks entirely useless if all it can do is tell time. Hopefully they fix the network and power issues soon.

Vogue fired missiles at our power plants.

Will every thought lead me back to my torments?

I walk until evening clouds cover the sun and it's too chilly to be out without a jacket. I suppose I should stop by uniform issue (the very thought of getting clothing there is appalling), but I'll deal with that later. When I return to the hotel, the power is on. That's an improvement. Jase is sitting on the bed when I walk in.

"There you are," he says.

"I went for a walk."

His hands shake as he leans into them and takes a deep breath. "Next time, take a jacket. I picked up some things for you when I stopped at uniform issue."

"Thank you." His ability to anticipate my needs is impressive. "Are you sick now too?"

"I'm fine."

"I'd ask you how the meeting went, but I'm afraid the answer will be too much to add to the day." Not that I want to talk about my own conversation today either, but eventually I'll have to verify how much Jase can know since he's here.

"There isn't much to note."

I twist a lock of my hair as I sit down next to him. "Do they need to talk to me again?"

"Not for now." A minor reprieve for my nerves. "Since Vogue is gone," he says, "I asked them to send someone to take Snowflake until we get back."

Guilt pulls my chin to my chest. "I didn't even think of her. Thank you for taking care of that."

His smile is labored. "That's what I'm here for."

Despite claiming he's fine, Jase skips dinner. My parents, grandfather, and I hardly speak during the tense meal. Back at the hotel, Jase doesn't take me up on my offer to get him anything, and I find I now have cotton t-shirts and shorts to wear to bed. I miss my silky nightgowns, but I'm not sure I want to wear them in front of Jase, anyway. He is doing everything right, but my feelings have gotten buried under the avalanche of change I'm wading through.

Again, we sleep in the same bed, but apart.

Chapter Six

BRAM

Before the sun is fully risen, we're on our way to Gladstone. Aren drives. Our four Kaycians and Carista fill the second and third rows of the shiny vehicle which was manufactured for the city. Keeping the nice stuff will be quite the change for Lawson. More follow behind us.

We ride alongside the train tunnel and see the breach which threw our train around the other night. Gladstone is just beyond the damage. The seawall is partially collapsed at the northeast corner of the isl—town. Countless fingers of smoke curl into the sky. Everyone is silent as we get out of the car.

"First, we look for survivors," I say. "Radio if you find anyone. Be on the lookout for hostiles."

We walk through the quiet street in silence. Buildings all around us are in various states of destruction. Houses and stores are indistinguishable in the rubble. Any building still standing is checked. Inside one, I find a dog curled up next to a dead old woman who is half buried under the remnants of her fireplace. In the city center, bodies are abundant. In person is nothing like seeing this on a screen. I'm surrounded by gasps and stifled cries. The front of their Townhall is decimated, trucks are overturned, and the concrete square is a checkerboard of scorches.

There's no response when we call out for survivors. We go to work checking for pulses, tiptoeing around to avoid stepping on anyone. More are in marshal uniforms as we get closer to the building.

"This would be so much faster with a heartbeat scanner from home," Krisalyn murmurs as she checks bodies.

"I've got one!" Dixon shouts from my other side.

A doctor, an assistant, and Krisalyn rush toward him. "It's okay," Dixon says to the young man. When help arrives, he backs away.

Krisalyn sits on her heels behind the man. "Drink some water," she says, tipping a bottle toward his mouth and wiping his face with a cloth.

"I'm Brenna. Can you tell me where you're hurt?" He points to his left leg and lays a shaky hand on his ribs. The doctor cuts away his bloody pant-leg. His shin bone juts out through the skin, and I whip my head away.

"We can take care of that," she assures him. "Let's check those ribs." As she prods, he winces, and Krisalyn pets his hair. "A few broken ribs, probably. I'll give you something for the pain."

The assistant hands Brenna a syringe which she injects into the crook of his elbow. "You'll feel a lot better with that. Can you tell me your name?"

He takes a few labored breaths and whispers, "Thane."

"Thane, we're going to give you something so you can sleep while we move you, okay? I don't want you to be uncomfortable."

He nods weakly.

Brenna unfolds a plastic tarp with handles along the edges, and they move Thane onto it. Frey and a few other volunteers carry him away to send him to Lawson. The rest of us keep searching.

A knot builds in my throat as I walk through the fallen marshals. Are we going to find Reid or Travick? Carista's gaze darts around.

Maybe she shouldn't have come. Finding one of her brothers like this would be traumatic. The sound of something dropping near my foot pulls my attention from her. A grenade rolls away from me. The pin still around a finger. *Shit.*

"Grenade!" I scoop it up and throw it before diving behind a truck. My arm grates against the concrete. The explosion resounds through the square. Then a bellow of agony rings out. I jump up to see where it's coming from.

"Dixon!" Vogue screams, running toward him.

We all converge at the spot. Dixon throws his head back and grinds his teeth as his left hand grips his right arm. A large shard of glass sticks out from his bicep. Blood pours from the wound.

Brenna kneels down next to him and pulls out a long elastic band. She binds it above the wound as Krisalyn and Vogue mutter reassuring things to him. "Pain killer," Brenna says, holding out her hand toward her assistant. She gives him the injection and waits a moment for it to work before carefully pulling the glass from his arm.

Dixon groans and presses his eyes closed as the girls squeeze his other hand. A tear falls from Vogue's eye.

"Pat, don't leave yet," Aren says to his radio. "We've got another injury to send with you."

As Brenna cleans and dresses the wound, Dixon's face starts to relax. "Of course, I'm the first one of us to get hurt."

Vogue smiles through a few tears. "No you're not." She points to the cut over her eyebrow. "I *bled* when the train tried to flip over the other night."

"Oh good. I didn't want to be first."

"You'll need stitches," Brenna informs him.

Krisalyn helps him sit up. "Let's get you into a car."

The girls help him to his feet. "I didn't hurt my legs." He stumbles despite his words.

"No," Krisalyn scolds him, "but the pain killer won't do your legs any favors right now."

"We'll be back," Vogue says as they start to walk him away.

I rub my eye and shake my head. "Let's take a break."

Most of us find space as far from corpses as possible to drink some water and munch on granola bars. Aren takes a group to clear the interior of Townhall instead. Carista comes to sit next to me but notices my bloody arm. "Let me get Brenna to bandage that up for you."

"It's nothing. Just a scrape."

She goes to Brenna anyway, but only to retrieve supplies. "Arm," she says when she sits next to me. I lay my hand palm up on her lap. "What's this?" she asks as she takes off the blue and purple leather band from my arm.

"Nothing." I take it and grip it in my other fist, leaning my forehead against it. Serenity's gift was supposed to remind me I was fighting for the marshals, but now it makes me think I should have put up a fight for her.

"How did the grenade go off?" Cary brings me back to the present.

"I nudged the hand that was holding it. It rolled out leaving the pin around a finger."

"Lovely."

I nod.

"You okay?"

"Yeah, fine."

"That's convincing."

"You've got worse to deal with, Cary. Don't worry about it." Carista's cousin died in the uprising—right before her eyes. Plus, she's waiting to find out about her brothers. I don't know if she's still active in this as a distraction or what.

"Only old people call me that, now."

"I *am* older than you."

She rolls her eyes. It's only a year, but it's still true. "All done," she says.

"Thanks."

"What's going on?"

I drop my head into my hands. "I didn't know the uprising coincided with problems with Montica. I didn't even know Montica existed."

"I'm sorry you couldn't know."

"That's not the worst part. None of the Kaycians who helped us were told either. I might have still gone along with the plan—it's my mom's. I don't know if they would have, though. Now Dixon is hurt, we all almost died on the train, Tori did die, and Serenity..." My fist tightens around the leather band. "And they did it all under false pretenses. Maybe none of them would have participated."

"Maybe it was for the best then. We needed them."

"They'll find out eventually, and I'm not sure how they'll take it. I don't want them as enemies."

"Oh." Carista pales.

Damnit. I shouldn't have said that. I don't need her being suspicious of them. They're on our side, and I mostly trust them. Not as much as Serenity. This would be easier if I could go through her to clear everything up. *I wish I knew what you were doing.*

Chapter Seven

SERENITY

"Let's see what's going on, shall we?" Tevin Hickey clips a monitor on my fingertip. Two pads are secured to my head. He watches a couple of holoScreens as he asks me how I've been feeling.

Papá stands next to the large mirror opposite the examination table I'm seated on.

"I feel confused mostly." How do I word this? "Like I've woken up and vaguely remember a dream, but not completely. I remember slices of it, but I can't work out what all happened, or what it was really about. But it's not a dream; it's months of my life."

The beeping indicator of my heart rate keeps a steady rhythm like a pendulum.

Tevin has a soothing nature, perfect for the practice of medicine. He leans against the wall casually. "Did you know we have a drug that can erase memories?"

"No." A slight increase in the speed of the beeps.

"It's useful in the case of information leaks. If someone hears something they weren't meant to, one can eliminate ten, thirty, sixty minutes of the person's memory to protect the information. There are few if any side effects. However, when it wipes out a longer period, the person can be left in an unsettling position."

The machine beeps faster. "Are you saying someone drugged me?"

"Actually, sweetheart,"—my father comes to lean against the exam table and hold my hand—"you chose to take it. You removed all of your memories since the beginning of the year."

"That's ridiculous. For one thing, I'd never do that. Also, I *do* remember things from this year!" My heart, my lungs, and the infernal beeps race.

"You *know* things from this year, which you told yourself to replace the lost memories, but do you truly *remember* them?" He takes a deep breath. "Do you remember living in the townhouse after I got my promotion? Do you remember going to the symphony with Jase, your mother, and me?"

"I *remember* plenty about Jase." Am I defending that part first because it's been the most questionable?

"I know this isn't easy to hear, but you must believe me."

"It's not that I don't trust you, Papá, but you're wrong." I blink away stars as the room starts to tilt around me.

"I wish I was." He opens a holo from his cuff. A video projects from it. The plaza fountain. Jase running around in it, and... me. The girl in the video is playing in the plaza fountain, spinning around a sculpted horse, and kissing Jase more enthusiastically than I've ever kissed anyone. That can't be me. There's no way...

My hand covers my gaping mouth. The lack of beeping would be a concern if I couldn't feel my heart racing in my chest. Tevin must have silenced the machine. "Why would I have wanted to forget that?"

My father wraps an arm around my shoulders. "You didn't want to, but you thought it was necessary."

A thunderstorm erupts in my mind. Pieces that don't fit together quite right, whirling around to find the missing bits. I clutch the sides of my head as if I might contain the chaos with my hands. My chest feels like it's being crushed.

"Anton, this is dangerous."

I don't look up to give any attention to Tevin and my father's interaction.

My head may very well explode.

And then darkness falls over me.

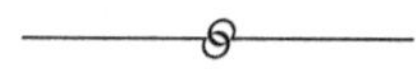

Tevin Hickey removes the clip from my finger. "Well, my dear, the concussion will leave you with some gaps in your memory, but you'll be fine."

My father dips his chin. "Thank you, Tevin."

"Of course." He turns to me. "Try to keep busy. Do things you enjoy. That will help."

"All right. Thank you."

Papá walks me out of the examination room. Jase is waiting outside with my mother. His hair is disheveled and his eyes bloodshot. "How are you feeling?"

"I'm fine. This wasn't anything terribly exciting."

My mother rubs my arm. "Your father and I need to talk to Tevin for a bit. We'll catch up with you later."

"All right."

Jase walks out of the hospital with me. "Are you still not feeling well?" I ask.

"No, I'm okay. Just a little overwhelmed. I have a lot of work to do while we're here."

Chapter Eight

BRAM

"The building is clear," Aren says when he emerges from Townhall. "I don't know if the Establishment manager got out or what."

"She might not have been here," I say. "It was the middle of the night on a Friday. She was probably back in the city."

Vogue, Krisalyn, and Frey return, so it's time to continue our search. We head north and come to the limestone quarry—a white stepped canyon with heavy machinery at the bottom.

"Look there." Frey points to a dark area at the bottom of the quarry wall.

I squint, trying to discern what it is. "A cave?"

"Maybe some people hid in it," Krisalyn says.

"Only one way to find out." Vogue starts toward the sloping path that winds down the quarry.

We hike down, spiraling around as we go. When we get close, I call out, "Hello! Is anyone in there?"

A man wielding a shotgun appears from the darkness of the cave. "Who's there?"

"We're from another island," I say. "We're here to help."

"It's mostly kids in here," the man shouts. "There's no reason for them to get hurt!"

"Oh, thank God," Vogue breathes.

Carista steps forward. "We're not going to hurt anyone. We started the uprising. We want to make sure you're all taken care of."

He examines us. Hopefully, our disheveled appearance gives us points in our favor.

"I'm Bram Eros. Who are you?"

"Eros?" the man says.

"Yes. Kolina Eros started this. She's my mother."

The man disappears into the cave, and we glance at each other while we wait. He comes back out followed by a multitude of children, elderly, and a few scattered young or middle-aged adults. We let out a collective sigh of relief before jumping in to assess needs.

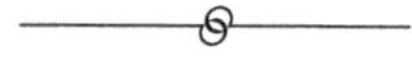

All of us who are able, carry little ones up out of the quarry. They were hungry and thirsty, but no serious injuries. Frey has a boy sitting up on his shoulders, Vogue bounces along, making the little girl on her back giggle, and Krisalyn carries a baby for his tired mom. Seeing them like this makes me think I'm crazy to suspect they'd turn on us.

Carista watches the Kaycians suspiciously as she carries a toddler up. *Crap.* I don't want her paranoid and sharing my concerns with Mom.

Elsie, my four-year-old charge, keeps insisting she wants to walk, but only for a few minutes, then she asks to be picked up, and a few minutes later she wants to walk again. It's slow going, but I appreciate the attempt and her independent spirit.

There isn't enough of Gladstone left, so we bring the survivors to Lawson. A bus arrives, and I talk with Elsie's grandmother as the little girl sleeps on her lap.

"We were told it would be late the following night, but then the broadcast started." Magdala may be in her early fifties, the dark knot on her head is peppered with gray and she looks exhausted. "I told my daughter to take Elsie to the quarry, but she wouldn't hear of sheltering during the struggle. Stubborn as anything, that one." She wipes a tear from her eye. "I can already see it in Elsie. It's a wonder the Foster family has survived so long."

Foster? "Any relation to Aldan Foster?"

Her face pales. "My brother. He was selected to go to Kaycie. I guess he became a marshal."

She'd have no way to know he was the exception to the rule. Aldan Foster was moved to Kaycie without wiping out his memories. They kept his mind intact so he could work in the Department of Health. The vaccine he developed for the extirpation drug saved me, and his daughter trained me.

Elsie's determined independence is no surprise—her mother was Tori's cousin.

"We didn't expect them to have that kind of fire power."

Thane's nephew crawls around the hospital bed back in Lawson. Mom and I listen to the story of Gladstone's battle with rapt attention.

After the broadcast, people rushed to stow away the young, old, and infirm in the quarry cave and marched on Townhall. Explosives opened the doors, but getting through the blanket of gunfire was impossible. Armed with grenades they had fashioned from their mining supplies, the uprising tried to push through, but the marshals returned with shell launchers that flattened the town.

"It was chaos," Thane says. "Smoke, fire, and blood everywhere. I saw a launcher look like it was taking aim toward the quarry—about pissed myself knowing that's where this little guy and all the others were—but a woman leapt at it and sent it firing up and out to sea." Or maybe to the train tunnel where we were passing through.

"That woman saved many lives." My mom's sad smile bears the weight of the lives lost in her plan. Not that it's her burden alone. Gladstone didn't receive the weapons that *I* was supposed to deliver. "Thank you for your sacrifices. Your nephew will never be a marshal thanks to your efforts." She picks up the squirmy toddler.

"Tell Maggie I said thanks for watching him."

"I will. You'll be back on your feet and chasing him around in no time. Get some rest now."

We bring the little boy and dinner to Magdala who is settling into a house on our street. Libby has already befriended Elsie, and they play hide and seek outside. Mom tells her to come in for dinner, and she begrudgingly drags herself inside.

Chapter Nine
ADWIN

Never have I asked this man for *anything*. If I get this, I won't ask for anything else ever again. I *must* have this. This may be a once in a lifetime opportunity. How to ask, though? A childlike, *Grandfather, I'd really like to go with you,* could play upon his regret that he missed my childhood... or annoy him. An assertive, *I insist on going with you,* could either impress him or anger him. If I can get him talking about the trip, it can sound like the idea just pops into my head. *Oh, yes, I forgot you were going. Would you like some company?*

Idiotic.

I tug at the bottom of my jacket, smoothing out wrinkles. There hasn't even been time to have my fleeing-Kaycie outfit cleaned, but I refuse to dress like one of those drones this evening. Grandfather needs to remember who I am. Who he's molding me into. There's no better way to learn than hands-on experience. I must make him see that.

As I walk through the restaurant, I meet Serenity's gaze. She averts her eyes quickly and blushes. Quite the contrast from the last time I ran into her in the city. Then, she was all embarrassment and aggravation, running away from me to wrap her arms around that boyfriend who sits with her now. He looks up and narrows his eyes at me. Though I don't want her back, I rather enjoy his irritation. She doesn't remember her relationship with him, but she remembers me. I'm the one who warms Serenity's cheeks with blushes again, and it's his own doing. It's less than either of them deserve for sinking us into such a mess.

My grandfather looks up as I arrive at our table, eyeing me with unaffected coolness.

"Good evening," I say as I take a seat. "Were there any updates today?"

"Due to a serious lack of other options, it appears I'll be going to Montica."

"That's probably for the best."

He nods, and I push the words past a block in my throat. "I'd like to go with you."

The range of emotions that flash through his eyes is enough to make me regret the words. Surprise, annoyance, anger—faster than anyone should be able to shift.

"Relations with Montica will fall to me someday." I square my shoulders and paint my voice with all the confidence I *don't* have in this. "The opportunity to meet the leaders there is invaluable."

His mouth pinches. There are many words he won't say here, on the chance someone can hear him. "This is over your head, Adwin."

"How else could I possibly remedy that, other than to jump in?"

"And what of your responsibilities here?" What responsibilities? He glances toward the Wards' table and back to me. *Oh, you've got to be kidding me.*

"That is not a responsibility," I hiss.

"I suppose that's how you felt when you started seeing her, and look how ignoring me turned out."

This is a pathetic excuse. She's broken, and even if her parents were up to anything, they aren't likely to tell her because they know she's broken. He just doesn't want me to go.

"What if I find another babysitter here?"

He arches an eyebrow at me in a skeptical glare.

There has to be someone else he'd trust with such a silly thing. "Lanelle Kemp. Her father is one of your biggest supporters." Plus, she can be near Serenity without stepping on the boyfriend's toes.

Grandfather runs his tongue over his teeth, searching for excuses, no doubt.

Under my breath I add, "Kemp's designs align with yours."

"Your mother would be furious."

That's not an angle I expected. "When did that begin to matter?"

She'd be furious about the entire last two years. She excused herself from participating in any of this, so I don't imagine she wanted me to be a part of it.

Grandfather puffs out a breath as he picks up his wine glass. "Talk to the Kemp girl. I hope you'll be honest with me and yourself about her merits."

A working commCuff would really come in handy right now. The hotel gave me Lanelle's room number, but she wasn't there. There aren't many options on how to track her down here, but Rollin Karan is usually around her. I try his room next.

After a couple of knocks on his door, I'm about to walk away, but the door opens. Rollin stands in the doorway with a towel wrapped around his waist, bronze curls in a wild mess around his head. "Adwin, what are you doing here?"

"I was wondering if you knew where Lanelle might be, but I can see—"

"Come in," a lyrical voice calls from behind him.

He glances over his shoulder with an exasperated look but swings the door open.

Lanelle sits on the bed, combing through her mussed hair with her fingers, the sheets wrapped around her otherwise naked form. "Fancy seeing you here."

"If this is a bad time—"

"I'm not shy."

Rollin scoops up a pair of shorts and disappears into the bathroom.

"He is a little," she says with a smirk. "What can I do for you?"

Well, why not? "I was wondering if you might do me a favor. I may have the opportunity to go with my grandfather to Montica, and while I'm gone, it would be helpful if someone here was keeping an on eye on Serenity Ward."

She clicks her tongue. "Oh, she's already on my list. Though not my highest priority."

"What did she do to earn that?"

Rollin comes out of the bathroom then. "Lani, I told you, Serenity is a doll, and she didn't actually do anything to you."

"Fine," she sighs. "It wasn't technically Serenity who got me into trouble with my father, but I won't stand for any objections against my intent to destroy Jase Delgado."

"I don't care who you destroy," I say. "So long as you can also monitor Serenity and her parents."

Lanelle twists a lock of rose gold hair around her finger. "I'm sure befriending Serenity can support both our goals."

Chapter Ten

BRAM

Last night was busy with preparations for Gladstone. Tonight feels like we're trying to establish how life will be moving forward. Mom delivered dinner to the Kaycians so we could have a 'family dinner.' If it was awkward to live in Sophos' Kaycie home, it was only because I couldn't have imagined ever having Sophos live with me in my Lawson home.

Libby is, of course, over the moon to have everyone here, but Aren hasn't warmed up to Sophos yet. Mom keeps a probing eye on me. Maybe she's worried about me since I'm the only one who was kept in the dark about all this, or maybe she expected me to be the link between the Lawson and Kaycian sides of our 'family.' But having lived with Sophos doesn't make this more comfortable for me. It makes it that much more awkward.

Sophos can't stop staring at Libby. It's easy enough to see why he was willing to jump on any option to get back here. We both missed Libby's first three years, but I wasn't aware of what I was missing. It must have been torture to be away from her.

Libby is the only one who makes this feel like a family. She is a little ray of sunshine and quite the chatterbox—clearly half Kaycian. At least there are no awkward silences with her present. She tells us all about how she can do somersaults, she can spin around eleven times without getting dizzy, and she sings us the alphabet a thousand times.

Maybe my sister will be the person to brighten me up. Tori said I needed that. The idea that Serenity might do it seems ridiculous now. She has Jase—who better have kept her safe—and she probably doesn't even remember me now. The thought is nauseating.

After Libby goes to bed, I go outside to try to clear my mind. I don't want to think about Serenity, but as long as we don't know what's happened to her, how can I stop? I pace up and down our street, not wanting to go into town and get stuck talking to people.

The door of the Kaycian outpost (as they've decided to refer to it) opens and Vogue emerges. She comes over and hands me a beer, keeping one for herself. "We're going to need to get wine from Gardner, but I guess this will do for now."

"What brings you out here?" I ask and take a sip.

"Someone is prowling around. I thought I'd check it out."

"You seem like the obvious choice to come out and secure the area." We both sit on the curb, legs outstretched in front of us.

"Didn't you know? I'm quite dangerous."

I do. It makes this even more complicated. If Serenity were here, would I worry about her turning on us too?

"I'm also restless," she adds. "It would be easier if Serenity and Jase were here."

It's strange to be on the same page as Vogue. "I should have stopped her."

"You couldn't have."

"She's tiny. I could've thrown her over my shoulder and carried her to the train."

"As amusing as that would have been to see, I don't think you'd have been successful. She's more feisty than she looks. Did she ever tell you she almost gave you amnesia once?"

"What?"

Vogue laughs to herself. "When she confessed to telling Adwin about the uprising. She had a shot in her pocket and kept it in hand in case you were going to sell her out."

She had paced so calmly when I blew up at her—hands in her pockets. A small chuckle bursts from me. "Nice." Serenity has never failed to surprise me. And the surprises keep making me want her more.

Vogue nudges my arm with her shoulder. "You can't blame yourself."

"That would be easier if we at least knew where she was and what's happened to her."

She frowns. "It looks like Kaycie and Leavenworth aren't even online. Apparently, their solution to my hacking was to go dark and give me nothing to hack."

"They found your only weakness."

"There are disadvantages to being this good."

"Like the risk of developing an ego?"

"No, I'm definitely immune to that." She takes a swig of her beer. Vogue looks comfortable in jeans and a loose sweater. I figured she'd be the first to demand proper Kaycian fashion—which we'll have access to once we organize things from the textile factory—but she's content to dress down. She looks at me earnestly. "So, how do we get her back?"

Chapter Eleven
SERENITY

At one point in history, these families came together to create the world I knew. The peaceful, happy one. Today most of them seem ready to tear out the others' throats.

"Espy, we are all well aware that you are only joining us because you want to get your daughter back." Alima Karan sits at the opposite corner of the hollow square table formation. "But if we spend resources to retrieve your little traitor, it will be to arrest her."

Vogue's mother tenses next to me in the outer ring of attendees. "Bitter that your cybersecurity was no match for a sixteen-year-old?"

Alima's glare could burn a hole through the wall.

"My granddaughter was pardoned," Adelle reminds her.

Similar exchanges are thrown about the room. Nine representatives of the families sit at the table. Sophos is, of course, not present to represent the Verity family as its only living member. The rest of us sit behind them in elevated seats, making this look like an arena. Any moment now there will be a gladiatorial battle in the center, I'm sure.

This melee isn't what I pictured when my parents told me the Establishment families were meeting. I shouldn't be included yet, but they decided to include those of us who are still in our transition age—sixteen or seventeen years old. Rollin Karan and Lanelle Kemp are the only other ones besides me. Vogue isn't available.

Watt Kemp's mother argues with Governor Martel's daughter on the far side of the arena, Platinia Rinne accuses Flora Prosper of a cover-up regarding the dropping of the sea, and my grandfather debates the ethics of the extirpation drug used on the marshals with anyone who will listen. How did such a peaceful society ever come out of this chaos? Well, I suppose it wasn't *quite* as peaceful as I thought it was.

Adwin sits in the corner behind Lieutenant Governor Agnar. I didn't even know they were related. His conversation with Rollin seems convivial enough. His eyes meet mine, and I blush at being caught looking at him. He flashes me a grin and I look away. Why did he break up with me? That's not something I should be thinking about. I have Jase. And plenty to distract me from that mystery.

Martel stands and the dull roar fades. "We are not here to lay blame for our current situation. Now is the time to delineate our problems and find solutions. Flora, how long can we feed Kaycie and Leavenworth without receiving anything from Gardner or Eudora?"

"Three months based on normal consumption."

"And with comfortable rations?"

"Six."

Tevin Hickey's mother puffs out a breath. "Rations in the city. That will go over well. You'll need to move the marshals back to Kaycie to control our own people rather than sending them to recover the islands."

"We aren't sending them to the islands anyways," Watt Kemp says.

Another dull roar builds as people express their shock and disapproval. Some are concerned about keeping the city afloat. Some of the fuss is only injured pride—needing to prove ourselves as the sovereign governing body.

"We do not need to control all of the islands," Agnar says. "Not as an immediate priority. All we need to do is strike a deal with Eudora and Gardner to secure our food supply. Sophos can play house in the rats' nest of Lawson all he wants. That can wait until we've secured matters with Montica."

"Who *will* be cleaning up Watt's mess?" my father asks.

"For the hundredth time," Kemp says, "our marshals can't fire missiles without approval. I don't know how they'd have shot down that Montican craft."

"Maybe it was another teenage hacker," Tevin says with a smirk.

Alima glowers at him, and I shudder thinking of Vogue's role in this. Her parents grasp each other's hands to my right.

"I will go to Montica," Agnar says.

Many suspicious eyes point at Martel who nods his agreement. "We only have any relations with Montica because of Casimir. He is the one to smooth this over." The room is silent for a tense moment.

"What do we know about the sea, or lack thereof?" Adelle asks.

"It's under investigation," Martel replies. His wife and daughter exchange a concerned glance behind him. The latter rests a hand on her swollen belly.

"I'd like to aid with that investigation," my mother says. Others murmur similar sentiments.

"It's under control," Agnar says.

Discomfort radiates through the room. Casimir Agnar is not the most popular person in this group, but apparently, he has enough power to keep anyone from arguing. I start to see the lines drawn between these people. Rivalries, ambitions, infighting tearing them apart. Sophos knew they were like this. Of course he was able to orchestrate an uprising.

"Now then," Martel says, "who will go to Gardner and Eudora?"

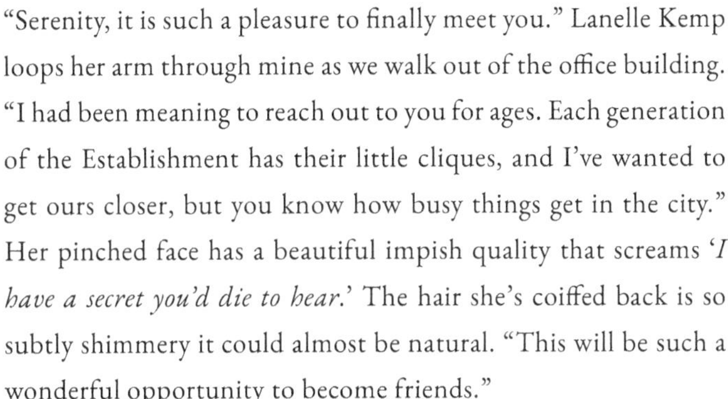

"Serenity, it is such a pleasure to finally meet you." Lanelle Kemp loops her arm through mine as we walk out of the office building. "I had been meaning to reach out to you for ages. Each generation of the Establishment has their little cliques, and I've wanted to get ours closer, but you know how busy things get in the city." Her pinched face has a beautiful impish quality that screams '*I have a secret you'd die to hear.*' The hair she's coiffed back is so subtly shimmery it could almost be natural. "This will be such a wonderful opportunity to become friends."

"I'm sure it will."

The strategy to send fresh young faces to Eudora and Gardner means Lanelle and I will be going on an adventure together. My parents didn't love it but didn't stop it either. I can't help but agonize over the idea that Vogue should be included as well. Between what I've learned about Kaycie over the last few days and my faith in Vogue, it's difficult to condemn her actions. There is so much I don't understand, though. If only I could talk to her.

"And while we're all stuck here,"—*At least I won't have to worry about filling silence around Lanelle.*—"we should all get to know each other. We'll all be working together for the rest of our lives, and I don't ever want us to clash like everyone did at that ridiculous meeting."

"Absolutely. I have no desire to be part of anything like that ever again."

"Of course, so we'll make sure we all get along. You're friendly with Rollin and Adwin already, anyway."

Did I just agree to spending time with Adwin? I don't want to alienate Jase. "To be honest, I'm not sure it would be very kind to Jase..."

"Come now, we're all adults here. If Jase and I can still work together, you and Adwin shouldn't have a problem."

"Oh. You and Jase?"

"We broke up years ago. Anyway, he's more than welcome to join us. If you marry him he'll be part of the Establishment anyway."

Marry him? I hardly know him. The mentioning of it, so casual, raises my blood pressure and tenses my muscles. How did I end up in this strange place, walking around with this girl I just met as if we're the best of friends, talking about marrying my boyfriend who might as well be a character I've read about? I should be in Kaycie, walking with Vogue, talking about Adwin.

The fog bears down on my mind.

"We'll plan a little get-together soon," Lanelle continues, not noticing my mood shift. She releases my arm and kisses the air as she taps her cheek to mine. "Have a lovely evening."

She flitters away, leaving me uneasy. I brace myself on the railing by the drying sea floor. So much buzzes through my mind that it blurs—so unfocused it might as well be blank. I don't know what to do, what to think, how to feel. How am I supposed to help get anything done for Kaycie in this state?

My father appears next to me. I look up to see his warm smile with sad eyes behind his glasses. "You're very brave, Serenity," he says. "I'm so proud of you." Brave... Me?

"Why?"

"Agreeing to go to the isl—towns." He lays his arm around my shoulders, and I lean my head against him.

"I don't feel brave, Papá. I'm scared and confused."

"That's what makes your actions all the more courageous." I'd like to believe that.

"I got you something that I think will make you feel better," he says. "Come with me."

Chapter Twelve

BRAM

"Command Verity-8491." Sophos stands before the marshals, hands clasped behind his back like a military commander. "New command codes are as follows: Lawson-1870, Blue Springs-1880, Greenwood-1867, Gardner-1857, and Eudora-1857. All command codes prefixed Martel, Agnar, Kemp, Karan, Prosper, Hickey, Rinne, Nemes, Taylor, Ward, and Verity are null and void. Stand by for transfer assignments."

"Will that work?" Aren mutters to me.

"It should. They won't act like humans, but at least they'll take orders from the right people now."

We may not know their names, but we know where each marshal is from. They each have a town they aren't allowed to go to—the one they're from. We can identify them by their tattooed ID numbers and send them back. Then each town can sort out who is who among them. It sounds fine for the living marshals, but we'll also be swapping bodies between the towns. No one is looking forward to the shitshow which will be the identifying of corpses.

"Why didn't he just reprogram them to begin with?" Carista asks. "Would've saved a lot of lives."

"There was no stealthy way to get to enough marshals. To reset command codes, they need to see him in person."

"Hmm." Carista picks at her cuticles, coming up with another work around, no doubt. "Now that he has more support, maybe we could get him into Leavenworth to reprogram the rest of them."

"That would end the war," Aren says.

"*This* one." I shoot him an annoyed look. "They'll have voided his code by now, anyway. But nice try. Going to Leavenworth would be suicide. I've tried to convince myself otherwise, but it's pointless."

Vogue and I are at a loss on how to get Serenity back. And Jase. I keep forgetting about him. Any plan we come up with is shredded by Frey and Dixon immediately. Krisalyn remains silent on it all. She wants it as much as Vogue and I do, but she's reasonable enough to admit we're screwed. None of us are willing to wipe out our memories like Serenity and Jase did. It would make the whole thing pointless, and we don't want to. So, we can't hand ourselves over to the Establishment.

Carista questions me with her eyes, then glances at Aren and back at me. "Bram, can I speak with you a moment?"

"Sure."

We get out of earshot from Aren, and she asks, "Why have you been trying to find a way into Leavenworth?"

"I had gotten Serenity into trouble back in Kaycie, which is why she was ready to wipe out her memory." All while I was inadvertently starting her relationship with Jase, as *I* was falling for her myself, which is so ironic it should be funny, but I'm too stupid to get over her. Which is also why I want to get her out of Leavenworth. Because stupid begets stupid begets stupid.

"I thought that might be why." Carista bounces on her feet. "And if you haven't come up with a way to get to Serenity and Jase, then... I guess you don't know either." She presses her fingers over her eyes and shakes her head.

Damnit, what are they keeping from me now? "Just tell me. I'm getting used to this."

"The Establishment sent word that our resident Kaycians were pardoned. Sophos excluded, of course."

"What?" I stop in my tracks.

"Apparently they believe Vogue and the others were manipulated by Sophos. They are supposedly in the clear."

"How would the Establishment know that?"

"I have no idea."

"By not telling them, we are basically holding them hostage." Why do we keep creating rifts between us and our *allies*? Mom and Sophos are digging us into a hole we won't be able to climb out of.

"We are *not* holding them hostage. For one thing, this is the Establishment we're talking about. Do we really trust their word? They could go back and be greeted by marshals and handcuffs."

"That's not our judgement call to make, Cary! Shit."

"I agree with you on that. That's why I wanted to talk to you about it. I was considering telling them. What do you think?"

We continue walking away from Townhall. "I don't know. I have to think of a way to tell them everything without highlighting the fact that a mound of secrets have been kept from them."

Carista sits on a bench and pulls her feet up to sit cross-legged, leaning her elbows on her knees. "After going to Greenwood with them, I think we can trust them. They're good people. They won't be our enemies unless we make them our enemies."

Maybe her field trip with them helped pull her from the suspicions I planted. They got Greenwood on-line and figured out the towns were hardly getting any electricity from Kaycie. I guess that makes sense since the 'power plant' is actually a military base. They only had to redirect some things, and the towns generate enough electricity to keep us up and running. Where would we be without them?

"Well, despite all they've done for us, we've been doing a great job of treating them like enemies," I say. "Maybe I'll talk to them when we go check out the missile mystery." Two-hundred-fifty miles from civilization seems like a good place to incur Vogue's wrath.

Carista's eyes widen. "You'll actually go there, right? You're not going to go rogue and sneak off to Leavenworth?"

"Yes, I'll actually go out there. *I'm* not pardoned by the Establishment, and we're all anxious to see if we can officially blame Vogue for draining the sea." Seeing what it is she bombed should prove whether or not it was a coincidence.

"Okay." She looks back at Townhall where they're sorting the marshals. "I should get going."

"Why did you insist on going along for marshal sorting and reprogramming?"

"I'm basically part of your family, Bram. I figure I should get to know Sophos." She stands to leave. "And I do have a job in this mess."

"Good luck then, Major." I give her a careless salute, and she rolls her eyes as she walks away.

I sit in her place. Will it make things better or way worse to tell the crew everything? If I could remove my personal feelings from the equation, I might be able to look at it objectively. That's not going to happen, though. I lay my hand over the leather band on my arm. The card it came with said remembering Emrys and the others would make me stronger. I'd like to think remembering the girl who gave it to me would do that too—give me something to fight for. But when everything brings me back to thoughts of Serenity, I feel helpless.

Chapter Thirteen

SERENITY

The tune fills my empty spaces, wraps me in warmth, soothes me. My fingers dance over the keys—the choreography imbedded into my muscle memory. I was born in the wrong century. I'd like to have known the composer of *Lost Soul*, but he lived long ago. Back in a time which I had believed to be complicated and dangerous, as opposed to our peace and tranquility.

Perhaps it was actually better back then. RIOPY died long before the flood, but really, he outlived the masses, the monuments, the land. His songs are still played, and that makes him immortal. I wonder if he knew that as he wrote them.

My father's gift of musical therapy was exactly what I needed. Piano is the only normal thing I have. Being here, not knowing what's going on with any of my friends in the city or Lawson, and no access to buzzChains, has left me unsettled. Ironically, the islands are now all connected by land, but I feel more isolated than ever. Maintaining my reputation has always been my primary occupation. What am I without that?

This solitary space is my haven now. Away from the world, the people I'm supposed to be friends with now, and Jase. Yesterday, I'm sure I saw him walking away down the hall when I left this small office my father gave me. The idea of Jase knowing I play feels like a violation. I don't want to confront him about it, though.

As my mind drifts to him, my fingers change course and start a different song. Ten notes in, I realize what it is and clench my hands into fists. Some part of me is ready to fall into Jase's arms and let him carry me through this chaos, but it still feels foreign to me, and our *relationship* is so lopsided.

Jase is perfect... and it's maddening. How can he anticipate my needs when I wouldn't be able to think of anything for him? He downloaded some music I can listen to without a network connection, had Espy Taylor take in my uniforms so that they aren't completely horrid on me, and I wake to tea every morning. This would all be great if I could reciprocate, but I don't feel anything. Except guilt. I'm plagued by guilt.

Letting myself really be with him would be reprehensible. I'd be enjoying all the benefits of his adoration without giving anything back. I suppose that's what I'm doing now anyway, but it would be worse to encourage it. The least he could do is give up on me. He could tire of the burden of pulling all the weight in this relationship and just leave me. Not that I want him to leave me. It's comforting having someone care for me this way, and I'm endeavoring to bring back the feelings I know I had, but with each day that passes their return seems less likely.

Despite my indifference, he remains steadfastly devoted to me. Which increases my guilt.

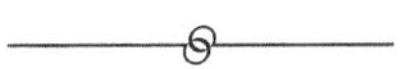

"Why are we doing this, again?" I make my final attempt to wriggle free of my mother's plan as I don my white mask.

"We both need our exercise and a distraction." She unsheathes a sabre from the rack and swishes it around to get a feel for the weight.

"If this is just for exercise, why are you in black?" The instructor uniform foretells that this is more than friendly practice. The very idea is exhausting.

"How long has it been since you fenced? Two, three years?" I don't respond as I select my weapon. "I shouldn't have let you drop it."

Not that I hated fencing, it just wasn't my cup of tea. My mother effortlessly balances power with feminine elegance, but my scale has always tipped away from the physical strength side. Few realize my mother does her own stunts—seeing her only as a delicate rose, but she has thorns.

"Being that I am out of practice, wouldn't VR suit you better than me?"

She lets out an exasperated breath as she takes her stance. "A virtual opponent is never on par with a person, and what would you do with your time if not this?"

"Anything."

A wind chime of a laugh comes from the black metal net of her mask. "En garde." I groan to myself. "Prêtes?" As if she cares if I'm ready. "Allez."

My confusion and uneasiness have been more persistent than I would have imagined possible. Fencing has to be the worst thing I could do in this state. She thrusts and gets an easy point. The next I parry, but she makes an immediate riposte, scoring again. At least this will be over quickly.

"Serenity, if you aren't going to try, we can go to fifteen instead of five."

"Mamá, it's been years!"

"And?"

She continues to dominate the match. I'm down by four at the three-minute break. If I don't score, this will take three times as long. She takes off her mask and flashes a perfect smile at me. "You knew I wouldn't go easy on you. Irrigated vines make bland wines." That's her favorite saying to remind me that struggling strengthens. Except I've had little opportunity to put it to practice. Who has? Until I got dropped on this military base, life was easy. I'm not prepared for my role in the world or this family now that I know what it entails.

"Not going easy on me is part of the reason I did not want to participate." At another time I might enjoy the competition, but sorting myself out is challenge enough for now.

"Come now, where is your fire?"

Where is any part of me? My father's version of helping me by giving me a piano is much better. This is exasperating, but she is done with my sulking. I suppose she's harder on me because she was born into the Establishment too. She wants to prepare me. Perhaps she's always been doing that.

"Back to it!" My mother springs to her feet.

I put up a better defense in the second bout, turning to avoid a counterattack by the narrowest of margins. I get one point on her after a feint, regaining my confidence. It's a dance— graceful and smooth, but instead of reading my partner's movements to follow, I sense my opponent's to deflect. The loss is unavoidable, but catching my breath and stretching neglected muscles is easier than solving my mental and emotional distress.

No reason to tell my mother she's right—she always knows. And perhaps she found a spark of the fire she was looking for, because now I have to continue until I can beat her.

⑨

A dream already forgotten wakes me up, and as I shift in bed, my eyes fly open. How am I tangled up in Jase's arms? His chest rises and falls steadily under my hand. My head is nestled between his shoulder and his neck. I'm about to move back to my side of the bed, but a deep breath fills me with his scent of warm spices, and I let myself relax again.

This is the most we've touched since we've been here. Despite his attention, affection and intimacy have been locked away. He hasn't so much as held my hand since the day after we arrived here—likely his altruistic way of giving me space to get comfortable. At least, we don't touch in the light of day. When we get into this bed, we keep to our sides. He might as well be on the other side of a wall. Now that I'm here, though, I wonder if this is typical. I've woken up in the middle of the bed, but he's always gone before I get up. Has he been waking up to this?

Lying here with him asleep, I feel like this is my secret. I wonder if he thinks it's a secret he's keeping from me. That's a conversation I don't have the nerve to start. I don't even know what he does with most of his time here. He's working with Lanelle on something, but I haven't asked about it. Asking him if we frequently cuddle would be all sorts of awkward.

To my surprise, the cuddling itself isn't awkward at all. The two of us together feels like a song I can't quite remember. The idea is in my head, but I can't pull the lyrics or melody from my memory. Even if I can't place the song, I'm comfortable with my body pressed against his. Could we be like this always? Close enough to leave no room for anything between us? It sounds nice, but in the light of day there will always be walls. I was born to carry and protect terrible secrets. I have to have walls. Even if we got to the point where I could tell him everything, what would he think of me when he finds out who I really am? Not to mention the terrible burden it would put on him. How could he love me then?

A tear rolls out of the corner of my eye, mourning the impossibility of holding onto this. This contentment is doomed to be restricted to my sleeping hours. Jase and I will only be a dream, and by day I'll have to face the real world. It isn't fair to either of us, but for now I let myself enjoy the dream. Using his breaths to pace my own, I relax myself back to sleep.

Chapter Fourteen

BRAM

"You can't tell Sophos. If he changes his mind about my involvement, he'll wipe out my memories." Serenity squares her shoulders toward me. For someone so small, she's surprisingly fearless.

"I'm about to do that!"

She whips a vial out of her pocket, but I catch her wrist. She gasps as I pin her back to the wall. Her gray eyes bore into mine with a stubborn fury. "I'm not letting you take my memories."

"Good idea. Both of us should remember this."

She tenses between my body and the wall as I press my lips to hers. After a heartbeat, she relaxes, and her lips part with mine. My tongue explores her mouth. Her free hand slides up my neck, pulling me closer. The other releases the vial...

The imagined sound of shattering glass jerks me awake. My heart races as I pull my palm down my face. That's not quite how that happened in real life. *Shit.*

When Vogue told me Serenity had an amnesia shot ready during that fight, I didn't realize my imagination would take off with the idea. I sit up and lean onto my knees. The image won't get out of my head. I *need* to stop thinking about her this way.

Sleep isn't going to happen, so I go out back. Maybe fresh air will clear my mind. At a thud from the treehouse, I reach for—*no gun*. Because I'm home. And rattled by rogue thoughts I can't control, so I didn't automatically put it on. The sound repeats. And again.

"Who's there?" I say.

There's a gasp and crash before Carista peeks out. "Shit, Bram, you scared me!"

"You scared me. What the hell are you doing out here?"

"I couldn't sleep. What are you doing out here?"

"I also couldn't sleep."

She huffs out a breath and hops down.

"I can't believe this thing is still standing."

Cary looks up at it with a thin smile. "Well, don't you go trying to climb in. I don't know that it can support your weight anymore."

"Gee, thanks."

She rolls her eyes. "Like you'd rather still be a gangly teenager instead of sporting all those muscles."

"Why can't you sleep?" I care, but I also want to direct this away from her asking why *I* can't sleep. Carista has a lot to deal with. She found Reid in Gardner but having him back as a shell of himself is a struggle. A lot of families are having a hard time coping with their returned loved ones.

She sighs and sits with her back against the tree. "I went to see Janey and her mom today."

"Oh." Also that. Janey is Carista's surviving cousin. Her sister died protecting Carista during the uprising.

"I wish I could give Hensley back to them. I wish she were alive, but even more I wish it wasn't my fault she died. Is that horrible?"

"No. Guilt might be the hardest part to deal with. I'd tell you it's not your fault, but I know me saying it won't change anything for you."

"You are correct."

"But it still isn't your fault."

She shrugs and shifts as I sit next to her. "It's just... it's everywhere. There it was Hensley, at home it's Reid, at your house it's Emrys. There are a lot of ghosts."

In Leavenworth, it's Serenity. In Kaycie, it's Tori. Yeah. A lot of ghosts.

Chapter Fifteen
SERENITY

A gin martini appears in front of me at the officers' bar. I'm fairly certain they only have cocktail onions because I was mildly disappointed there were only olives earlier in the week. Jase was speaking with the bartender as we left that night. Even my remedy is garnished with guilt now. Maybe I *would* feel better if he just broke up with me.

Lo-and-behold, the last person to break up with me comes walking in. "Is this seat taken?" Adwin asks, pulling out the one next to mine.

"Go right ahead." I keep my eyes on my martini. Lanelle has tried to get us all together, but I was trying to avoid Adwin. Clearly this base is too small for that plan to work.

He orders scotch and turns to me. "You're loving it here too it seems."

I look up at him, and his damn blue eyes ensnare me. I find myself smiling back at him. "Well, this wasn't my first choice of vacation options, but at least there's a bar."

His drink arrives, and he holds it out to me. "Cheers to having a bar."

I clink my glass against his and pour more than I should down my throat. I suppose if I'm already here with him, I might as well clear up some of the fog. "You're related to Casimir Agnar. Why didn't I know that?"

"My mother likes to forget he exists, so I try not to mention it either. But he and I have gotten close over the last couple of years, and now that I'm eighteen, I'm part of this."

"I wonder if not getting along is common in Establishment families. My mother and grandfather butt heads, but not so thoroughly as to estrange themselves from each other." I hope that doesn't happen to me and my parents. We've always been so close.

"There is a lot of pressure on all of us. If there are cracks in a relationship, it seems the pressure could easily break it."

I sip my martini as I think about which of my relationships will be consumed by this.

"Speaking of relationships, how is it that you got to bring your boyfriend?"

The less-than-subtle transition from breaking relationships to Jase riles me. This is a perfect example of why I should not be around Adwin. I will not talk to him about Jase. Just sitting here with him while Jase is probably off doing something unbearably thoughtful for me is enough to pile onto my guilt.

"He was in the wrong place at the wrong time." The night we left Kaycie is still a blur thanks to my concussion, but that's my understanding of it. *Plus, your grandfather thought we were both involved in the uprising. That probably helped.* I bite my lip.

"Lucky for you." The sharpness in his voice says he is anything but happy that I have Jase here with me.

"Indeed." I press my lips together as the guilt washes over me again. "I should go find him, actually."

"Oh, please don't let Lanelle and Rollin find me drinking alone. That would be pitiful."

Like how you just found me *drinking alone?* "I'm sorry, but I—"

"See Lanelle, I told you Adwin Lebeau never lacks for company." Rollin comes toward us, dark bronze curls falling over his forehead and framing his long face.

"That doesn't excuse your tardiness." Lanelle gives Adwin a kiss on the cheek before greeting me warmly. "I'm so glad to see you out, Serenity. I had started to worry we wouldn't get any time together until we go off to the towns."

"I'm sorry," I say. "I haven't been feeling particularly sociable."

Rollin orders two drinks and turns to me. "Understandable in the current state of things."

"I think the current state of things is all the more reason for us to be social," Lanelle says. "How else are we to keep our spirits up?"

What a perfect snapshot of Kaycie: worrying about being social and keeping our spirits up as the world burns around us. I *should* disagree, but it's so tempting to just let things seem normal. And we do all have to get along. I find myself settling in and ordering another round as we chat. Nothing has changed between Adwin and me. Why did we break up? I'd feel guilty for being more comfortable with my ex than with my boyfriend, but the martinis are doing their job. Alcohol induced fogginess masks the fog that already existed in my head. Having something to blame makes it tolerable—almost funny.

"I'm so jealous," Rollin says. "The rest of you have adventures coming up. Has yours been decided, Adwin?"

"Has what been decided?" I ask.

"I'm going with my grandfather to Montica," he says. "We leave in a couple of days."

"Wow." Going to a foreign country sounds incredible, but since they are currently threatening war against us, it seems like a dangerous place to visit. My upcoming little trips are probably more than enough excitement.

"And then you two"—Rollin gestures to Lanelle and me—"will go off to the towns, and I'm the only one left here to rot."

"We are going on day trips." Lanelle rolls her eyes. "Don't be so dramatic." Her gaze jumps past us and a curious smile creeps onto her lips.

I turn to see Jase walking in. "Here you are," he says when he reaches me.

"Jase Delgado, just the man we were missing. Rollin, get another seat," Lanelle orders. "Please join us."

"Maybe some other time." He turns to me. "Your mother is looking for you."

"Grace isn't one to worry," Adwin says.

Jase's eyes narrow at Adwin. "Well, I'm sure Grace wants to be sure *she* doesn't lose Serenity."

I gasp, but his eyes remain focused on Adwin with a confident stare. "Let's go find her then," I say as I stand up. "I'll see you all soon." I storm out of the bar with Jase at my heels. Outside, I halt and turn to him. "What was that?"

"What?"

"If you have something to say about what I'm doing, say it to me. Don't be passive aggressive to other people, just get angry at me!" He has to start getting angry or disappointed or resentful of me. I've been waiting for it.

"I can't be angry at you," he sighs.

"Why not?"

"Because it wouldn't be fair. None of this is your fault, and I'm too busy being angry at myself."

"Stop acting like this is your fault. I'm the one falling apart and dragging you down with me. I've been awful and you keep taking it. Give up on me already!" I need to cut him loose. He deserves better than my inattention, better than this world of lies and manipulation.

His honey-colored eyes beguile me, but I look away. No need to remind myself of what I'm giving up. He tilts my chin up to meet his gaze again. My skin prickles under his touch. "It'll take more than that to get rid of me. I know you're hurting, and I'm so sorry for that, but I want to help you through it. You're still the bold, surprising—"

"Stop!" I twist away and storm off to the railing at the former waterfront.

Jase follows, looking at me with pleading confusion.

"You're hanging onto a vision of me that I can't be. You know it, so stop lying to yourself, and don't bother lying to me about it."

He drops his head and rubs the back of his neck. "Fine." His eyes meet mine again, but they aren't soft anymore, they're resolute and sad. "You're right. You haven't exactly been pleasant company, Serenity. You've been sullen and dismissive, you've scoffed at my attempts to help, and you've shut yourself away from humanity." *Be careful what you wish for.* I wanted this, but watching him leave tears a hole through me. "You are so determined to be miserable that you're willing to turn your back on me. I understand you want to be stronger, but shielding yourself in armor doesn't make you strong. It's too heavy to keep on all the time." He takes my hand in his and gives it a squeeze. I brace for goodbye. "I'll be here when you take it off, though."

What?

"Whenever you're ready." He turns and leaves me gaping after him.

Chapter Sixteen
ADWIN

"Isn't there enough conflict going around without adding a chauvin-istic territory campaign over a fair maiden?" Lanelle looks bored to death by the idea.

"You know that isn't the case," I say.

"Jase doesn't."

"All the more reason you are a far more appropriate babysitter than I am."

"Actually,"—she crosses her legs and leans in like she has something devious up her sleeve— "I was thinking Rollin could slip in and pull Serenity right out of his hands. Then she's cut off from all of her accomplices."

And you get your revenge on Jase.

Rollin cocks his head. "What?"

"Oh, don't be a baby about it." She swats him on the arm and drops her chin to look at him through thick eyelashes. "You know I hate to share, but it would be worthwhile to see the look on Jase's face when he walked in on you two."

Guilt seizes me. Lanelle keeping an eye on Serenity is akin to letting a wolf watch a lamb. I can practically see Lanelle sharpening her claws. "No, that's too far."

"It's exactly what they did to me. Sending Frey Dempsey to seduce me so they could steal from me." She crosses her arms with an indignant huff. "If they want to fight dirty, I'll fight dirty."

"Again, that wasn't Serenity," Rollin says. "So you can do your own dirty work."

"So much for teamwork then." Lanelle pops up to her feet. "Perhaps our generation of the Establishment won't be any more productive than the current one." She bustles out, leaving Rollin and I shaking our heads.

I tell myself she'd be on this war path without my request for her assistance. None of these people are my problem, anyway. As much as I regret not realizing I was anyone of any significance for most of my life, Lanelle does make for a good example of why children perhaps *shouldn't* grow up knowing they're special. Even though her parents couldn't tell her about the islands and everything until she was sixteen, she grew up in one of the council townhomes, having more than anyone around her. Her sense of superiority drips off of her.

"She's a handful," Rollin sighs.

That's an understatement. "I'm not Serenity's biggest fan, but in her current state, she *is* innocent. Could you try to keep Lanelle from getting out of hand with her?"

"I'll try. It's hard to believe Serenity turned on the Establishment the way she did. She was always such a perfect poster child for the city."

Rollin had been in the Leadership pre-program with Serenity for six years before Verity got his claws into her. I wonder if his family is blaming him for not noticing anything was off about her like I'm getting from Grandfather.

"I suppose Verity spun it just right," I say.

Rollin nods. "I can understand why Casimir would want eyes on her. Even if she doesn't remember, she chose to go that direction once. She could do it again."

That's true enough. Underestimating Serenity Ward proved problematic already. It's not a mistake I can make again.

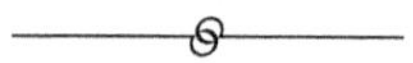

What a strange time it is to be able to tell people I'm going to *Montica*, but not that I'll be visiting Kaycie. Lanelle would no doubt pitch a fit if she found out I got to stop by. Thanks to the uprising, the train isn't an option at the moment. Flying into the middle of the city with the sun still shining over the horizon is surreal. Secrets such as our aircraft aren't worth hiding anymore when much bigger ones have been revealed.

The fountains are off early. Not for the weather this year, but to conserve power. The monorails aren't running. Though there isn't much to do in the city, foot traffic is actually higher than I've ever seen it. Electricity is too scarce now to use it on all the in-home entertainment systems, so in their boredom Kaycians have taken up going for walks.

We land on the rooftop pad of the EC, and Grandfather reminds me that I have precisely three hours before we return to Leavenworth. He goes to his office in this near-abandoned building. Only essential workers are still here. Seeing how very few Kaycians are 'essential' should be the big wake up call, but I doubt many will recognize their own insignificance.

I go to see my mother first. She doesn't look at me when I come in—keeping her eyes focused on the wall in front of her—dark, sunken circles under them.

"Mother." I sit next to her. "Are you angry with me?"

"No." She still doesn't turn toward me. "I'm angry at *him*. He had no right to drag you into his world."

"I chose to be in his world." Now she turns to face me. "Too much looms over us. I want to keep us safe. That's what Grandfather wants."

She puffs out an incredulous sound from between her teeth.

"It's true. Especially now that turmoil abounds, you must see how important it is."

"Being involved puts a target on you. Connections to important people put you at risk. Anonymity is safety. It's peace." A tear rolls down her cheek.

"Not necessarily."

"So you're going back to Leavenworth?"

For now. "Yes." My trip to Montica is likely too much for her to handle. I won't burden her with that worry. I glance up at the painting behind her. The mountain scape which always mesmerized me.

"I don't know why this life isn't enough for you," she says.

I don't know how you've settled enough to believe it is. "Are you sure you want to stay in the city?"

"Yes. These are only minor inconveniences. I'm fine."

"All right. I may be unreachable for a little while. There are things to do around the towns."

"Okay."

At least I can count on her to sink into her own misery enough not to bother questioning me. "I'll call when I can."

She dismisses me with a nod, and I leave. The next person I mean to call will no doubt be less quiet about her disappointment in me.

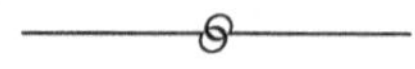

"I cannot *believe* you didn't tell me." Parisa paces my bedroom as I pack my suitcase—a sea of orange ruffles rustling around her. A lack of things to do has not stopped her from dressing extravagantly.

"It was unequivocally confidential."

"You trusted me with plenty of other secrets."

For goodness' sake, she can't honestly think to compare my personal secrets to the ones which molded Kaycian society. Had I already forgotten how exhausting she is?

"Parisa—"

"And then you just disappear! You leave me here to rot as the city falls apart, and I don't even hear from you."

"I didn't have a way to reach you. This is the first time I've come back, and I got in touch with you right away. What more do you expect?" I hang a shirt in the bag, thrilled to be wearing real clothes again.

Parisa scowls at it. "You have better options than that." She makes her way to my closet.

"I can't be in high fashion right now."

A groan sounds out and she comes back to lean against the door. "These have to be the signs the world is ending."

Her melodrama is almost endearing. To be fair, the world as she knew it has certainly met its end. It isn't her fault she can't see past the borders of the city—those were meant to be the edges of the world.

I squeeze her hand. "I'll try to get life here as close to normal as possible."

"Are you going to visit with Liam while you're here?"

"No." Her interrogations about the islands are preferable to this.

"Why not?"

"I don't have time."

"You had time for me. I don't know if I should be honored or sad for you."

I give her an incredulous look. "Would you have allowed me *not* to see you?"

"Oh, there'd have been hell to pay if you didn't see me."

"Exactly." I offer her my arm, and we walk out. "I can't deny you this opportunity." She's always enjoyed being seen with me.

Parisa rolls her eyes. "It doesn't even matter anymore. Our arrangement is rather one sided now that Serenity has a boyfriend." Her using me for the bragging rights of taking something from Serenity Ward is fine—I'm using her too.

When it comes time for us to part ways, she kisses me lightly on the lips. "You're absurd, Adwin. I hope you're better at managing politics than your personal affairs."

Me too.

Chapter Seventeen

The lobby of Townhall is always a weird place to be. It's where we gathered to find out if we were going to Kaycie or not. This was the last place a lot of people saw their loved ones. Including Carista, who sits against the wall in a daze.

"You okay?"

She sighs. "Is anyone?"

"Probably not." I sit next to her.

"I got in a fight with my mom."

"About Reid?"

She nods and picks at her fingernails absentmindedly. "How did you react when you saw Emrys the first time?"

It's a memory I'd rather not relive, but Carista is one of the few people who might understand. "I panicked, had to be thrown into a closet to keep from making a scene and giving myself away, and then got drunk. A few weeks later I threw in a one-night stand for good measure. So... all the mature ways to deal with grief." Thinking about Tori now is bizarre. That night, I thought I knew her, but I really didn't. Not until right before she died.

"No judgement here. At least someone else had to take you away from him. I was too spineless to face Reid. I walked away."

"Remember, I didn't technically *know* Emrys was a marshal. My reaction was all shock. I don't know how I'd have acted in your shoes."

"Not sure if that's better or worse." Her heels bounce against the floor, and she presses her hands onto her knees to stop them. "I've known for years, but I can't handle the reality of it. I mostly got what I wanted out of the uprising, but I still feel empty. Maybe more than before, because now I don't even really have any ideas on how to improve the situation."

"There isn't any right way to handle this. Everyone just needs to do whatever they can to survive it. That'll look different for each person. We all had expectations of the uprising, but most of those have gone right down the drain."

"Down the drain... like the sea?"

"Ha. Ha. That is the biggest quirk in *my* expectations."

"At least trying to figure that out means you still have plans and goals to keep you occupied."

"Yeah..." I drop my gaze to the floor. The ocean mystery is definitely one goal, though not my only one. "So do you though. My mom is keeping you close as she tries to iron things out with the towns, right?" Carista nods. "How did you get that position?"

"I put myself into it and didn't give your mom any other choice. I went to see her after Emrys' selection, and she was a mess. From anyone else, I'd expect that, but nothing ever gets to Kolina like that. Plus, she had already gone through it with you, and back then she really didn't seem too torn up about it. No offense."

"None taken. I know why."

"And she explained that to me. Possibly just so I wouldn't think she was a terrible mother who liked her third born *way* more than her first." She cracks a smirk at that, and I mirror it for a moment. "But when she told me what being selected to go to Kaycie meant and how you were saved from it, I started by being absolutely furious that she allowed Reid, Travick, and Emrys to go through that. She had tried and failed to save Emrys. But Reid and Travick are part of your family too, you know? I get that she couldn't very well let all of Lawson's boys walk around Kaycie without the brainwashing—someone would catch on, but…"

"Understanding the logic didn't make it any easier to swallow."

"Exactly. It's not like I could be that angry at her anyway, because she pretty thoroughly sacrificed Emrys by sending Sophos away when she did."

"What do you mean?"

"She found out she was pregnant and wanted Sophos gone before he found out. She realized we needed him to be on the council, and he wouldn't have left if he knew he was going to have a baby here."

My jaw clenches. There has been so much going on with my family and I missed it all. All of these links between our lives and the uprising, and I just sat there in Kaycie—unaware the whole time.

Carista presses her lips together. "I'm sorry. I probably shouldn't be telling you all this."

"I'm glad someone is finally telling me stuff. Go on."

"So, after I got over hating her for it, I glued myself to her side to do anything I possibly could for the uprising. I could lie and say it was to save all the boys coming up for selection, but I really wanted revenge. I didn't realize it at the time, but now that the uprising's success is so unsatisfying, I can see that my aims weren't as noble as I had told myself."

"Doing something good for the wrong reasons is better than doing something bad with good intentions. You still helped a lot of people."

"I guess so. Thanks." She doesn't sound encouraged.

"If you want to get away for a bit, you could come with us to investigate the power source bombing."

"When are you going?"

"Friday morning."

"Friday all the mayors are meeting. Have to get everyone on the same page to keep the Establishment from taking back control."

"I never thought I'd ever prefer spending time with Kaycians, but I don't envy you for being in meetings like that."

Chapter Eighteen

ADWIN

Flying over land feels like we're actually getting somewhere. There isn't anything to mark progress when I've flown over water. The destination makes it quite different as well. I wasn't sure I'd ever get to go to Montica. When I dared to hope for it, I never imagined these circumstances.

The topography changes below us. Past the rolling, muddy hills which were sunken under the sea, trees now spring from the ground. They huddle together in a dense forest and reach up for us as the earth rises. This small window is an inadequate outlook for the vista appearing before me. Earth shoots up in harsh juts of rock face and flows gently in majestic inclines. The clash of sweeping beauty against the natural exhibition of power leaves me feeling small, just like when I would sit and stare at my mother's painting. She still cries sometimes when she looks at the mountain landscape on her living room wall. It always attacked my identity as an artist. I wasn't sure I could ever create anything with so much depth, intrigue, and beauty. Now that I'm seeing mountains in person, the reason is obvious. To create art that lives and breathes, the artist must live, explore, feel the subject. Great art isn't born of isolation.

A white and green patterned hoverPlane appears outside my window. Another flanks our port side. We're almost there. My grandfather exits the cockpit and goes to the back of the craft. Minutes later he crosses through again, accompanied by the Montican pilot who will fly us in. Her uniform is like a second skin, flecked with dark green and white as if paint brushes were flicked at it. Dark hair ends at her jawline and sweeps across her forehead, nearly obscuring her side-glance at me as she passes by. Brown boots are the only bulky thing on her. Despite their hefty look, her steps are silent as she walks down the aisle and disappears into the cockpit with my grandfather.

The two marshal pilots come to take seats in the cabin. My stomach bubbles and I try to swallow my excitement. The view gets more dramatic as we continue on, rivers cutting through forests, waterfalls, lakes, cliffs, and boulders sharing the space. Then the view disappears altogether. Darkness overtakes the vessel when we enter the cave like hangar. We're now underneath Breck Fortress. The walls of the tunnel could be inches or miles from the wingtips for all I can see. Then it opens up to a maze of lights and docks. We decelerate as we glide over it and set down on a small pad. Many of the crafts dwarf ours.

Grandfather and the pilot come out as I rise from my seat. "Welcome to Montica," he says.

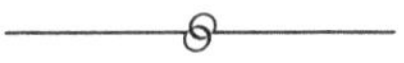

The pill-shaped glass car feels more like a mail shoot than an elevator. The pilot eyes Grandfather and me curiously as she wraps a brown shawl around her shoulders, securing it with a pearl clasp at her neck like a cape. I mirror my grandfather's uninterested appearance. My ears pop as we shoot up out of the hangar where mechanics fuss over planes, and people and machines load and unload cargo. That scene disappears when we pass out of the cavern and into the fortress above. The door slides open silently, depositing us in a room as wooded as the mountains. Wood, iron, and stone dominate the space, dark and warm as opposed to Kaycie's cool, crisp design schemes. Beams too big to have ever been trees cross the vaulted ceiling, flames dance up a stone wall like a reversed waterfall, and a grand staircase with an intricate iron railing rounds a far corner.

"They are ready for you in the boardroom," the pilot says.

"How very impersonal," Grandfather replies. He leads the way across the atrium, the pilot and I following side by side. Without the curtain of hair on this side, I see that rather than dangling down, her jewelry wraps up along her outer ear. When my grandfather stops at a large double door, he looks up at a small red light. Nothing happens until the pilot steps up next to him and does the same. This time the light turns green, and he purses his lips as the door opens.

In the room, four people sit at a trapezoidal table. The women wear shawls similar to the pilot but wrapped fittingly around themselves. The men wear thin sleek jackets with high collars. They both have long hair and bearded faces, one more surly than the next.

The woman at the top of the table glares at my grandfather from under a crown of braided sandy hair. "Casimir."

"That's how you greet your father after thirty-five years?"

"It's more than you deserve."

Grandfather turns to the man at his daughter's right side. "Son."

The man inclines his head briefly. The pilot has taken the seat at his side. He gestures to her and says, "You've met my daughter, Minea."

"Clover," the young woman corrects. She's my cousin then.

"Yes," Grandfather says. "It's a shame it took so long. And I suppose these two"—he gestures to the people on the other side of the table—"are your son and daughter, Ismene?"

"They are," she replies. "I was hesitant to introduce them to you, but there is much they can learn from you. You've always supplied valuable lessons on misconduct and repercussions, and it would appear you aren't done yet."

My cousins look on with curiosity rather than their mother's contempt. "I'm Priam, this is my sister Nemora."

"It's a pleasure to meet you both. This is your cousin, Adwin."

Ismene's shoulders rise with a deep breath and her eyes meet those of her brother. "Perhaps we should allow the four *cousins* to get acquainted. The three of us have old business to tend to."

"I couldn't agree more," Grandfather says.

Priam, Nemora, and Clover rise and lead the way back out to the atrium.

Chapter Nineteen
SERENITY

"Celia, you amaze me." Lanelle lounges in the back seat of the vehicle like a princess in a litter. "You can drive, you're willing to go to the towns without any marshals for protection, and all with a baby on the way."

"Showing up with marshals would hardly warm them to us." Celia Martel fidgets with the seatbelt which can't be comfortable against her bulging belly.

"Of course, but the governor's pregnant daughter would be a valuable hostage."

I find it hard to believe that Lanelle thinks anyone is more valuable than herself. Even if she couldn't know about the Establishment structure until she turned sixteen, she grew up with her father on the council, and has an inflated sense of self-importance.

"Either of you would serve the same purpose," Celia replies. "Anyway, the entire point was to send trustworthy emissaries. Vulnerable young women fit the bill. We're negotiating for food. No one will deny a pregnant woman food."

I press my lips together to suppress a smirk at the infallible logic. Celia seems to be a no-nonsense kind of person. It was a struggle to get her father and husband to agree to the scheme, but she wasn't going to accept 'no' for an answer. They felt she had enough excitement in her escape from Blue Springs when the uprising began. She used it to strengthen her argument that she was perfectly capable of this.

Blue Springs didn't actually attack at all. They were the only town that didn't. Celia is—or was—the manager and happened to be staying at her apartment there that night. After Sophos' broadcast, she got word of attacks on other islands' Establishment Centers and barricaded herself and the marshals in. It proved unnecessary, but if the town had risen up, she might have saved lives by taking a defensive stance rather than offensive.

She tried to get back to Kaycie via the trains, but the system was down. Nineteen miles separate Blue Springs from Kaycie, but she started to walk down the tunnel only to find it impassable a couple of miles down. The walk brought her through a transparent section, and she saw she was no longer under water. Back at her Establishment Center, she slipped out and took a truck to drive back to the city, leaving the marshals with orders to surrender if attacked.

Celia Martel may become one of my favorite people in the Establishment.

Gardner comes into view, and I try to channel Celia's confidence. It's hard to imagine this is what I was born into. My Leadership program did nothing to prepare me for this, but maybe my parents did in ways I didn't notice at the time. They raised me to care about people. I do, and I can help with this.

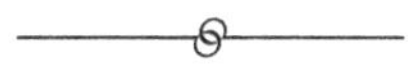

The mayor waits at the top as we walk up the makeshift ramp at the seawall. "Welcome to Gardner. I'm Aster Rigby." Dressed down as we may be in our security-issued dresses, we are still stiff and formal compared to Aster's relaxed look. Her sleeves are scrunched up her forearms and her jeans are threadbare at the knees. Loose strands from her auburn ponytail blow around her face.

"Thank you for having us. I'm Celia Martel." She shakes Aster's hand. "This is Serenity Ward, and Lanelle Kemp."

We exchange pleasantries as Aster looks at me, wide-eyed. "I had heard Kaycian ladies were more frilly."

Lanelle grins. "We have our moments."

"But we're all more alike than we've been allowed to know," Celia says. "Difficult as this has been for all of us, I'm sure we'll come out of it more unified than ever."

Aster raises an eyebrow. "Dare to dream, I guess. Let's go find a comfortable place to talk and get you off your feet." Her gaze drifts to Celia's belly.

"I'm up for anything," Celia says with a smile, "but thank you."

We board a truck, and Aster passes the modest Establishment Center, continuing down the road. Rolling green hills sprawl in every direction in a breathtaking view. There's so much open space. Swaying fields of corn, tall round silos, a bright field of sunflowers, and endless rows of crops and trees sweep by the window. Platinia Rinne showed us images of Gardner as we prepared to come, but those holos didn't do it any justice. This is a different world.

The truck stops in front of a pretty little house with a big porch. Across a field, a red barn stands on a low hill. Rows of winding plants stretch in between. It all looks like it's straight from a movie. Aster leads us to the porch and offers us lemonade. The idea of these people taking us as hostages seems more and more ridiculous every second.

"What do you grow here?" I ask.

"Grapes," Aster says. "Kaycie's demand for wine keeps us busy."

Lanelle looks at the vines skeptically. "Those scraggly plants make wine?"

"Those vines are scrappy. They work hard to survive, but the wine is better for it. Irrigated vines make bland wines."

The phrase snaps my attention to Aster. "My mother says that all the time."

"Is that so?" Her countenance tightens, but she moves on quickly. "Well, tell me. Why should we trust the daughters of the councilmen who run this system?"

"We are trying to remedy the mistakes of generations of Kaycian leadership," Celia says. "Several members of the council have been working to make slow corrections to the way we do things for years, but the uprising made it clear that drastic changes cannot wait. I'm very sorry you had to sacrifice so much to make us see that, and I thank you for being brave enough to rise up."

"You're thanking us... for the uprising?"

"Yes. It was necessary."

Aster glances around at us, no doubt debating our sincerity.

"You're all as much a part of Kaycie as we are," I say. "I for one am outraged that I never knew all of this was here. Our isolation was based on obsolete concerns from a world long passed. We all just found out about one another, it seems a shame to continue to keep ourselves separated."

"And what do you want out of a relationship with us?"

"We would, of course, love for the city to not suffer starvation." Celia rubs her belly lightly, and I nearly laugh at the theatrics of it.

"What do we get in return?" Aster asks.

"All of your people from the last two selections," Lanelle offers.

Aster's eyebrows pop up and her eyes widen. "As they were?"

"No, I'm afraid we don't have a way to do that." Lanelle drops her gaze and sighs like this is the saddest thing in the world. I'd have preferred Celia or myself to deliver that information, as it truly saddens us. Lanelle doesn't care.

"I want them all back." Aster's lips set in a hard line.

"I wish we could." Celia's earnestness shows. "We can certainly work out something for the future, but right now we need the marshals."

"What for? To come take back the towns by force if we don't agree to work with you?"

"To protect us all." Lanelle is doe eyed as she seizes the opportunity Sophos and Kolina left us. We had hoped they didn't tell the other towns. Now the Establishment isn't the only liar in the game. "Didn't you know?" she asks with feigned surprise. "The uprising isn't the only war we're facing."

Chapter Twenty

ADWIN

"And I thought the air was thin on the peaks," Priam says when the door closes behind us. He makes my six-foot-one stature look small. His thick beard and hair wrapped into a knot at his neck make him appear alien by Kaycian sensibilities.

Clover turns to me and smiles for the first time. "Nice to meet you, Adwin." She shakes my hand with more strength than I'd expect.

"It's a pleasure, though the sentiment doesn't seem to be shared through the family."

Nemora scoffs. "He isn't really our cousin, and Mother does not care if we get acquainted. She just didn't want us to see her erupt at *him*." She tilts her head back toward the boardroom, the ends of her sandy hair brushing over her shoulders.

"You're a miserable hostess," Priam says. "Don't mind my sister, she's cursed with our mother's temper." He turns to her. "I don't suppose you'll join us for a tour?"

"Of course not. I'm going to the security office to watch that fight."

"She'll have scrambled it," he says.

"I can get past that," she calls over her shoulder as she walks away.

"And then there were three," Clover says.

"Probably for the best." Priam's gaze falls on me. "So, Adwin, have you really never seen a mountain before?"

"Kaycie only has small hills."

Clover frowns. "Sounds awful. Let's get you something to wear so we can go outside."

"Is it that cold up here? I have a coat if you know where they took our things."

They both smirk. "It's not the cold so much." Priam eyes me up and down, noting my suit. "More a range of motion issue."

"And you won't get far in those shoes," Clover adds.

I glance down at my brown dress shoes and wonder what going outside entails.

Twenty minutes later, I'm in a fortress suite wearing a temperature-controlling layer similar to Clover's flight suit under loose-fitting pants and one of those thin jackets. The boots are as heavy as they looked. The clothing may be able to move more fluidly, but only if the body in it can. I shuffle out of the bedroom to find Priam and Clover in the living room.

"Ah, he *is* half-Montican." Clover hops up off a robust leather armchair and pulls on a pair of stretchy gloves. "Yours are in the left boot."

"What?"

"Feel for the pocket inside."

I slide my fingers into the boot and find a pocket just big enough to pinch the fabric inside and pull out two gloves. "Oh, they're storage too. Is that why these things are so heavy? Are there rocks in there too?"

"Priam, you oaf."

"I forgot." He crouches by my feet and adjusts a latch on each which I thought was only holding the laces in place, but somehow makes the shoes lighter and more flexible. "Much better," he says, standing up.

I take a few steps in place, trying to figure out how these bulky, solid boots can flex with my feet like socks.

"Now then," Clover says, opening the balcony door. "Shall we?"

"Shall we what? I thought we were going out?"

She walks out, steps up onto a chair, and hops to a nearby tree branch. "This is the most direct route."

"We're six stories up."

"Is that too high or too low?" She crouches to grab the branch and swings herself down onto another one, nine feet below.

I look at Priam, waiting for the punchline of the joke. "She's show-ing off," he says. "The gloves and the boots do the work. You'll be fine."

"Are you kidding? At least Nemora was forthcoming about dislik-ing me. You two are actually trying to kill me."

"No, really. The gloves and boots will keep you from falling to your death. They feel like magnets. It's fun."

Kaycie has a very different definition of fun.

"We'll go straight down and then keep to the ground if you prefer."

I'd *prefer* the elevator, but if this is some kind of family initiation…

I step up onto the chair and make the obvious mistake of looking down. The ground is awfully far. The branch that Clover stepped onto with ease now appears to be yards away. "I jumped to your moving plane earlier," she calls up from the ground. "Don't be such a pika."

"What's a pika?" I ask Priam.

"A mousy little creature that shrieks when it spots a predator."

Excellent. I take a deep breath and launch myself off the balcony. Regret hits me like a slap in the face. This is insane. One foot after the other lands on the branch, and I slap both hands against the trunk. There's nothing to grip, but the gloves do feel magnetically connected to the tree. I'm surprisingly steady.

Priam touches down on a branch a few feet over. "Not so bad, right?"

"I guess not." My heart races in contradiction to my words.

"Follow me."

He takes a less dramatic route down than Clover did, choosing branches which take us down like a spiral staircase around the tree. The boots and gloves release when I start to pull away from the tree and attach at every touch. To my surprise, I make it down in one piece.

"Well done, cousin," Clover says with a smile. "We'll make a tree-walker of you yet."

"What is a tree-walker?"

"Clover's self-awarded title to reflect her preference for traversing tree branches over solid ground."

"You are a tree-walker too." She sneers at him.

"I will never identify as that."

"Is that why Nemora doesn't consider me to be family?" I ask. "Because I'm... human?"

The tree branches weren't so bad, but walking is considerably more comfortable. Clover and Priam lead me down a foot-worn trail winding through the trees, past small creeks, and over large rocks. I'm interviewed as we hike.

"What have you been told of the family break up?" Priam asks. "I imagine Casimir and your mother's story is quite different from my mother and Rocco's."

"I was never told much of anything," I say. "All I had ever known was that she hated him, but that was supposedly due to his disapproval of my father. Then Grandfather told me about Montica when I came of age, and that he and my mother were exiled after a family feud. I think she intentionally chose my father to spite Grandfather, because she was already furious at him for her removal from her home."

"Who could blame her?" Clover says. "To have lived here and be sent to the flatlands is cruel. And she was innocent in the whole ordeal. It wasn't her fault Casimir snuck off to have a second family behind his wife's back."

"That was the feud?" Grandfather told me I might hear stories, but that nothing would fully encompass the truth. How many sides could there be to this, though? He either did or did not have two families. And why have two? He's never even seemed terribly interested in one.

Priam nods. "After discovering the secret family, our grandmother—the Director of Montica at the time—executed the mistress, and exiled Casimir and his daughter."

They start to climb a rock formation. I follow, ruminating on the awkwardness. Their grandmother killed mine, but here we are, cousins getting to know each other.

"I can't believe your mother never speaks of this place," Clover says as she hoists herself onto the top.

"I think it was too depressing." I catch up, and a breathtaking view of snow-covered rocky slopes, a sweeping green valley, peaks, plateaus, and lakes opens up before me. "She misses it too much, and how could she describe this, anyway?"

Chapter Twenty-One

BRAM

Krisalyn and Dixon cheer for Libby in front of my house. Libby takes a deep bow after showing off a somersault, then runs headlong into me, wrapping herself around my legs. "I wanna go with you!"

"Maybe next time." She holds on tighter, proclaiming I can't leave. Tickles loosen her grip, and she lets go, giggling. "Go on in, I'll see you later."

"Okay." She pouts and stomps into the house where Mrs. Campbell waits.

Vogue and Frey join us mid-banter as usual. "You could stay behind," Frey says. "As much as I'd *love* to see your face when we verify you drained the ocean."

"Well, aren't we giddy about today's field trip?" Dixon says with a laugh.

"Being proven right is one of my favorite past times." Frey smirks. "Sad that it usually comes after I'm ignored. No one wants to accept that I can look this good and be intelligent."

I know well enough that he and Vogue are both as intelligent as they are attractive. They won some kind of genetic lottery.

Vogue lets out a haughty laugh. "*Too Pretty to be Taken Seriously* is already the name of my autobiography, so you'll have to come up with something else and find *someone else* to complain to."

The rest of us are content to ignore them at this point.

"Shall we?" Dixon says, tossing the key in the air and catching it.

We pile into the sleek black truck we acquired for the trip.

"I'm now considering acronyms," Vogue says.

Everyone groans.

"For what?" I ask.

"Our name."

"Huh?"

"Vogue had been trying to give us a team name." Frey shakes his head. "But until everyone is present to agree to one, I guess you'll have to put that project on hold."

"I can still run options through you, so there are fewer when we get Serenity and Jase back."

Frey mumbles something about capture being preferable.

"You'll like these, Frey. They're rather flattering, not that your ego needs it. *Gorgeous and treacherous: GATS. Captivating and treacherous: CATS. Beautiful and treacherous: BATS.*"

"You're batty," Frey says under his breath.

It takes five hours to go the two-hundred-fifty miles to the nearest power site. It would be faster if we had a road instead of the uneven, semi-dry sea floor to drive on. The smell of the unfortunate sea-life which didn't get washed away keeps the windows closed. That lesson was learned quickly. I keep expecting us to reach a beach, but the sea has receded the entire distance. We've gone three times the distance between the farthest towns. How much more has the world grown? Up ahead we see our destination—a metal behemoth stretching to the sky at the shoreline.

Waves lap up against the back of the tower as we walk around, looking for a way in. It would dwarf any building in Kaycie. The first seventy or eighty stories of it are windowless metal. The top is all windows, though. Something hangs down from the bottom of the glass section. A sheet of wood maybe?

No damage is visible on this building, but debris litters the beach next to it. I run my hand along the metal wall. The western side is carpeted with algae and crusted with barnacles, the eastern wall facing the beach is clean.

Frey stops at the middle of the tower's side, examining a panel in the wall. "Look. I think this runs all the way up the side." The foot-wide strip shines against the dark metal, splitting the algae covered side from the other. The west side was under water, but not the east side. There's a door on what would have been the dry side of it. "We need to get inside and find out what it is."

Krisalyn glances at Dixon. "Can you open that door?"

Dixon runs his hand over a rectangular outline on the metal. "This must be a control panel, but it's locked somehow."

"I'm sure you have some kind of key," Vogue says.

"I'll see what I can do." Dixon walks back to the truck, and I continue around the perimeter of the tower. A matching strip splits the other side.

As I reach the beach side, a scream rings out. I take off running through the surf. Cold water shocks my feet as it soaks through my shoes and socks. Near the other side of the building, Vogue comes into my view as she kicks Frey in the shin and yells at him. She's soaked from head to toe. I groan and shake my head as I trudge the rest of the way to them.

"I'm going to get pneumonia!" Vogue bellows. "Insufferable ass."

Frey rolls on the ground laughing, clutching his leg as Vogue and Krisalyn storm to the truck.

"I forgot CATS don't like water," Frey calls behind them.

"Are you sure you aren't brother and sister?" I offer Frey a hand to help him up.

The girls stay away while Dixon attempts to breach the tower. I glance at my cuff, wondering if we have time for this. As it is, most of the drive back will be in the dark. By the time he brings the panel to life, and Frey hacks through the security protocols, the sun is setting.

Vogue and Krisalyn return, the former warning Frey to sleep with one eye open when we get back to Lawson. Inside, we illuminate the cavernous space with our cuffs—sounds echoing as they rise endlessly above us. A thin steel tower rises through the core of the building, holding a large cage at the top. That elevator would be helpful, but we'll need power for that. There are switchback stairs on the far side, so we still have a way up. On each side wall, a large transparent half cylinder seals off bundles of wires up the height of the metal wall. Dixon, Vogue, and Frey huddle around one of them.

"This is the inside of that panel," Frey says.

"What could it possibly do to hold the sea back?" Vogue asks.

"How far apart were they?" Dixon asks.

"A hundred miles."

Dixon scratches his scalp. "I think it's some kind of electronic dam, but our tech is nowhere near capable of that."

I glance up the stairs. "There has to be a control room or something up there. Let's start climbing."

Vogue looks up and laughs. "You're hilarious. How about you and Dixon climb the million stairs and get the elevator turned on for the rest of us."

"You are such a diva," Dixon says.

"What if he can't get it turned on?" I ask. "Then we'd be up there and have to wait for you."

Somehow, Vogue isn't the one put off by my suggestion. Dixon's jaw drops. "Ouch. So little faith in me?"

"You have no idea what's going on up there!"

"I love a challenge."

"Have a lovely time." Vogue flicks her fingers in a wave to us. Even if he can turn the elevator on, we should make her walk. But Dixon and I make our way up without the rest.

Even though I know Sophos kept secrets from me, I'm sure he didn't know about this. He and my mom were genuinely shocked by the drop of the sea. Nothing should surprise me anymore, but manipulating the very face of the planet? This goes beyond anything I could have dreamed. How did it come to pass? Did the oceans even rise, or was it all manufactured?

By the time we reach the top, I'm glad Vogue didn't come. The two of us are feeling all those steps in a bad way. Vogue's complaining wouldn't have been worth it. The metal stairs lead us to a level several stories high containing enormous turbines.

Dixon lets out a tired breath. "Wow. Well, we didn't bomb the power plant after all."

"Yeah, just stopped the water flow that ran it."

"Guess we'll see." He gets to work and soon lights flicker on. "Good thing that grenade didn't kill me, or you'd all be helpless."

The elevator goes down to get our lazy counterparts. Vogue, Krisalyn, and Frey arrive in a tense silence. Wonder what fight they were getting into now.

We spread out between the forty-foot turbines. Our footsteps echo through the cavernous space. Dixon crosses the catwalk over them, contemplating the machinery with the appreciation of an enthusiast. Frey gravitates to the equipment and computers around one of the clear tubes. Vogue and Dixon follow suit and hover over his shoulders. The three of them mutter to each other as Krisalyn and I lean back against the adjacent wall. "I find it's best to leave them to nerd-out together," she says.

Bits and pieces of their conversation slip through to us. *Ion wall?... Seven hundred feet high and a hundred miles long?... Just because you can't do it doesn't mean it isn't possible... Giant arch...*

Dixon straightens and takes a flustered step back. "Sure, if they rewrote the laws of physics."

"I gather you've solved the mystery of the disappearing ocean?" Krisalyn says.

"Your girlfriend did indeed bomb a dam." Frey looks at Vogue incredulously.

"First of all,"—Vogue's hands come up in a graceful defensive gesture—"you helped. Secondly, if a false sea was isolating us, this is a victory."

"But the missile didn't even hit," I say. "Could it have been a coincidence that it failed simultaneously as we attacked?" The odds would be miniscule.

"No," Dixon replies. "We destroyed some huge arch that was part of it, and other towers were probably hit."

"All right, mission accomplished then." I push back against the wall to stand upright. "Let's get going so we aren't getting home at sunrise."

"Are you crazy?" Vogue asks. "I want to see what's on top of this thing."

"Fine, but make it quick."

The next level up resembles a basement. Dixon identifies mechanical equipment, the same as residential automation appliances found in every building in Kaycie. Machines to prepare and deliver food, clean, and run entertainment and sensory tech seem out of place here. On our way higher, we pass the metal base of the structure and enter the building at the top. The door opens and we're transported back to Kaycie... only more luxurious.

Chapter Twenty-Two
SERENITY

Martini glasses tap against each other with a high-pitched *clink*. "I knew we would make an excellent team."

The frosty gin goes down easier than the idea of Lanelle and I being a team. All I can do to half-heartedly agree is grin. Even though we did something good for Kaycie, Lanelle being proud of it makes me cringe. *We did a good thing, right?*

"The Establishment is the glue that's held this country together," Lanelle continues. "Anyone who'd think they could cut us out must be truly foolish." She flashes me a sharp smile.

"Dividing the towns was not our purpose." It may be a side effect of revealing the uprising's lies, though. But we couldn't let them cut off Kaycie and Leavenworth. There doesn't seem to be any obvious right and wrong with this. Most of it is gray area.

"Hello, ladies." Jase walks up behind me, and my heart picks up.

Lanelle's eyes sparkle. "It's a brave man who wants to spend time with two ex-girlfriends together."

I throw back some more of my martini. *Make this more difficult, would you?*

"Or a smart one." Jase sits next to me at the high-top table. "Shouldn't I make sure you aren't gossiping about me?"

My speeding heart sinks. Does he really believe I would do that? I don't even have a negative thought about him. "We're celebrating securing Kaycie's resources from the towns," I say.

"Great." He looks back and forth between me, my drink, and Lanelle.

Her eyelashes flutter. "Alas, I was only here for one round." She stands and puts a hand on my shoulder. "Unless I'm a terrible friend for leaving you alone with Jase."

"Of course not. I have no problem with him."

"That's wonderful. You certainly shouldn't." She whispers something to him before walking away.

Jase's knuckles blanch as his fist raps lightly on the table.

"I hope you're only actually concerned about one of us being mean behind your back."

He lets out a breath. "I was only teasing. I know you wouldn't."

"What's all the tension for then?"

"I worry about you spending time with Lanelle."

"I see what she is. And I can take care of myself."

He rubs the back of his neck. "I know."

The acidity of a cocktail onion washes through my mouth. "Are you still waiting for me to come around?" Why would I even ask that? I'm a horrible person. But what else can I think of when that conversation simmers between us unresolved?

"Do you want me to?"

Yes. "No."

"Well, I am anyway."

"I don't understand why." But my heart skips at the idea.

Chapter Twenty-Three
BRAM

The great room of this tower-top mansion has ceilings vaulted up to the second floor. Through two story floor-to-ceiling windows, the moon hovers over the ocean. A cascade of crystal and glass hangs down from the ceiling over a plush sitting room which is anchored by a mosaic-tiled fireplace. We make our way past a chaise lounge and a silver bar cart to the glass door on the other side of the fireplace—all held in awed silence. The door leads to a large room walled in by glass. The double-sided fireplace adorns the wall out here next to a long dining table. A small round pool stands raised from the floor, with stone steps curling around it. It overlooks a large rectangular pool which appears to flow right over the edge of the building. Dixon activates a control, and the glass outer wall lowers to become a balcony rail, opening the room to the ocean air.

"It's even better than being home." Vogue leans against the rail and drinks in the extravagant surroundings.

"What is this doing out here?" Dixon says. "It's the definition of the middle of nowhere."

Krisalyn sinks to a lounge chair and wraps her arms around her knees, closing her eyes and dropping her head.

Vogue sits next to her. "What's wrong?"

"I looked down," Krisalyn says between her teeth. "This is much higher than any building in Kaycie. Don't like it."

"Awe." Vogue rubs her back. "I didn't know you were afraid of heights."

"I've never had the opportunity to be this high up."

"You can't even see anything down there," I say, peering over. Hard to believe we're perched on top of that spartan tower.

"That's no better. It looks like you'd fall forever."

Frey comes out holding a small picture frame. "I think I know who's place this is." He hands it to Vogue who breaks into a satisfied laugh. She turns the picture around so we can all see the picture of Casimir Agnar with his grandson, Adwin Lebeau.

"I believe we've stumbled upon the lieutenant governor's vacation home." Vogue tosses the frame over her shoulder to send it sailing out of the building. "Oops."

"Where did you find that?" I ask.

"In his study," Frey says. "It's magnificent. Come see."

Krisalyn closes the glass wall with a sigh of relief on our way back in. The room Frey leads us to would be better defined as a library. In contrast to the coolness of the crisp décor we left, the dark wood dominating the room gives it warmth. Intricately carved posts break up the wall of bookshelves and a ladder leans against it, connected to a track at the top. A bulky desk is set back against the wall and four chocolate leather chairs surround a low, round stone table.

"Would you like to see the best part?" Frey's smile is playful as he takes a screen from the wall and taps it. Fire slithers up from the round table in a single stream, coiling as if it were in a clear spring. It flickers and flows but maintains the shape.

"How on earth?" Dixon stares wide-eyed.

Frey taps the screen again and the flames converge to a vertical trunk and spread at the top to form a tree canopy. The tree of flame glows before us like a breathing sculpture.

"That's incredible," Krisalyn whispers. "What did Agnar do to get all this?"

"Maybe it's not the only one," I say. "How many of these sites were there?"

"Ten," Vogue replies.

"There might be other matching retreats."

Vogue flashes a smile at Frey. "Wouldn't it be fantastic if we blew up Martel's villa? Beautiful though it may be."

Our exploration continues and we find the sheet of wood we saw from outside. Only it isn't a sheet of wood. It's a planked deck but hanging vertically below a set of double doors. Krisalyn jumps back when I open one. "Why is there a door to certain death?"

"It wasn't always a drop off." I hold on to the doorframe as I look down. "This is the western face of the building. The sea came up to here. I think this deck floated on it." I close the door.

"I wish I could have seen it like that," Vogue says.

"Well, now it's a deathtrap." Krisalyn crosses her arms across her chest. "Someone put furniture in front of that door please."

Dixon and I laugh as we slide a console table to block the doors. Frey reports finding four suites from the overlook above the living room and makes his way down the stairs back to us.

"I think that concludes our tour," I say. "We should be heading back to Lawson."

Four pairs of eyes glance back and forth at each other. Vogue purses her lips to the side. "Why?"

Outnumbered, I never stood a chance in this debate. We're staying the night.

My Kaycian cohorts pilfer Agnar's food and beverage stores for a decadent dinner. They've all been enjoying the food in Lawson, but they light up for shaved raw tuna with greens and lemon oil, Frenched rack of lamb, and balsamic glazed mushrooms.

"Vogue, I can't believe you haven't said it yet." Dixon smirks at her from across the table.

"What?"

"A name like *dam destroyers,* or something."

Her gasp is the most ridiculously dramatic thing I've ever seen. Vogue's eyes light up.

"What is wrong with you?" Frey demands. "Do *not* start her on dam puns!"

"Dam Decimators. Dam Demolishers." *Here we go.* "Or if we don't like alliteration—"

"We don't like any of it."

Vogue ignores Frey. "Dam Annihilators. Dam Rebels. Oh! And since the ocean created all the borders between towns, we are also Border Breakers."

I shake my head. "You're not going to give this up, are you?"

"She doesn't know the definition of *give up*," Krisalyn says.

Vogue's answering smile drips with adoration. "That's why you love me."

Afterward, everyone strips down to their underwear and hops into the pool and spa. They claim it reveals just as much as swimwear, but I think modesty just doesn't matter to them because they all have perfect bodies. Despite their invitations to join, I remain dry, looking out at the stars. There are more here, so far from civilization.

Frey peruses the screen by the spa and clicks his tongue in a judgmental way. "The insults just keep coming. Agnar has all kinds of hidden treasures."

"What is it?" Krisalyn asks as the glowing water of the spa shifts through the color spectrum around her. She refuses to go into the pool due to the glass walled side with the view straight down to the beach.

Frey holds their attention with a dramatic pause. "Tequila."

Three jaws drop. Dixon leaps up to confirm Frey's claim. "Real tequila?"

"Why is that a big deal?" I ask.

"To be called tequila," Vogue says, "it has to be made in Mexico, which doesn't exist anymore."

"They must still have some preserved." Dixon walks to the table as a bottle and five short glasses of ice appear. It figures that as the world was ending, Kaycie's ancestors were hoarding liquor. Dixon admires the bottle and starts filling glasses.

"Not for me," I say. "Tequila and I don't get along."

"You've had tequila?" Krisalyn looks cheated.

"Sophos had it. He doesn't drink it, but it was in the townhouse's system."

"Now that's going too far." I'm not sure if Vogue is being sarcastic or not.

"Is there nothing the Establishment won't keep from us?" Frey distributes glasses and they all hold them out to each other for a beat before taking a sip.

Dixon melts onto a lounge chair. "There are four bottles of this. I'm taking them all."

Vogue pops out of the water to peruse the inventory. "Oh, sweet heaven. There's champagne. Why wasn't I hacking the Establishment's liquor cabinet? This is unbelievable."

"Let's give it a try," Frey says.

"No. Not without Serenity and Jase."

The mood darkens as guilt crashes over us. I'm hardly even partaking in the party, and I feel guilty for being here while Serenity's fate remains unknown.

"We'll take the bottles," Krisalyn says with a thin smile. "We can open the first one when we're reunited."

Vogue presses a fingertip against the bridge of her nose, pushing her misery back down.

"I'm turning in for the night." I rise to go inside. "You're not going to try to extend your vacation tomorrow, right?"

"No," Frey says. "We'll leave."

I plod up the arcing stairway to a guest suite. The excuse of waiting until we figured out the situation with the dam has expired. Once we decided to just take it easy tonight, all that stopped me from telling them everything was cowardice. Maybe I could leave them. They can't do any harm if they're stranded here, and it's a nice enough place to be stuck. Of course, Dixon could probably fashion a car out of whatever he finds here. And it's not even that I don't trust them or like them, they're just unpredictable and headstrong. All the reasons Sophos recruited them are the reasons to keep them at arm's length. But the longer I put it off, the worse it will be. Tomorrow I need to bite the bullet and tell them. It's not like I'll be able to get Serenity back without them.

The room is better appointed than Sophos'. A chandelier hangs over the bed which is layered with varying textures of sheets and blankets. Light glows from behind a marble panel on the wall as water flows down its surface. This was never intended for someone like me. Serenity would make sense here—her hair fanned over a silky pillow, hands in a constant state of motion as she tries to figure everything out.

Thinking about her in this bed is not helpful. Before trying to sleep, I take a cold shower. What the hell is wrong with me?

Chapter Twenty-Four
ADWIN

The cold air and hot coffee soothe the dull pounding in my head, and the view from my balcony distracts me well enough. At least the irritatingly early wakeup call gave me the chance to see the range glowing in the morning light. It's the kind of scene which both inspires and humbles an artist. To capture this landscape on canvas would be a triumph, but I'd be afraid to try. The beauty of this place is so complete, I know I couldn't begin to replicate it. Self-doubt is a feeling I thought I had rid myself of.

Hangovers, on the other hand, are an old friend. And I thought Kaycians could drink...

After Nemora advised us to keep our distance from Grandfather, Ismene, and Rocco, the shackles fell off and the *real fun* began, as Clover put it. She and Priam distill their own spirits, which were incredibly good. I accused them of being over-achievers, but they don't actually have any other options. Montica is dry. A concept I have a difficult time comprehending, having grown up in Kaycie. Living in the fortress, being who they are, offers them some privileges.

A body swings down from the balcony above me, and I choke on my coffee in surprise. Clover lands lightly on her feet, eyeing me with a cocky grin. "Are you all right there?"

"What is *wrong* with you?" I try to shake off the prickling sensation at my pressure points. "Oh, don't be so dramatic. This is the fastest way from my suite."

"You live above me?"

"Yes, but don't worry, I'm a quiet neighbor."

A quiet neighbor with no sense of boundaries. "Your parents must be so proud."

"Parent. Singular. And I vex him terribly."

She says it casually, but I may have stumbled into sensitive territory. "I'm sorry. I didn't know. What happened to your mother?"

"I never had one. Casimir's actions had wide-spread consequences. And speaking of which..."

The balcony door opens, and Grandfather joins us, wearing a sweater and slacks rather than his typical stiff Kaycian suit.

"Casimir," Clover says with a greeting nod.

"Good morning, Minea."

Her lips twist, but her eyes weigh the options, and she doesn't correct him. Her name and this mention of never having a mother due to Grandfather are on my list for a later conversation.

"I'm told we'll all be meeting in the boardroom again?" he says.

"Yes," Clover replies. "I'll see you both there." She nimbly jumps onto the rail and up to her balcony.

Grandfather gapes a moment.

"She's a bit of a wild thing," I say. She may have heard me, but I don't think she'd take offense.

Grandfather shakes his head to rid himself of that idea. "Does it feel like home?" he asks, looking out at the vista.

"It depends on your definition of home. If home is a place that belongs to you, then no, this could never belong to someone. I'd be content to feel like I belong to it, though. I'm not sure I ever would, but I can see the appeal."

"Get dressed. It's time we deal with the real reason for our visit."

Ismene is at her place at the top of the trapezoidal table in the board-room—Rocco on her right, Nemora and Priam on her left. Grandfather and I sit at the bottom of the table, opposite Ismene, and Clover saunters in shortly after.

"Now, then." Ismene taps her fingertips together. "Let's settle our business with Kaycie. I don't want to keep our *guests* here any longer than necessary." She may as well be carved of ice. Her rigid solemnity is unflinching, and I can't help but wonder if she was always like this or if her father's betrayal made her this way.

"Let us back up," Rocco says, "to the attack on our MA-816."

"That was an accident," Grandfather says. "If you had told me you were sending a craft into my airspace, I could have prevented it."

"Your airspace?" Ismene arches an eyebrow.

"It has been my home for some time. Obviously, I have to take ownership of it."

"Why does Kaycie have weaponry that can destroy one of my crafts?" Ismene asks.

"They may not be at your technological level, but they aren't cavemen."

"They shouldn't need them, though."

"When has a lack of need ever slowed the advancement of weapon-ry?" Grandfather's rhetorical question goes unanswered. "Anyway, what was your craft doing out there?"

"Reconnaissance," Rocco says. "Looking to see what kind of weapons Kaycie has. We didn't expect to get such an up-close look."

"Again, some notice would be helpful. Sneaking around in the night is dangerous."

Rocco bristles. "So is bolstering your military behind our backs."

"You can't possibly feel threatened by Kaycie? They're nothing. Clearly they need to strengthen themselves to maintain control over their own country. They're not aggressive, and they're in no position to be."

"What about the dam?" Rocco looks skeptical.

"The fault for that lies with all of us," Grandfather says. "It wouldn't have been attacked if the Establishment had known about it. The rebels only thought they were taking out Kaycie's power grid."

Priam smirks. "The beachfront properties at the base of the mountains are furious."

Ismene shoots him a sharp look and his grin melts away. Our generation is here to observe and learn, not to speak, and certainly not to make jokes. It is somewhat jarring to hear it joked about anyway.

She steeples her long fingers. "I will only ask this once. Have you shared our technology with Kaycie?"

"Of course not. They can't handle that. My Mo-accumulator is at my residence at the dam. You can take it back if you wish. It isn't as if it's needed for the dam anymore."

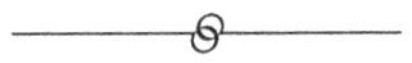

More stars than I would have dreamed possible hang over us. The sky here is darker and deeper than I've ever known. At this elevation it feels like I could fall into it.

"That could have been worse." Clover stokes the fire she built herself. Not that she needed to. Apparently, she just likes to.

I keep my eyes on the sky. "You sound disappointed."

Perhaps Ismene's rage burned out yesterday when they spoke in private. Today went well enough. After a couple of highly scientific explanations that soared over my head, Clover paired down the accumulator to an energy storage device. It was essential to the dam that kept the Kaycian region of the continent flooded.

Once Ismene retrieves it, we'll go back to Kaycie and both sides can act like the other doesn't exist again. After I leave, how long will it take to feel like this place is all a dream? How soon will I forget the taste of crisp mountain air and these incredible views?

Clover chuckles to herself. "Perhaps I am disappointed. If their fight is still going to dictate my life, the least they could do is actually fight. For a moment I let myself hope that if everyone calmed down about it, things would change, but Ismene doesn't change. Not quickly. She's like a mountain. It would take millennia to wear her down."

"Are you going to keep alluding to whatever it is that Ismene is holding over you, or will you actually tell me?"

"I thought Kaycians enjoyed dancing."

"Being used to—or even skilled at—this kind of dance doesn't mean we *enjoy* it. Plus, I'm only half-Kaycian."

"You seem to think that's a curse. As was intended. You're lucky, though. Your life is your own." She twists herself around to lie on her stomach, spinning a ring around her finger. "You get to have a family if you so choose. We can't marry. Any children of mine will be conceived and grown in a laboratory. Biologically mine, but..."

"Why?" My options aren't as open as she assumes, but hers are bizarre.

"Casimir's treachery devastated Grandmother. The last thing she said to my father and Ismene was, 'don't ever get married.' They took that to heart and decided that our family would only grow with people born into it. That's why I never had a mother, and Priam and Nemora never had a father."

Silence falls over us as I struggle for anything to say to that. I wonder if Grandfather knew about this. Does he know how his betrayal affected the entire family? The fear of being forsaken now shackles his whole line. He and my mother weren't the only ones punished for his indiscretions.

"I'm sorry." It's a weak response, but anything would be.

She shrugs. "We all have our lot in life. I get mountains, but you have the option of falling in love. I don't think I'd trade. This place is more a part of me than any person could ever be." She picks a small red-purple flower, gazing at it with tender affection. "This is where I can grow."

"What is that?"

"Dwarf clover. The namesake I choose to identify with. My first name weighs too heavily with expectations. 'Minea' is a variant of 'Minerva.' Intellect, wisdom—and war, oddly enough—are what I'm meant for. But clover is wild. Free."

"It suits you."

Chapter Twenty-Five

BRAM

Caffeine may not be a requirement for Dixon, but this morning he drinks black coffee to counter the effects of the bottle of tequila he hardly shared. Krisalyn joins us for a breakfast Dixon won't touch. Vogue and Frey are still asleep. A door closes upstairs, and Krisalyn reaches for the menu screen. Getting something for Vogue, I'm sure. But when low, unfamiliar voices float down to us, she freezes.

My heart races as I unholster my gun and wave Dixon and Krisalyn into the alcove under the stairs. They press their backs against the wall next to me, gripping each other's hands.

"Who could be here?" A voice resounds from upstairs.

Did Agnar send marshals to check his villa?

"Search the rooms." A door clicks as it opens.

Shit. I can't wait for them to come into my line of fire. They'll find Vogue and Frey first. Before I can make a move to go upstairs, Krisalyn's shout makes my heart stop.

"Who's there?" she says as she pulls her hand from Dixon's and steps out toward the stairs. God damnit, she's trying to pull them away from Vogue.

"Hands where we can see them!" Footsteps speed down the stairs. Krisalyn grabs something from her purse and slides it under her cuff.

With her back to the console table we moved yesterday, she blocks her bag and holds her hands open at shoulder level. What is she doing?

Dixon points to his wrist and mimes sleep. Krisalyn keeps sedation pellets in her purse? Go figure. Well, if the marshals go to bind her hands, she could release it and knock them out. It gives us a chance to get information from them. Even if we can't, she probably has amnesia shots too. Two tall figures reach the bottom of the stairs in sleek, form-fitting dark green jackets. These aren't marshals. Rather than clean-shaven faces and buzz cuts, these men wear thick beards and long hair.

"What's this?" one of the men says. "Where did you come from?" The gun he points at her is unlike anything I've ever seen. Its bulk looks like it would be too heavy to aim, but this husky man keeps it steady with one hand.

"Kaycie." Krisalyn is the model of resolute calm.

"A pissant Kaycian, in the flesh."

They aren't Kaycians. They aren't marshals. Townspeople couldn't have dropped from the roof, so they must be Montican. *Shit.* This isn't how I pictured everyone finding out about Montica.

They debate what to do with Krisalyn as I slink around the corner to take aim at the gunman. A heartbeat before I squeeze the trigger to send a bullet through his skull, Krisalyn reaches for her cuff.

The men see it. "Really, now?" One fires lazily, as if inconvenienced.

Instead of the familiar blast of a gunshot, thunder erupts from the gun, shattering the windows throughout the villa. Glass shards rain from the enormous chandelier. Krisalyn is thrown backward into the console table and disappears with it through the now empty doorframe.

Time stops. *Oh God, Krisalyn.*

I deliver a bullet to the shooter's brain as Dixon cries out for her. The other Montican turns around in time to watch my next bullet go through his left eye.

Vogue and Frey sprint down the stairs as Dixon leapfrogs the fallen men to look down where Krisalyn fell. "Kris!" Dixon turns to me. "I can't reach her, find something to pull her up."

She's alive? I scramble to the living room and snatch a throw blanket. Vogue screeches at the ledge as Frey pulls her back when I return. Dixon lies belly down in the shattered glass, head and shoulders extended over the edge of the building. Krisalyn hangs from the end of the wooden deck. Her grip on the edge is all that keeps her from being splattered on the ground below.

"Keep your eyes on me, Kris." Dixon lowers an end of the blanket to her. I drop to the floor to hold his end with him. "Grab the blanket. We'll pull you up."

"I can't." Her entire body shudders.

"You can do it," I say. But can she? *If* she can overcome her fear to pry a hand off the deck, she'll be suspended by one hand, if only for a second. We'd be better off dropping someone down to grab her. This blanket won't cut it though.

I take a breath to think and jump to my feet. "Tell her it's going to be loud a second."

Dixon obeys and I fire three shots into the ceiling to bring the chandelier's skeleton crashing down. Vogue jumps in Frey's arms. The chain breaks away from the chandelier easily enough. I toss one end to Dixon along with plastic wrist restraints and tell him to tie the chain around himself. He understands and doesn't hesitate. We need the length to get Dixon to Krisalyn, so I can't secure the other end.

"Frey, I'm going to need your help."

"Do not move," Frey says to Vogue. He comes and wraps the end of the chain around his wrist and hand.

Dixon takes a breath and nods to us. "I'm coming to get you," he says down to Krisalyn. He sits with his legs hanging over the edge and turns to lower himself, facing the building. Frey and I step forward slowly. "Keep going," Dixon calls from below. We're four feet from the edge. "Almost there." Two feet. "Stop!"

I lean over to see Dixon wrap his arm around Krisalyn's waist. "I've got you. Come on." I brace for the added weight, little as it may be. There's hardly a change. "Okay, bring us up!"

We pull the chain back, inching our way from the deathtrap Krisalyn was so scared of last night. When their heads appear at floor level, Vogue rushes over and pulls Krisalyn in. Once she's safely on the floor, Dixon hoists himself up too. He rolls onto his back with a sigh of relief. Krisalyn and Vogue skitter away from the opening and lock in a teary embrace.

Dixon takes Frey's hand to rise from the floor, and I help him undo the restraints which secure the chain around him. The three of us trudge to the stairs, where they both drop to sit on the bottom steps. I catch my breath as I lean my forehead against the wall. No one speaks for a while.

Frey breaks the silence, speaking quietly as to not disturb the sobbing girls across the room. "What the hell happened?"

"They dropped in from the roof," I say. "We didn't hear anything until they were walking around upstairs."

"Krisalyn drew them down so they wouldn't find you and Vogue in your beds," Dixon adds.

"Well," Frey says, "so they wouldn't find Vogue, really."

Dixon's mouth turns up at the corners as he shakes his hair, making it rain fragments of glass.

"They were probably from some black-ops squadron of marshals." The lie comes easily. I'm too unnerved by this to deal with a big reveal right now. Somehow, I'm more relieved Serenity isn't here to listen to my coverup than I am about her missing the danger. I don't know what that says about me.

"They have those?" Frey asks.

"Wouldn't surprise me. We should get out before they're missed and someone comes looking for them." This one isn't a lie, but I also want to minimize our time around these corpses before the Kaycians find clues about them.

"I need to see how they got here." Dixon starts up the stairs.

"Oh, me too." Frey stands to follow. "And what was that weapon?"

"We don't have time," I say.

They continue up.

"We'll be quick," Dixon says.

Shit. "Two minutes!" Not good. God knows what they'll find. Hopefully they can't get into whatever craft is up there. At the very least, I can claim ignorance. I was supposed to be a soldier, not a spy.

This sucks.

Vogue gets Krisalyn to a couch and gives her a glass of water. It splashes from side-to-side in her shaking hands. Vogue tucks Krisalyn's hair behind her ear and whispers something to her before rising to come to me. Tears stream from her eyes as she wraps me in a hug. "Thank you."

The gap I've always felt between myself and Kaycians seems superficial now. As Krisalyn sits sliced up on the outside and falling apart inside, and Vogue recuperates from her terror, their humanity is all too obvious. None of them are the glamorous, perfect figures who got on the train to flee their home. They're ruffled and battered and tenacious. It feels like a lifetime ago that Serenity told me Kaycians weren't my enemies.

The idea might finally be sinking in.

Dixon and Frey photograph the vessel on the roof, snatch the weapons off the bodies to study later, and we all get cleaned up to leave. Dixon stops in the basement to retrieve the tequila and champagne before we take the utilitarian elevator down to ground level. I drive this time to give myself something to do. Dixon sprawls out in the third row, and Krisalyn falls asleep on Vogue's lap in the second.

"Okay, Frey," Vogue says. "Since you helped save Krisalyn's life, I'll forego my planned retaliation. Throwing me into the water is forgiven."

He turns back to look at her. "What am I spared from?"

"I was going to drop a laxative in your coffee one morning."

Chapter Twenty-Six

ADWIN

"We brought you a parting gift." Priam hands me a bottle of his craft whiskey.

"I'll need to make it last, but smaller portions might increase my enjoyment of it." I put the bottle into my bag.

"Are all Kaycians so weak?" Clover drops into a chair and flings her legs up over an armrest.

"Weaker. I'm only half-Kaycian, remember?"

"Don't you get bored there?" Priam asks.

"There are plenty of diversions." Though sitting in a theater might be dull now compared to flying through the trees. Everything here is larger than life. Kaycie already feels small in comparison.

"Priam, maybe we should go visit."

Seeing Priam stroll through Kaycie would be diverting in and of itself. His appearance would be more surprising to Kaycians than the existence of the towns or the ocean's disappearance.

"You may want to wait until we sort out our little civil war," I say.

"How long could that possibly take? We could end it in a minute if my mother wanted to get involved," Priam says.

"I'm sure they'll sort it out." Talking about Kaycians like this is bizarre. People in the city may be the pinnacle of society there, but compared to Montica, everyone there is insignificant. I've felt separate from them for some time, but I'm far more Kaycian than Montican.

"In the meantime, we'll work on our parents," Clover says. "You should be able to come here as you please."

"That would be nice. There's really no opportunity to practice tree-walking in Kaycie."

"Do *not* encourage her."

Clover grins at Priam victoriously. "Oh, this will be the call that you're leaving." She points to her ear and soon her expression morphs into concern. "Why?" she says. "What does that have to do with—I'll just lock him in here then... Because that's ridiculous... Yes, I'll bring Priam." She taps behind her ear and sighs. "I don't think you have to pack up just yet, Adwin. You're going to need to stay in here until further notice. Sorry."

"What happened?" Priam asks.

"The agents we sent to get Casimir's accumulator were killed."

Being detained in here is certainly more comfortable than a cell which was Ismene's initial plan. The transition from guest delegate to prisoner is a little jarring, though not nearly as unsettling as not knowing what's going on. I pace the living room and consider opening the whiskey. It's a beautiful day out, but Clover locked the balcony door too. She couldn't have thought I'd actually go running off into the trees, could she?

I drop into the chair she had occupied, and something pokes my thigh. In the seat is a three-inch metal cube.

I turn it over in my hands, examining its smooth, reflective surface. What does this do? Two of the sides depress slightly under my fingers and a holo springs up from it, displaying the boardroom.

"Who did you have there?" Ismene shouts at Grandfather.

"Ismene, I didn't—"

"You may call me Director Agnar."

"Oh, get over yourself."

Did Clover leave this for me on purpose?

"The second team is reporting no Mo-accumulator on the premise," Nemora says.

Ismene glowers at her father. "What do you think you're playing at?"

"If it isn't there, then it was stolen from me," Grandfather says.

"We should close the dome until it's retrieved," Rocco says.

Clover jumps out of her seat. "That's not what it's for! Is it even worthwhile to close it for a short period? You can't leave it up until spring; we're only just getting into autumn."

"Stop being so damn dramatic," Nemora says. "It's been used for defense before, and it does no harm to leave it up for more than a season."

Clover glowers but holds her tongue. What does the dome do, and why does Clover hate it so much?

"You should get to work on retrieving it, Casimir," Ismene says. "I'll be keeping your grandson as collateral until you return it to me."

Grandfather bristles. "Adwin is your family."

"He is no family of mine."

"Mother," Priam says, "he is family. And what is his crime?"

"Being related to that snake."

"A crime we are all guilty of," Clover says. "May he stay as a guest rather than prisoner?"

Ismene looks back and forth between her son and niece. "If he steps a foot out of line, he goes into a cell and I will hold both of you accountable."

They nod their assent. Nemora remains conspicuously out of it.

I set the cube on the coffee table as they discuss my grandfather's immediate departure.

How long will I be a *guest* in this well-appointed prison?

Clover knocks only to announce her entrance. Waiting for me to answer the door is unnecessary, apparently. She finds me sitting in the living room and glances at the cube on the table. "Did you figure out how to use it, or do I need to update you?"

"I figured it out."

"Good." She picks it up and presses the corners to compress it before sliding it into her pocket. "It's old, but that means it goes unnoticed. I find it handy."

"Do you frequently find yourself aiding criminals?"

"You haven't committed any crimes that I'm aware of." She looks at me incredulously.

"I think my record is clean."

"Let's keep it that way. Come with me, please."

"Am I allowed to leave?"

"With me, yes."

We descend to a lower level under the Breck while Clover tells me about the dome. Every winter it controls the weather, keeping it comfortable at the high elevations. It can also serve as a shield, using a similar energy force as the destroyed dam. The Mo-accumulator has enough power to act as a bomb. If someone figured out how to use it, its single burst could take down the dome, but then it wouldn't have anything to attack Montica with.

"It's like living in a cage," she says.

"A cage several times larger than the city of Kaycie."

"Which was also a cage, so I don't know why you accepted that. Anyway, it doesn't matter the size. It changes the whole feeling of the mountains. The sunshine isn't as warm, the air is stuffy, and we need winter. I've gone out past the border during winter before. It's beautiful."

Part laboratory, part hospital, this lower level is brightly lit and blindingly white compared to the rich tones of the fortress. I'm taken to a room to get a communication chip implanted. The anesthetic injection is the only thing I feel. The incision behind my right ear is sealed, and I sit up to receive instructions.

"Tell it to call Clover," the technician says.

"Call Clover."

Clover taps hers. I hear a faint beep then, "Testing, testing," echoes as I hear her say it in front of me and in my head.

"This will take some getting used to."

Clover taps again, hanging up on me. "Is the volume all right?"

"It's fine."

A tone sounds in my head, and an automated voice announces Clover's name in a soothing tone. I tap the chip and hear the beep.

"Well, done," she says, echoing again. "Tap to hang up."

I do it.

"Thank you," Clover says to the technician. "I'll give him the full orientation."

We return to the surface and go outside. She drops her head back a moment, looking as relieved as I felt every time Serenity didn't take me up on my obligatory invitations to spend the night. "I hate it down there in the recycled air."

"I'm surprised you don't *live* in the trees."

"My balcony door stays open at all times. I'll wear a heap of blankets rather than cut off the mountain air."

Priam and Nemora catch up with us in a sitting area set up around a fire sculpture of an eagle, soaring in flight. "Are you chipped?" Priam asks.

"I am indeed." I rub the dull itch behind my ear.

"You'll get used to it," he says.

Nemora goes on to explain that the chip tracks my location. If I leave my suite without one of the three of them or a guard, I'll be arrested. "Don't expect me to be coming to take you out, though. I did not volunteer to babysit."

"I'm not surprised."

Priam and Clover tell me how to mute it, ignore calls, and find their locations with it. Nemora makes it clear that she is not sharing her location with me.

"We get it, Nemora!" Clover grumbles. "Why are you even here?"

"To make sure *you two* are staying in line."

"So you will be babysitting, after all," Priam says. "Go report to Mother already."

"Don't do anything stupid," she says and stalks off.

Clover smiles mischievously at Priam. "It's like she doesn't trust us or something."

Chapter Twenty-Seven
BRAM

I had hoped to return home on better footing. We were supposed to know what happened to the sea, and the Kaycians and I would have squared away all the misinformation. We were going to be able to move forward. Focus on a plan to get Serenity. Instead, we're all shaken from our brush with death, and there are even more secrets between us.

This is going really well.

At least we know what happened to the sea. One step forward, several back.

Mom's luck hasn't been any better than mine. She rubs her forehead, pacing alongside the kitchen table where Aren and I sit. "Years to get the islands on the same page; *weeks* for the Establishment to split us up again. This is ridiculous!"

Gardner, Eudora, and Blue Springs are cooperating with the Establishment now. They've got seats on the council and are keeping trade open. Due in part to the Establishment telling them about Montica before Mom did. Now *we're* the liars after everything the Establishment did.

"Without those three, we have nothing." Mom wrings her hands. "Gladstone is a wasteland, they could flatten Greenwood's town without destroying their forests, and why *not* wipe Lawson off the map? They could replace us with automation in the city easily enough. The only reason they haven't exterminated us is because we aren't worth the energy and resources right now."

Sophos tries to calm her. "There are also people in the Establishment who would not stand for that."

She lets out a frustrated sound from behind clenched teeth.

"Let's look at it this way," Sophos says in a soothing tone. "Even if the Establishment retains control over the country, they can't possibly continue selection and the marshal program now that everyone knows what really happens. And even if only those three towns are represented in the council, there will be enough reasonable people on it to keep them from avenging their pride. Life would improve, which was the real goal—not to govern the nation."

"The Establishment shouldn't be able to keep their power." She sinks into a chair, looking defeated. "We can't trust them."

Aren taps his fingers on the table. "We need someone higher up on the food chain." We all look at him curiously. "Montica has them shitting their pants. Maybe they would take our side."

Was he paying attention when I told him about what happened this morning? "Monticans just tried to kill me."

Aren shrugs. "They don't know that was *us* at their dam."

"Montica could be worse than the Establishment!"

"They're far away and probably wouldn't bother with us."

"Then why would they *bother* getting involved in this?" Holy shit, it didn't take long at all to jump back into butting heads with my brother.

"The Establishment pissed them off. Maybe they want to oust the Establishment too."

"Or maybe they want to get rid of us all." Which is more dangerous? An enemy I know, or a friend I don't. A false friend can do more damage.

Mom scratches her chin and looks at Sophos. "Do you have a way to contact them?"

"No, Casimir has always been the only one to communicate with them."

She chews her lip as she considers.

"The ocean is gone," Aren says. "We could probably just drive there."

Are they ignoring me because I've been in the dark for so long and can't *possibly* have a good idea about any of this? "Or we could send our four *pardoned* Kaycians back to the Establishment to infiltrate them."

Sophos rests his chin on his knuckles. "Vogue didn't make any theories about Montica at the dam?"

"How could she? She doesn't know it exists."

"Well, actually..."

The door slams behind me as I storm out into the cool evening. *I cannot fucking believe him.*

"Hey, what's going on?" Carista approaches me from the direction of the house the Kaycians are staying in.

"Just another happy day in the Eros family—finding out more of the bullshit lies."

"What now?"

"You were visiting the Kaycians, right?"

"Yeah."

"Did they seem suspicious about the Monticans we ran into at the dam?"

"No. I don't think so. They said you told them it was marshals."

I tap my teeth together, mulling it over. "Well, since they aren't idiots, I have to assume they're hiding their suspicions. Vogue already knew Montica existed, so she's bound to put it together."

"Vogue knows about Montica?"

"Yeah. Apparently, her grandmother told her about the islands and Montica when she turned sixteen. So, when I got pissed at Serenity for spilling the beans, Vogue had actually known it all and then some."

"And you're really angry about this because?" Carista's eyes are glassy.

"Are you okay?"

"I'm fine." She shakes her head. "Dixon let me try tequila."

I'm surprised he'd share. "Well, I'm angry because Mom is insistent that we don't come clean with the Kaycians until we have secure footing with the Establishment. Now that the entire uprising is down to Greenwood, the remnants of Gladstone, and us, she is absolutely panicked. I had to fight them against the idea to give all the Kaycians amnesia to wipe out the whole damn uprising." As if giving Vogue back to them without any memory of the last six months would piss them off any less.

Her eyes widen. "We can't do that! They're our allies and friends. That would be horrible."

"Well, they agreed not to so long as I don't reveal their lies yet."

"But you don't like this compromise?"

"They need to know they're pardoned. They deserve to be able to leave and get back to Serenity."

Carista purses her lips. "Sounds like you and this Serenity Ward got close."

Is this becoming obvious? "She was the one around the most. And she was manipulated even more than the rest of them."

"How so?"

"Vogue's family, Serenity's, and Sophos were working together. I just found *this* out, too. They were setting up Vogue to be Director of Research and Technology, and Serenity to be Governor or Lieutenant. Vogue's family took a more direct route with her, but the Wards had been grooming Serenity with her sense of justice, and then Sophos was supposed to introduce her to the way things were so they could see how she'd react without her parents telling her how to feel about all of it. But Sophos went behind their backs and planned the uprising with my mom and dragged Serenity into it. He's probably made enemies of all our allies."

Will Serenity lump me in with this? Is she going to hate me for it? No. She doesn't even know me. Somehow her indifference is worse.

"So now we're talking about trying to get Montica to back us," I say. And as much as I hate that idea, we might be screwed if they don't."

Chapter Twenty-Eight
SERENITY

The meeting room feels somewhat less like a battleground this time. Agnar's absence has the effect of keeping some claws tucked away. The Kemps and Karans aren't quite as bold without Agnar present.

"That's absurd." Well, Watt Kemp is still a bit bold. "They can't expect us all to step down. No one else could run anything."

Celia folds her hands on the table in front of her. She sits next to her father in Agnar's place. "You've been grooming our generation for this, and *we* haven't given the towns any reason not to trust us." *Yet* goes unsaid.

Flora bristles. "You're the only one with any experience. The rest, no offense,"—she gestures to Rollin, Lanelle, and me—"are practically children." Flora is scarcely older than Celia. If she hadn't already taken a position on the city council, she could be included in those of us who haven't lost the towns' trust.

"They don't actually need to run anything," Alima Karan says. "They only have to be the face of the council."

Estrella Rinne bobs her head back and forth. "Put them on stage but continue controlling things from the wings."

"My daughter is *done* being a puppet." Fury rolls off my mother like I've never seen. Certainly not in front of others, but everyone's attention is on me. Looks ranging from pity to disdain land on me. Eyes on me is nothing new, but not with these sentiments.

"Grace, it's really no different from how we've always run things." Governor Martel remains calm and stoic. "We've always made the important decisions together and let those in the council seats implement them."

"This is different. Alima makes it sound as if we'd throw them out there without any power to do anything."

"They must have *some* power." Tevin fixes my mother with a firm gaze. "If they are to meet with the representatives from the towns, they need to be able to make decisions."

"Of course," Martel says.

My mother's shoulders roll back as she lets out a breath. "Fine." She turns to me. "If you want to do this, of course."

The choice isn't mine now any more so than when I was placed in Leadership at age ten. This has always been my future, whether I knew it or not. Now there are even fewer of us available to do it. Vogue and Adwin should be a part of this, but Adwin is in Montica and Vogue…

"Of course, I will. Anything to help. Which, I assume, includes retrieving Vogue Taylor? She is obviously part of this."

Espy gives me a small, grateful smile. "Thank you, sweetheart. We're trying. You don't need to worry about it."

"I'm going to worry about it! Let me go to Lawson. You sent me to Gardner and Eudora, and I was fine."

"Lawson is a different story," Cornell Prosper says. "They're actively hostile. Holding Vogue and the others proves that."

Alima Karan frowns and says, "We're trying to contact them, but they've set up the networks in such a way that we can't get through." Is she trying to get Vogue back without calling for her arrest now? That's a nice change for her.

"Fine. What will we be doing in the meantime?"

Black is not a color Millie Gersemi wears. Ever. I wouldn't have thought she owned anything black. Her skirt suit is missing the sparkle, sequins, and bright colors I've come to associate with her. Even her hair is more subdued—purple being mostly hidden in the bottom layers of her long curls. She lights up as Celia, Rollin, Lanelle, and I enter the room—another meeting space that's clear of furniture aside from several wheeled racks of clothing and a five-top table.

"My darlings!" She holds me by the shoulders as she appraises me. "Oh Serenity, they're ruining all my years of hard work. Who throws a diamond back into a pile of coal?"

"Good to see you too."

"And you!" She either ignores or fails to notice my sarcasm as her attention turns to Rollin. "How many times have I told you, I do not like you in shades of blue? It's too common, and you are *not* common."

"There isn't much of a choice here, Millie."

"I'm here to change that. Celia, it's a pleasure to see you. Lanelle, I know we've scarcely met, but I'm thrilled to be working with you all. Please have a seat."

We do so, but Millie remains standing. This promises to be quite the show then.

"The four of you were always going to be the face of our lovely city someday. The nation, apparently." Her smile masks her anxiety over these developments, just as she always taught me to. "It pains me that in our current situation this image needs to be subdued, but even if you can't quite sparkle, you can still shine.

"I have new wardrobes for each of you—simple and somber to reflect the current mood. You will present yourselves as humble and gracious, *but* do not forget the upper hand is yours. In ways you haven't even noticed, you've been preparing for this your entire lives."

The subtle ways my parents prepared me have been occurring to me. They demanded my best in everything I do, sharpened my mind, gave me outlets in music and fencing, and most importantly, taught me to be compassionate. Celia seems to have had similar experiences. Lanelle has certainly been developed in different ways. I don't think a strong sense of justice was embedded into her. Oddly enough, the one I've known the longest is the biggest mystery. Rollin has always been decent, but I know which side his family is on.

Oh. This is why my mother relented about my participation. To balance the scales.

"Not that you need so long," Millie says, "but we have one week to prepare before you meet with the mayors. The four of you will present a united front to this new council and the country."

Maybe on an individual basis we don't need a week to prepare, but the four of us being on the same page will take some work.

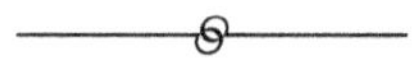

"This is not the first impression I envisioned for my entrance onto the world stage." Lanelle tugs at her blouse to reveal some cleavage from under her dark purple suit.

Our new wardrobes may be a touch boring, but they're better than Leavenworth's uniforms.

Celia sighs from the front passenger seat. With her husband driving, and the rest of us in the back, I can't help but feel we're being babysat. Lanelle seems to make Celia feel that way, too.

"This is not a theater stage, Lanelle."

"You know by now the world is a theater."

It always has been, but we are supposed to be changing that.

"It's never been my favorite part of the job, though," Celia says. "Are you so disappointed to not have been in the performing arts?"

Lanelle brushes invisible dust off her sleeve. "Not at all. I'm eternally grateful to be in a department where I can do so much good. I only wish I could do more." She spares a glance at Rollin and me. I never wanted my Leadership placement, but for everyone's sake, I'm glad it was me instead of her.

I roll my shoulders back as we exit the vehicle in front of Blue Springs' Townhall. The gray cloudy day makes me feel even more out of place than I already did. Celia and Rollin are in dark colors, too. I'm the one in ivory. To show that this isn't 'all doom and gloom.' To be the sign of hope and peace. Or as my mother and I agree, to be the shiny distraction. *Let them think that's all you are. Being underestimated can be invaluable.*

My mother would be great at this. She stepped aside, stayed in the background of the Establishment, so now they hardly know what to make of her asserting her power role. I'm her daughter. I can be like her.

Vaiana greets Celia with a handshake. She's the only one I haven't met. Celia took care of this town on her own since she already had connections here. Blue Springs is the most neutral territory since there was no uprising. Celia introduces us all, and we go into a meeting room where Aster and Cole are already waiting.

"Thank you for meeting with us," Celia says.

Cole's gaze sweeps over us as we sit down. "We're a touch outnumbered."

No matter that all four of us are young enough to be his children. "We aren't on different sides, though." *Be an olive branch.* "We all want the same things."

"To your point," Rollin says, "it would appear more even if the other towns were willing to come to the table. Do you have any insight into their refusal to work with us?" He sounds so grown up. We always knew we'd be doing this, but seeing it happen—and so much sooner than we expected—is strange.

Vaiana clears her throat. "Greenwood doesn't trust anyone from the Establishment, but they are probably the least hostile. Kolina and Sophos won't bring Lawson over easily, and there isn't enough left of Gladstone for them to have feet to stand on." Her gaze falls on Lanelle. "But the survivors from Gladstone consider this to be a blood feud now."

Thank God for Millie. It would be so hard not to smirk without those years of training. Lanelle's grandmother was the one who had her marshals lay the town to ruins rather than surrender. I wouldn't be disappointed to have the Kemps displaced based on it.

Lanelle has the good sense to look ashamed. "That's precisely why the people who were running the Establishment are no longer part of this."

"I'm not sure this is going to be enough separation for them," Vaiana says. "But being that they are in Lawson, it may not matter."

"Should we worry about the safety of Blue Springs?" Celia asks. "You are tucked in between the two hostile towns."

"They aren't hostile toward *us*. And they wouldn't act against anyone at this point. Kolina is no fool."

"She is bold enough to hold on to some Kaycians, though." All eyes land on me. "Four Kaycians who aided Sophos are still in Lawson. They've been pardoned but haven't returned. We believe they weren't informed of their status."

Cole leans forward onto his elbows. "Kolina wouldn't hold hostages."

"Then why haven't they contacted us to tell us they've *chosen* to remain in Lawson?" Vogue wouldn't disappear on me like this. Not by choice.

Aster sighs. "I'll try to get word to them. Tell them they're pardoned."

"Thank you." I give her the names and finally feel a twinge of relief that I'm doing *something* to get Vogue back. The rest of the group discusses the continuation of trade with Lawson and Greenwood while I mull over what else I could do. There's no point volunteering to go to Lawson myself. They've blocked all our attempts to go meet with them. There has to be someway though...

"As a collective," Celia says, "our region was once known as the KC Metro. What are your feelings about using that again?"

"I don't like it." Aster is the first to shoot it down. "It sounds like we all still revolve around Kaycie."

Rollin maintains his professional demeanor. "What do you suggest then?"

Chapter Twenty-Nine

BRAM

Every screen in town came on, saying an announcement was coming soon. It wasn't long before Lawson looked like a ghost town. Vogue bounces her foot, Dixon paces in the kitchen, and we all wait to see what this is about. I can barely stand to be around Sophos at this point. All the ways he twisted information and people make me sick. Even Vogue has grown on me enough that telling her everything races through my mind constantly. Her temper and unpredictability are all that's keeping me from it. It can't be much longer, though. Every day I care less about the ramifications and more about getting Serenity out of the Establishment.

To say my priorities are shit would be an understatement.

The blank screen changes to a view of a lake and a small dam. Frey lets out a breath. "Oh. They got through because they're in one of the towns. I feel better now."

I'm glad someone does. Dixon rushes over, and we all focus our attention on the broadcast. A soothing, feminine voice says, "We are coming to you live from Blue Springs, for an announcement from our leadership council."

"That's Millie," Vogue says. "The Establishment's public relations guru and molder of young leaders' images."

That voice drilled into Serenity that she had to look and act a certain way to be 'perfect.' The woman must be an idiot. Serenity is better without all of that.

Seven people step into view. I would've only seen the one anyway, but she's probably caught everyone's attention being the only brightness in the group of dark suits. Blood pounds through my ears, but I keep stone still on the outside. Not like I needed confirmation of my steadfast feelings for Serenity but seeing her locks it up tight. I'm going to be useless for anything until we get her back.

"Thank you for joining us as we find a way forward together." Vaiana's refusal to participate in the uprising seems to have worked out well for her. "Our towns rose up to stop the injustices we faced under the previous Establishment, not to make us each independent, but so we could unite. The fallen sea water has cleared our physical barriers, and we must tear down the rest."

Are they going to tell everyone about Montica? Do I play dumb if they do? They don't... yet. Others blab about healing old wounds, and my attention doesn't really snap back to it until Serenity speaks.

"Our new Union is incomplete without the remainder of the towns—the rest of our family." Her gray eyes plead through the screen. My breath hitches in my throat. "We want to move forward as a whole. Lawson, Greenwood, and Gladstone are vital parts of our nation. We hope every town will join us as we come together to officially unite as one. The signing of the Union Compact will take place on—"

Vogue turns it off and buries her face in her hands, where she sits on the floor at Krisalyn's feet. As much as seeing Serenity and hearing her voice were a relief, I understand her aversion. *Not like this.* Seeing her as an Establishment puppet after everything she did to take it down...

Frey leans back on the couch and crosses his arms. "Who would *actually* believe the sons and daughters of the ousted council would do anything differently?" Vogue glares at him. "I know Serenity *would*, but not if she's re-learned everything with their spin."

I worried about her becoming the person she was before she learned how the world works. The real danger was this, though. Is it worse for her to learn it from someone else? Her parents should be keeping her on the right side of things. Well, one of the right sides. They don't align with the Establishment or Sophos. There are too many sides to keep track of now.

"We need to tell her everything." Krisalyn's knees bounce against Vogue's back.

Vogue reaches up to her shoulder to hold Krisalyn's hand. "Not we. Me." She drops her head back to face the ceiling. "I shouldn't have waited this long. It was my responsibility to tell her the truth of what happened this year. I need to go to her."

Dixon stops his agitated pacing. "Not by yourself you don't."

"She doesn't know any of you. Not really."

That statement is like a knife to the chest. The idea of Serenity not knowing me is a physical ache. Vogue voicing it tears it open into a bleeding wound. Serenity was one of the few people who knew me. She saw me when I was invisible. Everyone sees me now, but it doesn't mean anything if she doesn't.

"Jase knows me," Krisalyn says.

"We don't know where he is," Dixon points out.

"He'd be near her."

"Not if they don't really remember what they were."

"It doesn't matter," Frey says. "We've already decided we can't get into Leavenworth."

"Serenity isn't in Leavenworth." Vogue gestures toward the now blank screen.

"We need *a little* more notice."

My priorities and options race through my head: Who to trust, what the goals are, where does this all lead. "That signing ceremony probably won't be in Leavenworth."

Townhall without marshals patrolling is still hard to get used to. Walking right in and having free rein of the place where they hid the train station for so long is surreal. Luckily, Sophos is alone. He sounds exasperated when he greets me.

"Is everyone this excited about the news?"

He sighs. "Your mother is scrambling. Greenwood is considering going along with this Union, which would leave us high and dry. How are our resident Kaycians feeling about it?"

"Mostly hating how Serenity is being used. And guilty that we let her fall into that." *I* let her fall into that. Regardless of what Vogue says, I could have stopped her. I should have.

"I hope you don't share that guilt, Bram. This was always going to be Serenity's role."

"Until you changed it for her."

"She was always going to end up back with them. Do you really think *Serenity Ward* could be kept away from the Establishment? It's a miracle they haven't come after Vogue. Both of them here would have invited fire to rain down on us."

What is he saying? "But the plan was for her to come here with us?"

"No, the plan cracked and splintered when my agents all befriended each other, and crumbled when Tori died." He massages his temples.

"What does this have to do with Tori? Why was it a problem for them to be friends?"

"Bringing Serenity and Vogue here was out of the question, but then they all found each other and I knew Krisalyn, Dixon, Frey, and Jase wouldn't just leave the other two behind, so I was going to have to lose them all."

"How?"

"I was going to have Tori wipe their memories and leave them in the city."

My pulse is like a rip current as that sinks in. When he was done with Serenity—with all of them—he was just going to discard them. I left her for *him*. And this is what he was going to do? Of course, he didn't mind her carrying an amnesia shot around—she was making it easier for him. *Son of a bitch.*

I meant to feel it out, to see if I could suggest a plan to go to the signing to get Serenity, but I figured there was a chance I'd end up just doing it. Easier to ask for forgiveness than permission and all that. But now the choice is simple. *Thanks for teaching me to hide everything, Tori.*

"I take it Tori didn't know about that?" I ask.

"She didn't need to know ahead of time. Tori was always quick to act."

Would she have done it, though? She had just told me she understood my attraction to Serenity. Not that Serenity was mine anyway, but would Tori have been willing to take that away?

Chapter Thirty

SERENITY

I roll over, reach out, and wake up to find myself seeking Jase. Again. Flat on my back, I rake my fingers through my hair, tugging at the roots. It doesn't take a genius to discern the correlation between Jase's departure and my sleeplessness. It would appear I had enjoyed the warmth of his embrace more often than my conscious mind knew. Now I can't sleep without him. Knowing he's in this building doesn't help. Every night I consider knocking on his door, sliding into his bed.

When I thought he was going to leave me, my feelings for him finally hit me. The idea of losing him was excruciating. Failing to recognize it until then was shamefully childish. I'm in love with him. It should be like walking on clouds. I love him, and he loves me. He said he'd wait for me. But instead of euphoria, all I feel is pain. How can loving someone hurt so much?

A weight on my chest threatens to smother me. I press my hand to it, wishing I could grasp it and pull it away, but it's under my skin. I'm over-complicating this. It's my own fault I'm in this position, but I can't pull myself out of it. Feeling like I don't deserve something is new to me, and I don't know how to get past it.

I thought I'd have the world in the palm of my hand soon, but the world is too big now, and the truth about the Establishment affirms that none of us should hold it anyway. So fine, I won't have the world. Can't I allow myself this little slice of happiness in it, though?

Let him love you. You do *deserve to be loved.* I wrap my arms around a pillow and repeat that to myself as I search for sleep's embrace.

This braid is hardly noticeable in my monochromatic hair, but I do it anyway, just to make it look like I'm trying. There aren't a lot of options, but I'm putting more effort into my appearance today than the month and a half I've spent here. Not for Jase—I don't need to do anything like this for him. It's for me, and it feels good, because it's never been for me before. How I presented myself was always to satisfy everyone else's expectations of me. Millie did a remarkable job, considering she didn't realize what she was really training me for.

Today, I'm forgetting her lessons though. Today I will do something just for myself, without concern for outside opinions. I want something, and I'm going to let myself have it. I'm going to let myself have *him*. I'll shove down all of my internal negativity that tells me I don't deserve it and let myself be happy. This shouldn't be a difficult thing. So, why am I nervous?

We're connected to a secure local network now which only serves Leavenworth. My detox from the buzzChains continues, and my cuff is mostly a vessel for Lanelle to nettle me, but at least I can find Jase. It lets me into the Department of Health building adjacent to the hospital. I take a deep breath before opening the door to the laboratory Jase's cuff shows him being in.

He is here.

So is Lanelle. With her arms wrapped around his neck and her lips pressed to his.

All of the air is pushed from my lungs. On impulse, I relax my face into a stoic expression. It's well practiced. For all anyone should see, I might as well be watching a history lecture. The wall is up. It's only one agonizing heartbeat before Jase pushes her away, but it feels like an eternity.

"What the hell are you doing?" he yells at her.

She notices me then and gasps, doe eyed and blushing.

Jase whips his head around to see me, and his jaw drops. "Oh my God, Serenity." I turn around. "No, wait!"

I slam the door and hear muffled shouting before I dash down the hall. My breaths are shallow as I race down the stairs. In through my nose, out through my mouth. Alone, I can let the façade slip. My heart thrashes and I blink back tears as they start to blur my vision. All of my self-encouragement was false. I didn't deserve him, and karma has caught up. Not that Lanelle deserves him, but that's not my problem.

Outside, the cool air bites my lungs. Jase calls for me, but I keep walking. I take a deep breath and let it out slowly. My face pulls back together before I turn around.

"Serenity, I'm so sorry. That wasn't—"

"Sorry for what?" I color my voice to be completely disinterested.

He tilts his face up toward the sky and clenches both hands into fists. "I know seeing that hurt you."

"Why would it? I told you to give up on me. I have no claim on you."

"You have every claim on me. Lanelle is vindictive, and determined to crush me, and she knows you're my highest priority."

The knot in my chest loosens ever so slightly. That makes more sense than the notion that Jase had moved on. I know how dedicated he is to me, and I know what Lanelle is. His adverse reaction to her was before he realized I was there. I'm almost certain.

"She's a liar, Serenity. She's manipulative and vicious. Even if you can't trust me, *please* don't trust her."

My fingers fidget, even with my hands tightly clasped. I swallow the lump in my throat. "I know I can't trust her. And I do trust you."

His shoulders relax. "Thank you." He reaches out for me, but I step back.

"No. So much of what you hate about her... I'm the same."

"You are *not* the same as Lanelle Kemp."

"I am though. We're both born and bred liars. All of my training on how to present the best possible image of myself was really so that I'd be able to sell the best possible image of Kaycie. Even if it was all lies. And I would have excelled at it."

"No you wouldn't. You never would have concealed everything."

Part of me believes him. It's probably just wishful thinking. I'd love to be as good as he thinks I am, but would I have uprooted generations of tradition and my own ingrained education? My parents wanted to change things, but that's a slow process and in the meantime, I'd have covered it all up.

"Jase, I think you should go back to the city. This is no place for someone as honest as you."

He huffs out a humorless laugh. "Don't practice your lying on me."

"I'm not lying." And it's true. "You'd be better off going home."

"Is that what you were coming to tell me?"

Now I do have to lie. "Yes."

His expression falls and my heart plummets. I don't want to hurt him. He comes toward me, but I match his steps to keep my distance. Not because I don't want him to touch me, but because if he does, my resolve will melt. This is the right thing to do. I can't let him pull my focus from that.

He raises his hands in surrender and backs off. "Okay. Whatever you want."

None of this is what I want, but I don't let that show. "I wish you all the best, Jase." And as I walk away, I silently add, *I love you.*

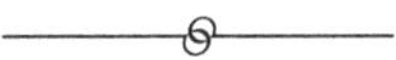

Victory against a VR opponent doesn't mean I can beat my mother, but I *am* improving. A goal to focus on eases my nerves, and strengthening my body settles my mind, though it's still a mess. I suppose that was my mother's plan all along.

The program resets and I go again against a higher skill level. It demands more work, but I still win quickly. I put my mask down and start to stow my sabre when—

"It must be seen to be believed."

I jump as Lanelle comes up behind me. "Do not sneak up on a person holding a sword!"

"You are much too pretty to be playing with swords."

I shake my head as I put the blade away. "If my mother isn't too ladylike for it, then no one is."

"It serves a purpose for Grace. You never have to portray a medieval heroine. You live only in this world."

Because this world is so peaceful. "All the same, it's something to do."

"Serenity, about earlier... I owe you an apology." Had I not been witness to her acting in Gardner and Eudora, I might believe her—glassy-eyed as she is. "Everything feels out of control, and Jase is something familiar... But I—"

"Jase and I aren't together anymore. It's none of my business." *But if you think I don't see what a conniving snake you are, you'll never win games like this.* We have to work together so we can't be openly hostile. If she wants to keep acting like we're friends, I will too.

"Are you sure? I'd hate it if his leaving is my fault."

"He's going back to Kaycie?"

She nods.

"Good. I told him he should."

"You're not angry, then?"

"Not at all." It's not even a lie. I'm not angry at Lanelle. This has been a perfect lesson in being cautious of whom I trust. I'm not angry at Jase for leaving, even if he said he'd wait for me. It's for the best.

No, I'm not angry. Just empty.

Chapter Thirty-One

BRAM

Fried food and alcohol are effective bait to get Vogue Taylor alone. She takes another miniature doughnut from the bag in my hand and pops it into her mouth then chases it with a sip of hot chocolate spiked with spiced liqueur. "Are we finally going to do this?" She doesn't look at me when she speaks. Brown, knee-high boots crunch leaves with each step.

"Do what?"

"Lay our cards on the table. Although, I have to admit, I'm surprised you chose me for this. I'm not ashamed to be the most difficult of the four of us—or perhaps tied with Frey. Krisalyn or Dixon seemed like the obvious choices."

I've never doubted that Vogue—that all of them—know more than they let on. Still, her confidence is unsettling. She thinks herself a step ahead at all times, and she may very well be. Dixon or Krisalyn wouldn't have rubbed that in my face though, so she has a point there. But Vogue is more involved, and I don't have any options to deal with this without her.

"You know more than them," I say.

"Than my friends?" She looks at me now with a sly smile. "Not at all. I'm an open book."

"Would Serenity agree?"

She laughs to herself. "Oh, that's why it's me. Because Serenity hasn't been used enough. You'll drag her into this too?" Vogue is better at this than I am. She knows where to cut to draw blood. Her words take the immediate effect of making me feel like I'm using Serenity. I've been furious at Sophos for it, but am I doing it too? I'm doing it for the greater good, but he'd have said the same. Actually, I'm doing it for *her* good, but that's too stupid to admit.

"Vogue, I'm not the enemy."

"Are you sure?" She halts and turns to me, stopping deep enough in the park to ensure privacy. "Weren't *lies* the Establishment's primary crimes against me?"

This would have been easier with Dixon. "Are you going to let me speak?"

She swipes the bag of doughnuts from my hand and plops down on the ground against a tree, cross-legged. "Go ahead." She pops another doughnut into her mouth like she's eating popcorn at a movie.

"I didn't even know Montica existed when we left Kaycie." She looks slightly bored by my statement. "I felt used too. And Tori was my friend. She wasn't aware of the conflicting plans, and she died without the chance to choose one. You're the only one who knew the options."

Vogue's head cocks slightly. "What other plan are you talking about?"

"Your grandmother's plan for you to fix things from within the council. Serenity was in it too."

"What?"

Knowing something Vogue doesn't is too satisfying. And this is why it had to be *her*. "Adelle planned Serenity's placement with the Wards. Did you think you were going to rise into the council and change it all by yourself?"

"I can be persuasive."

"You're too smart to think you'd be the only plant in the council. Adelle's plan included Sophos." Vogue's eyes pop wider. This makes Sophos' actions even worse. "Your families are two of only ten families that can be on the council and run the towns. That's why you could find out after you turned sixteen. Serenity was meant to be governor or lieutenant governor someday. Her parents raised her to be pre-disposed to our side. Sophos knew that and twisted it to insert her into his own plans, but she was already in the other version."

Vogue covers her mouth with the back of her hand. For once, she doesn't know everything. She blinks slowly before boring into me with her gaze. "When did you find out about this?"

"I found out about Adelle's plans with Sophos and the Wards after we got back from Agnar's villa."

"And what's going on with Montica?"

"They were threatening war against us before the uprising. We took advantage of the Establishment's distraction."

She glances away and scratches her scalp. "Telling me Sophos and Kolina—I assume your mother was aware of all the deception?" I nod. "It's pretty risky to tell me this. I could take the towns back to the stone age."

I bear my weapon too, presenting the vial from my pocket. "Maybe I didn't tell you anything." I'll hate myself if I have to give her amnesia, but I've done worse things.

Her face doesn't betray any hint of emotion. "What did you hope to accomplish with me?"

"Getting Serenity back."

Vogue's satisfaction about being feared is nauseating. I hate giving her that pleasure. We go back and forth over who knew what when. Of course, she mocks me for ever thinking they were dumb enough to believe those were marshals at the villa. I don't know if I feel bad for Frey, or if I'm impressed by his tenacity, because arguing with Vogue is exhausting. I don't know how he does it all the time. It almost falls apart when I tell her she and her friends have been pardoned by the Establishment. Being kept here against her will is nearly too much for her to take. Our only common ground is our distaste for Serenity's role in all of this and wanting to free her from Leavenworth. Fortunately, that's all I need to get Vogue on my side.

"My mom is hoping to get Montica to help now, but I don't like the idea."

She puffs out a breath. "Montica shouldn't want to ally with any of you. You tend to lie to your allies and threaten them. It's adorable you thought you'd give me amnesia, by the way."

My eyebrow cocks up as I look at her. "Why?"

"It's been clear that you've all been keeping secrets from us since we went to Agnar's villa. Krisalyn has us all taking amnesia vaccines." *Always one step ahead.*

"But I'm thrilled you had a false safety net to give you the courage to tell me everything." As if Vogue needed anything else to bolster her ego. "The only truly new information you gave me is the Establishment structure, the games played with Serenity's position, and our pardon though."

"How did you find out about the Montican threat?"

She taps her nose. "In the spirit of openness—and Krisalyn will be angry if I don't confess it—we got it out of Carista and gave her amnesia when we returned from the dam."

"What the hell, Vogue?"

"You were about to do it to me!"

I rub my forehead and sigh. "You're out of control."

"Hence I was helpful in a rebellion." She flashes a cocky smile.

"So what have you been doing all this time?"

"Tinkering with the Montican weapons and tech we found. Since we didn't know they *pardoned us*"—her eyes narrow—"we were trying to see how it might help us abduct Serenity and Jase from Leavenworth, but it didn't seem reasonable."

"Well, now that the cards are laid out, do you trust the Establishment enough to go back?"

She shakes her head. "I don't want to be stuck with them. I want to get Serenity and get out."

"Kidnapping seems like the kind of thing you'd add to your resume at this point."

"I like it. Master hacker, drainer of the sea, abductor of celebrities. Let's do it."

Chapter Thirty-Two
ADWIN

Never did I think I'd be a fan of the outdoors, but Clover's love for the trees is contagious. Truth be told, being a prisoner here is more pleasant than being in Leavenworth. Montica has a certain magical quality about it, with or without the shield-dome. I don't notice it even when I try. Clover insists it bears down on her, though.

Again, I clear my head and try to control my commChip without speaking. Pulling thoughts from the background current of my mind and making them as clear as if they were spoken. *Call Clover.* When it *pings* in my head, I let out a triumphant snicker.

"*He can be taught.*" Clover's voice sounds the same even when it's silent to the outside world.

"I better not get arrested because you're too far up in the trees." A beep marks the end of the call, and leaves rustle as Clover does a flip off a branch, landing lightly a few feet to my left. "I thought you were a tree-walker, not a tree-gymnast."

"Tree-gymnast doesn't have the same ring to it."

"What would you be doing if you weren't babysitting me?"

"This. But I wouldn't be on the *ground*. You're getting good up there. I don't know why you prefer this."

"Because I am not of the genus squirrel." Though it has gotten easier and more fun since Clover pulled back on the restraints controlling the gear. Not that I'd admit that to her. The learning curve with the boots propelling me in proportion to how hard I push off on them was rather embarrassing. Now it's a bit like flying.

"If Nemora and Ismene would get to know you, they'd probably prefer you to Priam and me. You've got the serious, straight-edged Agnar genes they value so much."

"There is something to be said for order."

"There is *much* to be said for order: it isn't ours to arrange, imposing our order defies its own purpose and creates chaos, it can only be maintained by disorder."

"You prefer chaos?"

"Does this look like chaos?" She opens her arms wide and twirls.

"A little." The artist in me appreciates that there is no rhyme or reason to this place. Vegetation mixed in any which way it chooses, fallen trees left to lie wherever they land, water forging its paths downward. People can't live like that, though.

"You are mistaken. This is the natural order. We keep trying to take the reins, but we aren't capable. We act like we're being more mindful of the planet now, but we've just found different ways to oppress it. As if keeping a quarter of the continent flooded was a gift rather than an imposition. Minimizing Kaycie's acreage wouldn't hinder them from causing environmental catastrophes anymore than humanity was when they had thirty percent of the Earth."

"It sounds like you've made this speech before."

"Of course. I'm the crazy anarchist in the family. I'm surprised they didn't accuse *me* of destroying the dam."

"I don't think Vogue was trying to free Mother Nature, but if I see her again, I'll send your regards."

Even with the help of the boots, Clover reaches the top of a rock formation swifter than I ever will. When I catch up, she's sitting with her legs hanging over the edge, looking out over the vista of slopes with the capital city below. Where Kaycie flaunts its technical and architectural abilities, Nyberg's modesty veils the advanced society it holds. Rather than glossy towers, low buildings in earth tones stand in clusters tucked into the wooded slope of the mountain.

"You think I'm a radical nonconformist, but it isn't only the natural world I worry about." Clover's eyes soften as she gazes over her capital. She braids her fingers together before turning to me. "Want to go on a field trip?"

"Am I allowed to?"

She drops her chin to her shoulder, looking at me from under arched eyebrows. "Do you think I care?"

Nyberg may look the part of a small, cozy town, but it lacks the feeling. People zip by on hovering panels, focused on holos. Those who walk do so in a stiff, brisk pace, keeping their heads down. It's incongruous with the bright flower beds, charming steep sloped roofs, and wooden building façades. Such a lovely city, but no one seems to enjoy it much.

"Does the inherent *order* here make you feel all warm inside?" Clover's pursed smile gives her an elfin appearance as she strolls through the city with contradictory nonchalance.

"There isn't a thing wrong with this city."

"I couldn't live like this every day. Busy bees always buzzing about. Work, work, work. Do what you need to get ahead. Practicality governing every moment. I dare say it would exhaust even you."

"Well, aren't you lucky to have been born into the ruling family then?"

"I am. But I'm responsible for this." She presses her teeth into her bottom lip.

A trip to Kaycie would do wonders for her. If she could see what happens when people have no responsibility, no drive, she wouldn't feel any guilt.

"I assure you," I say, "the alternative isn't better. Do you think people utilize free time to improve the world? They don't. They laze about seeking nothing but pleasure."

"Is that what you did?" I glance at her sidelong, and she smirks. "I can't picture it."

"Don't *judge* me. I'm half-Kaycian. I can't be held accountable for my actions."

"Oh, I judge you much more harshly for your stringency."

Easy enough to say when she doesn't know the other side. Sure, parties and pampering are fun, but I'm not proud of it. All of it was just something to do. Ways to wile away the time. If not for Grandfather stepping in and giving me a purpose, my brain may have melted.

"Kaycie still has religion, right?"

"Yes."

"What's it like?"

"I wouldn't really know. I never participated. In the city, few do. I'm told it's bigger in the towns. It gives people hope, and the people in the city don't see the need to hope for anything more than what's in front of them."

"At least they have the option." Clover leads me into a white building with a spired bell tower protruding from the roof. Inside, sunlight pours through elaborate stained-glass windows, illuminating the room in ethereal color. Paintings line the walls, and statues create aisles through the space. A church turned museum. This is the kind of religion I can get behind.

I walk in with slow, deliberate steps, masking my excitement as my pulse rate doubles. Ancient masterpieces, one more stunning than the next, pull my attention in every direction. I could spend hours staring at just one or bounce back and forth among all of them erratically. Every muscle in my body tenses to stop me from running around like a child. After a breath, I realize Clover is examining me. When I meet her gaze, she cocks an eyebrow, then strolls away.

Still lifes, landscapes, portraits reach for me as I walk past them, following Clover. She stops at one. "Doesn't this make you want to believe in something?"

The paintings of ancient gods or glorious angels might, but of course Clover would stop at one of a gnarled tree spirit. "Even you couldn't actually *believe* in that."

"I never said I do. I just don't see why people shouldn't be free to believe whatever they wish. How does it affect anyone else?"

"Growing up in this family, there is no way you don't know the answer to that." She's had her entire life to learn the actual histories. She knows the arguments against religion.

"There are two sides to every story," she says. "I know religion was an excuse to divide people and forge wars, but it also inspired most of this." Her green eyes bore into mine. "It can't be all bad." The mountains may suit her, but she struggles against everything else about Montica. "Perhaps there is a sweet spot in between our approaches."

"Wishful thinking. You give people an inch, they take a mile."

She rolls her eyes, then stops short, listening for a moment. "I'm on my way." She taps her chip and sighs. "It would appear people take many miles, actually. We have someone on the ground coming to pay us a visit. Without our watery barrier, I suppose this will become the new vacation destination for Kaycians."

"Well, there goes the neighborhood."

In my suite-prison, I pour myself whiskey and sit down in front of the cube. It's already showing Clover's view from the cockpit. She's over the foothills, heading east to head off whoever is coming. If the Establishment were sending someone else, they'd fly. But why would someone from the towns be trying to come here?

Clover's fingers glide over the control sphere as she descends to the would-be seafloor. A truck drives toward her and comes to a stop some thirty yards away. Clover exits onto the wing and jumps down to the ground, landing lightly with the aid of her boots. *Show off.* A girl comes out of one side of the truck, and a man comes out of the other—Sophos Verity. Bitterness bubbles up in my chest. Hasn't he churned up enough trouble? Betraying the Establishment was one thing, but he's in way over his head if he thinks he is at a level to play games with Montica.

Chapter Thirty-Three
SERENITY

I'm finally back in Kaycie, and I haven't even seen it. The track between Leavenworth and the city is cleared and repaired, so they brought us in on the train. That put us directly into this ancient building from its lowest levels. It's all I can do not to bounce on the balls of my feet in excitement. *Home.* We even get to stay here tonight. I'll stay at my parents' house so I'm closer to the EC, but that's for the best—it would be strange to go to my empty apartment without Vogue there. Maybe being back in the city will make me feel somewhat normal again. The city itself is starting to get back to normal—monorails running and everything. I can't wait for this to be over with.

All that's standing between me and Kaycie is a few excessive speeches and signing this piece of parchment, as if that's all it takes to undo generations of damage and unify us. I'm glad we're trying, but this is more smoke and mirrors.

Lanelle speaking to Aster and Cole worries me. Hopefully, they're good enough judges of character to take what she says with a grain of salt. Millie fusses over Rollin, and Celia and Vaiana have stepped away for a private conversation. The council—the old one, or is it the real one?—is keeping their distance, as they are *supposed* to be out of the picture. I wander through the dank warehouse. How was all of this and the train station underneath it here all along without anyone noticing? It's not even as if the building is unassuming.

Aster approaches me, and I greet her with a handshake. "Can we speak in private?" she asks.

"Of course."

We get to a back room, which features a picture of Union Station back before the flood. The old name is back since we're re-naming the nation after it. It was old even then, but it looked majestic, with its three soaring arches. This was where the city—the whole area which makes up our country now—came together to celebrate, as we're doing now. The picture shows hundreds of thousands of people crowded here. For what, I don't know.

"I finally got a hold of your friend," Aster says.

My heartbeat picks up. "You spoke to Vogue?"

"Yes. I had to break some things as an excuse to get her there, but it worked."

"When?"

"A few days ago. She said she was working on a plan to get to you today."

"Didn't you tell her she's pardoned? Why is she waiting?"

"She already knew she was pardoned."

What? That doesn't make any sense. Why wouldn't she come back? "Oh. All right. Well, thank you."

Aster nods and leaves me alone in this historical room.

Vogue knows she's pardoned, and she's not here. Why? I can't believe she'd abandon me like this. She wouldn't. Aster had to be wrong. There's no way—

"Serenity?" An unfamiliar voice breaks my train of thought.

I turn to the stranger at the entryway. He's tall and handsome in a crisp dark suit. The polished kind of beautiful Kaycians always are but different in a way I can't place. Rough around the edges somehow. He's also tense from head to toe. Nervous, I suppose. That's nothing out of the ordinary for me, but his intensity is startling. His eyes bore into me. He looks more like he's seeing a ghost than a starlet. My panic attack about Vogue will have to wait. I bury my unease under my usual smile.

"Hello. I don't believe we've met." I offer my hand, which he shakes tentatively. "I'm Serenity Ward."

"Bram Eros."

Chapter Thirty-Four

BRAM

My name scrapes out, even though it feels like a hand is wrapped around my throat. Why did I think I could do this? She doesn't know me. I brought her here once—showed her this place, but that's gone. The one person I had opened up to knows nothing about me. Last time I saw her, she said she'd meet me at the train station. Here we are, but a month and a half too late. She looked glamorous then, running from a night out into calamity. Today she looks like the princess the city has always seen her as—beautiful and regal in an ivory dress. A caricature of her name, looking every bit the representation of peace. I hope she gets that someday. But today's not the day.

"Oh." Surprise flashes in her eyes, but her expression is controlled. She lets go of my hand and it aches to hold hers again. "I wasn't aware Lawson had agreed to cooperate with us."

"They haven't."

"They? Aren't you from Lawson?"

"Yes."

"And you're Kolina Eros' son, I take it?"

"Yes."

"So aren't you here to represent Lawson?"

"Not exactly."

"Is there someone here who *does*? Because I need to speak to someone about Vogue Taylor."

Serenity snapping at me like this is oddly nostalgic. She had this fire before Sophos dragged her into the uprising. So my favorite thing about her is still intact.

"I'm the person you'd want to talk to about Vogue. She's waiting for me to bring you to her."

"Vogue is *here*?" Her perfect countenance shakes at that.

"She's close by. We can slip out through the train tunnel." Because if Vogue and the others aren't quite as pardoned as the Establishment claims, then in a bizarre twist, it might be safer for me to be here than them. Acting like I'm here for this bullshit ceremony gives me an in. If everything goes terribly wrong, Dixon is the most likely to be able to break someone out of prison, so he's keeping his distance unless shit hits the fan.

"You're the plan?" Serenity is all business now. "Vogue would not expect me to follow you through a dark tunnel. I don't even know you."

Obviously she doesn't mean that as an insult, but it stings like one. *Yes you do. You trusted me to follow me through these tunnels before.* She did ask if I was going to kill her then, but that was a joke. What can I say to make her trust me? Nothing about her. That would be creepy without our friendship.

"She would have come herself, but she doesn't want to fall back in with the Establishment. Vogue and I are friends." It sounds weird, but that's actually true now. "She trusted me to come get you."

"Why should I believe that? You've basically been keeping her prisoner."

"I haven't..." *Ugh.* Okay, the fun of fighting with Serenity is over. "Look, Vogue will happily tell you about all the ways I've screwed up, but she won't be able to do that unless we get you to her."

"You're not taking her anywhere."

I whip around to see Rollin Karan storming toward us, flanked by two marshals.

"I was under the impression people from the towns are allowed to be here now."

"You are." He doesn't sound pleased by that. "But *you* specifically, cannot be speaking to Serenity Ward."

"What?" I say at the same time Serenity says, "Excuse me?"

I nod toward the front of the building. "Your friend Kemp didn't seem to think it was a problem."

He sighs. "Of course she didn't."

"What's the problem?" Serenity comes up beside me to face off with him. "Why is there anyone I can't speak to?"

"Serenity, don't you trust me?"

"Yes."

Another wound she doesn't mean to inflict. She trusts Rollin Karan over me.

"Well, I'm telling you to stay away from this person," Rollin says, "and Lanelle told him where to find you. What does that tell you?"

Serenity steps away, looking back and forth between Rollin and me.

Shit, shit, shit. I didn't want to do this, but even if I can't get her out of here now, it'll get her thinking about things differently. She'll get suspicious of these people she trusts. Can't hurt, anyway. "You don't remember, but we're *friends.* We—"

"No!" Rollin reaches for Serenity as the marshals grab my arms. "Get him out of here."

In the commotion of everyone yelling over each other, my wrists are bound. I throw my elbow back into the gut of one marshal, but the other locks his arm through my own, and the cold metal of a gun barrel presses against my neck.

"What is going on?" Serenity screams.

"Nothing." Rollin turns towards me and says to the marshals. "Take him to the EC." To me he says, "Someone will come explain things to you."

"Bullshit! Serenity, you took amnesia! You were—"

"Shut him up!"

Rollin's command is obeyed immediately—a hand covering my mouth as I'm pulled away.

Serenity looks at me with wide eyes. "I..." Her chest rises and falls with quick breaths.

Rollin rubs his forehead. "Damnit." He pulls some items from his pocket, looks at them, and keeps one out. "You're fine, Serenity." He injects her neck.

I try to yell against the palm covering my mouth. Serenity wobbles, and Rollin catches her elbow. "You were wandering around, and now it's time for the signing," he tells her.

No! No, no, no.

She shakes her head and blinks rapidly. "Okay, let's go." She smooths her dress and follows him away.

I stop fighting against the marshals. They take me to a staircase and down to the tunnel. Numbness washes over me as I walk the familiar path toward Marshal HQ. When I was here with Serenity, I was the one in a marshal uniform. She was in those ridiculous boots, playing spy, and I told her about Emrys. Maybe I was falling for her then and didn't know it yet. If I had, maybe things would have been different. I could have been the one at her side on the night of the uprising. I could have gotten her away from the EC. She could still know me now.

But that's not the way these things go.

We go up to the main level and exit HQ. Which would be worse: not knowing Serenity ever again, or having to *meet her* again? Both options are horrible. The first one would be horrible forever and may not be possible. The thought of her introducing herself to me again makes my chest knot up, though.

First thing's first. I need to get out of this mess, back to Vogue and company, and figure out a new plan. Should I wait until someone here 'explains' this crap to me? I may not have a choice. Being handcuffed limits my options.

The marshals lead me into the EC lobby where the *someone* in question is waiting for me. "Thank God you're here. Where is everyone else? Take the handcuffs off him."

The marshal obeys. I rub my wrist as I wonder *why the hell* Serenity doesn't know me, but Jase does.

Chapter Thirty-Five

ADWIN

"Well, that was interesting." Priam helps himself to the whiskey he gifted me. "I'll get you more before you leave."

"If I'm ever allowed to."

"This is the better place to be anyway, but you've got some convoluted problems going on back home. I'd think you'd be begging to stay."

I'm certainly not dying to get back to Kaycie's mess, but being a hostage isn't an ideal escape. Sophos' latest attempt to dissolve the Establishment while 'the Union' joins together was a diverting paradox. The city celebrates without realizing the uprising isn't over. Although, even without that, anyone who believes Kaycie's reins have switched hands is deluded. The course of action taken by the rebels is foolish, but the motivation is sound.

"Are they going to tell Grandfather?"

Priam sits on the sofa and crosses an ankle over his leg. "Probably not."

"Your mother cannot possibly prefer those people running Kaycie." Sophos is proving himself to be completely unreasonable. *My family* runs Montica, and I still wouldn't agree to demilitarize Kaycie. These rebels trust too easily. "Regardless of her feelings toward Grandfather, he is family."

"He has also failed to keep Kaycie under his thumb, and all she cares about right now is getting the accumulator back. If they can do that, maybe they're more useful to us. We'd go get it ourselves, but most of Kaycie still doesn't know we exist, and we prefer it that way."

"Yes, Kaycians function better when they're uninformed. Hence, keeping the Establishment in place would behoove Montica. The rebels don't want to keep secrets from the people. The Establishment is quite comfortable lying."

"Don't you find it all petty?"

"Yes, but someone has to maintain order."

Priam's eyes flash with amusement. "Clover is right. Nemora would like you."

"Should that sentiment offend me?"

"It would offend me."

Nemora. Perhaps I should try to bond with her.

"What?" Can the commChip transmit emotion? I swear I feel Nemora's aggravation.

"Are you available to come talk?"

"I thought I made it clear—"

"Not a social call. Business."

She sighs. *"I'll be there in ten."* The beep marks the end of the call.

Nine minutes and fifty-eight seconds later, a knock precedes Nemora letting herself in. She is certainly precise. "What do you want?"

The lack of pleasantries is almost a refreshing change from the constant blabbering of Kaycians.

"We should tell Grandfather about Sophos' intentions," I say.

"Why?"

"Because keeping him and the Establishment in power is more stable for you. Sophos' request shows how illogical they are. You don't want neighbors like that."

"I don't want neighbors at all, but my suggestion to eradicate the world of Kaycie all together was rejected."

Oh. I guess Clover and Priam weren't around for that one. Nemora seems heartless, but that's further than I thought she'd be willing to go. It's fine. I can work with that.

"Then you can't want people as emotionally driven as Sophos and Kolina to be in charge over there. Grandfather is more like you than you realize."

She narrows her eyes as if I dealt her a thorough insult. "The rest of the Establishment isn't, though. Sophos was one of your own and he blew up the whole thing."

"Get rid of the Establishment then. Make Grandfather king. But do not give Kaycie to the rabble."

"Do you want to be a prince, Adwin?" Her expression is equal parts annoyed and amused.

"I don't care. You come be queen if that sits better with you."

"*Psh,* queen of the flatlands, what an honor."

"Are we going to call him or not?"

"We just need the accumulator back. I don't want to get in the middle of Kaycie's schoolyard quarrel."

"If Grandfather retains power, you'll never have to again."

Communications with Kaycie are limited, so Nemora takes me to an office where we can call out. Grandfather's holo appears. He's in his Leavenworth office. "Adwin, are you enjoying your stay in Montica?"

"Yes, it's like a vacation. Everyone is fine."

"Is Nemora being convivial now?"

"Hardly," she says.

"Hello, granddaughter."

"Casimir," she replies.

"So you've let the towns have a hand in government, I see."

He rolls his eyes. "People have never known who controls this country. What do I care for the optics?"

"I'm not here for Kaycian gossip," Nemora says. "Any luck finding our accumulator?"

"Kemp assures me no one has gone out to the dam. I can't imagine the rebels being bold enough for any of it, though."

"Oh, their boldness knows no bounds," I say. "Sophos came here for a visit."

"Verity went to Montica?"

"Yes," Nemora says. "And thank you again for using *our* family name out there. Having to use a pseudonym is infuriating. Your rebels are looking for an ally against the Establishment."

"Nemora, please tell me your mother isn't so resentful as to actually consider that."

"My mother will entertain any option that maintains our separation from Kaycie and regains the accumulator. However, I wouldn't prefer to have those people in any sort of power. They are a rather irrational bunch."

"They will let Montica dissolve the military all together so long as they get the marshals back," I say.

Grandfather laughs humorlessly. "They're happy to trade one ruling power for another? What a pointless rebellion."

"They think they'll keep their autonomy."

"Idiots. They're either lying or they're idiots." His hands work a holoScreen we can't see. "Oh. Or she wants her son back."

Nemora and I look at each other.

"Sophos' lady-friend. She has a son in the marshals." He rubs his chin. "Perhaps I'll return her son to her."

Chapter Thirty-Six

BRAM

My mind races but keeps coming back to two things. One: Jase is going to regret having the handcuffs removed if I punch him in the face. Two: Serenity can get her memories back.

Priorities.

I stop pacing the meeting room to look at Jase. "Okay, so we need Krisalyn?"

"Yes."

"Let's get everybody together then." Another benefit—with Vogue around, I won't be the only one pissed off at Jase. I'm a terrible person for being excited about how much she is going to lose her shit.

"Where are they?"

"They *were* waiting by the tunnel that heads toward Lawson, but they've never been big on following directions." Vogue had messaged me when she saw I was going the wrong way from the station. When I got here and saw it, I told her to stand by but knowing her...

Oh, yeah. I put my cuff back on—its incessant vibrating was driving me crazy while I was listening to Jase's story. Now I have too many messages from Vogue to count, plus the pleading, less angry ones from everybody else, but the newest ones sound like they'll be here any minute anyway, so—

The door flies open, and Dixon bursts in, sweeping a gun across the room. He stops and gasps when he sees Jase.

"Thanks for that," I say, "but I think I can handle this."

"Jase?"

Krisalyn, Vogue, and Frey come in behind him. Krisalyn squeals and rushes to hug Jase.

Vogue's shoulders relax as she looks at them, but then she turns to me. "You are the *worst* accomplice."

"There's one person here who you're about to think is worse."

She looks at Jase again, then back at me. "Wait, does he know you?" I nod, and she turns back to Jase again. "Jase, you know all of us?"

He releases Krisalyn and sighs. "Yes. I didn't take the shot."

Krisalyn shakes her head. "But we saw Serenity with the council. She...?"

"She took it."

Vogue's lips press into a hard line. She leans forward on the table, glaring at Jase. "What. Have. You. Done?"

Jase gestures to the table and everyone sits. He rubs the back of his neck and sighs. "Okay, so on our last day in Kaycie, Krisalyn created an antidote for the amnesia shot."

Krisalyn shakes her head. "No, I tried to, but it didn't work."

"It did work. I remembered the day the Establishment picked me up after our night out on the train."

Her jaw drops. "Why didn't you tell me?"

"They told me about Montica that night. When the memory came back, I panicked. I didn't know if they had lied to me, or if we were really being threatened. Kemp thought we were doing something to aid them. When I remembered it in September, I had to figure out if it was real, so I went to see Adelle Nemes."

Vogue's eyes bulge, but it's Krisalyn who speaks. "Why her?"

"Because I didn't trust anyone on the council besides Anton, but Serenity would have killed me if I dragged him into this."

"Instead,"—Vogue's voice is frighteningly low—"you risked me killing you for dragging my grandmother into it."

"Obviously I'd rather have you angry at me than Serenity."

"Bad choice," Frey says. "I don't care if Serenity is your girlfriend, choosing to piss off Vogue is stupid."

"You constantly seek out ways to piss off Vogue," Dixon says with a sideways glance at Frey.

"No, I only do little things to irritate her. Throwing her into the surf was easily pardoned—all I had to do was help save Krisalyn's life."

Jase turns to Krisalyn. "When was your life in danger?"

God, I'm glad I got to hear this without all the interruptions.

"I'll tell you later," Krisalyn says.

Jase shakes his head and goes on. "So, Adelle confirmed the information about Montica, and I told her about Sophos' uprising. At that point I didn't tell her who was involved, but she insisted I couldn't tell Serenity without tearing apart the Ward family. She said she'd take care of it. But then Serenity tells me that we're leaving the next night and the uprising is starting. I panicked again, and when I left to get ready to go out, I called Adelle. She asked me not to say anything to any of you, especially Vogue, and that she would call Kemp that night."

Frey looks taken aback. "You were selling us out?"

"Not everyone." Jase drops his gaze.

"Just Sophos," I say.

"Our foreign enemies were likely to take advantage of us if we were distracted by a civil war," he argues. "It was the wrong time."

"Kemp came after us that night! Sophos was shot and Tori died because of you!" The first time around, I let him narrate the whole thing. Now, I have some points to add.

"That was not because of Jase," Dixon says.

Krisalyn shakes her head and taps her fingertips together. "Then after you spoke with Adelle?"

"We went out, and all hell broke loose. I didn't have time to explain the whole other side of everything, and Serenity went barreling off to the Establishment Center."

"That's convenient," I say, "since you were aligning with the Establishment at that point."

"That's not why I went."

"Of course not. You went to protect Serenity, and you did a great job."

"I tried everything to get her out of there! I practically knocked her unconscious to carry her out, but it didn't work. I still didn't trust the Establishment, but once we were stuck I..." He drops his head onto one of his hands. Krisalyn rubs his back. "I wanted to tell them you were all sort of innocent, but I was still scared of their reaction. I couldn't let Serenity be at risk too, and I knew it could be reversed." He rubs his eye with the heel of his hand. "It was a huge mistake, though. It was too long of a time to cut out. Telling her what happened gave her a panic attack. Her brain was short circuiting trying to piece it back together."

"Which is why Rollin wiped out me talking to her today."

Krisalyn gapes at me. "What?"

"I started to tell her she took amnesia—that we were friends." I can't believe I'm the reason they screwed with her brain even more.

Jase sighs. "Well, that's only a few minutes. No harm done."

My shoulders tense. How can he dismiss that? I don't care how long it was. Serenity deserves better than to be thrown back and forth between alternate realities. Her panic was real. Even if she doesn't remember it, I don't ever want to be the cause of that for her.

"Anyway," Jase continues. "Tevin and I can't reproduce the antidote. I need your help, Kris."

On the train to leave Kaycie, Krisalyn told me Jase would do anything to protect Serenity. Instead, he let her surrender to the amnesia drug. "Oh, has it been so hard for you?" It's kind of low, but I don't care. "Because it sounds like you got to keep your memories and your girlfriend."

All but Vogue stare at me wide-eyed, trying to get me to back off. I don't feel any pity for him, though. He should feel this guilty.

Jase lets out a sardonic puff of a laugh. "Not exactly. Serenity broke up with me."

"It would have happened anyway," Vogue says. "Why drag it out until she finds out you lied to her?" Krisalyn gives Vogue a pleading look. She's stuck in a tough spot now.

"And what about you?" Jase asks. "She knows Adelle told you about the islands."

If not for Krisalyn, Vogue would dive across the table at Jase. Her knuckles pale as she grips the edge.

Frey laughs. "So, if we reverse Serenity's amnesia, she's going to have a flood of memories and find out the two most important people in her life were lying to her. Would it maybe be more kind to just... not?"

"No!" we all respond together.

"Okay." Frey puts up his hands in surrender. "Just a thought."

"I didn't hurt her by withholding information," Vogue says. "You pushed her into harm's way."

Krisalyn sighs. "There's no use in you two arguing over who was worse. We'll get Serenity's memories back, then she can be angry at Jase if she chooses to be."

"She will be." Vogue glowers at Jase.

"I'm willing to take that risk," he says. "Even if helping her means losing her forever, I want what's best for her."

"Fine." Vogue stands. "You figure out how to fix your mess. I'm going to see my best friend."

Chapter Thirty-Seven

SERENITY

Confetti flies, fireworks blast, but it feels forced. The atmosphere isn't truly celebratory. Maybe because marshals are still security here—the people of Kaycie blissfully unaware of what they really are. Maybe it's because three towns still won't work with us. Whatever it is, I feel unsteady. We're supposedly unified now, but I'm still in a thousand pieces scattered on the floor.

Rollin asks me if I'm all right as we go back into Union Station.

I nod. "Yes, I'm fine—just eager to get into the city."

Millie appears at our side. "Serenity, dear, you're wanted at your parents' townhome."

"Are they back?"

"Not yet, but they're coming. Vogue Taylor is there, now."

My hand covers my gasp. "Vogue is back?"

I'd have walked to my parents' house just to soak in the city, but adding another minute would be torture now. The Establishment vehicle stops to let me out and for a fleeting moment, I don't remember which is my family's house. The time away has really done a number on me.

Vogue comes rushing out to me. "Serenity!" Tears fill my eyes as she sweeps me into a hug.

"I missed you so much." Being with Vogue again pulls some of my pieces back together. I pull back and wipe tears from my cheeks. "It feels like forever."

"I know. I've been so worried about you." She loops her arm through mine to guide me inside. Her pant legs are tucked into soft, flat boots which allow my heels to narrow our height difference a little. She looks cozy in a cable-knit sweater. She's probably enjoyed dressing down, away from Espy's critical eye.

"Me? You were the one accused of treason!" She shrugs that little detail off as we walk into the house. "Do you realize how much Sophos manipulated you?"

"Yes." We sink onto a sofa together. "We befriended Kolina Eros' son. He's been very helpful in illuminating the situation."

"Oh." How could they have gotten so close to Kolina Eros' son that he'd tell them about his own mother's duplicity? "Well, tell me everything."

"First of all, I owe you an apology. I hated keeping secrets from you. I'm so sorry."

My heart sinks. "Adelle and Espy said you couldn't tell me about the islands. I understand." What I don't say is once she was going behind their backs, she might as well have told me. But I don't want to mar our reunion. On the thought of reunions... "Where is everybody else?"

"They're with Jase." She hesitates. "I hear you aren't together any-more?"

I sigh and lean back. This is a topic I've been trying to avoid even with myself. "Vogue, I just couldn't. He shouldn't even want to be with me. I've been such a mess. I didn't give him anything worth the hassle of sinking himself into this life. I don't know why he tolerated me as long as he did."

Her jaw clenches. "You are *never* someone to be tolerated. The world is crazy, but that doesn't mean you have to close yourself off to everyone."

"Don't I though? Isn't that what we were born into by being in these families?"

"Yes, to a degree. But that's changing, anyway. Don't get me wrong, it's totally fine if you don't end up with Jase, but it's okay to let *someone* really know all of you. You're amazing, and anyone would be lucky to share your life with you. The right person will want to help you through this mess."

"Isn't that what I have you for?"

"Of course! But having a lover is nice." She grins sheepishly. "Krisalyn and I are together, now. It's going really well."

"Awe, I'm so happy for you! That's great." I mean it, unequivocally, but it also means Jase and I will probably find ourselves around each other quite a bit. Not that I don't want to see him. The problem is I do. Could I let myself have what Vogue has with Krisalyn?

"Thanks. She's wonderful, and we've been through so much to-gether, now."

"What have you been up to since you left?"

I'm awestruck as she tells me about the tunnel on their way out of Kaycie, Gladstone and Dixon's grenade injury, Greenwood's forest, and Krisalyn's near-death experience at the dam. Despite the danger-ous parts, I wish I had been there with them. Why did they exclude Jase and me from the uprising?

"You're sure the villa is Agnar's?" I say. "He said the dam is Mon-tica's."

"That was obvious. The technology is ages beyond anything here. We haven't figured out the connection between Agnar and Montica."

"Well, he went there shortly after we left Kaycie. He returned without Adwin."

"Interesting." She taps a finger on her nose.

"You know, I *can* be around Jase if we want to get everyone back together."

Her smile hides *something* but what? "Maybe tomorrow. Today, I want you all to myself."

The door opens and Snowflake comes bounding in and onto my lap. "Oh, my darling! I missed you!" My sweet little white fluff ball kisses me enthusiastically, jumps over to Vogue, and then back to me.

My parents have come in behind the dog. "Hello, Vogue." My mother hugs Vogue, then looks at her reproachfully. "You need to go to Adelle's, love."

Vogue groans. "You'd send me off to my death like that?"

"You'll be fine."

"You all have just as much explaining to do. I know about the champagne and tequila."

Mamá gives her an incredulous look which ends the conversation.

Vogue turns to me. "If I survive, I'll come back."

"Good luck."

Papá takes Vogue's place on the sofa. "You did well today, sweetheart."

"I didn't do anything."

"That's how these things tend to be, but people look to you. People will follow you, and you're showing that we should unite."

"We aren't though. Not really." I bury my fingers in Snowflake's fur. "There's division amongst the towns, amongst the Establishment—which isn't supposed to be in power but is."

My mother sits in an adjacent armchair, glass of wine in hand. "Lasting change takes time. It's something Sophos failed to recall. You're doing everything you can. You should be proud of yourself. We certainly are."

"Thank you."

While I appreciate their words, I'm not sure I deserve them. All I've done is gone where I'm told, doing what they tell me to do. I'm still just an empty symbol to this city. But I *can* let a select few people know more, like Vogue said. And I do want that. So after the three of us have dinner, I make a call.

Chapter Thirty-Eight

BRAM

Vogue goes to see Serenity alone. No need to confuse her with the rest of her friends she doesn't really remember. And me... I can't possibly face her again until she remembers me. At least that should be soon.

Krisalyn leans her face forward into her palm. "After we retrieve Serenity's memories, what's next? We kind of broke the country."

"What are you talking about?" Frey smirks. "The Union is a shining beacon of cooperation where we'll all live in peace until the end of time."

The rest of us do a collective eyeroll at Frey's remark. *United, indeed*—with the old council running things from behind their children, Kaycians still not knowing about the marshals, three towns dissenting, and Lawson trying to pull Montica's support. The Union is a time bomb.

Krisalyn whispers something to Dixon. He does something on his cuff, and says, "No, we're fine."

"Great." She turns to regard the group at large. "It seems to me the marshals are the key to all of it. Control over them is the only source of power left to the Establishment. So, what if the marshals remembered who they were? Maybe we can reverse extirpation."

She's trying to snowball off her success in reversing amnesia. It shouldn't surprise me that she'd keep pushing for more. The thought almost hurts though, like I'm already feeling the disappointment of failure.

Jase sighs. "Kris, extirpation is a different beast than amnesia."

"I know, but it's a start."

"Someone tried before," I say. "He poisoned himself in the process."

Tori's dad died for this years before she did. I can still smell her blood. Still feel her eyelids from when I brushed them closed.

But Krisalyn's determination won't falter. "I wonder if there's any way we could get our hands on that research."

"You could ask Adelle," I say. "She was close to him."

Krisalyn and Jase agree to check it out after they've finished their first task. I can hardly let myself hope for it to work, though. This idea is too good to be true. I need to accept the fact that Emrys is gone.

Kaycie didn't seem to hear the news about two wars on the horizon. Outside of the EC, life practically goes on as usual. Krisalyn offers me her apartment, since she's planning to stay at Vogue's.

"Thanks," I say. "And hey, would you like a lab rat tomorrow?"

She arches an eyebrow skeptically. "Jase and I are usually our own test subjects."

"But you need to have your minds sharp so you can get the job done. You lose time every time you take an amnesia shot."

I can't believe I'm offering this. I thought it was crazy that they test this stuff out themselves, but I want to get Serenity back as quickly as possible.

"If you're sure," she says and shrugs.

"Yeah. How bad could it be?"

"All right. See you in the morning then. Meet me at Vogue and Serenity's?"

"Is Serenity going to be there?"

"No, she's staying at her parents'."

"Okay then, sure."

She taps around her cuff and mine buzzes, having gained access to her apartment. "See you then."

Dixon hangs back and turns to me when everyone else is gone. "What do you think you're going to accomplish by that?" He inclines his head in a patronizing look.

"Helping Serenity."

"Not saying this because I'm friends with Jase, but Serenity loves him. The best-case scenario is them staying together. If she remembers everything and they break up, she's going to be destroyed. Please tell me you aren't hoping to piece her back together and sweep her off her feet."

I scratch my forehead and avoid his eyes. "I don't know what you're talking about."

"Really? I love her and I'm not thrilled about what's happened to her, but *you* were fired up. You nearly matched Vogue in rage, which no one should ever be able to do."

"Well, I'd never *hope* for her to be destroyed. Give me some credit."

"Okay. Keep in mind, as much as I'd like to orchestrate a prison break, you might push your luck staying here."

"I won't be here long."

"Whatever you say. Proceed with caution." He goes a different direction. "Good night."

I make my way toward Krisalyn's apartment. Dixon is right, but I can't bring myself to leave.

My stupidity will keep me here until I see recognition in Serenity's eyes.

Chapter Thirty-Nine
SERENITY

"Serenity... hi." Jase couldn't sound more surprised to be hearing from me.

"Hi. Is everyone still around?"

"No. I need to be up early, so we've called it a night."

"Oh, all right." God, I feel like an idiot.

"Is everything okay?"

"Yes, I just wanted to talk to you."

"We're talking now."

"No. In person."

The silence kills me. Of course, he wouldn't actually wait around for me. That was ridiculous.

But he said it, so I thought...

"Serenity, I'd love to, but tomorrow would be a better idea. I'll be there tomorrow, okay?"

"Sure. That's fine." I've brushed him off in worse ways, so I have no right to feel slighted now. "I'll see you tomorrow then. Good night."

"Good night."

But as I sit on the bed I have here at my parents' house, I think about sharing a bed with Jase in Leavenworth. The way I slept peacefully in his arms. And I don't want to wait until tomorrow to get that back.

I walk out into the chilly evening with more certainty of purpose than I've felt since I landed in Leavenworth. Nervous energy fills me as I tap the elevator button. My cuff grants me access, and I go up to the apartment number saved into my contacts. When the door slides open, Jase stands there with a desperate look on his face—sad and torn.

"May I come in?"

"Serenity, tomorrow would really be better." The content of his internal struggles is a mystery to me, but his indecision is obvious.

"Please. I don't want to lose my nerve." I step past him, my nails digging into my palms. "I'm sorry for how I treated you. You deserve better."

He blinks slowly and takes a deep breath. "You don't need to—"

"I do. I *have to* apologize for the way I acted in Leavenworth and for lying to you."

"When did you lie to me?"

"After the incident with Lanelle. I wasn't planning to tell you to go." It's on me to make the first move after shutting him down before. I step toward him and slide my fingers through his. "I was going to ask you to come back... to *our* room... to me."

He squeezes my hands and lets them go. "Serenity, I can't... Can you please give me a day?"

"What difference would it make?"

"It could make a big difference."

"I'm sorry." I wring my hands together and step back from him. "I shouldn't have assumed you'd actually wait around for me." He may have said that, but he had to have a limit. I completely shut him out.

"No, I still..." He rakes his fingers through his hair and looks away. "My feelings for you haven't changed, it's just..."

"It wasn't as if I ever didn't want this." His amber eyes meet mine now. "I was just confused and scared. I didn't want to deceive you. I couldn't act like everything was okay when I was so torn up."

He presses his lips together, shaking his head. "You're not that good an actress."

I close the distance between us and tilt my face up to bring my lips to an inch from his. "Don't you want this?"

"Of course I do. That's not the—"

I kiss him hungrily. All the pent-up longing finally pouring out in a rush as our mouths move together. If there is such a thing as a perfect kiss, it's this. We've been apart too long to reunite with anything less than magnetic force. His hand slides up my back, pressing my chest against his. My heart races as if it hadn't been beating at all and has been restarted by electric shock. He's playing the melody of that song I couldn't quite remember, and now that I hear it, I feel ridiculous for ever forgetting. Why did I fight so hard to keep us apart? We're not meant to be apart. We're meant for this.

A buzzing at my wrist pulls my attention. Vogue calling. I decline, and she immediately calls again. This time, I take off my cuff and toss it aside.

"Who's that?"

"Vogue."

He pulls back from me, lips scrunched to the side. "Do you want to get back to her?"

"No." I brush my fingertips down his neck. "I want to be right here."

His eyes devour me, but from where his hand sits warm on my lower back, I feel his cuff vibrate. He puffs out a breath when he glances at it. "Are you sure?"

"Oh, she's being ridiculous." I take his cuff off and toss it aside too.

"She's going to kill me."

I shake my head and pull his face back toward mine. "I've missed you. I don't sleep well without you."

"Neither do I."

"Can I stay?"

He pulls me in tight against his chest. The warmth of him relaxes away any remaining tension I was holding on to. Into the top of my hair he says, "Obviously, I'm incapable of saying no to you."

Chapter Forty

BRAM

Morning comes, and I meet Krisalyn as she and Jase walk out of Serenity and Vogue's building. They keep a tense silence on our way. I don't ask, or care, what's going on with them. Maybe Vogue's fury bled through to Krisalyn.

Boards cover the hole Tori put in the EC. Repairs are slow with everything going on. Seeing it brings up memories I'd prefer to forget. My stomach tightens as we enter. Krisalyn gets me a guest pass to go up to her office with them, and suddenly I'm walking around like any other person. In the EC. This is surreal. People nod and smile at me in the hallways, and not one of them would guess I was a marshal. I've seen plenty of these people before, but they've never really seen me.

Krisalyn pulls the bottom of a drawer out in her office to uncover a microchip, and Jase groans. "Why didn't I know about your hiding place? I searched but came up empty-handed."

"Not the kind of research I wanted floating around." She takes a seat, ties her hair up in a messy knot, and sets the chip into her cuff.

"What was it like when you got your memories back?" I ask.

"It was like a time lapse with several months playing in high speed. Not just the memories I had lost, but everything."

"How far back?" Krisalyn asks.

He presses his eyes closed and thinks about it. "About six months? The first thing I remember popping up was the film awards, and those were in March."

"Not bad." Krisalyn nods. "We need almost a year for Serenity, so we aren't terribly far off. I think adjusting the amount of memantine should move the timeline."

"Could we add some ondansetron to counter the nausea?" Jase asks. "I'd like to make this easier for her."

"Sure." She scribbles some notes and pops up from her chair. "I'll be back in a minute." She leaves Jase and me alone in her office.

"To test the antidote," Jase says, "you have to take the amnesia shot first."

"Obviously."

"You don't need to do this. I'm not supposed to remember the time, anyway."

"I'm already here. Might as well."

He looks at me inquisitively. "You were as angry as Vogue was about me not taking the amnesia shot with Serenity." It's half an observation, half question.

"It was a shitty thing to do."

"I was trying to protect her. It may not have been necessary, but I was acting in her best interest. I get the feeling you might act the same way in such a scenario."

Does he see my desperation to keep her safe? I wish I could say I'd do anything to protect her, but when it came to it, I let her walk away. Before I can come up with a response, Krisalyn comes in.

"I won't judge if you change your mind," she says.

I shake my head.

She raises her hands. "If you say so." She pulls out a vial and hands it to me. "This will wipe out the last ten months of your life."

"I trust you to get it back."

"No pressure," Jase mutters.

"Last chance to back out."

I shake my head and open the vial. After avoiding getting my mind wiped out five years ago, who would have thought I'd volunteer for it now? After a deep breath, I swallow it down. I lean my head into my hands as my vision blurs.

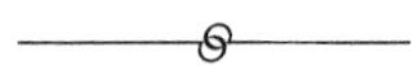

I squeeze my eyelids tighter before opening my eyes. This is definitely an Establishment office, but it's much smaller than Sophos'. What am I wearing? I stare at the gray sleeve before noticing the jeans. Where is my uniform?

"Hi Bram," a familiar redhead says in a soft, friendly tone.

"Krisalyn Laska?"

"Yes. And Jase Delgado is with me, too. You're probably feeling a little confused."

"That's an understatement."

"Take this for me." She holds out a vial, but I don't take it from her. I barely know her. She's one of Sophos' little helpers, but I don't trust her. "It'll help. You just took the amnesia drug."

"What?" My pulse picks up.

"You wanted to help us test something," she explains.

"I wouldn't agree to that." What did they do to me?

"You did. But we're going to get your memories back now."

She can make her voice as soothing as she wants. I'm not buying it. She just drugged me! There's no way I consented to that. I stand on wobbly legs and back away from her. My hand goes to the gun at my hip on instinct.

"Should have been me." Jase rubs his forehead.

"The biggest *should have* right now is that we should have had him give us the gun first."

I tighten my grip around it, and Jase places himself between Krisalyn and me.

"Bram," he says, "we're trying to help you. See your clothes? How could you be wearing that?"

I have no idea. My heartbeat pounds in my ears.

"What day is it?" he asks me after I don't respond.

I blink a few times. "December 13th."

"Look at your cuff."

I glance down to see that it's October 13th... of next year. "That doesn't prove I took the amnesia by choice."

"If we could force you to take something, we'd force you to take this antidote!" He turns toward Krisalyn. "This was a bad plan."

And the room goes dark.

I open my eyes to see Krisalyn sitting on the desk with my gun in her hand. My hands are restrained behind my back. *Shit.*

Jase shakes his head out. "Seriously, Kris?"

"It was ten minutes! Would you rather be sedated or shot?" she says. "Sorry, Bram, you'll understand in a minute." She keeps the gun pointed at me as she hands Jase the vial. He injects it into my neck, and the room blurs around me.

I clutch my hands together and press my lips shut. God, I might throw up. What the hell are they doing to me? Like watching a movie, I see Friday meetings with Sophos and Serenity Ward, every meal I ate in between, meeting Vogue when Serenity snuck me out to their apartment, confusing run-ins with Tori, selection, seeing my mom. She's in charge of the uprising, Tori dying, getting to Lawson. The sea is gone. Montica, Gladstone, the dam, coming back to Kaycie.

Serenity doesn't remember me. Oh... volunteering to test the antidote.

I take a deep breath and look up. Krisalyn and Jase stare at me expectantly. "Sorry about that."

She smiles. "In hindsight, I probably should have laced your memory with something about trusting me and taking the antidote." She frees my hands and gives me back my gun. "How far back do you remember?"

I holster the gun and rub my wrists. "March, I guess. Do you have water?"

Krisalyn hands me a glass and turns to Jase. "The first version was six months, this was seven. Now we can figure out the dosing."

The cool water going down my throat settles me a little.

Soon Jase has the formula figured out and they depart for the lab. I stay put, trying to pull myself back together. Now that I've had a taste of this mental torture, I feel even worse for Serenity.

Chapter Forty-One

ADWIN

"I know she's your mother," Clover says, "but your denial is absurd." She launches herself from one tree to another as Priam and I simply hop over the small creek.

"What do you want from me?" Priam sounds exasperated. "You make it sound like she's out for world domination. She's just trying to get the accumulator back."

"She's going to use that as an excuse to conquer Kaycie. Don't you see the glitter of excitement in her eyes when she considers extending her power?"

"As a Kaycian—"

"Half," Priam corrects me.

"As someone who grew up in Kaycie," I begin again, "may I point out they'd be better off under Montican rule? You make it sound like Ismene would burn the country to the ground, Clover. Kaycians are clearly not capable of keeping themselves under control, why not let them into this more prosperous nation?"

Clover groans. "Adwin, you are turning out to be quite the disappointment. Why do they need to be controlled at all?"

"Because most of them are like spoiled children who need a firm hand."

I stumble when I'm cutoff mid-step by Clover landing right in front of me. "You really look remarkable for your age, Adwin. How old are you? Seventy? Eighty?"

"I'd rather think and act beyond my years than like a *child*."

I regret the words the moment they escape my lips. Clover's eyes widen, smoldering with rage. She may be considering the most convenient way to kill me.

"I'm sorry. I—"

She disappears into the trees, leaving a trail of swirling leaves in her wake.

Priam shakes his head at me. "Poor choice of words. Rocco and Nemora are always on her about being childish. She's constantly being told her free-spirited nature is an impediment rather than a merit."

"What do you think?"

"She's probably the best of us, though her eccentricities *are* excessive at times. Her optimism may be childish, but I think that just lets her see more possibilities than the rest of us. I agree with her... I just don't have the passion she does to try to change it."

"I should go after her."

"You should leave her alone. You won't be able to catch up to her, anyway."

I ignore his advice. Following Clover's tracker through the trees is akin to playing Marco Polo. My chip tells me which direction to go, I don't follow the directions well apparently, and I swear it is actually getting frustrated with me. The corrections sound angrier as I go. I don't see the routes from branch to branch as easily as she does. These aren't the kind of possibilities Priam meant, but I have no doubt her way of looking at things helps guide her through.

I call out for her when I'm close enough to be within earshot. She doesn't answer, but her signal doesn't dart away, nor does it shut off. Stopping on a branch to catch my breath, I look down from the greatest height I've been. My stomach does a little flip, but I'm surprised that I actually feel steady up here. Clover's signal seems to be directly above me.

"Clover!" No answer. "Please come down."

"I think I'll just stay up here and pout like a *child*."

I lean my forehead on the tree trunk. "I'm sorry."

She only whistles a light tune.

Ugh. Here we go. The good news about being higher up is that there aren't gaps between branches to jump across. Rather, I have to slither along, finding spaces big enough to squeeze through. "Where are you?" I'm nearly at the top of the tree, but I can't find her.

"Out here."

Beyond the tree I'm in, Clover reclines on a large hammock tied between this and another tree.

I maneuver out away from the trunk, feeling nauseatingly unstable. "What is *that*?"

"My home away from home."

In a testament to self-control, I don't call her crazy. It wouldn't help things right now. "I'm sorry I called you a child."

She glances at me over her shoulder, waiting for me to continue.

"Your vision of how things can or should be sounds great, I just don't think it's realistic."

"Don't you see it isn't realistic *because* of people like you?"

"No, it's because most people are neither like me nor you. Most people are in the middle, unsure of their own opinions. They need structure."

"You underestimate people, Adwin Lebeau. What do you think would happen if you let the masses choose for themselves? It isn't as if the world would come crashing down."

Beep. Beep. Beep.

The magnetic hold between my boots and the tree disengages. My foot slips and I wobble as if on a high wire. "Clover!" I grab a branch, but it doesn't connect to my gloves. "My boots and gloves are dead!"

"What?" She checks her own and mutters a curse under her breath. "Get to the trunk. I'll come help you." She drops her boots as I creep deeper into the tree. The distance of their fall turns my veins to ice. She crawls to the end of the hammock and takes a deep breath.

She can't possibly make that jump without the boots.

"Clover, no!"

She springs into the tree, wrapping herself around a branch rather than landing gracefully on her feet. "It's fine." She shimmies over to me, looking nervous but not all-out panicked like I am. "What happened?"

"I don't know. I heard some beeps, and I felt the connection die."

She frowns and squints as she looks up to the sky. "Let's get out of here. Dump the boots, they'll only weigh you down now."

"Can't we call someone for help?"

"Our chips are dead."

I tap mine, but she's right. How did she know that? With one arm wrapped around a branch, I pull the boots off and let them fall to the ground. Watching them bounce off branch after branch turns my stomach. It's an awfully long way down.

"Have you ever done this without the gear?"

"Not quite this high up," she admits, "but it'll be fine. Just follow me. We'll go very slowly."

The tight spaces of the upper branches offer safety, but the larger ones look like they're insurmountably far from each other now. Clover hops down to one, crouching into her landing to hold on.

"I can't do that."

"Yes you can." She moves to another, giving me room. "Go on. We're nearly there."

"We're forty feet up!"

"Exactly." She smiles, but her confidence isn't there.

I take a deep breath and sit to get a little closer to the next branch. Shaking from head to toe, I push off. My feet hit it, but I teeter forward. I reach for the branch ahead of me where Clover is perched. Her outstretched hand grazes mine before I fall.

"Adwin!"

Branches beat at me, but don't catch me. I don't belong here. This isn't my place, and even the trees want to throw me back. The ground welcomes me like a bolted door—Trespassers will be broken.

Chapter Forty-Two
SERENITY

When Jase enters the townhouse, Snowflake loses her mind. I'm not sure she was this excited to see *me*. He picks her up, and she licks his face while he apologizes to her. "I know. I missed you, too. I'm so sorry we left."

I stay on the sofa to wait for my turn. "She likes you better than me."

"She has terrible taste in people then. Hello, Grace. Vogue."

"Hello, Jase." My mother takes something from Jase and thanks him.

Vogue only glares at him. Though she hasn't killed him, she had much stronger feelings about me spending the night with him than I expected. Oh well. It was worth it. I wanted more to happen, but lying in his arms was such a comfort. And this time, he was still there when I woke up. The relief of waking up next to him was overwhelmingly sweet.

"What's that?" I ask regarding the item Jase delivered.

My mother smiles tentatively at me. "Sweetheart, the last couple of months have been difficult. This will help with your confusion."

I turn toward Jase. "Is that what you had been working on?"

He nods. His honey-colored eyes glisten, but he blinks it away. "Are you all right?"

"Yes. I've just been worried about you. You've had a hard time and I want you to be okay."

I turn to Vogue and my mother. "Can we have a moment?"

Vogue frowns, but Mamá places the vial Jase gave her on the coffee table and leads Vogue out of the room.

"Come here," I say, patting the cushion next to me. Jase sits, and I run my hand through the back of his chestnut hair, resting it on his neck. "What's the problem?"

"Nothing."

"If this is what you've been trying to do, why are you so worried about it?"

"Would you kiss me one more time?"

Not a subtle change of topic, but since I enjoy this one... "I plan to kiss you many more times."

His hands clutch the sides of my face as his lips crush against mine. My arms reach up under his, and I press my fingertips into his shoulder. What do I care about gaps my concussion left me if I have this? Breathlessly, I pull my face away from his. He pulls me into a tight embrace and takes in a deep breath against my neck.

"Are you sure this won't kill me? It feels like you're saying goodbye."

"You'll be perfect."

I take the vial and look at him skeptically. He nods, and I pour the contents down my throat. My stomach does a little flip and my vision blurs.

Deep breaths.

Deep breaths.

I press the heels of my hands onto my eyes to try to stop the spinning, but it doesn't help.

My first glance at the map flashes by. Meeting Bram, meeting Jase, then Krisalyn. Telling Adwin, telling Vogue, our housewarming party, the train. Stopping Jase, the symphony with my parents, rain, piano bar, fountain. Running to the burning Establishment Center, hoverPlane, Leavenworth, Papá telling me I took the shot. Forgetting again. Fencing, Gardner, Eudora, Blue Springs. The entire year flies by me.

I drop my hands down to cover my mouth, but I don't open my eyes.

Deep breaths.

I asked them to send someone to take Snowflake until we get back. Deep breaths.

I can't be angry at you. None of this is your fault, and I'm too busy being angry at myself. Deep breaths.

You're not that good an actress.

The very words I said before our first kiss—repeated back to me before we kissed last night.

If I don't open my eyes, maybe it won't be real.

He didn't take the drug. He handed me mine, and he didn't take his. Why would he do that to me? God, please let this not be real.

I can feel his eyes on me. Just like I had my eyes on him at the symphony, but he didn't turn to meet my gaze. That's the kind of will power I do not possess.

The moment my eyes open and meet his, the tears come.

His arms wrap around me, and I sob onto his chest.

Finally, when I can control my lungs enough to speak, I push him back. His face is wet with tears too.

"Serenity, I—"

"What the hell happened on the hoverPlane?"

His fingers rake through his hair as he launches into the story of the last day in Kaycie. I hug a throw pillow and avoid looking at him while he speaks. My mind is a five-thousand-piece puzzle being assembled at dizzying speed. The knot in my chest throbs with each breath. I hear him, but every word translates to betrayal.

"I still didn't trust them, and I wanted to keep you protected."

I glare at him. "I hadn't agreed to the plan to protect myself." The words come out slowly. "It was to protect everyone involved in the uprising." My volume increases as I go.

"I know. I knew you wouldn't take it for your own sake, but—"

"But what?"

"If you weren't going to protect yourself, I had to!"

"It wasn't your choice to make. Do you realize how awful it's been for me?"

"Yes, I do."

"No, you don't!"

"I was there. I had to watch you falling apart, and I couldn't get the antidote right, and I couldn't make you feel any better. It was killing me! I realized it was a mistake, and all of your suffering was my fault. It was awful for me too because I love you."

My head drops back, and I stare at the ceiling. *Oh, he loves me. Right.* Wait.

I snap my focus back to him. "Why did I know you love me? That wasn't in my recording."

He releases a sigh. "I told you after you took the shot."

I spring to my feet and throw the pillow onto the couch. "Why not just go all the way and tell me I love you so you could guarantee I'd jump right into your arms?" I storm over to the coat closet while he tries to answer me.

"I didn't want to tell you anything that may not have been true." He grasps my shoulders, turning me toward him. "I wanted you to know that I love you, because it's the truth."

"And the truth was clearly important at that moment." I twist out of his hold. Fury burns through me.

My mother and Vogue come back in. The former starts first. "Serenity..."

"I don't want to speak to you either! You could have told me everything and saved me from the entire thing!"

"Serenity, we—"

"I don't care."

Vogue only wrings her hands.

"You knew. When I told you. You already knew." Before she can reply, I whip the door shut behind me. My lungs burn with the cool air rushing in and out.

How many times can a person's world shatter? I thought mine had come back together so perfectly, but what has Kaycie taught me if not to question things that are too good to be true?

I return to the boardwalk near the theatre. I wasn't thinking about it, but it's fitting. This was where I came after that first day with Sophos. This time there isn't any water to look out over. This time I'm not in denial of what I just learned. I didn't think I could ever be so crushed, but here I am again.

Leaning on the rail, I may cry enough tears to refill the sea.

Chapter Forty-Three

BRAM

She flies by in a fury like I've never seen before. After getting my brain set back into my head, I got a burger and sat by the boardwalk. The weather is nice, and it's a novelty to be out and about, acting like a normal person in the city.

Serenity's coat billows open around her until she stops at the railing. Her face drops into her hands and her shoulders shudder as she breaks down into hysterical sobs.

Damnit, Jase.

Before I go over to her, I pop into a coffee shop to get her a cup of tea. While I'm in there, I shoot a message to Krisalyn and Vogue to let them know I'm with her. I place the tea next to Serenity on the railing, and her head turns toward it slightly, but she keeps her eyes down.

"I really don't want to—" Her eyes widen when she looks up and sees me. "Bram!"

"I guess you're back?"

She throws her arms around my neck, and I wrap mine around her back. After all this, I can't believe I have her in my arms. This is what my mind has come back to constantly, even in my dreams, and I don't want to let go now.

"I missed you." Those words undo yesterday's wounds. Serenity knows me. She trusts me. *She missed me.* "Or... I would have. If I had known who you were." She sniffles and pulls back. "Was meeting me awful?" Her smirk makes me feel lighter. "Did you hate me as much as the first time we met?"

"I didn't hate you the first time." The question is even more ridiculous than she means it to be. I'm glad she's the only person unaware of my feelings for her. "Yesterday was... hard though."

Her hand runs up and down my arm. Kaycians being touchy-feely always annoyed me, but I understand the appeal now. "I'm sorry," she says.

"I won't hold it against you." I slide the cup closer to her. "Isn't your stomach in knots? That stuff wreaked havoc on me."

She wipes her eyes and takes a sip. "Why did you take it?"

"I volunteered to help them test it."

"You don't even *drink* out of concern for maintaining your clarity. You took an amnesia shot?"

"Well, I've eased up on my no drinking rule. And yeah, I did."

"Why?"

If this was a movie, I'd tell her I did it for her. I'd confess my feelings, and we'd... But this isn't a movie, and she's in a bad place right now.

"I couldn't do much else to be useful," I say.

She combs her fingers through her hair and puffs out a sarcastic laugh. "Being useful. That would be nice. I've been completely useless. Maybe detrimental. I'm still too scrambled to judge."

We walk toward a bench and sit down as we talk. Many curious eyes follow her, whispers spread, pictures are taken. She doesn't seem to care at the moment.

"You aren't blaming yourself for that, are you?" I ask.

"Oh, certainly not. But I don't want to talk about that. You…"—she shakes her head—"You came to get me." Her disbelieving smile stirs something in me. She's pleasantly surprised by the simple act of *finally* coming to get her. Wonder what she'd think if she knew I hardly thought of anything else the whole time?

"Of course I did."

"Thank you. And by the way… Sophos and your mom?"

"Yeah… I've gotten used to it."

"Did I hear they have a daughter?"

"Libby. She's awesome."

"Wow. Was it great to go home?"

"It was a little weird, actually. I didn't feel like I fit in there anymore."

"I'm sorry to hear that."

Her genuine concern when she's in the middle of her own life-shifting drama makes me smile. I convince her to eat, and she gets us a private room in a swanky bar, claiming she doesn't usually use her notoriety for things like this. She only nibbles on food, preferring gin at the moment.

"Do you like olives? Here." She places the skewer of olives on a napkin in front of me. "They probably sent all the cocktail onions to Leavenworth for me," she mutters over her third martini.

"Maybe you should slow down."

"Maybe I've gotten used to having my brain in a fog."

"Frey did offer up the suggestion to just not reverse your amnesia."

She rolls her eyes and laughs. "Of course he did. Although I'd think it would be Jase and Vogue who should have desired that option."

"No. They shot him down immediately."

Her eyebrows pop up incredulously. "Can't imagine why."

"They wanted the real you back. We all did."

"Well, I don't know which version is preferable at this point. I'm not Serenity 2.0 anymore, that was when only the Establishment had been lying to me." Her hand gestures are as expressive as her face—a jarring change from her usual careful composure. "Now I'm at 3.0 or 4.0? I don't know. But the surviving-betrayal-by-loved-ones version might not be so fun to be around." She's in rare form.

"You'll be okay."

She shrugs. "Maybe with Vogue. But you took the amnesia shot. You understand how miserable that is! How long were you without your memories?"

"I don't know. Fifteen minutes?" Probably less.

"And how were those fifteen minutes?"

"Well, Krisalyn sedated me for ten of those minutes so I wouldn't shoot them."

"See! I had almost two months. He shouldn't have done that to me."

"He was trying to keep you safe." Wait, why am I defending him?

"I don't require protection."

False. You ran into the arms of the Establishment. "I should confess I had considered slipping you the vaccine so you couldn't wipe out your memories."

"Why didn't you?"

"I figured you'd kill me if I made that choice for you."

"Exactly!" She leans forward and takes my hand. "*You* get it! You didn't try to save me against my will. Thank you. And anyway, how could Jase's method be called saving me? Oh, there's a bear coming so let me save you from it by pushing you off this cliff!"

"Okay, I think it's time for you to go home." Although that is a funny and fairly accurate metaphor.

After some convincing, I get her out and walk her wobbly form onto the monorail where she falls asleep on my shoulder. Her hair hangs over her face like a curtain. At her stop, I lift her up as gently as possible, and she nudges her head into my chest. *Don't get any crazy thoughts. Don't think of her that way.* God, I'm a terrible person. I can't possibly *enjoy* her like this. She's devastated!

I carry her to her apartment, where Krisalyn and Vogue are waiting. Vogue leads me to Serenity's bedroom and pulls back the sheets so I can lay her down. I rip my gaze away as Vogue tucks her in and smooths her hair out of her face. *Stop it, stop it, stop it.*

Back in the living room, Vogue asks me if Serenity hates her.

"No, she already said she'd get over her issues with you. Jase is a different story."

Chapter Forty-Four
SERENITY

The water in the fountain is cold, but my adrenaline keeps me warm. Then his kisses keep me warm. On the walk back to my apartment, he drapes his soaked blazer around my shoulders as if that will help.

"Everyone in Kaycie will know we're together by this time tomorrow," I say. "Mission accomplished."

"Oh, so we're done now?"

"You're going to have to try harder than that to get rid of me."

I open my eyes. He isn't here.

A sharp pain rises in my chest. I try to take deep breaths, but everything hurts. It's not just the emotional pain—I feel like a train hit me. Dragging myself up, I see there's a glass of water and two small pills on my nightstand. I take them and lean forward onto my hands. I'm not sure whether it's my mind, my heart, or my body that's in the worst shape today. They're all battling for my attention.

Let's sort through this influx of information, my brain orders.

Might throw up, my body points out.

Jase...

No, heart. Not yet. It's too much.

There's a soft knock on the door and Vogue peeks in. "May I come in?" I groan an affirmative sound, and Snowflake perks up.

Vogue pads in and hands me a mug as she sits down on the edge of my bed. "It's ginger," she tells me. "Krisalyn said you probably wouldn't be feeling great."

I only nod and take a sip of the tea.

"Apparently you weren't supposed to mix alcohol with the antidote."

A glare is all the response I give.

"But I completely understand why you'd need a drink."

I take a deep breath. "How did I get home?"

"You fell asleep on the monorail and Bram carried you home."

I pinch the bridge of my nose and let out a slow breath. That's embarrassing—but one thing at a time. "Why didn't you tell me you already knew?"

Vogue's lips twist to one side. "You were upset that Adwin hadn't told you, so it felt like it would be sort of horrible to say 'neither did I.' I'm sorry. I meant to tell you other times, but it just never happened."

"You took it really well. I should have realized."

"No, you were upset, and until then I hadn't given you any reason not to trust me. I don't suppose you still trust me explicitly." She looks down at the floor until I take her hand.

"What's one little lie in a lifetime of friendship?" I say.

Her arms wrap around me in a hug. "Not to exploit my influence, but I'm not the only person who really wants to speak to you." She grimaces in preparation for my answer.

"I don't know what to say to him."

"How are you feeling about it?"

"I don't know." I rub my forehead. "I'm angry, but sad. I finally remember those perfect moments, but I can't forget what he did." A tear escapes from my eye and I wipe it away. "As far as our relationship is concerned, those months in Leavenworth were wasted, and now I'm back to feeling like I can't be with him."

She rubs my hand. "You know how much I didn't want you to end up taking that amnesia shot. And you can ask around—I was completely enraged when I found out Jase didn't take it with you. But I really do believe he had the best intentions, and your best interest at heart."

"Doing the wrong thing for the right reason doesn't work. The Establishment has been doing that forever."

She frowns. "I know."

"Thanks for the tea. I'm going to shower. I'll be out soon."

"Okay. Do you need anything else?"

"I don't think so."

She leaves my room with Snowflake in tow, closing the door softly behind herself.

Steamy water rains down on me. My mind betrays me, turning the drops of water into the rain after the symphony and the spray of the fountain at the plaza. I turn it off and wrap myself in a towel before sitting there on the shower floor with my head on my knees.

Vogue is right. I need to talk to Jase. If my brain keeps focusing on all of the best times, maybe I can push aside the bad. I want to try. I send him a message before getting ready. The forget-me-not necklace on my vanity stares at me. I can't bring myself to put it on, but I slip it into my pocket. My mother calls me, but I ignore it. She has plenty to explain too, but I'll deal with that later. When I venture out of my bedroom, I hear Bram from the hallway.

"... tell Dixon and Frey to keep their distance?"

When I enter the living room, he, Krisalyn, and Vogue go silent and turn toward me.

"I'm so embarrassed," I say to Bram. "Thank you for dealing with me yesterday."

"No problem."

"Hey stranger," Krisalyn says, approaching me. "I missed you."

We wrap each other in a hug. "I missed you too. Thanks for taking care of Vogue."

"It is a full-time job, but not my only one."

"Oh, what else are you up to these days?"

She sucks in a breath through her teeth. "I'm going to see if I can reverse extirpation."

"Oh my gosh!" My eyes meet Bram's, but he looks tightly wound. *His brother. That would be amazing.* I look back at Krisalyn. "Do you think it's possible?"

"I'm not entirely sure. Adelle has some research from the last person who tried." She shrugs. "We'll see what I can figure out."

Why doesn't Bram appear excited about this?

"I'm going to Frey's," Vogue says. "We have Montican tech to figure out."

"Sounds good. And what are you doing today?" I ask Bram.

"I'm probably going to need to go back to Lawson soon. I thought maybe you'd like to get lunch first."

"That sounds great."

Once Vogue and Krisalyn leave and we're alone, I ask, "Why do you look miserable about Krisalyn's plan?"

His hand drifts to his opposite forearm as he shakes his head. "I don't want to get my hopes up."

So much has been taken away from him. I don't blame Kolina for holding her ground about removing the Establishment root and stem. How could anyone feel safe around them after everything?

"Where is Emrys?"

"Leavenworth."

"Maybe I can get him out of there." They *did* say I'd have some actual power.

"There's not really any point." Bram sighs and sits on the sofa. I sit next to him. "People are having just as hard a time with the marshals who came back. Having a family member back as a shell of themselves is... tough. There's no good situation to be in."

Tears sting my eyes. I blink them away, but one rolls down my cheek. Bram's hand beats mine to it, and he wipes the tear away with his thumb. He shakes his head—a curious grin on his face.

"Well, one of us should cry about it," I say.

"I'm not a crier."

"Of course you're not."

The elevator chimes. "I need to do something before lunch," I say. "Can I catch up with you in a little while?"

"Yeah, that's fine." Jase walks in and Bram tenses. "Oh." He rises to his feet. "All right, I'll see you later."

Bram and Jase pass by each other to switch places. Bram disappears into the elevator, and Jase sits down next to me. Close, but not touching. His face sallow, his eyes shadowed.

"You didn't sleep last night."

He shrugs.

I keep my gaze down and my hands clasped together in my lap. His hand wraps around both of mine. "Serenity, I'm so sorry."

I look up to meet his gaze. His eyes are glassy, and I think mine mirror that. "First, let me just say... thank you." His expression suggests this wasn't something he expected to hear. "The other night,"—*God, this is awful*—"you *tried* to stop me from rekindling our romance."

His chin drops to his chest. "I just didn't want it to be like that—without you knowing everything."

"I know." My cheeks burn with my embarrassment. "And I didn't make it easy for you, but thank you for not letting anything happen which I would have regretted." His reneging on the idea that he couldn't say no to me stung but I understand it now.

"You have nothing to be embarrassed about."

"Really, because I feel like I was acting like a drunk idiot throwing myself at someone who didn't want me."

"Not a single part of that is accurate. What we are—or were…"

I run my hands through my hair, tugging on it at the base of my skull. "It was so intentional. That's what kills me. It wasn't as if I grabbed the vial and took it before you had a chance to stop me. You put the pod in my ear and handed me the open vial. You didn't even try to give me any more information on what was going on."

He leans his forehead onto his hand. "You're right. It was stupid. If I could go back, I'd do a hundred things differently. But we can only go forward."

"I don't know if I can yet." A shudder rolls through my chest. "When I'm not with you, all I think of is why I want you, but now that I'm with you, I just keep seeing you handing me that vial. It was so sad in the moment. Now it's crushing."

"Take as much time as you need. We can start over if you want."

"We can't start over. Everything that's happened will always be part of this." I shake my head and try to control my heaving lungs. "One of the two times I fell in love with you was based almost entirely on lies. That's not a great record."

"But"—he glances away and back to my eyes—"you fell in love with me twice."

I bite my lip as my heart twists itself into a painful knot. "Don't do that."

"You don't want to try for best two out of three?"

"I'm really not ready to laugh about any of this."

"Okay. I'm sorry. I'll follow your lead."

Should I kiss him or hit him? I settle on not touching him at all. "I presume you're going to help Krisalyn?"

He nods.

"Good. That antidote would be the best thing any of us have done in this whole mess."

"What are you going to do?"

"First, lunch with Bram. Then find more excuses not to speak to my parents."

"There's a lot they need to talk to you about."

"I'm sure they do." And Jase knowing more about it than I do adds to my fury with them.

He bites his lip. "Oh, I should give this back to you." He holds out my bracelet. "It seemed like it would be confusing if you didn't understand it."

"And the forget-me-nots weren't?"

"I guess that was wishful thinking."

I take the silver phrase and put it in my pocket with the necklace. The two sweet gifts aren't outweighing the horrible one right now.

When he stands, he offers me his hand to help me up. I give him mine and he squeezes it as he seems to debate his next move. My heart pounds painfully as I look at our joined hands. But when I remain still, he releases me. I ball my hands into fists as I step away to grab a coat. We get into the elevator in silence. The air buzzes between us, and breathing is a challenge.

Outside, Jase turns to me. "I tried to prepare myself for losing you..." He shakes his head and clenches his hand.

Silence stretches, but I'm frozen. Love and fear, desire and anger, threaten to rip me in two. Today fear and anger win.

"We'll... talk soon." It sounds pathetic, but what am I supposed to say? I'd like to tell him he hasn't lost me, but I'm not sure if that's true.

Chapter Forty-Five

BRAM

After I leave Serenity's, Dixon tracks me down and we meet at Crown Center. Apparently, Jase spent the night on his couch after the fallout with Serenity.

"But you know all about consoling people after a breakup," he says. "Or was it only a fight? Did they actually break up? Jase wasn't sure."

"Why do you think I know about it?"

"Besides us all being together when you told Krisalyn and Vogue you were with Serenity, there are also pictures of the two of you everywhere ."

"She happened to pass by me."

"How convenient. You were probably the worst person for that role, you know that, right?"

"Worse than Frey?"

"Okay, fine. Frey might be worse. Jase freaked out, so we had to talk him off of *that* ledge. Thanks."

"Why would he worry about me being with Serenity?"

"Because he isn't an idiot. The only person who hadn't noticed your crush was Frey, but now it's common knowledge."

Why is this blowing up? If people know, it becomes a thing, and it shouldn't, because nothing is going to happen. Damn Kaycians.

My cuff buzzes, and I tap it to respond to Serenity. "Well, she's on her way here, so if you could stop talking about pointless shit, that would be great."

"Why is she coming here?"

"We're meeting for lunch before I go back to Lawson."

"Why eat here if you're going to Lawson? The food is better there. In fact, maybe I'll go too. I need some burnt ends."

"I don't remember inviting you."

Serenity arrives and rushes to hug Dixon.

"She's back!" he exclaims.

"I'm so glad you're here. I missed you so much. Well, I didn't... because... Well, you know. What are we doing for lunch?"

"You can have whatever you want," he says. "I'm waiting for the good stuff in Lawson."

"You're going too?"

"The food is better. We aren't islands anymore. We can hop around the whole country whenever we want. That was the point, right?"

Serenity smiles and shifts her gaze to me. "Can I come too? I'd really like to speak with Sophos."

"Sure." The word only sounds half as unsure as I am.

Dixon shakes his head at me subtly. "Are you sure?" he asks her. "Don't you have things here to take care of?"

She rolls her eyes. "I think I've earned the right to avoid my problems." She turns to me. "You don't mind, do you?"

Dixon's eyes widen in an exasperated look at me.

"Of course not," I say. "The more the merrier."

"Great. How are we getting there?"

"The car we brought from Lawson is over by the train station."

"Okay. I'm just going to the ladies' room here and we can go." She walks away and Dixon looks at me suspiciously.

"I didn't do that," I say in my own defense.

"You *will* back me up when I tell everyone I tried to talk her out of it. Jase is going to lose it."

Is he really so threatened by me? The thought shouldn't be satisfying, but...

Serenity comes back toward us, saying, "I'll be back soon. I want to talk to Sophos... No, I'm not avoiding him, but some time to clear my head wouldn't hurt... Oh stop it, you love Snowflake... Well, we're leaving. Tell my parents. Thanks, bye!" She taps her cuff and removes it, putting it in her pocket along with her ear pod.

The defiant smile tells me the Serenity I knew before the uprising is definitely back. Stubborn and independent as can be. "Shall we?" she says.

My cuff vibrates against my wrist.

Vogue: What are you doing?

More buzzing when Krisalyn calls, but I ignore it as we walk to the station.

Frey: Don't tell Jase I said this, but well played.

Okay, if Frey approves it is probably a horrible thing to do. But at this point, I don't think I could stop Serenity even if I wanted to.

Dixon slows down to let Serenity get ahead of us. He pops up a message from Jase.

Is this a joke? It's not funny.

I shrug and say under my breath, "Think you can stop her?"

"I'd back out, but at this point he'd probably see that as even worse," he whispers. "At least this way I can keep an eye on her or something."

"What?" Serenity asks.

His voice goes back up to full volume. "I'm getting yelled at for kidnapping you."

"You're leaving too. Why does anyone care where I am?"

"I keep trying to tell you. You're a very big deal."

She shoves him playfully.

Per Dixon's demands, we eat upon arriving in Lawson.

"Okay, burnt ends did not sound appealing, but *oh my God*," Serenity says as we walk toward Townhall.

Dixon smiles. "I told you. I'll catch up with you later. Tell Sophos I said 'you're welcome' for not letting Frey and Vogue destroy him." He splits off to see if he can start working on antidote administration devices.

Serenity and I continue on. She rolls her shoulders back as we enter the building.

"Ready for a fight?"

She smirks at me. "Just because I can't throw a punch like you, doesn't mean I can't fight."

"Oh, I've been on the receiving end. I know what your mouth can do." *Shit.* That sounded dirty. *Kill me.*

She doesn't seem to notice. Or she's more mature than I am. Or it only sounded like innuendo because it's her.

I'm all too happy to separate from her when she goes to Sophos' office. Why does this girl make me such an idiot? As I approach Mom's open door, I hear Aren and consider trying back later. But I guess I can't avoid him forever.

"Wow, the prodigal son returns... again." Aren's glower makes me wish I'd gone with my first instinct.

"Good to see you too."

"Bram, where the hell were you?" Mom asks.

"Kaycie."

"Did you speak with anyone from the council?"

"He wouldn't remember if he had," Aren says. "They'd have wiped his memory of it."

"If you qualify the new generation, then yes. I have all my memories from the time I was gone, though. Calm down."

Aren doesn't look convinced. "Well, how much did you tell your Kaycian friends? Maybe they told Agnar."

"Told Agnar what?"

"He knows Sophos and Carista went to Montica," Mom says. "He knows what we were trying to accomplish with them, and he's negotiating with me to back off."

"What? What is he offering you?"

She takes a deep breath. "Emrys."

"Uh, well..." I sit down, thrown completely off course by this. "It's not like you can base your decisions on just Emrys. There are thousands of them."

"I know."

"And... it wasn't any of us who told Agnar. So how did he find out?"

"Cary thinks it was Montica," Aren says. "Playing both sides."

"That kind of makes sense," I say. "He seems to have a pretty strong relationship with them."

"I think they care more about their battery than him though," Mom says. She explains about a device taken from Agnar's dam villa.

I scratch my eyebrow and take a deep breath. "They did take some tech, but I don't know—"

"I knew it!" Aren slams his hands down on the desk. "You knew too, didn't you? Didn't think we might want to know that before sending people to Montica? You're just like them now! You back-stabbing asshole."

"Aren!" Mom shoots him a look that would shut up anyone with *any* sense, but this is Aren.

"*If* I was betraying someone," I say, "would that make me like them or like us? We're the ones that used them and lied to them at every turn."

"You deserve those shallow shits. Did you get your girl? Are you going to go live happily ever after in the city? I hope she's worth it."

"You're a moron."

"Both of you, stop it! Aren get out."

"I'm not the one—"

"Out!"

Aren sulks out. The look in his narrowed eyes assures me this isn't over. The door slams shut, and I look at Mom.

"Bram, if we give Montica the battery, we might still have a chance to get their help and dissolve the Establishment."

"What makes you think they'll follow through?"

"It's the only chance we have." Defeat colors her words. She doesn't have faith in their help, she's just clinging to this last resort.

"What if it isn't? Krisalyn is looking into an antidote for the extirpation drug." Mom stiffens. "If she pulls it off and we can wake up the marshals, we'd unite everyone against the Establishment instantaneously."

"Sophos said it can't be done. Someone died trying."

"Yeah, Maggie's brother. But they have his research, and Krisalyn is the only person who managed to create an antidote for the amnesia drug. If anyone can do it, it's her." As much as I didn't want to get my hopes up, I'd rather we try for this than Montica.

"If she can't, will you get the battery?"

"I'll try, but Montica doesn't seem like an option we should hope for."

Mom swipes her hand across her face. "Revitalizing the marshals is an option I can't *afford* to hope for."

Chapter Forty-Six
SERENITY

"This is cozy," I say as I walk into Sophos' office. "A tad smaller than what you had in the city."

All of my pleasant feelings from my reunion with Bram and Dixon melt away when I see Sophos. Even with my memory intact, I can't begin to guess how many lies he told me. Maybe I'm more like my mother than I realized, because I feel myself shift from the happy, fun version of myself, into a sharpened arrow intent on my goal.

"Serenity. How did you— And you remember my office?"

"I remember everything."

"Ah, you're here to admonish me then. Would you like some tea? I'd have to go get it—it doesn't pop out of the desk here."

"All I want is answers." I sit across from his desk, ready for a verbal bout. "It would appear you misrepresented some things as my *mentor*."

"May I say, I *am* glad to see you're well. Jase is too, I hope? And I gather the rest of your friends found you?"

"Everyone is fine, despite being used as pawns in this game."

"Serenity, you're familiar with how the Establishment families work now. We're all toyed with. Dragged to places we don't want to be for the good of the game. I simply wanted to reset the board with some new players. The opportunity to work with you was too good to pass up."

"How lucky for you."

"Luck had nothing to do with it. Your parents' plan for me to tell you about the islands was perfect for my own goal."

My sense of control over the situation falters. "They *knew* you were telling me about the islands and marshals?"

"Haven't you spoken to them yet?"

"No."

"Why would you come to me before them?"

"Because I'm angrier at you!" My heart picks up as that anger seeps through me.

He looks at me with a warm smile. "You are so much like your mother."

I keep my focused gaze on him, unwilling to be distracted by such sentiments.

"Yes, your parents knew I was telling you everything," he continues. "Adelle, your parents, and I had planned for you to be in the Leadership program. Grace and Anton raised you with our morals, intending that you'd take your place in the council with a determination to change things. They wanted me to reveal everything to you to see if you would choose the right side without their influence and how keeping the secret would affect you. They were worried at first but ultimately proud of how you handled yourself. Of course, they were unaware I had recruited you into an uprising. Everything I told you about Kaycie was true, except that I didn't tell you about the Establishment families. Every horrible thing you wanted to uproot was real."

"I realize that, but Leavenworth being a military base was no surprise for you."

"No, it wasn't."

"And you knew all along what the Establishment was in a tizzy about."

"Yes, I did."

"You had a plan to change things. A plan with other members of the Establishment supporting it. Why go rogue and rush it all behind their backs?"

"I have no doubt you'd make a wonderful governor someday, Serenity, but that day would be too far in the future. I missed the first three years of my daughter's life. I wasn't willing to miss it all."

My anger softens until I consider something. "When I went to *rescue* my parents from the EC, you knew that was unnecessary at best—ridiculous at worst. Why did you let me go?"

"*Let* you? Who lets you do anything? Did you need someone to *let you* come here, or carry that amnesia shot, or—"

"That amnesia shot tore up my life, and I took it because I didn't know what was really going on."

"I thought you didn't—"

"I did. Krisalyn developed an antidote. But I spent nearly two months drowning in confusion only to come out of it and find that everyone I love had a hand in putting me there."

My pulse drums in my ears. *Everyone I love.* I do love Jase. I got angry at him for saying it to me—I didn't say it back—but I do. How funny that I thought it hurt to lose Adwin. Loving Jase hurts infinitely more. My heart wrenches. I'm done with this conversation. I can't hate Sophos for what he did, even if he could have done better. Desperate people do crazy things.

"I'm sorry, Serenity. Truly, I never meant for you to get hurt in this." I nod and try to swallow the lump in my throat. "How long will you be here?"

"I don't know," I say.

We should go back tonight, but facing Jase feels impossible, and I don't want our group to have to take sides. Of course, they all have work to keep them busy. Jase and Krisalyn working on the extirpation antidote, Vogue and Frey on their Montican toys. Dixon probably needs to get back to help them, but I've dropped back into uselessness. Keeping busy would be so helpful right now. I hug my arms around myself as if I could physically hold myself together.

"You're welcome to stay as long as you'd like," Sophos says.

"Thank you. I'm going to find Dixon. Bram was telling Kolina about our alternative plan. You should go see them."

On my way out, I double-take, thinking I see Bram, but it's not him. His doppelgänger glares at me with chilling sharpness. The girl with him watches me with surprised curiosity. I guess even Kaycian-casual is a little fancy here, but the guy's reaction is overkill.

I hurry out and message Dixon, who says he'll come meet me. Waiting on a bench, I find myself lost in a daydream.

"If you could choose a superpower, what would it be?" Jase asked when he took one of my igra pieces.

"Hmm, I'd like to be able to transform into any animal I choose. That way I could fly or swim across the ocean. What would your superpower be?"

"You didn't get one of my pieces. You don't get to ask a question."

"I haven't cared much for rules lately," I said with a defiant smile.

"I'd want ability to read minds."

"That doesn't seem necessary. You can already read mine."

"No, I can't."

"Really? You don't know what I'm thinking about?" I slid the game away.

"You're a complete mystery."

When I crossed over the ottoman to sit on his lap, I whispered in his ear. "Still can't hear my thoughts?" He kissed my neck, sending a shock wave down my spine. "See?" I breathed. "I knew you could read my mind."

Our lips met for a perfect kiss. My fingers in his hair, his hands pressed into my back.

"Hey." Dixon snaps me out of my reverie.

"Hi." My brain is so happy to have these memories back that it's playing them on repeat for me. It hasn't gotten the message from my heart that they're painful right now. "What do you want to do?"

"I can manage putting together devices to release the antidote from here, if you want to stay."

"I do, but you don't need to stay with me."

"Of course, I do. Though I don't condone avoiding Jase."

I rub my forehead. "I realize you're trying to help him out, but—"

"Not just Jase; you too. You're happier with him."

"I was." My voice cracks. "I hope to be again, but this morning when I was with him, I was just sad and hurt. It should have been my choice, and he took that from me."

"If he wanted to disregard your choices, he wouldn't have let you go to the EC in the first place."

My lips purse together. "This isn't your fight."

"True, but you're less likely to walk out on me."

Seriously? That was a low blow. I guess the gloves have come off. I'd be glad he's not treating me like I'm made of glass, but some extra care on this topic would be okay.

"Look," he says, "he didn't ask any of us to pull for him. He actually told us to stay out of it, because he didn't want you to feel pressured. So, I guess I'm not that good a friend to either of you. I'm just telling you how I see it."

"Did you know he snuck in saying he loves me after I took the shot so I'd have that in my new memories?"

"Why does that upset you?"

"Because it further manipulated my mind."

"Do you think it isn't true?"

"That's not the point."

"Isn't it though?"

For a while, I only knew he loved me because he artificially planted it in my brain. What if they hadn't been able to retrieve my memories? That would have been the entire basis of our relationship. Could we have spent our entire lives together with that massive secret between us? Dixon's attempt is backfiring. I'm getting more upset with Jase the deeper we go.

"Can we drop it, please?"

"Fine. I'm sorry I brought it up. I can show you the house we stayed in if you want to stick around."

We walk away, his arm around my shoulders. "You know I'm only meddling because I love you, right?"

"I know."

Bram joins us to go back to the house. So, this is where everyone lived all this time. It would have been crowded if Jase and I had managed to come along. Potential alternate realities play through my mind—all the what ifs and could have beens. It's silly, and things could have gone so much worse, but the regret still lingers.

Not long after we arrive, there's a knock on the door. Dixon answers it. "Hi neighbor. Did you miss me?"

"Yes!" The tall girl I saw in Townhall wraps him in a tight hug. "You ditched me!"

"I'm sorry. I knew it wouldn't be for long. Carista, this is Serenity."

She comes in and looks at me curiously. "Serenity Ward in person."

Great, I'm famous here too. "It's nice to meet you. I hear you grew up with Bram and his brothers."

"I did… for better or worse. Aren—he's the middle brother—was the person glaring at you as you left Townhall earlier."

"Oh! Well, that figures. I guess I repel Eros men." I look over at Bram who's pulling food out of a to-go bag. "Bram hated me when we met."

"You didn't like me either," he says.

"You insisted on calling me a *puppy*."

The four of us lounge around the table after we eat. Explaining that even the Director of the Department of Health couldn't reverse my amnesia seems to make Carista more hopeful about Krisalyn's chances with the extirpation antidote.

"Speaking of Krisalyn and drugs, don't you have something to tell Carista?" Bram looks at Dixon patronizingly.

Dixon sighs and runs a hand through his hair. "I have a confession to make. Though it wasn't actually me!"

My jaw drops as Dixon tells the colorful story of Vogue and Frey weaseling information out of Carista and then wiping her memory of it.

I smack Dixon's arm. "I can't believe you."

"It was thirty minutes," he says. "Krisalyn and Jase did that all the time. We knew it wasn't a big deal." Says the person who's never taken it.

Carista's outrage turns toward an unsuspecting Bram. "You knew about this?" She whacks him on the arm.

"Not for long!"

My friends are crazy. "I'm gone less than *two months* and you pull stuff like that."

"Clearly the six of us should stick together," Dixon says with a smile.

"There are eight of us now." I gesture toward Bram and Carista. "I don't think I can balance out everyone's absurdity myself."

Chapter Forty-Seven

Muffled voices roll over me like waves. They're far away. So is my body. I don't feel it. I don't feel anything.

The voices slowly come into focus, as if my brain is tuning an ancient radio, finding just the right frequency. The sounds are familiar and—despite whispering—are noticeably angry.

"You had no right to bring him here—to drag him into your drama like I was. Get out."

"He's an adult, Emmaline. He makes his own choices."

Mother? I try to pull myself back into my body. My mind swims through darkness to find my limbs. I sense where they are now, but can't will any movement from them. I picture my little finger—picture it moving. Nothing happens. What about my eyelids? I could open my eyes. They tingle faintly as I concentrate on them. If my face could move, it would contort with the effort. I focus on my breathing—control it rather than just letting it happen. If I can do this, I can open my eyes. It could be seconds or hours of trying. The voices rumble in the background, but I can't focus on so much at a time. Finally, I open my eyes.

Blinding light leaves me seeing as little as when my eyes were closed. I blink away the glare, and my mother's eyes meet mine. She gasps and leans over me, trailing her fingers through my hair. "Adwin, can you hear me?"

The only sign that my head actually nods is the rush of dizzying pain. It wobbles, and I wince. My mother looks like she's the one who felt it. "No, no. Don't try to move. I'm sorry."

I inventory myself and my surroundings to see the stark hospital room. Bigger than the one I went to for my commChip. Grandfather stands behind my mother, worry tainting his ever-stoic expression. From my neck down, I'm submerged in a blue gel of some sort, floating.

"You're going to be fine," my mother says. "They've already mended the broken bones and nerves. This allows your body to settle into the changes. You should be out of it tomorrow." My lips creak open, but she shakes her head. "Don't speak yet." Dark circles shadow her eyes, but her eyes themselves are clearer than I've ever seen them. Her hand shakes as she fidgets with her necklace.

A doctor enters and asks how long I've been awake. Grandfather tells him, and he says I should go back to sleep. He does something on a holoScreen and warmth runs through my spine.

My mother's sad smile blurs as I fall back into darkness.

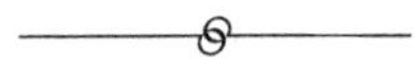

When my eyes open again, I'm in a normal hospital bed. Dim lighting glows through the room. I pull myself up, feeling stiff, but otherwise all right. I stretch my arms in front of me and rotate my elbows.

The door clicks open and Clover pads in. She doesn't look surprised to see me up. "Good morning. Do you need an oil can, tin man?"

"How—" The word scrapes out of my throat like a pumice stone rubbing against it.

"Shh. Here, drink this." She hands me a steaming cup smelling of licorice and honey. Sipping it takes immediate effect of soothing my throat, though speaking will still be rough. "Were you going to ask how I knew you'd be awake?"

I nod in response, saving my voice as she sits on the edge of the bed.

"They scheduled the meds to wear off in an hour, but I modified it. Otherwise your mother and a doctor and Casimir would have been here."

Grandfather came back. And my mother is here. I'm surprised she spoke to Grandfather long enough to find out I was hurt.

"Now we have a full family reunion," Clover says with a smile. "But I wanted to talk to you before anyone else did. Don't strain yourself trying to speak. We can save what you remember for later on. For now, I just wanted to tell you not to mention the gear dying." I tilt my head. "I'm still looking into how it happened, but I don't want anyone else digging into it. They think your commChip failed as a result of the fall. I got mine changed out discreetly. Priam knows, but that's all. Sorry to tarnish your reputation, but they think you fell despite the boots and gloves. Honestly, you call yourself a tree-walker."

I give her an incredulous look over the tea. I do not call myself a tree-walker.

"I'd appreciate you keeping this to yourself. I'll explain later. Will you do that for me?"

I nod again.

"Thank you, Adwin. You should be out of here this afternoon. I don't think Ismene is still intending to keep you hostage, but the doctors want to follow up, so you'll be stuck here for a while." She rises from the bed. "I'd better get going. Are you done with that? I don't want them asking who brought it to you. I'm already in plenty of trouble for almost killing you."

I hand her the nearly empty cup. "Thank you." The whisper is scarcely audible.

"I'll come see you when you're back in your suite."

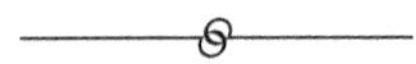

My mother creeps into the room, careful not to disturb me. I sit up, arching my back to stretch it.

"Oh!" She hurries to my side. "How are you feeling?"

I clear my throat and whisper, "I'm all right."

"Oh, wait." She taps the screen by my bed and summons another cup of the tea. "Here you go. I can't believe you're here." Her forehead wrinkles with worry as she chews her thin bottom lip. She squeezes my left hand, but her trembling is strong enough to shake both our hands. I think she's *clean*. And probably in greater need of a hospital bed than I am.

The door opens, and a doctor enters, followed by my grandfather. The latter gives me a thin smile. "Apparently you'd have been better off in a cell."

Mother looks daggers at him.

"Does anything hurt?" the doctor asks.

"Just my throat." Though it's already much better than when I croaked a word at Clover's arrival.

"That's to be expected. A few cups of that will set you right." He examines my eyes through a tool and tests my motor skills and range of motion. "Looks like you're good as new. I'll schedule you for a stretch and massage before you leave, but you can go back to your suite upstairs later today. I'll want to see you in a couple of days to make sure everything is in order."

Grandfather thanks the doctor as he leaves, then turns to me. "*What* were you doing?"

"Trying to keep up with Clover."

"More importantly," my mother says, "what was he doing *here*?"

"I wanted to come. I wanted to see where you're from."

She shudders. "I'm sorry you had to learn about all of this from your grandfather. I just couldn't... This place..."

"It's all right," I tell her. "How long was I out?"

"You fell six days ago," Grandfather says. "The same injuries in Kaycie would have killed you. You're lucky to be here."

She scowls at him. "In Kaycie this wouldn't have happened at all. Sweetheart, we'll get you back home as soon as possible. I promise."

"I'm in no hurry." Before I go anywhere, I need to know what happened when Clover and I were out there.

Chapter Forty-Eight

BRAM

My imagination had run wild with ideas that won't ever happen. But I never thought of the best things about Serenity being in Lawson. I kind of love seeing her outside of Kaycie. Away from the glitz and pretension, she slips into a comfortable, down-to-earth type.

Dixon wrangled her into his morning runs. I'd have thought she'd be more reluctant, but she's holding her own. In the afternoons and evenings, I show her around town, she plays with Libby, or tries to help my mom in the kitchen. She gets flustered, but her not being good at something is a fantastic thing to see. Not in the dark way I enjoyed Vogue being thrown off her game. This is just... cute.

Today, we have other plans. Carista and I go out to the park to meet Serenity and Dixon after their run. We find Serenity lying on the grass, sweat beading on her forehead. Dixon stands over her with his back against a tree and pokes her stomach with his foot when we approach.

She tilts her head back to look at me upside down. "Oh, you remembered."

"Don't sound so excited."

"But Dixon is killing me." She sits up and rests her forearms on her knees.

"Oh, please." Dixon offers her a hand and pulls her up.

"Catch." I throw her the ball, which she catches against her chest.

She examines it, then looks back up at me. "Is it technically a ball if it isn't a sphere?"

And so it begins.

I show them how to hold and throw the ball, which Serenity can barely wrap her hand around. It wobbles when she tries to throw it. Since copying me isn't working, I put my hands on her shoulder and wrist to guide her arm. Dixon eyes me suspiciously. She maintains that she's not generally this stiff and uncoordinated, as if I'd see her lack of perfection as a negative.

"There are supposed to be more people," I say. "But for two on two the offense would have a quarterback and a receiver, and the defense will try to block the pass or take down the receiver. Or in this case, two hands on a player equals a tackle."

"Oh good. I didn't want to hurt you." Serenity winks at me.

"Kaycie versus Lawson?" Dixon suggests a little too enthusiastically.

Carista laughs to herself. "You sure you don't want to be on my team, Dixon?"

"I'm sure."

"That'll put you at a disadvantage," I say.

"Don't underestimate us," Dixon says with a smile. "We're crafty."

"If you say so." I toss him the ball.

Dixon wraps an arm around Serenity's shoulders and leads her away from Carista and me.

"You know why he did this, right?" Carista can't hide her smirk. Her awareness of my situation is an inevitable annoyance.

"Yes."

"Of course, this is counterintuitive to his goal."

"Sure is."

"Are you going to behave?"

I look at her incredulously. "Car, I always behave."

Serenity misses the first throw entirely and catches the second only because it hits her in the stomach. Of course, while standing there to announce, "I got it!" Carista 'tackles' her, so she gets nowhere. The throw was long enough for a first down, but she doesn't really understand what that means. The next one I snatch out of the air before it reaches her and take back to score.

"He threw it to me!" she complains.

"And I intercepted it."

"Is that allowed?"

"Yes."

"You're making up rules as you go."

When she takes a turn at being quarterback, she accuses me of making up rules again when I sack her. She takes revenge by tripping me when I'm the receiver, sending me sprawling backwards on the grass.

"Oh, that's how you want to play?"

She shrugs with a smug grin.

The next time I sack her, it isn't a two-hand touch. I throw her over my shoulder as she laughs hysterically.

Dixon groans. "Oh, come on!"

"I think you win," she says when I set her back on her feet.

"Yes, I'm done." Dixon shoots me an agitated look.

"Did you two have a disagreement that I'm unaware of?"

Cary pulls Serenity's arm to lead her away. "Bram just has a way of getting under people's skin. Let's go get cleaned up and have some girl time."

Dixon glares at me as I pick up the ball. I shrug. "You were the one who put us on opposing teams."

"Clearly, I didn't think that through all the way."

"Clearly." When he doesn't soften, I add, "Calm down. It's just friendly. Not like playing is going to make her fall in love with me."

"Is that what you're going for?"

No. Am I? That sounds deeper than I've really considered it. I don't need her to be *in love* with me. Because I'm not...

"I just don't want her to be broken."

Chapter Forty-Nine
SERENITY

"What's their problem?"

Carista cocks her head to the side, her own unspoken question in her eyes. "Guys can always find something to fight about. Trust me, I grew up with five brothers if I include the Eros household."

"That sounds like fun."

"It was." She drops her gaze as we walk out of the park.

Compared to what's happened to her brothers, it seems ridiculous to fret over a couple of months of amnesia. That's been the case with everything, though. My problems are never *that bad*, but people still worry over me. It's unfair, but if my friends' dedication to helping me ends up helping other people then I guess it's okay. Would Krisalyn have ever tried to reverse extirpation if not for the amnesia antidote? I suppose my contribution can be needing to be saved. That sounds awfully pathetic, but whatever it takes to get Carista and Bram their brothers back.

"If Krisalyn wakes them up, what's the first thing you're doing with the guys?" I ask.

She laughs a little at that. "Well, if they remember everything that's happened while they were brainwashed, first I'll be getting ridiculed by Reid."

"What for?"

"My mom was freaking out about me ignoring him, and I didn't like it either. So, I started using him as a training buddy to blow off steam. We go for runs together, and…" Her mumbles are unintelligible.

"And what?"

She sighs. "And fighting practice."

"As in… you fight him?"

"Yep."

"Um. He's…"

"A trained marshal. Yeah. I've been getting my ass handed to me. Hence, expecting ridicule."

Wow, that is not what I would think of for sibling bonding, but I guess it works. "I'm sure it'll be an awesome reunion." We reach the end of her street, and it looks like I'm getting a reunion of my own. "I'll have to catch up with you later."

Carista glances back and forth between my surprise visitor and me, then goes to her house.

I reach the front of my borrowed house under watchful eyes. "Hello, sweetheart," she says.

"Hello, Mother."

She sits at the kitchen table, watching me as I make coffee for the two of us. "I thought once your amnesia was reversed, you'd be back to tea."

"It turns out remembering everything is overrated." I sit across from my mother. She looks so out of place here. Her attempt to dress down in a copper sweater and linen pants still looks too elegant. "So, what brings you to Lawson?"

"You've been here four days and made yourself unreachable."

"Dixon tells me when people call. I haven't had anything to talk about. Vogue was here nearly two months, and Espy didn't come knocking."

"I love Espy, but I *am not* her. I've only stayed away this long at your father's insistence."

"He understands me better than you do." He'd let me have my space. He was the one who gave me a piano to help me recuperate while she made me get back into fencing.

Her finger runs up and down the handle of the coffee mug. "He's better at being gentle and comforting. That's his way. He knows what it's like to find out about this insanity."

"As do you."

"I hardly remember. The rules were different then. I knew a lot of it as far back as my memory recalls."

"Really? Why did things change?"

She rubs her lips together. "It was deemed problematic." Her lips turn up as she gazes at me. "Anyway, dear, I'm afraid most of your problems are my fault." Maybe. But not *all*. "Of course, we couldn't have presented it to you as if the entire system was fine, but I didn't want to *tell you* it was wrong either. We wanted you to grow into it—to choose for yourself. Knowing you could be the governor who changes the country seemed like too much pressure to put on you."

"Sophos telling me everything and having to keep the secret even at home wasn't any pressure at all."

"That was supposed to go differently." She shakes her head. "We couldn't have known Sophos was radicalized. He was going to be the *impartial* party to explain things to you. That way you could come to your own conclusions."

"Do you realize how much I hated lying to you? And you were lying to me the entire time!" Just like someone else. Pieces come together in my mind. "It was you, wasn't it? You called Sophos about Adwin when Agnar introduced him into the Establishment." Someone knew enough to alert Sophos which concerned me. That being my own mother is unnerving. Everyone has always known more about what's going on in my life than I do.

"Yes, I did. I was worried about what you knew when you were with him. Of course, Sophos wasn't forthcoming about any of it."

"Oh, is it frustrating when people keep things from you?"

"Serenity..."

"Even with my memories back, it's a feat to decipher what was true!"

"I know. I'm sorry. We should have told you everything. Then you would've come to us. and we could have prevented most of this. I'm so very sorry for everything you've been through this year."

How would my year have gone if I had known? Would I have turned spy against Sophos instead of the Establishment? No, this only worked because he knew my parents weren't telling me. Without that, the uprising would've happened without me. I wouldn't know Bram, Dixon, Krisalyn, Frey... Jase. I can't long for that lost possibility.

"You might have prevented my suffering, but not the uprising. I'm not sorry for that," I say. "To expect the towns to go on that way for decades more is horrible. I'm glad the uprising happened, even if the timing was crazy."

My mother's eyes harden. "Don't think for a minute I ever forget how awful we've been to the towns." Her words crack like a whip. "I was trying to fix things without getting anyone killed."

The unexpected fury makes me drop my gaze. "Okay. But then we're all on the same side. Everything is fine."

"So come home."

A couple of weeks ago, I yearned to go back to Kaycie. I wanted Vogue and Jase, and my commCuff to work. Now, all of those are available to me, but I'm not ready to deal with them. "I will soon. Not yet."

She reaches across to hold my hand. "Your father and I are very proud of you." The sentiment makes me feel even worse.

I don't deserve it when I'm hiding away like this.

ADWIN

The stretch and massage loosen my stiff joints, and I'm surprised to find how perfectly normal I feel. I shouldn't have been able to walk ever again, but here I am a week later without so much as a limp. My mother sits in my living room, hugging her knees to her chest, staring sadly through the balcony door.

"Have you gone out since you've been here?" I ask.

"No. I've been with you."

"You didn't need to be at my side the whole time I slept."

"It was where I belonged. And truth be told, I'd rather not run into *the family*." She looks like a little girl, afraid of the older children on the playground.

"They're not all so bad."

"Maybe your generation. Plus, you're further removed from the insult. Ismene and Rocco hate me. Especially Ismene."

"It isn't really you. It's Grandfather."

"That's never mattered."

Ismene might actually get along with my mother on the basis of their mutual distaste for their father. I wish there was some way I could give her home back to her. Maybe she'd be better here. I assume the first thing she'll do upon returning to Kaycie will be to stop at the dispensary.

She retires to her suite after an early dinner, and my call to Clover goes unanswered. It's too early to go to bed, so I lie on the sofa and read a holoBook. I guess I fell asleep because I'm stirred awake by a sound outside my balcony. The darkness of the room throws me off balance. I thought I only shut my eyes for a moment, but it's the dead of night now. The room is freezing from the breeze coming in through the open door. As I shuffle over to close it, I hear something again.

Faint cracks of twigs snapping—wildlife of some sort. I start to slide the door shut when a light thud sounds on the balcony above me. Is Clover just coming in from a late-night tree-walk? I step out and crane my head over the railing in time to see two figures fly onto the balcony. Inaudible whispers drift down before the door snaps shut.

Clover never closes her door to the mountain air. What is she up to?

For a second, I wonder if she's gotten me new boots and gloves. It doesn't matter, that's a terrible idea. I just got out of the hospital. Bounding around the trees won't happen anytime soon. I'll ask about it tomorrow. I close the door and go to bed. The soft blankets, which are thick but not heavy, almost distract me from my thoughts about what Clover is doing... almost.

After breakfast, I go up to Clover's suite. She answers the door in pajamas, hair tousled and feet dragging. "Oh, good morning," she says with a sleepy smile.

"Did I wake you? I'm sorry, I should have realized you'd be sleeping in after your party last night." Her eyes catch in a surprised look for only a second before she puts on the appearance of not caring. "Or is it just that you aren't used to having guests come through this door?"

She smirks and drops onto her sofa, pulling a blanket around herself. "Did you hear them?" She clicks her tongue a few times and sighs. "Amateur hour. I can't wait to tell them."

"Who is it that travels via trees to see you?"

"Friends." I look at her expectantly. "I do know people outside our family, much to Ismene's chagrin."

"Is that why they come in the middle of the night through the balcony?"

"It's too early for this dance, Adwin. Sit and let's be straightforward about it." I follow her command as she wraps her hands around a steaming mug. "Those friends of mine helped me investigate *our* little accident. An EMP knocked out our tech. One of my tree-walkers found it—"

"There are more of you?"

"Of course. Why would I brandish the title by myself? And you know how they came to see me." She looks at me like I'm an idiot.

"Can I have a minute to catch up? I fell to what should have been my death recently."

"Fine. So, we found the EMP. It was short range, meant for precision targeting."

"Someone was *trying* to kill me?"

"Don't flatter yourself. Someone was trying to kill *me*. You had only just gotten there. I was alone when it was shot. Honestly, though, the audacity to think I wouldn't be able to get down safely without tech? So offensive."

"Trying to kill you *isn't* offensive though?"

She shrugs and takes a sip. "Being targeted means someone finds me threatening, which I rather enjoy. It also means I'm not as crazy as

Priam thinks. He may deny his mother's tyrannical habits when she's manipulating countries but going after the family—which she claims to put above all else—makes my case rather clear."

"You think Ismene tried to kill you?"

"Yes I do. Not just anyone can get those EMPs, and I've been stoking her flames lately. Not that I've actually committed treason, mind you, but I guess she sees I won't stop at complaining about things. Do you see why I like that she tried to kill me?"

"Because you are at least a little crazy?"

"Because she thinks I could actually mess things up for her. She loves her brother, and probably me in her way, but look what she's willing to do to secure her place. She *is* a tyrant. Trying to do away with me proves it. Failing to kill me will be her biggest regret, because far from scaring me into submission, it's emboldened me.

"You should go home as soon as the doctors release you, Adwin. Things are going to get messy around here."

Chapter Fifty-One

BRAM

Sophos watches Mom pace her office. He's been quiet since Grace's surprise visit. It seems like she was harder on him than Serenity.

"We agreed on one week." Mom is giving up on the antidote option.

Carista, on the other hand, is digging in her heels. "I know, but—"

"Cary, you know I'd *die* for this to work, but it's not realistic."

"I don't care about realistic. It's perfect!" Reid's presence doesn't seem to bother her as much anymore. I've seen her out walking or jogging with him. At first it seemed depressing, but she's making the most of the situation. Still, she would do anything to really get him back. "We would unite against the Establishment, take full control of the country this time, and we wouldn't have to involve Montica."

Unless Montica is invested in keeping Agnar in control. How can we find out more about him?

Oh!

"I've got to go!" I stand and leave without another word.

I let myself into the house without knocking. "Serenity! You dated Agnar's grandson!"

"Don't remind me," she says with an eye roll.

"Do you still talk to him?"

She sinks into a chair. "We were friendly in Leavenworth since I didn't remember he's awful and had cheated on me."

What kind of moron would cheat on her? *Shit. Focus.*

"Jase didn't tell you Adwin had cheated on you?" Dixon asks.

"Jase didn't tell me *anything*."

"So, he thinks you're still friendly?" Have to stay on track.

"I guess so. But last I heard, he was still in Montica."

"What is he doing there?"

"He went with Agnar. Except Agnar came back and Adwin didn't. He never volunteers details about anything, so I don't know what happened."

"If you could get a call to Montica, would he tell you anything of importance?" Am I horrible for asking her to talk to this asshole?

"It would be the first time. He wasn't exactly forthcoming with me when we were together."

"Would you be willing to try? I want to figure out the connection Agnar has to Montica."

"How could you get a call through to Montica?" Dixon asks.

"They gave us a device after Sophos and Carista went to meet with them. It's at Townhall."

Serenity shrugs. "It wouldn't be the worst thing I've done for this cause. Might as well try."

Chapter Fifty-Two

ADWIN

"You don't need to be here anymore," my mother insists. "Come home."

"The doctors want to monitor me a while longer."

"Adwin, I agree with your mother," Grandfather says. "You should leave while Ismene will allow it. I don't suspect her sympathy and goodwill will last long."

That's true enough. If she's willing to kill the niece who she held as a baby, my safety is far from secure. Still, I don't want to inform on Clover, but I can't stop her from doing anything rash if I'm gone. There probably isn't much to stop her from anything even if I am here, but my odds are slightly higher. After failing to notice Serenity's involvement in Kaycie's uprising, I can't turn a blind eye to my cousin's rebellious plans.

"I'm fine here. Maybe after enough time with me they'll remember we're part of the family."

Not that they treat family all that well...

"Adwin, I can't stay here." Tears threaten to pour over my mother's eyelashes.

"I know. You don't have to." I glance at my grandfather, who looks wholly uncomfortable with these emotions. "Could we have a moment before you leave?"

He nods and places a firm hand on my shoulder. "Be careful."

"I will."

"Goodbye then." He walks out, leaving my mother free to cry.

"I'm sorry you had to turn to him for stability. I should have been more present."

I hug her to my shoulder. "It's all right. I'll be back soon enough. Can you remain *present* back in the city?"

She pulls back and wipes her eyes. "I'm supposed to be the parent."

Better late than never. "Being here has helped me understand you, though. Ripped away from this, losing your mother and your home in one swoop..."

"Has been a decades long excuse." She rubs her temple. "I didn't even know what was going on at the time. I didn't realize who he was or that we were a secret. Then out of nowhere my life blew up and... It doesn't matter. It wasn't fair to you. I've given you as much reason to hate me as my father gave me to hate him."

"I don't hate you." *You taught me things too—like why people need to be cosseted.*

Is it unfair of me to want her to stay clean? She's miserable as she is. Why not let her be that happy, if absentminded, version of herself? That's why Kaycians are so cheery, because they can do that without care or responsibility. It's why Clover's ideals are flawed. They're based on the populous being better than it is.

"Please come home."

That home is already in shambles. Maybe I can fix that and prevent the same from happening here. "I will soon."

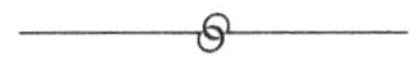

What will convince Clover things aren't as bad as they seem? From the chair on my balcony, the slight glimmer of the dome-shield is visible in brief flickers. Nothing feels different with it up, but she sees it as a horribly oppressive cage. Ismene is an exacting perfectionist, but her governing isn't cruel. Why would she try to kill Clover? It makes it rather difficult to defend her.

The door opens behind me, and I turn, expecting to see Clover—my most frequent visitor—but find myself in Priam's presence. "Hello, cousin. I'm glad to see you in one piece."

I should have known. Clover isn't likely to use the door. "Not half as glad as I am. I hear I have you to thank for that."

"No thanks necessary. It's lucky Clover found me so quickly. Did she tell you about the EMP?" I frown and nod. "She's been quiet since it happened. Has she said anything to you? Lately, her patience has been running thin, and I'm worried this will drive her over the edge."

Priam would be the one person I might tell, but if she isn't comfortable telling him, then I can't either. "Not really. I think it scared her more than she's willing to admit. She's sweeping it under the rug a bit."

He chews the inside of his cheek and shrugs.

"I'm sure she'll be fine," I add.

"Yeah." He seems to blink himself back into the present. "And you're okay?"

"Good as new."

"It's ironic. The story is you just fell, when actually you were so proficient in the trees as to catch up to Clover in time to get snagged in the trap meant for her. If you had been a little slower, you'd have spared yourself the brush with death."

"Such is life."

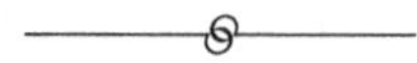

"To what do I owe the pleasure?" This visit is even more unexpected than Priam's.

"Can't a girl spend some quality time with her cousin?"

I raise an eyebrow at Nemora, who reveals a liquor bottle from behind her back.

"I come bearing gifts." She steps past me and to the bar for glasses. "I wasn't the most welcoming at first, but as it turns out, you might be the only other reasonable person our family has produced in this generation." She drops a couple of ice cubes into each glass and pours the whiskey. "I don't know how that's possible having been raised in Kaycie, but here we are."

Being on the side opposite Clover and Priam is unsettling, but I don't think Nemora is as bad as they make her out to be. I take the glass she holds out to me and tap hers before taking a sip. "Glad you're finally willing to admit me into the family."

"Blood is thicker than water, even somewhat diluted."

That's probably as far as I can expect her kindness to go for now. "Sorry you have to scrape the bottom of the barrel." My throat itches. I try to clear it and then to swallow, but my tongue tingles, almost numb in my mouth, like when I woke up from cosmetic dental surgery. I take another sip of the whiskey.

Nemora shrugs. "I can always make do with what I'm given. What is Clover going to do with her circumstances?"

"Dethrone your mother." My hand flies to my mouth. "Why did I say that?"

"Because you're reasonable, Adwin."

My flash of panic melts away. My heart is slowing down from a sprint, but why was it racing?

Was I worried about something?

"Why would Clover want to depose my mother?"

How does Nemora know that? "Ismene tried to kill her." Why did I say that? My heart rate picks up again, and I shove away the whiskey hard enough to knock it over and send it spilling across the coffee table. "What is that?"

"Just something to help you open up. You won't fret about it for long, you're forgetting the conversation while it happens."

"Why would I need to forget our conversation?"

A smile tugs at the corners of Nemora's mouth. "What makes Clover think Mother tried to kill her?"

Nemora knows? "The EMP knocked out our tech when we were high in the forest. It was targeting her." My mouth is dry. How did the whiskey spill?

"My mother wouldn't do that," Nemora says, shaking her head. What wouldn't she do? "What other grievances does Clover have against my mother?"

"Ismene controls the weather with the dome and the continent with the dam. She won't let any of you have romantic relationships or babies. She might take over Kaycie, which I tried to tell Clover would be better for Kaycie, but she doesn't listen, and Ismene tried to kill her."

"What are Clover's plans?"

"I don't know. I think she's still working on that."

"With who?"

"Who with what?" What are we talking about?

"Wow, you are highly susceptible to this."

"To what?"

Nemora tucks her hair behind her ear. "Who is Clover working with to depose my mother?"

"The tree-walkers."

"Who are the tree-walkers?"

"I don't know. I saw shadows going into her suite, but I haven't met them. Clover thought I'd be a tree-walker, but then I fell out of the tree. But that's because I was too close when Ismene tried to kill her."

"*Would* you be a tree-walker?"

"I prefer the ground."

Nemora sighs. "Would you help Clover depose my mother?"

"No! I'm trying to figure out how to talk her out of it. I don't want her to get into trouble, though, so I can't tell anyone." Wait...

"Is Priam involved with Clover's plans to depose my mother?"

"No, he's worried the EMP attack will make her do something rash, but I didn't tell him he's right. I want to protect her, even if it's mostly from herself."

"I'm so glad I can trust you, Adwin. Our family may be tumultuous, but we need to remain united. Those of us *capable of* guiding humanity can't shy away from our responsibility. But you aren't the one who doesn't understand that."

She goes to the bar and pours the rest of the small bottle of whiskey down the drain. She returns with a glass of water for me. "It was a pleasure speaking with you. I think we *can* be friends."

Nemora leaves.

It looks nice out. Maybe I'll go for a hike. Spending the *entire* day alone and bored won't do.

Chapter Fifty-Three

SERENITY

As the four of us go to Townhall, a thought occurs to me: Bram and Carista were Jase's and my replacements when we were stuck in Leavenworth. I bet Frey was happy to have me replaced with a girl he might have a shot with. I'll have to tease him about that later. The vision of having eight of us banded together flashes through my mind until I realize this four-and-four scenario will be more likely if I can't get past my issues with Jase. And we had just gotten back together…

Dixon gets the call through and says to the woman, "I have Miss Serenity Ward on the line for Mr. Adwin Lebeau." I grin at his secretarial performance.

It takes a moment to transfer it to Adwin's device and then he comes on over the speaker.

"Serenity?"

"Yes, hello Adwin. How are you doing?" My stomach twists. He must have known about my amnesia when we were in Leavenworth. I'm sure they all did. And there I was, ogling over him and wondering why he had left me. Maybe that was a stupid thing to put into my memories.

"I'm fine. I'm in a tree right now. Not as high as when I fell, but I figured I should give it another try."

"You fell out of a tree?" The voice sounds right, but the words don't make any sense for Adwin.

"I did. It was supposed to be Clover, but I was the one who almost died."

The four of us share confused looks and I mouth, *I have no idea.* "Well... I'm glad you're all right. Who is Clover?"

"My cousin. The slightly crazy one. She wants to depose our tyrannical aunt, and one of our other cousins might be okay with his mother's downfall, but Nemora wouldn't like it."

What on earth is going on? "I'm sorry, Adwin. I'm lost. How do you have cousins and an aunt in Montica?"

"Because my mother has a half-sister and a half-brother here. My grandfather was married to the Director, but he had another family with another daughter, so the Director killed the other wife and exiled Grandfather and Mother to Kaycie."

Dixon taps the screen to mute it. "Oh my God!"

"I thought you were barely friendly?" Carista says, wide-eyed.

"We weren't! I have no idea why he's telling me all this!" I tap the screen again. "Adwin..."

"Serenity?" He sounds genuinely confused to hear my voice.

"Yes, it's me. Um, why are you telling me all this?"

"Telling you what?"

Mute. "Okay, something is wrong with him."

"I should hope so," Bram says, "but is it something that's making him spew bullshit, or is he being way too honest?"

I pop my lips and unmute it. "Adwin, it's Serenity. Did you ever sleep with anyone while we were together?"

"Of course. I can't even tell you how relieved I was that you were clinging to your virginity."

A hot blush rises to my face as I gasp. I press my eyes closed to avoid looking at anyone. That's more information than I hoped he'd share on speaker, but it proves the point. He's being *very* honest.

"I didn't mean to cheat on you, but I ran into Liam at that Christmas party, and things got a little out of hand."

Dixon meets my shocked look with his own. My mouth opens and closes, finding no words to say.

"You're not angry, are you? No offense to you, of course. I liked you; I just wasn't attracted to you that way."

This is entirely off topic, but… "I thought you had been sleeping with Parisa." I wish no one else was here for this conversation.

"No! She kind of walked in on Liam and me at her Christmas party, and she covered for me."

"Why would it be any better for people to think you cheated on me with *her*?"

"My grandfather would not stand for me to be gay, Serenity!"

The air is sucked out of the room, and my hands tremble. Since when does anyone hide that? Why bother faking it with me? Could I have noticed?

Dixon mutes it and rubs my shoulder. "I know this is a lot to deal with, but can you get him back to the topic at hand?"

I nod and take a slow breath. Time to use Adwin's bizarre state to our advantage. "Your aunt who's trying to kill your cousin… who is she?"

"Ismene. She's only my half-aunt, I guess…"

Adwin retells us the story of Casimir's affair as we mute the call. How can the Director of Montica be Agnar's daughter?

Carista drops her head back to look at the ceiling. "Shit. Obviously Ismene isn't going to side with us over her own father. I knew they were playing both sides."

Unmute. "Adwin, is Ismene going to do anything to keep the Establishment in power?"

"She might hate Grandfather enough to help the rebels, but Nemora and I want her to keep Grandfather in power. Kaycians need a firm hand. They're kind of idiots."

"Adwin!"

"You're kind of an idiot."

Mute. "Okay, do we have enough? I'd really like this to be over."

"He doesn't seem to know what she's going to do," Dixon says. "I guess we've already got *way* more than we could have hoped for." I imagine '*or wanted,*' being silently added to that sentiment.

I hang up the call without a word to Adwin. It doesn't sound like he'll realize I'm gone, or that I was ever there, anyway. What on earth is happening over there?

The four of us sit in awkward silence for a moment. That was more embarrassing than I could have imagined possible, but also far more productive. "I will *kill* anyone who repeats the personal parts of that conversation."

"Don't worry, he called us all idiots." Dixon winks at me.

"So,"—Bram drags the word out as he changes tracks—"we're the only people in Kaycie who know about Agnar. That's something."

"Sure, but what do we do with it?" Carista says.

"Keeping this secret must be very important to him," I say. "Maybe we can blackmail him with it."

"That seems risky and wouldn't be as effective as waking the marshals," Dixon says.

"Yeah,"—Carista bites her lip—"but it's a nice option to have in case things get sticky with him."

"Huge as this is," Bram says, "I don't think it changes our plans. We're still banking on the antidote, right?" We all nod. "Is there anything to do until then?"

"Should we tell your mom about this?" Carista asks Bram.

"All she needs to know is Agnar should not be trusted."

"She's your mom…"

"And she knows all about keeping dangerous information close. What do you think Agnar would do with anyone who finds out? We'd be lucky to be given amnesia."

A shudder runs through me. "Maybe we should take vaccines. I can't lose pieces of my mind again."

Bram squeezes my hand. "That won't happen." At the time I couldn't place it, but he looked miserable when we 'met' last week. I don't doubt for a minute he'd do everything in his power to keep that from happening again.

On impulse, my fingers brush over my neck, but the forget-me-nots aren't there.

"Krisalyn didn't leave anything like that," Carista says.

Bram drums his fingers on his knee. "We should go get some, then. Cary, you want to see the city?"

She scrunches her lips to the side. "No, I'll stay—make sure Aren doesn't do anything stupid."

"Good luck with that," Bram mutters.

I manage a smile. "We'll give you a proper tour of Kaycie in calmer times."

"Thanks. That sounds great."

"So back to the city we go." It feels like just yesterday I was dying to be there. Now I dread going home.

Chapter Fifty-Four

BRAM

As we leave, Carista stops me in the doorway. I nod Serenity and Dixon ahead.

Carista looks grave. "Be careful."

"I'm just popping over there and coming right back. The Establishment won't even know I was there."

"I don't mean with the Establishment." Her gaze slides down the hall... the way Serenity went.

Ugh. "Car..."

"I'm on a very different page than Aren. I think she's great. I get why you like her, and I see how her exterior might lend to you feeling like you need to protect her, but she can take care of herself."

"I know she can." Sort of. It would have been better if I had dragged her out of the EC when everything blew up.

"Good. So, try not to get distracted."

Great, I needed everyone on my back about this. "I'll be back tonight." Walking away from her fills me with a sense of déjà vu—the night Tori and I discussed my feelings for Serenity. *You're getting distracted by worrying about her when there is the bigger picture to think of.* I know they're both right. I can only hope that if we find ourselves in a mess, I can keep my priorities in order.

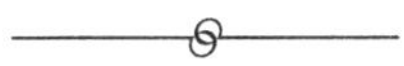

The ride back to Kaycie is quiet. Dixon tinkers with something while I drive. Serenity sleeps in the back seat. Apparently, she hasn't been sleeping well. Once she was out, Dixon said she really doesn't want to be back in the city, but she's desperate enough for amnesia vaccines that she'll do whatever it takes to get them. Everyone would lose their minds if I offered to bring her back to Lawson, but I'm still tossing the idea around in my head. It doesn't matter what everyone else likes, it's about what will help Serenity.

"Honey, we're home." Dixon reaches back to rub her arm when we arrive. She takes hold of his hand with a sleepy smile before blinking herself into awareness. Her expression falls when she sees Dixon. "Sorry to disappoint you," he says.

"Shut up," she mutters.

Dixon makes a call as we get out of the car and tells us Krisalyn is at the Wards' house. A thick blanket of clouds conceals the sun, and the wind whistles around the buildings, chilling our exposed skin. When we arrive, Serenity takes a deep breath before opening the door.

The townhouse is a near duplicate of the one I lived in with Sophos. Krisalyn and Adelle sit in the living room with Grace and Anton. I've seen Serenity run headlong into risky situations, but she's timid as she approaches her family now.

"Good afternoon," she says. "Krisalyn, do you have some amnesia and extirpation vaccines?"

"A few." She hands Serenity two small cases, one yellow one pink, from which Serenity immediately takes vaccines and swallows them. "Why do you need them?"

"We happened across some information," Dixon says. "If Agnar finds out, he won't want us to remember it."

"What information?" Grace asks.

"It's probably better if you don't know," Serenity says.

Anton waves Serenity over, and she sits next to him. "Sweetheart, withholding information to protect each other hasn't worked well thus far. Casimir will assume you've told us anyway, so please, what did you learn?"

He *would* assume they all know if he finds out we know. Planting the seeds to turn the Establishment against him can't hurt, anyway. "Agnar is Montican," I say. "The Director is his daughter."

I'm met with wide eyes and stunned silence.

Adelle opens and closes her mouth a couple of times before saying, "Are you sure?"

"Pretty sure." Dixon meets Serenity's gaze with a sympathetic smile.

Grace turns to Adelle. "How much would he have to forge to—"

"A lot." Adelle rubs her temple. "I don't even want to think about how many people he bought off to get in like this. The Establishment has had its disagreements, but *this*... The Establishment would crumble in on itself even without the antidote."

Anton nods. "Yes, but a clash would probably result in leaving the power in the hands of Agnar, Martel, and Kemp. They have too many resources."

"Not if they lose the marshals," Grace says with a glance at Krisalyn.

"Is that looking good?" I ask.

Krisalyn steeples her fingers. "I think Aldan Foster was successful—or at least very close, before he was killed."

"Killed?" I say. "His death was an accident. He poisoned himself trying to create the antidote."

"I don't think it was an accident. His formulas don't add up to how he died."

I sink into a chair as my mind reels. Someone killed him to stop the antidote. They all had the motive, I guess. Waking the marshals would shatter the whole system like we plan to do. And making it look like the research was dangerous would deter others from trying. His death is the reason Adelle and Sophos didn't want to attempt an antidote.

"You have his formula then?" I ask.

"Yes. Jase is getting the last one made now. We'll have to test it and see if it needs to be tweaked."

I thought we'd have to wait for Krisalyn to develop it, but she only had to find it. It didn't feel like we'd have enough time, but… "Can I wait and bring some back with me?" Carista would kill me if I came home empty handed when there was a chance to get it.

"I can't make any promises," Krisalyn says, wringing her hair.

"I'm not in a hurry."

Dixon, Krisalyn, and I head out, leaving Serenity to catch up with her parents. Krisalyn gives me a new cuff, taking my old one and snapping it in half before throwing it out. "We suspected you'd be back," she says. "Frey got you a fake ID, just in case. Congratulations, you're Kaycian now."

"Are you *trying* to pick a fight?"

She grins at me, and we continue to the EC. I get off at the tenth floor with Dixon, leaving Krisalyn to go up to the health department. She brings up the devices Dixon fashioned in Lawson. Bombs for large areas, grenades that could gas a room, marble-like spheres to treat two or three people at a time, and darts that we can fire from a gun. There's a good chance the next time I shoot a marshal, it won't be to kill. It doesn't get much better than that.

Dixon and I enter a workshop to find Vogue sitting cross-legged on the floor, flipping through holoScreens, and Frey sitting at a computer terminal.

"Dixon! Thank God you're back." Vogue closes the screen and pops up from the floor.

"You don't care that I'm here?" I say.

"*You* added to my headaches by kidnapping Serenity."

"I did *not*—"

"Don't bother. The drama has passed."

"Not really by Serenity's choice," Dixon points out.

Vogue groans and rolls her eyes. "Whatever. She's back. It'll all be fine soon." Vogue's position in all of this has to be making her crazier than she is naturally. She was angry at Jase, but he's like a brother to Krisalyn. Serenity and Jase breaking up would be pretty inconvenient for them.

"Anyway, Bram," she says, "you can't help me crack this literal egg, so yes, I'm more excited to see Dixon."

"Turns out Montica is pretty anxious to get this back," he says.

"That makes me want to understand it even more." The two of them get to work, tinkering with the accumulator.

"I'm out of here," Frey says. "Good luck with your alien technology."

"You're not going to help them?" I ask.

"That's not my area of expertise, and unlike Vogue, I prefer to be the best at one or two things rather than trying to master *everything*."

Vogue scowls at him. "You're just jealous because you aren't capable of mastering everything."

"That's it. You caught me." He puts his hands up in mock surrender. "It's getting late, don't kill yourselves over this thing."

Frey leaves, and Dixon turns to Vogue. "He's right. This isn't the highest priority. It can wait until tomorrow."

"Easy for you to say! This thing hasn't thwarted you all week."

"Have you ever met a puzzle you couldn't solve?" I ask.

"No. And I will not let this stupid thing be the first."

There's a knock on the door, and Krisalyn peeks in. "Hey, I'm out of here. We think we'll get it done tomorrow."

"See?" Dixon says. "Reasonable people know they can continue tomorrow." Vogue rakes her fingers through her hair and grumbles curses.

"Come on," Krisalyn says, pulling Vogue from her chair. "A good night's sleep might be just the thing you need to figure this out." She turns to me. "Do you want to stay at my apartment again?"

"That would be great, thanks."

She opens a holo from her cuff to give my new identity access. "All set. I'll be back here tomorrow, hopefully with goodies to bring back to Lawson."

Once we go our separate ways, I call my mom to tell her I'll be gone overnight.

Chapter Fifty-Five

ADWIN

A sound jolts me out of sleep and into that confusing moment of trying to place myself. Except today it's more than a fleeting instant. Why am I outside?

"Adwin!" Priam slinks through the trees, quiet as a whisper. He must have already been calling me—his voice the sound that woke me. "What are you doing out here?"

"I'm not sure, actually." I stand and stretch my back. It's sore from leaning against a tree trunk.

"Did you see Clover?"

"No, why?"

"There's a warrant out for her arrest. They tried to seize her, but she fled."

Arrest Clover? My stomach drops. Am I already too late to stop her from doing something crazy? "What has she done?"

"Nothing... yet. Nemora and Mother seem to believe she was planning something though."

"Like what?"

"*I* don't know." He says each word slowly, eyes boring into me.

Well, there's already a warrant out for her arrest, and she's already gone, so what damage could it do? "I don't know *what* she's planning, either. I only know she ran out of patience with Ismene. She told me things were going to get messy around here and that I should get out."

Priam's eyes flash. He isn't surprised, but I'm not sure what his feeling on the matter is. "Why didn't you tell me when I asked you about her before?"

"She didn't tell you, so I had to assume she didn't want you to know." I scarcely avoid saying *she didn't trust you*. That's a wedge I don't want to shove between them, though I'm sure he's figured it out himself.

He leans against a tree, scratching his forehead. "Well, she trusted you enough." He shakes his head. "She'll be hard to find."

"Can't we track her? Can't your mother?"

"She cut out her chip. Left the bloody little gift in the armory as her kiss goodbye." My face contorts in disgust, but Priam only chuckles. "It's not even the first time she's removed one."

I rub the little lump behind my ear, imagining taking a knife to the spot. My stomach reels. He says she'll be hard to find, but for me she was hard to find even *with* tracking. There isn't anywhere she can't go. It won't be *hard*—it'll be impossible. And what happens if we find her? We can't hand her over to the aunt who already made an attempt on her life. Maybe she's better off in the wild. She'll be free like she's always wanted. Except... she won't stay hidden forever.

"Her chip was in the armory?"

Priam nods.

"What did she take?"

The sun is low by the time we set out, making the autumn-tinged landscape glow red, orange, and yellow. The chill only bites at my face. Second-skin keeps the rest of my body as comfortable as a spring day—in temperature, anyway. Regulating my breathing, heart rate, and nausea is up to me. A task I'm not really up for as we fly over the treetops. My grip on the armrest of this deathtrap must give me away.

"You okay?" Priam looks at me with a mixture of concern and amusement.

"Please keep your focus on *not crashing*."

"It really doesn't require my full attention."

I'd beg to differ, but my stomach contents might come out instead of words. This elongated egg looking thing has no business zipping through the air. Big hoverPlanes I can handle, but this feels fragile, like a gust of wind could send us tumbling at any moment. Someone probably thought the sides and arching roof being glass from front to back was a brilliant design, offering panoramic views. I hate that person. I don't need to see how close the trees are, or the rock faces we could crash into. The only thing that makes it tolerable is the window cracked open, hitting me with a frosty stream of air.

"We'll slow down as soon as we're past the dome," Priam says. "I'm sure you'll be fine then."

Again, I keep my doubts to myself. I can't imagine being fine in this. When the silvery sheen of the dome looms ahead, Priam slows the avillipse and brings us down to hover inches over the ground. With some taps on the control panel, an arch rises in the shield, giving us a way out. We glide through and I turn to see it close behind us. I try to feel the difference Clover does between being in or out of the dome, but it's the same to me.

If Clover isn't out of the dome already, she will be soon. We assume she planned to collect her tree-walkers first based on her theft of darkComms—communication devices they'll be able to use on a closed network without anyone being able to track them or listen in. We assume she needs time to prepare whatever she's got planned based on her theft of EMPs. Using those would knock out all of her own tech too, so it'll take her some time to contrive a work around—too long to stay within the dome where it would be easier to find her. We go out on the southern edge, because Clover won't be prepared for an extended stay in the north with winter approaching.

These are ideas Ismene could deduce, but it's what Clover took from her own suite that makes Priam the only person capable of finding her. Only Priam knows the eCloak exists. It's what will hide her from Ismene's agents, but Priam knows how to find it.

"She thought she was so damn clever when she created it," Priam says. "It was the ultimate cheat for hide-and-seek, but I found a way around it."

"How old was she when she made it?"

"Thirteen."

Wow. "So, she is as smart as Rocco hoped her to be with her given name."

"Absolutely. She just doesn't use it the way the family would prefer." Another reason for them to be afraid of her.

We rise back over the treetops, but instead of darting off, we hover in place. It is actually much easier to stomach. Priam opens a holoMap with a grid over it, then drops an orb the size of my fist out of the window. I lean out of mine to see it explode into a snow flurry. Priam explains that each little piece transmits an electronic signal, which he monitors on his screen. When some fall into Clover's eCloak, they'll disappear from his monitor, and we'll know where she is.

"It's slow going, but we'll find her, eventually."

"And then what? We can't give her to your mother. Ismene already tried to kill her once." We disabled our own commChips so we don't lead them to Clover, thanks to Priam adjusting my permissions.

"In all fairness to my mother, executing Clover would be very different from having Clover die in an '*accident.*' Clover wouldn't be hurt if she were arrested." Priam flies us to another square on the grid and releases another orb.

"How comforting. But what do we do with Clover when we find her?"

"Find out how we can help her." He says this like it's the most obvious thing on earth. "I told you she's right about the whole thing. I wouldn't have chosen to go about changing things in this way, but now that the wheels are in motion, I can't leave her to do it all on her own."

I chew my lip to keep words from spilling out. Nothing I say will convince him, and I don't need him to think I'm against him. Why don't they see they're just going to create chaos? Kaycie should be a shining example of why *not* to have a coup. Instead, they sprint headlong to follow in the misguided footsteps of Kaycie's rebels.

Even if it were only for Montica—my ancestral home —I might feel this pull, but I also need Montica's stability to help regain control over Kaycie. My mother already lost this home, she can't lose her new one too.

For her and for peace in both nations, I have to betray my cousins.

Chapter Fifty-Six
SERENITY

Papá rubs my shoulder as my mother walks Adelle out. His presence has always been a comfort, but being back is a struggle. "I'm glad to have you home. How was your time in Lawson?"

"It was a nice escape." There we go. That sounds more like a vacation than a cowardly avoidance of my troubles.

"Well-earned."

If you say so.

"You amaze me." My mother sits adjacent to me with stars in her eyes. "Do you realize how much you've already accomplished?"

Is success supposed to feel so miserable? "It isn't really my doing. I just keep being put in strange circumstances which somehow result in *some* progress."

"Everyone has difficult circumstances thrown at them from time to time. It's what we do with them that defines us."

Without her voicing it, I still hear, *Irrigated vines make bland wines.* Now I wonder if the vines resent the winemaker.

"Is there anything we can help you with?" my father asks. Of course, he'd be the one to offer water.

In words, my conflict sounds absurd. I'm broken because I miss Jase. So, the obvious solution is to go back to him. He's mine for the taking. All I have to do is say the word. But he's the one who broke me. Can he be the cut, the blood, and the bandage? I squeeze my hands into fists to keep my fingers still, but that doesn't silence the music in my head—the notes I gave Jase along with a piece of my soul. Or was it a piece of my lung? Because breathing is a struggle.

"No, I'm fine." My lie isn't convincing.

"Jase worried about you leaving him when you remembered." Of course, my mother knows without me saying it. "I was sure the two of you would pull through, though."

"You didn't care when Adwin and I broke up. Why do you care about this one?"

"Adwin restrained you. You were content with mediocre when you were with him. Jase didn't make you want more—you got there yourself—but he encouraged it."

"Until he pulled it out from under my feet."

"Serenity, he knew he could undo it. We didn't think it would take so long, but—"

"I don't care!" How utterly stupid of me to be disappointed when my parents didn't care about my last break up. This is far worse. Papá is tight-lipped on it, but my mother is always the more difficult one to fight against.

"He didn't want you to suffer through the truth serum too!"

My jaw drops. "Too?"

"Grace," my father sighs, "that was Jase's story to tell, if he chose to."

"He took the truth serum?"

"Yes, that's why he was ill at the beginning of our stay in Leavenworth." My mother's jaw tightens. "It proved there was no reason to question you further."

That deflates my argument a little, but it really doesn't change anything. "I'd have preferred that to amnesia, though. He *knew* it wasn't what I'd choose. He had no right to make the choice for me." The words aren't as powerful as they would have been.

"I know." Defeat weighs my father's expression. "Too many choices have been taken from you. Obviously, we don't always know what's best for you. You should be in control of your own life."

"Thank you."

"But... it goes the other way as well. Don't make choices for us we wouldn't want. You thought the Establishment was a direct threat to us all, and you came anyway. You should know we'd never want you to put yourself in harm's way for our sake." His concern softens me. "Please, never do that again."

"Hopefully there won't be any more opportunities."

On my way home, I trace the parallels in my mind. I made decisions my parents wouldn't have approved of for their sakes, *but* those only put me at risk, not them. Jase's bad decision hurt *me* for my sake. Both of us, I suppose.

Why didn't he tell me about the truth serum? Even if I don't like it, I understand his desire to protect me. As we were evacuating that night, didn't I wish there was anything I could do to get Jase out of the situation?

Maybe we can try to get past it. What we had is worth the effort.

Third time's a charm, right? I call him, but he doesn't answer. Tomorrow then.

Snowflake jumps at my knees while I hang up my coat. In the living room, I find Frey. "Oh, to what do I owe the pleasure?"

"You're kind of a jerk, you know?"

That was unexpected. "What did I do?" I sit against the other armrest of the sofa he occupies.

"After you 'woke up,' you reunited with Bram, Vogue, and Krisalyn. You went out of town with Dixon, but I still hadn't even seen you."

Awe! I suppose I should feel guilty for slighting him, but I'm too touched that he cares. "I'm sorry. Things were a little crazy. I did miss you."

"Sure," he says with an eye roll.

I give his hand a squeeze. "Am I the first platonic friendship you've ever had with a heterosexual woman?"

"Of course not." He feigns offense. "There's... oh, no, that one night. But Pen—eh, well holidays shouldn't count."

I laugh to myself. "Exactly."

"Are you offended? Feeling left out? Want to join the ranks?" He bobs his eyebrows at me in mock seduction.

"Not at all. I consider it a place of high honor."

"Well, hopefully the band doesn't break up, because then there's no point in you ruining my perfect record."

The elevator opens and chatter floats in as Vogue and Krisalyn come in.

"Don't worry, I think we're all stuck with each other," I say.

Vogue sweeps in and plops down onto my lap, knocking the wind out of me. "Serenity, don't go running off like that again!"

"I won't." I look over her at Krisalyn who is shaking her head in a motherly way. "How much has she had to drink?"

"Enough. Not being able to figure out the Montican toy is too much to deal with, apparently. She had more wine than food at dinner."

"I don't *ever* want to go to Montica," Vogue says. "They're smarter than me, and I enjoy being the smartest person in the room." Her pout is *so* dramatic.

Frey smirks. "Since we've been friends, you're rarely the smartest person in the room."

"I'm smarter than you, Frey Dempsey!"

I pet her arm. "You're very smart, and so pretty." Drunk-Vogue loves compliments.

"Oh my God, do you think Monticans are prettier too?"

"Not even possible."

Krisalyn rolls her eyes and takes Vogue's hand to pull her off me. "Let's get to bed and take some aspirin."

"I love you," Vogue says as she submits to Krisalyn's wishes.

"I love you too. Now come on."

Vogue squeezes my hand before she goes. "I love *you* too."

"I know. I love you too. Goodnight."

"Frey's okay," she mutters as she shuffles out. "I don't *hate* him."

"I guess you're right," Frey says when we're alone. "We're probably stuck with each other."

Chapter Fifty-Seven

BRAM

"Bram, are you still in Kaycie?" Mom says when she answers.

Carista told her then. "Yes. I'm coming back tomorrow."

"I need you to bring the device."

There is no way I'm giving Montica anything now that I know Agnar is one of them. "No. We don't need them. Krisalyn may have the antidote ready any time now."

"Any time, is not enough. Time is not a luxury we have. I'm really feeling the pressure from all sides." Her voice drops to a whisper. "Agnar was here today."

"What?"

"He brought Emrys back." Her voice regains its strength when she says, "Anyway, it means he's desperate to stop us, so we can't wait around for a long shot."

"It's not a long shot. Foster may have developed the antidote before he died. She only has to recreate it." Emrys is there. He's home and we could get him back.

"Tomorrow. End of day tomorrow, I will go get the damn thing myself if this isn't going anywhere."

"Mom, Montica is playing both sides."

"They're our only chance."

I groan. "Is Cary there?"

"Yes, she just came to find me. She wants to speak to you. Hold on."

After some background mumbling, Carista comes through. "Bram?"

"Cary, what the hell?"

"So, you know about Agnar showing up with Emrys then?" The sound of the door shutting accompanies her question.

"Yes!"

"Yeah. This is insane. I feel like we need to tell your mom about Agnar."

"There isn't anything she can do with that information, though."

"She could drop the allying with Montica idea. As much as I hate to burst her bubble, it would be helpful if she saw the antidote as the only option."

"I guess. I mean, I told her Montica is playing both sides, I just didn't elaborate."

"Well, tomorrow probably doesn't give Krisalyn enough time, right?"

"It might, actually. She thinks an antidote was already created and she just needs to replicate it."

"Wow. That's incredible!"

"Yeah. How is everyone taking Emrys' return?"

"As well as they can. Libby is a little freaked out. I told her I'd stay with her tonight."

"Thanks, Car."

"I'm pretty used to being the one here for your family." She gasps. "Oh my gosh, I didn't mean to—"

"It's okay." She's absolutely right. She has been the one there for them. "If Aren said that, it would be an attack. You're fine. If you think Mom needs to know, go ahead. I'll be back as soon as I can. Hopefully,

I'll have so much good news everyone will forget how absent I've been."

"Bram, you haven't—"

"It's fine. Thanks again."

"Okay."

I tap my cuff to end the call.

Chapter Fifty-Eight

EMRYS

Carista takes the call outside. Mom looks at me and her face crumples, so she turns away. She's avoided looking at me today. Libby, on the other hand, couldn't stop staring at me. Mom stopped her like it was rude or something, but I was soaking it up. To have anyone look at me like I'm remotely interesting or like I matter... there aren't words for it after all this time. They had locked me away in this pocket of my mind so long I wondered if I was going to lose *it* too. Seemed like it was only a matter of time until my consciousness faded entirely. Would that qualify as dying of boredom?

Then Bram saw me a while back. Really saw me. I don't know how it's possible. He shouldn't have been able to show recognition or say my name. But he did. He looked devastated to see me, but I was beyond thrilled. He knew me. Which meant he was different. He's not locked away in himself like I am. I don't understand how, but that's amazing. And his recognition jump started me.

I started paying attention again. Not that anything interesting happened for a while. It was the same old thing until we all got sent to Leavenworth—which was exciting for a minute but quickly became more of the same in a different place. Then today the unthinkable happened. Agnar pulled me and brought me home. I never thought I'd be here again.

Clearly, he's using me as a pawn to manipulate Mom, but it's hard to care about that. I have a baby sister. Even if I just watch her from the sidelines like this, it's more of a life than I ever thought I'd get to have. She's in bed now, but the rest of the family is riled up. Mom is at the end of her rope, but I'm so proud of her for starting all of this. A lot of kids think their parents are heroes, but mine actually is.

I don't know what they're talking about, but as Cary comes back in, Mom tells Aren to plan on going to the city tomorrow.

"Kolina,"—Cary's voice is pleading—"Bram told you Montica is playing both sides. And Krisalyn really might pull this off. How can you give up on that option? On them?" She gestures to me.

Poor Cary. What hope is she holding onto for me or any of the rest of us?

Mom's jaw clenches. "I can't base this on emotion. That's exactly what Agnar expects, and I won't give it to him." Good.

"You're right. He thinks you'll act with your heart instead of your head, and he *thinks* that will be your downfall, but he's wrong. It's actually the only way you can win. He holds *all* the other cards. Montica is in his pocket."

"We don't know that," Sophos says.

"Yes we do. He *is* Montican. The Director is his *daughter.*"

What?

"Kill them all."

I've never heard another voice *in my head* before. Commands come from some unknown source within me—part of my mind I can't access, like the rest of my body. But this voice is unfamiliar. It growls the words, and my body reacts instantaneously.

Oh, God.

I tackle Cary to the floor before she even sees me coming. Her face reddens quickly as my hands squeeze her neck. *Why?!* Aren launches himself at me and we get tangled together in a fight. I wish he was stronger. I wish my skills in a fight didn't exceed his. But they do. *I'm so sorry, Aren.* All I can do is watch helplessly as my fist cracks into his jaw. His elbow strikes my chest, but I don't feel it. More than I've ever wanted to feel *anything* in these years trapped in my own body, I wish I could feel pain right now. I should experience every injury thrown at me for what I'm doing. Sophos makes pathetic attempts to pull us apart, getting knocked down in the process.

Where's Mom?

She rushes into the room and fires a shot into the ceiling. "Enough!"

I stop and stand to face my mother. The gun shakes in her hands, but she keeps it pointed at me as I walk slowly toward her.

Aren grunts behind me. "Mom!"

Tears streak Mom's face—she can't do a damn useful thing with that gun if the enemy is her own son.

"Shoot him!" my brother says, and I couldn't agree more.

Yes! Please. Please, shoot me. Shoot me!

She won't.

I wrench Mom's arm—taking the gun and dropping her to her knee. *Stop!* I plead to whoever it is making this happen.

She looks past me. "Don't hurt him!"

NO! I writhe, trying harder than I ever have to sense the nerves that control this useless fucking body. But there's no connection. I can't do anything. A high-pitched scream comes from the hallway. My finger pulls the trigger. Mom's head jerks back from the impact before she drops to the floor.

Blood pools around her. The same blood that runs through my veins. Mine should be spilled. Not hers! I'm already dead in almost every way. Why is this happening? If I cut my hand off, I wouldn't feel a thing, but this image burned into my brain is the most excruciating thing I've ever known. Even without nerves, this is more pain than I can handle.

My body is unfazed, though. I swing the gun toward the sound from the hallway. *Libby.*

No no no no no no!

Sophos flies at me, knocking the gun out of my hand. *Thank God.* While I knock Sophos unconscious, Carista snatches the gun and skids into the hallway. She scoops Libby into her room and shuts the door.

Aren sneers at me with fire in his eyes. Maybe his fury will power him enough to kill me. *Please just kill me.* He doesn't get the chance, though. The commotion has drawn the neighbors.

I scan the room, count the people streaming in, hear more voices coming.

Too outnumbered. Even for a killing machine.

But the crowd doesn't seize me. They stare in shock at the sight in front of them—gaping at the body which was my mom. Not understanding what's happened here anymore than I do. To them, I'm Kolina's third son. They don't know I'm the monster who just destroyed this family, so they don't stop me from walking right out the back door.

My legs move of their own accord—or that of someone else. I sink back into the little pocket of my mind left to me. Why can't I be as gone as everyone thinks? Why keep my senses of sight and hearing only to see Mom die and hear the gunshot *I* fired?

I killed her. She's dead, and I did it.

Somehow, even without being able to feel my body, it seems like I could throw up or sob. But all my body does is march across the dry seafloor.

I'm so sorry, Mom. I wish it was me instead.

Chapter Fifty-Nine
ADWIN

Clouds glow in fiery shades as the first rays of sunlight stretch over the horizon. Priam sleeps while I take my turn at the controls. I was hesitant, but it's all automated. All I have to do is tap the next square on the grid, drop an orb when we stop, and watch the screen for lost signals. The stash of orbs is running low. If we don't find Clover soon, we'll have to head back and try again another time.

Hours of solitary silence softened the guilt I feel about what I have to do. Clover and Priam are my family but not any more so than the rest of them. Even if they *were* the only ones willing to accept me at first. They'll be protected from their own stupidity if they get locked up. As immediate members of the governing family, Ismene will probably confine them to their suites. A slap on the wrists and systems access revoked—they'll be fine.

I'm the one who should be angry with *them.* Clover and Priam got to live their entire lives knowing they were important. Born to be leaders and innovators. Knowing who and what their family was, and their claim on their country. All to grow up and choose to throw it all away?

It's a slap in the face for me, who grew up only knowing a numb mother, a frivolous father, and a fluffy city. A city in which, even among idiots, I was no one of consequence. Getting my own apartment when I turned sixteen was even more of a gift than I had expected. When my grandfather showed up at my door to open my eyes, I cared little about the world being more than what it appeared. I was interested in my change of fate—in being more than what I had appeared to be.

My eyelids are heavy from only a few hours sleep in the avillipse, so I don't immediately believe what I see. One, no two, of the signals flip to red and show *Not found*. Three now. I shake Priam's shoulder to wake him.

"What?" He rubs his eyes.

"We might have found her."

He springs to attention, leaning toward the screen. "Really?"

"Did you doubt we would?"

"No, it's just a lot of ground to cover."

The last locations of the missing transmitters display on the map. Priam maneuvers us as close as he can, but it's densely wooded. *Big surprise.*

"Ready to earn back your tree-walker status?"

A silent laugh puffs out of my nose. "As in the ability to walk in the trees or the rebel group?"

"Both, I guess." He pulls his gloves on and steps out into the woods.

This makes the forest outside Breck Fortress look like one of Kaycie's manicured parks. Gnarled trees, boulders, and dense vegetation suggest Clover was never hoping for visitors. Not that I expected her to make this easy. A series of quick chirps startles me. Priam tenses next to me but remains silent. Instead, he puts his hand out to stop me, listening intently. His eyes sweep the area and narrow in a direction where I still don't see anything.

"You didn't even say 'ready or not, here I come.'" Clover materializes out of nowhere, walking up to us as if it's perfectly natural to run into each other here.

Priam hugs her. "You went beyond the boundaries of the game. All rules are null and void."

When she pulls back, Clover looks at me sadly. "What are you two doing here?"

"Well, you left without saying goodbye," I say.

"I was pressed for time. Terribly sorry. I hope you aren't going to try to bring me home."

"Would I attempt anything I can't accomplish?" Priam replies.

"No." Clover smiles. "So, why are you here?" She glances back and forth between the two of us. I wonder which one of us she trusts less.

"You know I've always been on your side," Priam says. "I want to help you."

She chews her lip and looks at me. I haven't always been on her side, and she knows it.

"Ismene may have been trying to kill you, but she almost killed me," I say. "I'm sorry it took that to see your point, but I do now. This is your world, your home, your family. I'm only a visitor, so I can't claim to understand the issues at hand the way you do. I trust *you*, so I'll trust your judgement."

"So, are you going to invite us in?" Priam asks.

"In where?" she replies.

"To wherever the rest of them are."

"The rest of *who*?" Clover sighs the word with perfect innocence and indifference.

Priam chuckles. "Your lookout made a tanager call. They've migrated out for the season."

"Intentional, so we know it's her. You're the only other person who would know that."

"There are plenty of things only I would know, for which you should be grateful. It's the reason *we're* here instead of armed agents ready to arrest you. So, again, are you going to invite us in?"

She bristles and waves her arm out with a shallow bow. "Right this way."

Priam flashes a self-satisfied smile as we follow Clover. To no one's surprise, she leads us in a vertical path up into the treetops. I keep my focus on where my hands and feet need to land—my fall fresh in my mind, though I know I'm safe with the boots and gloves this time. Up, down, and sideways we go. It isn't until my cousins stop that I look up and see where we're going. A large treehouse sits tucked behind a golden curtain of a weeping willow.

"How did you..."

"I *am* civilized," Clover says. "I know you think I'm part squirrel, but I do like having the option of a roof over my head."

Inside, three people sit on the floor around a short round table, a bear of a young man stands in the kitchen, watching us with suspicious intensity, and a tiny girl reclines up on a loft. She looks like she's fourteen, and is she petting a fox?

"Clover, what are you doing pulling *children* into this?" I tilt my head toward the loft.

"I'm sixteen, thank you *very* much," the small girl says.

Clover grins. "And Misty is not being pulled into anything dangerous. She's a fantastic lookout—like a ghost out there."

"She's left her post," Priam points out.

"Well, if we're going to let people walk in, I guess we don't much need a lookout." The hulking figure from the kitchen glowers at Priam and me.

"Please, Knox," Clover says. "They're fine."

"They're Agnars. I'm not terribly worried about the little Kaycian, but Priam is second in line for Director."

He should perhaps be more concerned with the *little Kaycian*.

"And *I'm* fourth," Clover reminds him. "Yet you trust me."

"Only as far as I can throw you."

"Which is probably quite far,"—she gives one of his large biceps a squeeze—"so I'll take that as a compliment."

Knox rolls his eyes before stalking out. Creaking sounds above us indicate he went to the roof. With his size, it's impressive that we don't hear thunderous clunks. The gear is incredible.

"This is your army?" Priam asks. "Six of you against the world?"

"I don't need an *army*. There are many things that a small, specialized group of people can do, that an army cannot." Clover gestures to the three at the table. "We can change the tide without brute force."

"How can I help?" Priam asks. "What do you need? I can go back to the Breck to help from the inside."

It's now or never. *Reconnect.* A shiver runs up my spine, but I have no choice. *Call Nemora.*

"Adwin, where the hell—" Nemora's voice is in my head, but she stops short to listen to the surrounding conversation.

"It certainly wouldn't hurt to have eyes and ears in the fortress now that I'm out," Clover says. "When we're ready, having someone to let us in would be helpful too."

"Of course," Priam says. "Whatever you need, but how would we keep in contact?"

A low snarl sounds in my head from Nemora at the sound of her brother's voice. My heart rate doubles.

"I have some fortress staff in my pocket. I can get messages to you. For now, it would be enough to keep them off my trail." Clover hasn't decided how far she can trust us yet. She doesn't want to show all her cards. Probably for the best. I don't want to get her into too much trouble.

"Where are you?" Nemora asks.

Send coordinates to Nemora.

After a moment's pause in which I have no doubt she is dispatching a team to intercept us, she says, *"Keep her talking. Get more."*

I swallow hard. Isn't she already incriminated enough? "Then what?"

Clover scrutinizes me. "Adwin, I know you're worried about us going the way of Kaycie, but I'm trying to do it with as little violence as possible. I only want to seize Ismene and my father, have them tried for their violations against our people's freedoms so they're forced to step down. Hopefully, they cooperate and can remain here, but if not, they'd be exiled. Having to go live in Casimir's world would be a punishment worse than death for Ismene."

"Would it, though?" Priam asks. "If anyone is even brave enough to find her guilty, do you really think we can trust her to be out there? She'd devote herself to taking back Montica."

"What do you suggest then?" Clover crosses her arms. "Let her rot in a cell?"

"No, she could garner sympathy from anywhere. Her very existence is a threat to freedom in Montica."

Nemora's gasp in my head echoes my own quick breath.

"She tried to kill you, Clover," Priam continues. "She can't be left alive."

Hang up! It's too late, though. My heart twists into a knot. An assassination plot is going to get them much worse than house arrest. That's much further than I thought either of them would go.

What did I just sentence them to by letting Nemora hear that?

Clover squares her shoulders to Priam. "I don't want us to turn into her."

"Get out." My voice is low, but it pulls both of their gazes to me.

"Why?" Clover asks.

"We've got company!" Knox's voice booms from outside.

Clover's eyes flash wide at me. "What did you do?"

Loud thuds rock the roof, followed by grunts and shouts indicative of a struggle. Clover points up at Misty in the loft. "Disappear," she orders. "Juniper and Willow split up. Aspen with me. Priam?"

"I guess acting like I'm on their side isn't an option anymore." His glower gives the impression he's ready to tear my throat out.

"I'm so—" His fist slams into my jaw, cutting off the useless explanation I don't have time for. I roll over the low table on my way to the floor. The taste of blood rushes over my tongue as I lay a cold hand on what is bound to become an impressive bruise.

"Bigger fish to fry," Clover says to him, avoiding my eyes. "Time to go." She throws a bag over one shoulder and tosses a cube at the ceiling where it sticks in the middle of the room. "Ladies, come out fifteen seconds after me. Adwin, you have thirty seconds to get out."

Clover leaps from a window, followed by Priam and Aspen. A thunderous rumble rolls through me. A scream slices through the chaos. Grunts and groans are echoes by sounds of branches hitting a falling body—sounds all too familiar to me. Someone bursts through the door in the green and white pattern of Montican soldiers as the two remaining tree-walkers escape through other hatches. Has it already been fifteen seconds? That means there's only fifteen seconds left.

The soldier points a gun at me but lowers it. "Lebeau?"

"Yes. I think this place is about to blow."

He gestures me to follow, and we spring from the door to the next tree over. As I jump to the next tree, the house erupts in flames, blasting my back with heat. I press my back against the tree trunk to watch as tree-walkers zip through the air like phantoms in the firelight, shooting strange guns at soldiers. Knox struggles against the three soldiers restraining him. They secure him to a tree for safe measure. His veins bulge as he pulls away from it, and the possibility of the tree uprooting flashes through my mind.

Aspen sits next to him, still as stone.

A soldier chases one of the other girls until Clover swings down, kicking him off a tree branch. He lands on his feet to shoot thunder back at Clover, but she leaps out of the way. The blast throws the girl, though. She yelps as she falls. I don't see where she lands.

Below, Priam and Nemora go at it hand-to-hand. He has strength on his side, but she is faster and exacting. She dodges his punches and gets in sharp hits with her knees and elbows. A soldier tries to get in to help her, but she waves him off. When she knocks Priam to his back, she drops her knee down onto his stomach and wraps a hand around his throat. "I'm in your way, too. Would you kill me next?"

"Can evil die?" he says through gritted teeth. He puts up little more fight as Nemora gestures to the soldiers to come in to restrain him.

"Stop!"

I whip around at Clover's shout and see her standing between a soldier and the other girl. She drops a weapon and holds her hands up. "It's okay, June," she says over her shoulder. "It's over."

The girl drops a weapon and pants heavily. Soldiers move in to restrain her and Clover. Two more carry the fallen tree-walker over to where the rest of the prisoners sit together. Is she unconscious or dead?

I descend to the ground.

"Is this everyone?" an officer asks.

"Yes," Clover says.

I glance around to take a mental inventory—Clover and Priam, Knox, Willow, Juniper, and Aspen. Misty is missing. I guess she disappeared as commanded.

The officer turns to me. "Is this everyone you saw here?"

Clover looks at me with a blank expression. Knox stares daggers at me. Misty could pass for his sister. I don't need him—any of them—to hate me more than they already do. And does it matter if the youngest tree-walker gets away?

"Yes, this is all of them," I say.

Nemora appears next to me and places a hand on my shoulder. "Thank you, Adwin. Truly." I don't have to look at the prisoners to feel their hateful stares on me. "I suppose I jumped the gun when I drugged you to get information about Clover's activities."

"You what?" My gaze jumps from Nemora to Clover. The latter closes her eyes and leans her head against the tree behind her.

"You bitch!" Priam tries to shoulder forward against his captors to no avail.

"*Someone* has to protect this family! You two will be the death of us all." Nemora turns to me. "I really am eternally grateful, and very sorry for my prior interrogation methods. You'd do the right thing, anyway."

The right thing. Is that what I'm doing?

Chapter Sixty

SERENITY

Krisalyn returns from Vogue's bedroom with a satisfied smile. Snowflake is the alarm clock of choice. Moans come from behind her. "That should do it," Krisalyn says. She sits next to me on the sofa as I sip my tea. "How are you doing this morning?"

"I'm hopeful." The tea works its soothing magic through me. "I want to talk to Jase, but he didn't answer me last night. Does he hate me for disappearing like I did?"

"Oh, no. Of course not. He was at Aurora's last night. Maybe try her if you can't get a hold of him?"

"Thanks." My fingers tap out a melody on my teacup.

"Everything okay?"

I sigh into the cup, sending a wave of aromatic steam back at myself. "Do you ever feel like if you put something off too long, you've missed the window? I was so stubborn and wouldn't face him, and now I'm going to be approaching him from this embarrassed place. And it's like the third time I have to do that. The first time Lanelle ruined—"

"Ugh, I heard."

"Then I sucked it up and got us back on track before I got my memories back, and now I have to do it again. It's such a hard conversation to start over and over again."

"It's Jase, though. You know he judges himself for all of this. Not you. You have nothing to be embarrassed about."

"Easier said than done." I shrug. "Where are you with the antidote?"

"We could have snagged a marshal to test it last night, but I didn't want to end up with a half-awake, confused marshal at that hour. Or at least, that's the excuse we used. I'm so nervous about it. If this doesn't work..." Thinking less of ourselves than others do is a common practice around here.

"I have faith in you."

Vogue comes shuffling out, coffee in hand, and eyes me suspiciously. "Tea? I'm glad to see your spirits are up. Did Jase sneak out already, or is he still in your bed?"

I roll my eyes. "If you hadn't been so drunk, you might recall Jase wasn't even here last night."

"Oh, that's right." She gasps. "Frey was here. Oh God, please don't tell me you're in good spirits because you slept with Frey! I'm already teetering on the edge of nausea."

Laughter erupts from me. "Please finish the coffee so your brain can join us today."

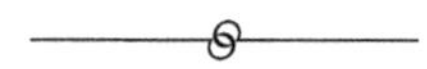

There's no real reason for me to go to the EC with Vogue and Krisalyn. I claim it's only to keep busy, but it's to see Jase who I still haven't heard from. As much as I'd love to look like a stalker, I did not resort to calling his mother to try to find him. Yet. Walking into this building makes my stomach flip. The hole where Bram and Tori blew up

Kemp's office is boarded up— an unnecessary reminder of the night the uprising ensued. I remember it all too well now.

I go with Vogue to the technology department, rather than tagging along with Krisalyn. Since Jase hasn't returned my calls, I don't want to show up at his office yet. Dixon and Frey are already here, and the three of them get to work trying to coax anything out of the accumulator. I check my cuff constantly, as if I could have missed a call or message. To keep from wearing a hole in my shoes pacing, I sit and pop a pod into my ear to listen to music while I scroll mindlessly through the buzzChains.

Oh, I can't believe I thought I missed this garbage. My return has caused quite the stir. People are speculating about Bram and me? Give me a break. Eventually I get back far enough to find a headline that reads *Serenity Ward Makes a Splash in Plaza Fountain.* I open it and watch clips of Jase and me playing in the fountain in August.

Tears well in my eyes as a smile stretches across my face. I brush my fingertips over the forget-me-not necklace at my throat. Not that I need to watch a holo to remember this. I can almost feel his lips on mine just thinking about it. Once I mused that the city's fountains should run with cocktails instead of water to better keep everyone in a hazy mist, but Jase was my intoxicant. Even involved in the uprising, things were more simple and straight-forward then. We had no secrets, no grudges, nothing to do but play in a fountain and fall—

A quick, low *buzz* hums through the room. The holo disappears and the lights go out. I'm snapped back into the present, in which I can't see my own hand in front of my face.

"That's *something* at least," Dixon says from the inky darkness.

"Something that killed everything in the room," Frey replies.

"*Hopefully* it's only this room," Vogue says.

As the person closest to the exit, I stand and grope my way along the wall to check the hallway. When I open the door, light pours in.

"Oh good," Vogue sighs.

Dixon smiles. "See? Just a small electrical surge."

"More like a small EMP." Frey takes off his cuff and tosses it.

Vogue shrugs as she removes her dead cuff. "Well, that could come in handy."

Without my cuff, Jase won't be able to call me. I'm tortured by our unresolved relationship status, and I already know what I've decided. I have to make it work with him. The memory of how perfect we can be together won't go away. Jase has to be miserable. I don't want to drag that out any longer than necessary.

"While you geniuses figure out if that can do anything besides kill our devices," I say, "I'll go check on Jase and Krisalyn."

Chapter Sixty-One

ADWIN

Nausea returns on the flight back with Nemora, but it's not motion sickness this time. I sided with the cousin who drugged me to get information. I turned on the cousins who welcomed me into the family and introduced me to their world. The first people I've ever been able to be friends with in any remotely open, honest way. Even if Priam was willing to kill his mother, I can't help but feel guilty for my role in this.

"What will happen to them?"

There is no emotion in Nemora's eyes. "They'll wait in prison cells for their trials. If Clover didn't already make her followers immune, we'll interrogate them under the same substance I used on you."

I look at her with one eyebrow cocked in question.

"It makes people very honest," she says, "but you forget the conversation as it happens."

"Like a combination of our truth serum and amnesia drug?"

An indignant hiss escapes her. "This is far more elegant than your crude Kaycian potions."

I slip back into silence, picturing Clover in a cell. She can't even stand the dome. She'll wither like a flower in winter without fresh air and sunshine. I wouldn't have involved Nemora if I thought it would go this way. It's too late to go back though, so how do I make the most of the situation?

"Do I get any compensation for helping you prevent this?"

"I'm sure something can be arranged. We *are* going to have two empty seats at the family council now. My mother may not like the circumstances of your birth—or more importantly that of your mother—but she can't deny the service you've done us here."

It's tempting. Reclaiming my place in my mother's native home with the part of my family that's strong and commanding paints a pretty picture of a future I never would have dared to dream of. The list of cons rattles off in my mind, though: I don't know if my mother would want to come live here, even if they'd allow it; if she stays in Kaycie, I can't let it go to ruins with the infernal rebellion; and I'm not sure I'd ever feel safe with Nemora and Ismene.

"I'd rather have Kaycie," I say. "Secure Kaycie for Grandfather and me. It gives you a nearby ally rather than an unruly neighbor. I helped stabilize Montica, help me do the same for Kaycie."

"Perhaps. We can discuss it with Mother later."

If Kaycie is under the family's control, maybe Clover and Priam can go into exile there. She'd hate the city, but perhaps Greenwood. The lack of mountains would be a problem, but better that than an underground cell. I owe it to her to do what I can to keep her from spending her days down there.

Back at the fortress, I'm torn between relief and anxiety when the prisoners go a different way and I don't have to face them. The angry glares are something I can live without, but I worry about them. It shouldn't matter. They were wrong. It doesn't matter who they are, they brought on the consequences themselves. So why can't I shake the urge to protect them from it? I wanted to solve things without hurting them, but I guess that isn't possible. What am I willing to sacrifice?

It's too late to answer that question. I made my choices already.

Exhaustion sets in as Nemora and I make our way to the board-room. Ismene and Rocco are arguing when we enter. Nemora goes to her place while I remain standing near the door.

"For the hundredth time! I. Did. Not. Try. To. Kill. Her." Ismene is on her feet, leaning over the table in a rage. I didn't realize she was capable of this level of emotion, much less that she would ever show it. "How can you possibly think that of me?"

"Minea and Priam believe it enough to stage a damn coup!"

"They are *wrong*. It's a set up to turn them against me. A rather successful one as they are willing to kill me over it."

"*They* didn't want to do anything. That was *your son's* idea." Rocco whips his head around to me. "Did Minea agree with him? We didn't hear her response."

I swallow hard. "No, she didn't."

"See?" He turns back to his sister. "Your son."

"Please, sit down, Adwin." Ismene doesn't appear softer. She's still stone, but cracking. That's the gentlest tone she's taken with me. I do as she asks. "What did she say to Priam's... suggestion?"

"That she didn't want them to turn into you." I drop my gaze, too uncomfortable to hold hers as I say it. This isn't the first time she's watched her family tear itself to shreds. Ismene isn't an easy person to like, but I don't have to like her to sympathize with her.

My estranged family members jolt to attention and exchange tense glances. They've all gotten a shared message. Strange how these silent communications already seem so natural to me.

"Well," Rocco says, standing, "they're secure and *safe*, so let's deal with this and then figure out how to handle our rogue children."

Ismene rises, pressing her lips together. "Adwin, someone has acti-vated the missing accumulator in Kaycie." Oh, she's sharing information with me now? "You may join us in the situation room... if you'd like."

This is my invitation to be a real member of the family. I've earned her trust by betraying Clover and Priam's. It's not how I'd have preferred to achieve this.

"Thank you. I'm exhausted, though. I don't want to get in the way." Plus, I'm not ready to cement my position on their side. It's probably too late anyway, but I can't help hesitating all the same.

"Of course, go rest. I'll circle back with you later. Thank you for your assistance."

On their way out, Nemora gives me a small, reassuring smile. As I go to my suite, exhaustion is a comfort—it makes it easier not to think about what's happened today. I make it only to the sofa, sprawling out and letting my mind go blank.

Chapter Sixty-Two

BRAM

Carista's name pops up on my cuff as I get into the EC's elevator. "Hey, what's—"

"Where are you?"

"EC. Going up to see the techs."

"Go to Krisalyn's office. Now. They know she was working on something to undo the

Establishment. I tried to warn her not to go to there, but I was too late, and they just seized her."

"I'm on my way." No time to understand *why* she knew to warn her.

I race up the stairs to Krisalyn's floor. As I check around corners, the irony occurs to me. Why is it when shit hits the fan I'm at my best and most focused? Will the rest of the marshals be the same when they wake up even though they underwent training while they were brainwashed? One can only hope. It would be so satisfying to see the Establishment regret how well they trained us.

That's only going to happen if Krisalyn is okay and finishes her work, though. Someone killed Aldan Foster over this antidote. The same cannot happen to Krisalyn.

Back to the wall, I peek around the corner toward her office. There's no one outside her door. They must be inside waiting to catch anyone else who comes in. Unless they took her away? A search will take too long. I wonder if Jase had arrived yet?

So, I don't know anything. Perfect. Going in blind isn't ideal, but here I go. I slip my gun from its holster and throw the door open.

The marshal poised by the door—as I knew one would be—is the first one down. Shot before he has a chance for anything. A sweep of the room gives me three more marshals and Krisalyn bound and gagged in her desk chair.

Two marshals draw guns to point at me and another swings up toward her. I drop the marshal who would use Krisalyn as leverage before he can level the gun at her head. Two gunshots ring out as I bolt toward Krisalyn. A bullet grazes my thigh. I wince as my pant leg dampens with blood. Practically falling into her lap, I shield Krisalyn so they don't have two separate targets to play off of.

One of the last two remaining marshals is bleeding on the floor, scrambling for his gun. The other is finding me in his sights again, earning him my next bullet. I kick the gun away from the injured marshal and knock him out with a blow behind the ear.

A few seconds is all I give myself to catch my breath. Taking out four marshals—three really, the one by the door wasn't even fair—took all of a minute. These were trainees. All that's left in the city while the rest of them wait in Leavenworth for war to come. Still, they were formidable enough. The Establishment created quite the army for themselves, but there is something to be said for having a fully functioning brain.

A chuckle escapes me. I can just hear Tori's response to that thought: *And you think you have a fully functioning brain?*

Back to work.

Krisalyn's face glistens with tears. I remove the gag and she sniffles out thanks. "Are you okay?" she asks while I unbind her wrists and ankles.

"I'm fine. Are you hurt?"

"No... I'm all right... We need... The others." Her words break through her panting.

"Relax. We'll get them, okay? We can't stay here."

She nods, steadying her breathing. Now that no one is trying to kill me, I realize they tore her office to shreds. They were looking for her work.

Krisalyn injects something into the neck of the unconscious marshal and looks at her watch. Before I can ask what she's doing, she says, "I'll be right back," and disappears through the door.

Meanwhile, I call Serenity, but there's no answer. Dixon doesn't answer either. Neither do Vogue or Frey. Each unanswered call increases my anxiety. They need to get out of here.

Krisalyn returns with a wheelchair. "Help me get him into it." I cock my head at her. "I need a test subject."

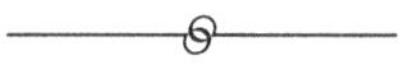

The sedated young marshal sits with his hands bound behind a chair. Krisalyn brought us to an empty lab to finish up so we can get out and find our friends. This kid couldn't be over fifteen years old. Maybe even just got selected this summer. After patching up a bullet wound in his arm, Krisalyn made sure I was diligent in securing him—remembering what happened last time she played with a marshal's brain... mine.

"Sit. Let me see your leg."

I do as I'm told, though hanging around here makes me nervous. She takes out a couple of vials, gauze, and bandages from the well-stocked medical kit which she had already taken from her bag.

"You keep all this in your purse?"

"I was always kicking myself for rushing off to Lawson without all the supplies I had planned to bring. I won't allow myself to be caught off guard again." She gives me two pills for the pain before cleaning and bandaging my wound, leaving as much of my pant leg on as possible.

I look up at the marshal while she works. "Why don't you just give it to him while he's out?" Based on the less-than-pleasant experience of having amnesia reversed, doing this in his sleep might be kinder.

"Because most of them will be conscious when we administer the antidote, so we need to know what happens in *that* circumstance." Krisalyn glances at her cuff. "Finally," she murmurs, and pops a pod into her ear. "It's about time! Listen, you need to find the girls, Dixon, and Frey. They were tinkering around on the tenth floor. Marshals came after me and—... I'm fine, Bram got me out... None of them are answering our calls either, but we're about to try the antidote, so I need you to get everyone out of here... Um, we could meet...?" She looks at me for an answer.

If we walk out of here with the antidote, we'll want to wake up as many marshals here as possible before we go to Leavenworth, so... "The train station." It's far enough from here, and we could take the tunnel into Marshal HQ.

"The train station," she says. "I will, you too." She taps her cuff and covers her face.

We need to focus on the task at hand and trust Jase to take care of everything else. It's all I can do not to go running off to find Serenity. But I can't leave Krisalyn alone, and the four of them won't be easy to catch.

A shuffling sound draws my attention. The marshal struggles against his wrist restraints.

"Ah, hello," Krisalyn says, approaching him. "This might make you feel a little sick, but I'm trying to help you." His lips are frozen in a hard line. He seems to look through her rather than at her. "You'll thank me later." She injects the trial-antidote into his neck and steps back.

The marshal squeezes his eyes closed and breathes heavily through his nose. His hands clench into fists behind his back, and his arms pull away from each other hard enough to make the restraints cut into his wrists. Krisalyn bites her lip, watching as his shoulders convulse forward. She gets a wastebasket in front of him just in time for him to vomit into it. He shudders and his breathing slows, his muscles relaxing.

"My name is Krisalyn." She makes her voice soft and soothing. "This is Bram. He's from Lawson. Do you know *your* name?"

My pulse pounds in my ears. Please let this work. This has to work. We don't have time to keep trying.

His eyes blink open. He opens his mouth but stops and swallows before speaking. "Oliver."

My heart jumps into my throat. *She did it.*

"Oliver," Krisalyn says with a smile, "do you know where you're from?"

"Greenwood."

I'm frozen in thrilled shock.

"I got to visit Greenwood. It's beautiful. Do you remember how you got here?" His glance darts around the room as he thinks about Krisalyn's question. "To Kaycie, I mean."

He takes a breath. "Selection. The train. The vaccine... it made it like I was sleep walking or removed from my body." He shakes his head. I can't imagine what it's like to come back from this.

"So, you remember your time here? Training?"

He nods. "Yeah. It was like I was there but couldn't control anything. If I tried to say anything, the words wouldn't come out. If I tried to move, I was paralyzed. My body was a puppet controlled by something else. How did you give it back to me?"

"I gave you an antidote for the drug that did that to you."

"But you're... *Kaycian*." He spits the word like it's vile on his tongue.

Finally, I force myself to be present. "She's been working to help all of us. She helped us take control of the towns from the Establishment. Not all Kaycians are bad." I undo his wrist restraints, and he winces as he moves his injured arm. "We're going to go wake up the rest of the marshals too."

Oliver looks around nervously. "Can you really pull that off?"

Skepticism colors his face. I push my own deep down. "We will. We have to."

Krisalyn gets to work making a massive batch of the antidote and filling the devices. I had hoped to see her looking like a mad scientist, but it's all automated. She inputs the formula, sending robotic arms to work. We only have to set the devices into trays to be filled.

"Ready to get back to Greenwood?" I ask Oliver as we work.

"I never thought I'd see it again. Even before we knew what selection and Kaycie really were, we weren't supposed to ever go home afterward."

"At least it hasn't been too long for you. I think the longer you're gone, the weirder it is to return."

"Aren't you only here because you were part of the uprising?"

"No," I say. "I lived here as a marshal."

"So, they woke you up first?"

"I was never out. Someone vaccinated me against the drug they used to wipe out everyone's minds."

"You were a marshal… but you were fully functional?" I nod in response to his disbelief. "That sounds impossible."

"It was difficult, but we do anything to survive."

Krisalyn comes around with the first batch of smaller devices. "Oliver, you take these and wake up the marshals here and at headquarters. I added a little anti-nausea medication, so *hopefully* we won't have a huge mess on our hands." She shows him how to activate the grenades and marbles and sends him on his way.

As we load up the last of the devices back into the bags, a storm siren begins to wail.

Our heads snap to look at each other in confusion. "No way there's a tornado," she says.

What kind of storm is coming then?

Chapter Sixty-Three
SERENITY

"Hey, how's it—" I stop short as I push Krisalyn's door open.

I press my hand over my mouth as hard as I can to keep myself from screaming. Three dead marshals are sprawled on the floor. Bloodstains abound in the ransacked office. A prickling feeling spreads from my neck over my entire body. I back out slowly, having no inkling of what I should do.

Where is Krisalyn? And who killed these marshals? Certainly not her. She could probably kill people, but it wouldn't be this bloody. She'd do it with pharmaceuticals. Who on our side would be capable of— *Bram.*

A hint of relief runs through me, knowing Bram would be her best chance at being safe. But where did they go?

"Don't move!"

I whip around toward the voice. Two marshals are heading my way. As fast as my feet will carry me, I take off in the opposite direction. Shouts call out behind me, authoritative but without emotion. I take the first corner to get out of their sights, winding through the labyrinth of the health department. I've gotten lost in these hallways before. Getting lost now could either save me or be my downfall.

The voices seem farther as I round more corners. When I reach an elevator bay, I hit the button and pant through my burning throat. It comes fast enough, and I jump in and press nine. That's where Vogue said they were going to move to after they blew out the power in their first workshop of the day. I have to trust that Krisalyn is okay with Bram. And Jase, if he was with her... God, I hate not knowing. Vogue, Dixon, and Frey are the only ones who wouldn't know what's going on. I have to get to them.

The idea of running out of the elevator blind terrifies me. How well can they track me through the building? When I lean back on the thin handrail, it wiggles. *Oh!* I turn around and grip it with both hands, pushing one foot up under it. All of my weight and force pulls against the rail until it snaps off the wall and I fall backwards against the door. A whimper slips through my teeth. I get to my feet and swing the rail. It's no sabre, but it's better than nothing.

The door opens and I peek out before exiting. It's clear. I walk quickly but try to appear normal—the rail laying up against my arm. When a voice behind me yells, "Freeze," I keep my pace. Not that it would be remotely normal to not turn and look, but I'm so close to a corner.

I slink around it and press my back against the wall as footsteps race toward me. The rail digs into my palm as I tighten my grip.

When the steps reach the corner, I step forward and swing out, hitting the unsuspecting marshal in the neck. His speed adds to the force of the impact. Another slash knocks the gun from his hands. I step on it and fling it back behind me. He dives for it, nearly taking my legs out from under me. I jump out of the way in time, but before I can secure my balance, the floor and everything else disappear as I fall.

―――⊚―――

My eyes flutter open to reveal another laboratory-like workshop.

Vogue greets me with a hopeful smile. "Are you okay?"

"What happened?"

"We heard the scuffle in the hallway. Dixon sedated the marshal but got you too."

"Sorry," he says.

"Not at all. Thank you."

"I don't know," Frey says. "It looked like you were holding your own pretty well."

My lips curl up in a satisfied smile, but the moment is short lived. The storm siren begins its eerie moan, and we all jolt to attention. There shouldn't be a storm worth sheltering for this time of year.

Dixon slings a bag over his shoulder. "Well, we needed to get out of here, anyway."

Frey leads the way to the department lobby where people run to and from the windows. The amount of sunlight coming through disproves the idea of a storm, but a crowd buzzes about something.

We get through to see the cause of the commotion. Aircrafts race over the buildings of the city. A dark green plane fires something at a navy blue one that sets its wing on fire and sends it tumbling to the ground. It crashes into a building in a fiery explosion. My heart leaps up to my throat as chills shoot through me. It's like that night the uprising started all over again. Watching destruction from the windows... but we're missing people. Jase's arms were around me last time. I look at Vogue in a panic.

"Kris and Jase," she breathes.

"And Bram. It looked like he was with them. Or at least Krisalyn." Was Jase there yet? My lip trembles.

"What?"

Frey interrupts us. "They'll be going down to the basement like everyone else." He pulls us away. "Let's go."

We follow the human current toward the stairs until people come to an abrupt stop by the door, stumbling backwards as hulking figures in green and black step out of the stairway. Frey grips my arm and pulls me away and around a corner. Vogue and Dixon follow suit.

Frey leans his head back against the wall and closes his eyes. "Not again."

"Monticans?" I say, though I know the answer.

A deep voice says, "The most recent signal came from this floor."

"None of these faces match the six we're looking for," another says. "Maybe it's back on ten where the first signal came from."

We've been on this floor and the tenth with the accumulator. They must have a way to trace it. *Six people?* The four of us, plus Jase and Krisalyn. They're looking for us. How would they know who we—Agnar... or Adwin, or both. This is bad.

"You lead them here with that damn thing," Frey hisses.

"Dixon," Vogue says, "what do you have?"

"A death wish, apparently." He pulls the bag from over his shoulder and takes out the accumulator.

"Are we just going to *give* it to them?" Vogue says.

"No, we're going to knock-out their weapons, so ours aren't so pathetic in comparison." He gives me a handgun and a smoke grenade, then takes a deep breath before running his hands over this thing they want so badly. He drops it like it shocked him and the lights go out—not that it affects the lighting level with sunshine pouring in through the windows.

Curses about dead equipment are exchanged as Dixon scoops the accumulator back into the bag. "Close your eyes. Hold on to each other. Frey, lead the way to the stairs when it goes." He pulls out the smoke grenade as the voices approach us.

I grasp Frey's hand in one of mine and Vogues in the other. The first Montican soldier comes into view. Dixon throws the grenade, veiling the room in thick, dark smoke before I can even seal my eyelids. Tears well up to soothe the sting from the millisecond's exposure. Frey pulls me and we slink along the wall, blind, as shrieks and shuffling feet sound around us. The sharp smell of the smoke burns my nose and throat.

We make it through the stairway door. I gasp in a breath of clean air.

"We need to get out of here," Frey says, pulling me toward the stairs.

I pull my hand out of his. "We have to find Jase and—"

"Vogue!" Krisalyn comes running down the stairs with Bram in tow, slamming into Vogue's arms.

Chapter Sixty-Four

BRAM

The bag of antidote-laden devices feels even heavier as I take in the view. A battle rages overhead, buildings turning to rubble as collateral damage. Krisalyn remains frozen against the far wall of the windowed office we found—ghostly pale and hyperventilating.

"Time to go." I grab her arm to haul her back through the door. "We have to find everyone and get this stuff out of here."

In the hallway, she stops to take a small container from her pocket. Her hands shake so hard she can barely open it, but she removes a pill and swallows it, holding up a finger to ask for a moment as her breathing slows down. She closes her eyes and takes a deep breath before coming back into focus. "Okay. Let's get everyone down to the basement."

"The basement isn't good enough if the building comes down," I say. "We need to get to the tunnel under Marshal Headquarters. It's deeper and it'll lead us out to the train station and the tunnels."

She nods and taps her cuff, calling over its speaker as we make for a stairwell. "Jase, are you with everyone?"

"No, I'm on my way to the tech department."

"Okay, we're on our way down the southwest stairway."

"I'm in the northeast. I'll meet you on the tenth floor."

"Okay. Just in case, we're going to Marshal Headquarters to get to the tunnel."

"Okay. Bye."

We take off down the stairs when we hear voices booming above us. "The active signal from fourteen is on the move."

We just left the fourteenth floor. What would they be looking for there?

"Delta squad is moving to collect the one from the northeast stairway." This voice sounds like it's coming through a device speaker.

Krisalyn gasps and pulls me through the door onto the thirteenth floor. "They're tracking *us!* Jase and me."

"Your cuffs. Come on."

As we race down the hall, she calls Jase again. "Lose your cuff and *get out!* They know you're in that staircase. Find another way." I slide to a stop and hit the elevator button. "Bram is with me; we'll get the girls. *Please,* go to the tunnel."

Before Jase can respond, I take Krisalyn's cuff and throw it into the elevator, throwing mine with it for good measure. I hit the button to send it to the top floor. "Let's go."

The next stairway we come to is noisy with panicked Kaycians, but I don't see any marshals. As we approach the tenth floor, the faint smell of smoke rises from below. *Shit,* what now?

I open the door to ten, but familiar voices rise with the smoke.

Krisalyn screams out and sprints down. "Vogue!" She throws her arms around Vogue. Serenity, Dixon, and Frey stand panting behind them.

"We have to go," Dixon says, taking the heavy bag from Krisalyn. "We just left some angry Monticans back there."

"Monticans are in here?" As if marshals weren't enough.

Frey smiles wryly. "Everyone wants us, apparently."

"Where's Jase?" Serenity looks frantic.

"He's going to meet us at the tunnel under Marshal HQ," I say. "Let's go."

Frey looks at Krisalyn wide-eyed. "I've got it," she says.

We start down the stairs. Serenity comes along, but protests. "He wouldn't leave. He wouldn't leave without me. Where was he? We have to find him."

"We had to ditch our cuffs. There's no way to find him," Krisalyn says. "I told him I'd get you. He'll meet us there."

Vogue looks at Serenity and then over her shoulder at me. I meet her gaze and imagine we're sharing the same thought. *This time we can't let her run toward the enemy.* We'll deal with the kicking and screaming if it comes down to it. Serenity will *not* go running into this danger.

We make it outside where the battle continues in the sky. The streets are deserted—we're the only people crazy enough not to be underground already. Debris litters the street, and smoke swirls toward the sky from countless points. Across the street from the EC, Serenity hesitates, looking back at it.

Vogue pulls her arm. "Serenity, *please*. We have to get underground."

"He wouldn't have left without me." Tears roll down her cheeks.

"He knew where you were going. That's the only place you'll be able to find each other. Come on."

Serenity moves away, but stops short, gaping at the building. I turn back to it as a dark green aircraft rise from the roof. As it ascends, something drops from it... and the Establishment Center erupts.

Chapter Sixty-Five
SERENITY

My racing heart comes to a full stop as I watch the Establishment Center's windows blow out one floor at a time, from top to bottom. The roof crumples, pulling the building in on itself with a deafening roar. A tsunami of dust rushes toward us, but I remain frozen. It disappears from my view, but it takes me a second to realize it's Bram shielding me. My nose is to his chest as he leans over me.

I feel separate from my body.

Krisalyn's scream snaps me back into focus. She struggles in Vogue's arms. I look up at Bram, and he grips my arms. Behind him, a crumbling pile of rubble takes the place where the Establishment Center once stood. His hands shake. My eyes meet his and find desperation. That worry for me I've gotten so used to seeing—magnified now.

"He wasn't there." I recognize the sound of hysteria, even if I can't control it. *He couldn't have been.* "He's in the tunnel."

Bram lets me go and I take off at a run toward Marshal Headquarters. The turmoil continues around us. Planes dart through the sky. Explosions and destruction rumble the ground. Glass rains down from a shuddering office building. I shield my eyes with a hand, running it over my hair to brush off shards after the glass-shower passes. The cuts on my hand don't bother me. All I can think of is his hands. They'll be holding my face momentarily, weaving through my hair—getting their own cuts on the shards still there—as he kisses me. *He's got to be there.*

Krisalyn screams again, and I turn to see Vogue splayed on the ground. Blood mats her platinum hair. Frey scoops Vogue up in his arms and keeps running. Krisalyn is frozen until Dixon grabs her hand and gets her moving again. I too have to take a breath to remind myself that the best thing I can do for Vogue right now is keep up with her as Frey takes her to safety.

We make it into the marshal building, which has no security at this point. Bram leads us down the flights of stairs to the tunnel. It's bathed in a red glow and several smaller lights shine within. Most are stationary against the walls where people sit and cry, gasping at every new rumble.

When we come to a stop, Frey lays Vogue down on the rough floor where Krisalyn orders us all to give her any light we can so she can examine the wound. None of us have cuffs, so she's stuck with the minimal ambient lighting until some strangers come to help. She declares Vogue is breathing and her pulse is all right.

I allow myself a sigh of relief and turn back to my other concern. "Jase!" I shout down the tunnel, scanning faces as I step through, picking up speed at the sight of every face that *isn't* his. I scream his name again, running past the point where any people are.

He wouldn't have continued this far. He'd wait for me. I run back the way I came. Tears pooling in my eyes. Dread settling into my bones. *If he isn't here...* I'm almost to the stairs, running when Bram appears in front of me and I slam into his chest. He wraps his arms around me and sobs tear through me.

Chapter Sixty-Six

BRAM

I'd give anything to see Serenity happy in Jase's arms right now. Holding her close has been on my mind for months, but feeling her shudder against me wraps my heart in an excruciating vice. Thoughts of her with Jase used to sting, but compared to this, it would feel like a kiss on the lips. She gasps for breath between sobs, and I wrap my arms around her a little tighter. She grips fistfuls of her hair in bloody hands, and I notice the silver words on her wrist. I can only see '*the journey be worth*,' but I know the rest. In this underground place bathed in red light I wonder... if the journey takes you through hell, can it possibly be worth it?

"Serenity!"

The shaking body in my arms makes no sign of noticing her mother's voice.

Over my shoulder I say, "She's here."

The Wards rush over. Grace pulls Serenity from my arms and runs her hands over Serenity's face, shoulders, arms, looking for injuries. "Are you all right? Where are you hurt?"

Serenity is unresponsive, so Grace looks up at me. I whisper to Anton, "We think Jase was in the EC."

His eyes widen under his glasses, and he turns to look at his daughter with regret and sorrow rolling off of him. He takes Serenity from her mother and walks her to the wall, where they sit down. Serenity buries her face in her father's shoulder.

Grace comes to me and presses her hands to her eyes. "Jase?"

"He was at the EC. We told him to leave and come here, but... he isn't here."

She wraps her arms firmly around herself and takes one shaky breath. "Is everyone else okay?"

"Vogue has a head injury."

"We need to get her to Leavenworth. The hospitals here are already being swamped." Grace's ability to compartmentalize and deal with problems rationally amid chaos is impressive. "Did the antidote work?"

"Yes." I hold out the bag on my shoulder. "We should have enough to wake them all."

"Good. I don't want to give Casimir the opportunity to silence those of us who know his secrets."

"So, what do we do?"

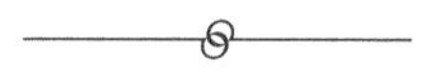

We look more like a funeral procession than an army going to battle. Oliver and a group of marshals in training march ahead of us, unpracticed at faking being brainwashed, but they only have to fool people for a few minutes.

Frey carries Vogue with Krisalyn at his side. The shell that is Serenity walks along with her father, and Dixon is by Grace and me. As we approach the train station, voices are audible, directing people to train cars or back to undamaged areas of the city.

Kemp spots the trainees and barks orders at them. "Go back up to ground level. Keep people off the streets. Department of Health officials will determine where injured people can be sent."

They march on to the stairs, passing the marshals stationed as security for the train. One of them is Travick. *Perfect.* I couldn't ask for more than to have one who knows me. The councilmen are too busy with the chaos to notice the light mist spreading around the marshals behind them.

Agnar and Martel are discussing something until Grace takes their focus. "Gernot!" Hearing the governor called by his first name is weird.

Agnar looks up from his place with Martel, running his eyes back and forth over us as if inventorying how many adversaries he has. "Arrest them!"

"Grace, Anton, are you all right?" Martel asks. His gaze finds Vogue. "Is that Adelle's granddaughter?"

Grace opens her mouth to respond, but Agnar cuts her off. "It doesn't matter who they are. They're traitors. They stole Montican technology and brought this attack down on us."

Behind them, marshals' faces twist in varying levels of discomfort and confusion. Travick leans his hands on his knees, panting. We've got them.

Grace flashes a contemptible smile. "How very bold of you to bring up Montica, Casimir."

Agnar's eyes flash with rage. Faster than I'd expect him to move, he snatches the gun from Kemp's holster and points it at Grace. I maneuver myself in front of her, but what actually stops Agnar is the gun pressed against his neck.

"I wouldn't," Travick says through gritted teeth.

Kemp wheels around to find himself staring down the barrel of a gun. He freezes. Martel slowly glances over his shoulder to see that the marshals have all turned their aim toward them. With inhuman coolness he turns back toward us and lifts his open palms to shoulder level in surrender.

"Drop it," Travick says behind Agnar. He obeys, too smart to jump into a fight he can't win.

One marshal points to Serenity's dad. "He's on the council too."

Another starts toward Anton, but I stop him. "No. The Wards are on our side."

"And who are you?" He looks at me like he's trying to place a vague memory. Disheveled and out of uniform, it's hard to recognize me as a marshal.

"He's one of us." Travick steps forward while others restrain the councilmen's wrists.

"Welcome back," I say, trying to swallow the emotion threatening to make my voice break. Neither of us were ever touchy-feely, but he throws his arms around me in a firm hug now. "I guess you were right," he says.

"About what?"

"Staying home being the better option."

I puff out a small laugh. "Well, I didn't know this was what we were getting ourselves into."

"The councilmen said you were never extirpated?" I shake my head. "Good for you. You went back home, right?"

"Yeah. Your family is fine. Cary's good, and Reid is home."

"But he's..."

"Waiting to be woken up," I say.

Travick's eyes light up. "Speaking of waking people up—you have a single dose of whatever you gave us?"

"Sure." Dixon takes a vial from his bag and hands it to Travick. "Who for?"

Travick's grin is sly and self-satisfied. He turns without a word and my jaw drops as he injects the antidote into Governor Martel's neck.

Each of Martel's panting breaths is audible through the stunned silence of the train station. He drops his face into his bound hands and shudders. When he straightens himself up, he glares at Agnar. "You."

Martel tells the story on the train ride. He hasn't earned anyone's trust yet, so his hands remain bound. The fact that he was extirpated moves Grace, but the marshals have no pity for him.

"You weren't blank like the marshals, though," she says, trying to piece together this development.

"Casimir couldn't let me be blank. He gave me enough to let me appear fairly normal, like the women who work at the town ECs. He set me up as a puppet whose strings he could control. His secrets were locked away with my full consciousness."

Agnar doesn't appear concerned. His face doesn't hint at any emotion at all. Whether because he's resigned himself to his loss or because he's still confident he'll land on top, I don't know.

Alternatively, Kemp's agitation radiates off him like a caged animal waiting for the chance to attack us all. A chance he will not get. "While I'm glad you've exposed this imposter, you must realize we can't just go reviving all the marshals." Furious glowers point at Kemp from all directions. "They'll tear us apart."

"We've already torn ourselves apart," Grace says. "Our collective ego over-inflated and it's popped. Our time to rule is over."

"You traitor," Kemp hisses. "How can you let this happen?"

"I don't imagine these men are going to ask my permission." She gestures to the marshals.

"Grace," Martel says, "I understand, truly."

"You don't." She looks at Anton and Serenity then turns back to Martel. "You never understood, but that doesn't matter anymore. It's over."

"Look at what Montica just did. We need our army right now."

"We'll still have an army," I say, standing. "It just won't be under your command."

I press my eyes closed as I pass Serenity. She looks lifeless as her father removes small shards of glass from her hands—looking at nothing, not seeming to notice what's happening around her, pulled from her body like Oliver said extirpation did. Only there isn't an antidote to breathe life back into her. I want to, but if I turn off my path to try to pull her out of her darkness, I won't come back to do what needs to be done.

Guilt bubbles up in me as I continue past her, but I shove it down. *The end goal isn't to save one person*, Tori's memory reminds me. Anyway, this time she's safe and I can come back to her after I finish this job. There isn't anything I can do to make it better, but I'll be around to be whatever she needs.

I grab the bag of antidote-filled devices from the floor by Dixon's feet where he holds Krisalyn's shuddering form. Frey sits on the floor with Vogue's head in his lap, looking up at the ceiling, jaw clenched.

Travick looks up from the group of marshals he sits with as I approach. "What's the plan?"

I drop both bags onto the seat next to him. "I'm going to need a uniform."

Chapter Sixty-Seven
ADWIN

Ismene's suite brings me back to my first moments in Montica. When Grandfather found out we were to meet with the family in the boardroom, he complained it was impersonal. Perhaps he expected to be received here. I certainly didn't expect this today. The invitation set me on edge in a wholly excessive way. This suite quickly replaces the anxiety with a sense of awe, though. Two-story windows overlook a vista as grand as any I've seen out in the forest with Clover. I soak in the mountain view. The city below. I'll miss it when I'm back in Kaycie.

Ismene leads me to a great room which features a massive fire sculpture in the center. The flaming angel stands so tall, the wings nearly lick the vaulted ceiling. She stares up at it in a reverie. "Religion pandered to the weak, giving them hope. The promise of ascension molds them. For the strong, the warning that our strength is hardly a drop in the ocean maintains our discipline. Feeling too powerful is dangerous." She waves a hand to gesture me to sit, and I do.

"Priam and Minea have been wrong about a lot lately," she says, still looking at the flames, "but they were right about one thing." She turns to face me. "My bias against you had nothing to do with you, or even your mother." Her eyes swim with more words she won't vocalize. "I'm sorry for that. You are undeniably one of us."

It stings like an insult, though it's meant to be a compliment. Do I really want to be part of a family that exiles, plots against, and arrests its own? "Thank you. No apologies are necessary."

When she sits down and pulls her shoulders back, she transforms from the woman trying to mend a family to the Director trying to manage a nation. Gone is the emotion, replaced by the familiar coldness. "Nemora told me you'd prefer to go back to Kaycie to manage things there." It isn't a question, but I nod anyway.

"You'll have our full support as the leader of Kaycie. We will retake the country with and for you and be grateful to have an ally and a member of the family in control."

My heart stops. *Me?* I didn't mean I wanted to be handed the keys to the kingdom—just that I want to help. To be a part of it. Grandfather should be in charge. Those words can't come out, she's still too angry at him to agree to that. I'm not sure if this is a tremendous gift or a horrible burden. Some combination, most likely. What's the catch?

I look up at her, words failing me. She shifts uneasily. There's something she isn't telling me.

"Part of our assistance," she begins, "will include rebuilding in your capital."

My brows furrow. *Rebuilding?*

"The situation with the accumulator went poorly."

A chill runs down my neck. The accumulator can level several city blocks. "How poorly?"

Ismene taps the end table next to her and a holo appears before us. Downtown Kaycie, scarcely recognizable through smoldering ruins. Damage to many buildings and at least three obliterated, including the Establishment Center.

My pulse rushes through my ears. I turn and enlarge the holo to see my mother's building. There's no damage. I let out a breath. Okay.

She's probably fine. Then the realization of what Ismene is offering comes into focus.

Sure, blow up my home and then act like you're giving me some lovely gift.

"Most of this was collateral damage. We did not set out to attack, but when we flew in to retrieve the accumulator, Kaycie's military engaged us." *Right, you thought you'd land a military craft in their capital and they'd just sit back and watch.* "When we couldn't retrieve it from the Establishment Center, we bombed the building to destroy the accumulator before we lost it again."

I keep my eyes on the holo, unsure of how I can possibly react to this without severing my fresh link to Ismene.

"Apparently the accumulator had already been removed," she says. "It did not detonate when the building came down."

If it had, I'd be looking at considerably more destruction—a cost Ismene was willing to pay. Clover was right about more than Ismene's bias against me. Clover sees Ismene for the tyrant she is. A tyrant I need to play nice with if I'm to right any of these wrongs.

"I'll have your aid in rebuilding and stabilizing Kaycie?" I ask.

"Absolutely. I wouldn't make you jump in blind and unprepared."

No, you wouldn't. You'd make sure to have a hand in things so that Kaycie and I are indebted to you. Kaycie will be under your control via the puppet you place as leader.

"Thank you," I say. "Together, I believe we can maintain a lasting peace across the continent." And the puppet shakes the hand of its handler.

She needs to think she's won for now. I'll need time to figure this out. And people. People who hate me now and are several stories below me in the bowels of this mountain.

Chapter Sixty-Eight
BRAM

Surrounded by revived marshals, I march to the assembly yard. Civilians rush around between the train station and the hospital, but there are no marshals to be seen other than our own. One team splits off to escort Dixon to the armory. It hasn't sunk in yet—the fact that this is real. It still feels like I'm walking through a dream, or a horrible nightmare if I include everything that just happened in the city.

The attack means we won't be waking the marshals to send them all home. This isn't over. We'll have to figure out what Montica is doing, how to respond to today's events, but we'll do it as a whole new country.

If we succeed here.

We reach the top of a small hill overlooking the yard, and the dreamlike feeling comes to a screeching halt. My jaw drops as I take in a crowd larger than I could possibly dream up. A sea of marshals in impossibly straight rows and columns stands before us. Grace's assembly order from Kemp's cuff was followed with perfect efficiency, of course. The number of marshals in the city always seemed high, but seeing the combined forces from all eight islands is nauseating. So many people taken. So many people erased. It has to be more than they need—like they keep taking more out of habit or compulsion, like Kaycians collecting more shoes than they could ever wear.

Our men take positions along the perimeter of the assembly. Every muscle in my body tenses in anticipation.

"Drones are ready to fly," Travick says. I tip my head in a single nod. "Send 'em up." He puts a hand on my shoulder. "You did good, Bram."

Vague feelings pass through me about this not really being my doing, how far we've skewed from our plans, how many marshals we killed in the process who could be revived now... but I don't voice any of that. I only clench my jaws as drones soar over the sea of people.

Travick speaks into his cuff. "All in position. On my mark. In three, two, one."

A gray-green mist showers down from the drones. More puffs up in staggered bursts from around the edges of the army as our men activate grenades. It encapsulates the field in a fog from which a low rumble of groans rises. The precise lines fall apart as if the ground under them was given a hard shake. An incomprehensible amount of time passes in tense anticipation, until too many voices talking at once drowns the field in sound.

My lungs deflate with a sigh of relief. *We did it.* I turn to Travick. "Ready to go home and wake up our brothers?" I get to put my family back together, then I'll see if there's any way to help my Kaycian friends recover from their loss.

Before he can respond, a gunshot rings out and a knot of people marks the source. We jump to attention and take off down the hill. Our sprint slows to a crawl when we hit the mass of marshals. Shouting and pushing our way through, people back away from the commotion and open a path for us. As we get closer, bits of conversations register through the buzz. "First thing I saw when I came to was the body."

A body? "He opened his eyes and put the gun to his head." Someone killed himself? Why now? Why would someone give up his life just when he got it back?

I get to the body and the rest of the world fades to black. My heart stops. Blood turns to ice in my veins.

All at once but somehow also slowly, my brain registers Mom's nose, the shadow of the scar on the chin, Dad's eyes which stare unfocused and lifeless now. The little boy who clung to me when our father died and cried when I left him too. The young man who didn't recognize me anymore, but finally had the chance to be with us again. The softest brother turned hard. The most lively turned corpse.

Emrys. My little brother can't be... *Why?... No. No. No!* He wasn't even supposed to be here!

An arm wraps around my shoulders, tensed to hold me up. It brings some sensation back into my numb body. The numbness was better. Rediscovering my place in my body makes every part of me ache.

"Bram!"

I don't turn in response to the desperate cry of my name, but the arm on my shoulder falls away.

"Cary? Reid?"

"Travick! Oh, God. Bram—" A horrified wail cuts off her words. Carista runs past me and drops to her knees, hugging Emrys the way I should be, but I'm frozen. Sobs wrack her body.

Our cycle of destruction continues, unavoidable as gravity. All of our attempts to fix things break more than we could imagine. We broke our country into pieces so it's fitting that we'd break along with it. I don't remember what the destination was supposed to be anymore. The journey veered off course, and I won't ever consider this to be worthwhile.

Chapter Sixty-Nine

SERENITY

The assault of memories we shared wasn't enough. Those just made me sad. Now my subconscious is going on a violent attack against me. This nightmare is outrageous.

I know! I know I need him. I am on my way back to him. Make this end and I'll never let him go again.

It doesn't end.

It should have ended when the building exploded. That would have been the obvious point to wake up, panting and panicked.

But it didn't end.

What I wouldn't give for the numbing fog of the amnesia drug.

This arrival in Leavenworth is infinitely worse than last time. Last time, at least, I had Jase's hand to steady me. Now my hands are wrapped in bandages and they'll never... I can't finish the thought without wanting to tear my heart out of my chest to stop its aching. If the words never fully form in my mind, I don't have to accept it. I can't admit any of this to myself.

As if in a dream, I follow as they take Vogue to the hospital. She is the only string connecting me to the world around me. She has to be okay. Fate couldn't possibly take... They couldn't both...

My legs buckle under me, but I don't fall. Krisalyn squeezes my hand, meeting my gaze with her large eyes, looking desperate and devastated. She and I share our loves. We both love Jase. We both love Vogue. Neither of us can fathom...

We sit together in silence in the crowded waiting room. Someone explains why my parents aren't with me, but it goes in one ear and out the other. It doesn't matter. Time passes with no marker of measurement.

A silent scream fills my head to block out the sound as someone tells us the initial search for survivors at the EC isn't looking good. I don't respond. To respond would unleash the floodgates, and I'd drown. Instead, I remain frozen. I need to wait to find out about Vogue.

Hours could come and go without my notice. Frey brings us news that Vogue fractured her skull, but she's already out of surgery and will be fine. My relief doesn't bring me joy, it only releases me from having to hold on to the string. That worry over Vogue—I can let it go now and plunge into the darkness that's pulling me down.

I rise without a word, walk out of the hospital and back to the hotel. I climb the stairs, biting my lip as the memory of running up the Establishment Center stairs with Jase flashes in my mind. It isn't until I get to my door—the door of the room I had shared with Jase—that I realize I don't have a key. I lean my head on the door, figuring I'll just collapse out here in the hallway, but a hand pulls my shoulder back to take my weight off the door. The unknown person taps a key against the lock and the door opens. I walk into the room, unaware and unconcerned about who is here with me.

My eyes take in the bed and my blood runs cold. This was a terrible place to come. The bed mocks me with the memory of nights spent with Jase. All those hours in his arms, but sleep kept me from holding the memories. Having his chest as my pillow before I remembered everything was the most peace I've felt in months. I'd never have thought it would be the last time. Just a glimmer of how happy I could be before every possible happy ending dissolved.

I sit on the floor with my head on my knees, my back against the bed. Someone slides down next to me, but I don't look to see who it is.

"I'm no good at knowing what to say at times like this." Frey's voice is heavy. "Sorry you got stuck with me. Dixon is with Krisalyn."

"There's nothing to say." My voice is unrecognizable. Barely a whisper and rough as it scrapes out of my throat.

"I'll just be here then." He takes my hand in his, and we sit in silence.

This silence is more complete than any I've ever known before. Even the perpetual music in my head is gone—I don't know any song sad enough to serve as the score to this scene.

The Story Continues...

Find out how Serenity and Bram overcome tragedy and attempt to stop Adwin from taking power in FRACTURED & RENEWED, the series finale.

MOSTLY AN APOLOGY

I'm sorry if this rambunctious middle child of the trilogy hurt you. I don't think you're entitled to compensation, but I've heard it helps if you make someone else read the book to share in your suffering.

But hey! You don't have to wait around to find out what happens next like people did when this book first came out. I'm so glad you won't have to be angry at me. (Cue the angry messages when you see the cast list at the beginning of book 3.)

Thank you so much for reading this series, reviewing, and sharing!

Nicole, thank you for existing. Megan, thank you for always bickering with me so we can be enemies to lovers. Robin, thank you for forgetting stickers exist since I'm not going to send any.

Gabby, thank you for thinking about my characters so much. You're their cool aunt, and they love you almost as much as I do.

About the Author

Natalie has a bookcase with a ladder and is on a texting level relationship with her local indie bookstore owner, so her life has peaked. In addition to writing books across a few genres (all with her signature banter), she is conducting a scientific study to determine if a human can survive on coffee and carbs alone. She's the only subject in the study. As of the time this is being written, she's successfully not died.

Join her newsletter or follow her on social media for updates on this important research. And her books maybe... if that's what you're into.

https://www.nataliecammarattabooks.com/contact